MYSTERY

"A co... ... ... a dark fascinating world, rich in menace and challenges."

Rowena Cory Daniells, author of the Chronicles of King Rolen's Kin novels

"Jamieson is a skilled writer who has earned his stripes in the short story craft and enters the novel scene with a bang – I see a big future ahead."

Australian Speculative Fiction in Focus

"I predict that Trent Jamieson will deservedly be Australia's next big genre export."

Chuck McKenzie

"Jamieson is an excellent writer, creating compelling yet flawed characters in his novels and short fiction. *Roil* is no different in this respect... The novel brings together elements of dystopian science fiction, fantasy and a touch of steampunk to create a gripping story."

Ticon4.com

THE NIGHTBOUND LAND

Also by TRENT JAMIESON

Roil

Death Most Definite
Managing Death
Reserved for Travelling Shows (collection)

TRENT JAMIESON

Night's Engines

THE NIGHTBOUND LAND
Part II

ANGRY ROBOT

ANGRY ROBOT
A member of the Osprey Group

Lace Market House,
54-56 High Pavement,
Nottingham,
NG1 1HW, UK

www.angryrobotbooks.com
No country

An Angry Robot paperback original 2012
1

Trent Jamieson asserts the moral right to be
identified as the author of this work.

A catalogue record for this book is available
from the British Library.

ISBN: 978-0-85766-186-9
eBook ISBN: 978-0-85766-188-3

Set in Meridien by THL Design.

Printed and bound by CPI Group (UK) Ltd, Croydon, CR0 4YY

To Diana

A Grand Defeat

Victory is certain.

GENERAL JH BOWEN

THE UNCONQUERED METROPOLIS OF McMAHON, TEN YEARS AGO
EDGE OF THE ROIL

"Victory is certain."

The words crackled and spat, springing from loudspeakers all along the front line and from loudhailers built into the shining bellies of the military class airships or clutched in the jagged-toothed fighting flagella of the Aerokin that floated, stately and predatory, above.

General Bowen's voice possessed such conviction that, for a moment, it was true and not a single soldier could doubt it.

Behind them the grand city of McMahon emptied. Its great bridges and northern roads strained with refugees – all fleeing, now that this last battle for their city was to begin. Smoke blackened McMahon's sky, and everything stank of it, there had been riots that morning and into the afternoon. But as the Roil's approach quickened, they'd quietened down. New laws (the Peace and Order Precepts, or as they were more popularly known, the Laws of Knife) were coming aggressively into play, as the dark curtain closed. Still, riots continued in some quarters, perhaps a final expression of denial or rage at what was being lost to them.

When the battle was won, those who had rioted would be dealt with by Verger's knife or hurled into prison to rot and consider their folly. But now sixty thousand soldiers, two thousand ice cannons, eighty battle Aerokin, and two hundred airships, the wondrous weaponry of the new age, were perched at the abyss of battle. All of that military force intent upon a single goal: the obliteration of the Roil.

"Victory is certain. We cannot fail. For if we fail here, we fail humanity and Shale itself. And enter that great darkness and become shivering meat for Quarg Hound and Endym, Flute and Floataotons. We will not fall as Tate fell, nor Chinoy or Carver. This time we are ready. This time we drive back the dark."

Surely Bowen was right, after all the Roil was a big dumb mass. It could not overwhelm this gleaming technology and the miles of soldiery arrayed against it, nor could it devour the grandest metropolis ever built. Yet, all it took was a turn of the head and the soaring terrible presence of the Roil and such arrogance was torn of its potency.

"Victory is certain," General Bowen said once more, and his voice echoed like a thunder-crack into the sky and faded just as quickly.

"Victory is bloody certain all right," Beaksley mumbled, checking his ice rifle for the umpteenth time, always checking his rifle, always. "Just not fer us."

Sergeant Harper smacked her palm hard against his head, enjoying the rather satisfying thwack! She realised that she and Beaksley were the only two not looking up at the armada in the sky, and flashed him a dark grin.

"Keep such sentiments to yourself, or you'll feel a knife in your spine. That is if you have one." She said it with some fondness.

"I've spine enough – standing here ain't I?"

No arguing with that.

The Roil was almost upon them, it had moved swiftly that day, as though anxious to meet them in battle. Harper shared that desire. She wanted this done. She wanted to go home.

Two minutes, no more, and the Roil would be in range, drowning out the sun with its great obsidian-like curtain, though it was already dark enough, a rank and bitter night. The air fleet overhead, made up of military class and converted merchant craft as well as Aerokin, hid the day almost as effectively as the Roil. Harper turned her attention a moment upon that drifting industry, the various ships' banners flapping in the wind.

There was strategy at work. They were here to deal with any creatures of the Roil that approached. The airships themselves were to attack the Roil airspace itself with endothermic jets and cannon. They would drive a wedge in the dark, as a series of moats were filled with ice, and coolant pipes running the perimeter of the city would be activated.

There was a furious signalling of flags across the sky; most of the airships were not fitted with the new radio technology. Endothermic weaponry had taken precedence over everything else; cannon protruded from the ships' bows and Aerokin's brain sections like the bristles of a Cuttleman. The guns made Harper feel uncomfortable, she didn't like this close fighting, didn't like the idea of all those munitions suspended above her head.

Harper spied a couple of Mirrlees dirigibles, the grey

teardrop painted upon their cabins; she yearned for the River Weep.

Thirty months ago her number had come up. Conscripted, she had seen a year in the north, stabilizing what the Council of Engineers called a "rupture of treaty" with the Cuttlemen. It had felt like war to her.

Through luck and a particular aptitude for survival, she'd lived and kept on living, rising in the ranks to sergeant, this motley crew hers to bawl commands at: glad to be in the company of someone who had the knack of not dying. But she could take no comfort that she had helped forge a peace in the north, because before it had come to a conclusion her troops had been transferred down to McMahon, and this new endeavour, one that made little sense to her. How could an army face off the dark?

"Soon enough dead, I reckon," Beaksley mumbled.

Harper was damned if she were going to let an idiot like Beaksley put an end to her chances now. She cracked him another blow to the back of his helmet.

The fool stared south, his jaw wide open. He pointed and Sergeant Harper's gaze followed his shaking hands. The Roil raced towards them, not all of it, just the lower strata: a shelf of darkness some forty feet high. She could hear it, a snapping, clicking, the friction of chitin against chitin, barbed and wild. A fierce and boiling wind rushed from the south ahead of it, so strong that she had to lean forward. Guns and armour creaked; the wind tugged at her gear. Sergeants swore, or bawled out orders. Harper blinked away dust and smoke, her eyes stung; she opened her mouth to speak and the sky exploded.

Rolling detonations thundered in the heavens. At first she thought it was the airships firing their cannon – too soon, they were doing it too soon – until she realised it was the airships themselves, rupturing, being torn apart by... she didn't know, couldn't quite comprehend its quick bulk, pale howling flesh, wings that beat hummingbird fast. Flaming remnants of craft, red-hot fragments of the rigid ships's skeletons, and flailing and screaming air troopers rained down upon the soldiers around her, killing those they struck.

The Roil hit them, washed over the chaos, with a deadening darkness.

All was quiet, a soft intake of breath, a widening of pupils or the dripping of sweat. More thrashing bodies fell, but it was as though all the sound had gone from the world. It didn't last.

She breathed out, pumped the action on her gun and fired.

"Fight, you fools," she shouted in the smothering dark. "Fight or die."

There was a third option. A mass of darkness struck her eyes and her mouth.

Darkness that burned.

General Bowen calmly called the retreat from the deck of the *Daunted Spur*. Everything was madness about him, but he kept his head, and considered his terrible failure.

The army was gone. Sixty thousand soldiers swept up in darkness as though they had never been, and the Roil rolled on like a storm front, if a storm could possess such dreadful silent majesty. On the edge of the Roil, chaos bloomed everywhere, behind it only the quiet of the dark.

In the air, over half his ships were down, torn from the sky by the savagery of the two attacking Vermatisaurs, their many heads pale and serpentine, snapping and striking – ruining Aerokin and airship alike.

But Bowen knew that, while showy, they were by no means the most of their problems. Endyms and smaller things, Hideous Garment Flutes amongst them, crowded so thickly upon neighbouring ships's hulls that their weight dragged them out of the sky. The hydrogen-filled ships hit the ground sedately and exploded, gas cells igniting one after the other, their fires darkening the ozone before the Roil and killing the troops beneath them.

Aerokin struggled and screamed too, overcome by the biting weight of all that dark. Flagella thrashed at the air and did not miss – Roil-things shattering almost at a touch – but there were always more to fill the spaces they made in the sky.

Already thousands of creatures raced towards the *Daunted Spur*. Gunners fired endothermic bursts at the beasts. Unlike the crowded front, his craft had room to shower the Roilings with cold; they fell away in a black rain.

His pilot, a Drifter, brought the ship hard right. Alarms rang out, and died down. The ship's control centre – built around a large diagram of the *Daunted Spur* – lit up, warning of engines overheating.

"Steady," Bowen hissed. "Steady or you'll burn out the engines."

"I've a lot of tailwind. The air's uncertain," the pilot said, between clenched teeth, and mumbled beneath her breath something about Aerokin, and the uselessness of dumb machines. Drifters dislike like being told what to do. Still she brought the engines back down.

Looking back, the Roil appeared perfectly still, but Bowen knew that it was not. That it washed over the city of McMahon as it had washed over Tate before it, and Carver.

As he watched, the Roil came bubbling out of Magritte Gorge. Rising up and crashing down over those who were trying to flee, clawing up into the air and striking down more of his air fleet. Bowen brought a hand to his mouth. He wanted to scream, but he forced that need deep. He wiped at his eyes and turned. His men stared at him.

"What do we do now?" his pilot asked.

"Signal retreat. Get as many ships out of there as we can." Though it appeared that those who could had followed the *Daunted Spur*'s example. Bowen noted it was Aerokin, mostly; they were faster, their allegiance to the Great Cities slighter.

"What about the troops on the front?"

Bowen jabbed a hand towards the south, at the darkness crashing over everything.

"There are no troops," he said. "There is no front."

The pain had fled, but with its passing had come the command.

Harper's eyes opened. The darkness was no longer that, she could sense everything, and it was a glorious beautiful power. All around her, soldiers were getting up. Those who had been ruined by the falling airships, their muscles and bones destroyed, stayed still. The Witmoths that had entered them, lifted and found residence elsewhere.

Rising in the light, eyes blinking, each man or woman that stood up broadened her mind and each mind echoed with a dry old voice. *South, south, you must come where the furnaces burn, where the air is thick.* She wanted to share this with those that she loved, the brilliance, the joy, the complete unification of will and action. But the voice was insistent.

The Beaksley smiled. "There are dreaming cities down there, all the way to the Breaching Spire, and heat."

"Yes," she whispered. "Yes. They slumber, but they're soon to wake."

Slowly they stumbled south, caressed and cajoled by the Roil, knowing and not knowing that ten years of preparations lay before them. Ten years of transformation, in cities fast asleep, but dreaming – furiously dreaming.

"Victory is certain," the Beaksley/Harper said.

All along the line the words were taken up, silently and whispered.

"Victory is certain."

When Bowen reached the city of Chapman, Stade's Vergers waited for him. How Bowen hated the mayor's knife men. Their faces revealed nothing, which ultimately said everything he needed to know. Even old Sheff – Stade's right hand killer – wasn't grinning, how could a habit so maddening become by its absence the very essence of terror?

They led Bowen from the landing field, away from his men – all of them were too shattered to offer any resistance, and perhaps they blamed him for what had happened – swiftly across the empty field, which, just two days before, had been crowded with airships. From what Bowen had gathered, amongst the garble of radio transmissions from the command craft, maybe six of the two hundred craft would be coming home. The vast hangars of the landing fields would remain empty. No fleet as grand as his had ever been gathered before, nor was one likely to exist again – who would pilot them? Who could afford to finance such a thing now?

That deserted landing field made it seem real in a way

that the flight from the battlefield had not. As their boots rang out on the scarred asphalt, Bowen's defeat rose in him like a fever; his face burned, he wanted to be sick. He turned his head and looked back at the *Daunted Spur*, its banners being torn down, the crew dragging it into the hangar. Vergers walked with them as well.

Bowen turned back to his crew, and a hand gripped his shoulder forcefully. "I wouldn't do that if I was you," Mr Sheff said.

Victory had been certain and they had lost. He had seen the end of the world. Whatever came next, whatever the following years held, it would be a pointless prelude to the end, to the darkness that was coming.

Stade stood in the hangar, by the offices at its far end, his face haggard, the bags beneath his eyes were dark, though lit with a callous humour. The mayor had been smoking a cigar, the remnants of which lay on the ground; puddles of ash that made Bowen think of his fleet, of the burning ships falling onto the troops.

Five days ago Stade had won the election in nearby Mirrlees. As Bowen's soldiers had formed a front along McMahon, Stade and his cronies had gained nearly as many seats as the Council possessed when it had been the only party. In one single election their rivals, the Confluents, had been gutted. The people of Mirrlees had given Stade almost absolute power.

Bowen did not like the man Stade. He was too much the chameleon. Too much of what people seemed to want. Stade's persona did not possess nearly enough substance.

But he would see the substance now. Clarity has come to him at last.

The mayor cleared his throat. "So we failed," Stade said.

"Well, you failed. No matter, I had little faith in all that wondrous weaponry, clever though it might have been. Tate is different from McMahon, and this idea was the grandest of folly." He folded his hands in front of him. "But you did your best. I truly believe that.

"There are dark days ahead, my friend. And for those dark days our people need a hero, a martyr. But what they do not need is a coward." Stade led Bowen into the nearest office. "When people hear that you fled, rather than stayed and fought, what do you think that will do for this city's morale? And more important, how do you think our allies in Drift will feel? After all, their Aerokin died. Screaming, I believe. You've simplified things for me." Stade allowed himself a smile. "And I must say it's nice to be rid of those progressive Councillors from McMahon: apologists and Confluents one and all."

"What are you talking about?" Bowen asked. "Flight was the only option."

Stade patted him on the back and the general fought the desire to flinch. "Bowen, my friend, and I'd like to think you are my friend, you never made it back. In fact you died most heroically, I will give you that, on another airship." He looked at his notes. "The *Raised Admire*, I believe, which crashed – all her great guns firing until she struck the ground. It was a defeat, but a grand defeat."

Stade drove a blade into the general's neck, and tugged it back out, ripping and tearing as he went. The knife's passage hurt in its awful taking of his thoughts and breath. Its blade was cold, a thing of ice. All that was hot and thinking and urgent gushed from him.

Bowen dropped, blinking, to the floor, fingers clenched around the wound in his throat. On his belly, dying, all he could see were Stade's shoes – scuffed old boots coated in ash – and his blood gliding towards them, as the Roil glided over Shale. The boots shuffled backwards and the mayor sighed.

"Now, Mr Sheff, clean this mess up, if you will," Stade said.

My fingers stiffen. The wind howls. The past is broken.

We snatch at our histories like the tattered storm-wrenched rags they are. All those victories and ruins, those scattered fleeting dreams. Shale is a world undone. Ten metropolises devoured; only two remained. One way or another, this is a Nightbound Land.

Let me write now of David Milde of the metropolis of Mirrlees-on-Weep. He was a Carnival addict, a drug whose comforts were popular in those last days. It cocooned him through the horrors of a city crashing towards oblivion, but not enough that he could stand and wait to be murdered by the Council Vergers that assassinated his father. He fled from his father's house – from murder to murderer, as it was Cadell, the Old Man that found him.

Cadell, what there is to know of him, a hundred volumes could but contain the merest whispers. Old Men are old as the world of Shale is old, the Old Men ruled, the Old Men fought the Roil once (perhaps more than once) and won and lost – cursed and blessed with near endless life. Cadell was an Old Man freed, a titan, and a fool.

Out of obligation (to Medicine Paul, a political ally of David's father) or cunning, Cadell took young David with him to the city of Chapman, on the storm front of that great monster-bearing cloud, the Roil.

In that city, David met the warrior Margaret Penn, sole survivor of the Roil-devoured city of Tate. And there he discovered that Cadell meant to destroy the Roil using a weapon of last resort – the Engine of the World.

When Chapman fell, they were forced to flee (again, always fleeing – be it Verger, Roil or politics), this time by air on the Aerokin the Roslyn Dawn. *And, in that flight, Cadell was fatally wounded in a battle with an iron ship. But the Old Man had one last trick up his sleeve. With a ring known as the Orbis, and a bite, he infected David with his purpose and found a sort of res-urrection within the young man's blood.*

And just in time, for more iron ships came, and David struck them down.

Safe in the far northern metropolis of Hardacre, with Cadell's allies Buchan and Whig, they sought to negotiate a journey into the Deep North to the Engine of the World. Of course, they were never safe: stern Margaret, cursed David. The Roil hunted them. Old Men freed at last, and raging, hunted them, and the Engine, that madness in the north, waited like death.

One way or another, this is a Nightbound Land.

The Weave & Fray of History, LANGDON MAGRITTE

PART ONE
HARDACRE

Murder Riots, there was plenty of those, but was it really murder? Certainly rioting, smoke and blood, and glass all a tinkle. The true murder came after. The Riots were a spasm, a final flinch before the killing stroke.

In Defence of Anarchy (a Primer), PYNCON

CHAPTER 1

We all have our limitations, and you meet me at the edge of mine. It is very sharp, careful, or you will cut yourself upon it. Limitations are to be honed: limitations are a weapon. Believe me when I say that it is a philosophy to hold to, in such limited times.

A Verger always gets the job done. That is my limitation and my creed.

And I always do.

The Stuck Pig & Other Capers, JACKSON SHEFF

THE CITY OF HARDACRE
973 MILES NORTH OF THE ROIL

An airship passed overhead, and an old man, but not an Old Man, pulled a knife on David Milde.

"Time to die, Mr Milde," the old man said.

David thought that as greetings went, at least it was to the point, and he couldn't resist: he looked at his watch. "Really?"

Of all the people David expected might try to kill him, and that included Margaret Penn, this grey and grinning man, eyes gleaming beneath his bowler hat, wasn't one of them, though there was a great deal of death in him. David still wasn't sure where he had come from. The street had been empty moments ago; then, as though bloomed out of the shadow of the airship, or sprang from the rhythmic beat of David's boots, the man had appeared, lips curled, and eyes bright.

A riot rumbled low and menacing in the distance like a storm. People shouted, sang and howled. Constables blew their whistles. Glass smashed. This was the third riot in the last week. David could taste smoke, and blood, and he had to admit neither was as repellent to him as they used to be.

"Do you think it's wise to do this alone?" David said, looking up and down the street, just the two of them, and a door some way back that slammed shut. "I can be... troublesome."

"Troublesome." The man lifted an eyebrow. "Perhaps, but not so much for me and mine." He whistled once, and three men dropped lightly from the rooftops.

These David recognized, Council Vergers – the cut-throat keepers of Mayor Stade's peace. They were a long way from home; from Mirrlees, the drowning city. Vergers had tried to kill him there, as they had killed his father.

Their movements were swift and jerky, as though they had been wound too tight, as though their blood burned. And maybe it did, rumour had it that Stade had transformed his Vergers with Cuttleblood. David wondered what that felt like. How might it burn? He thought he could understand it a little, after all something foreign burned in his blood, but he couldn't quite bring himself to pity them.

Both Buchan and Whig had warned David against leaving the *Habitual Fool*. The inn was safe, the rest of the city was most definitely not, but, then again, David wasn't particularly safe, either. He possessed certain hungers that he preferred not to reveal to either Buchan or Whig. David had but ten minutes ago procured a few grains of Carnival, it laid in a twist of paper in a hidden pocket in his jacket. He could certainly use the drug's calmative properties now.

The Vergers' leader tipped his hat. "Name's Sheff, man should know the one that kills him. I knew your father, shame about his get." He glanced at David's hidden pocket.

Was it *that* obvious? David thought he'd been subtle in his procurement of the drug; his cheeks burned. "Who are you to judge me because I take Carnival?"

"You don't take Carnival, it takes you," Sheff said, tossing his knife from hand to hand. It was an old-fashioned Verger's blade, the handle's pommel a black pearl. The sort you only saw on the covers of novels, and cheap ones at that. Didn't mean it wasn't perfect for gutting a man.

He wanted to argue the point, and explain that he took Carnival simply to keep at bay Cadell – the Old Man who had infected him with his thoughts. But it was too complicated and he didn't quite understand it himself, just that the Carnival helped keep a wall in his mind between him and Cadell.

"Stade's gone, and the Old Man he hunted dead. Mirrlees has fallen too, and I fled that city's politics weeks ago," David said, and even as he said it, he could hardly believe that only weeks bridged the gap between him in this northern city, and the frightened young man who had run for his life from murder and death at his father's house. "We don't need to do this, the Roil is hurrying to put an end to everything. The past is broken."

"I don't care about no broken past, or Old Men dead." Sheff's grin didn't slip. He lifted his free hand, gripped the brim of his hat, and pulled it from his head. Silver hair gleamed, close-cropped, on his skull. "A Verger always sees the job done. And you, sir, are the job. Stade wished you dead, and death by me would be a kindness compared to the other deaths that hunt you." He said that with no little pride, his face a weird melange of relish and stern disapproval.

Why did people always want him dead to redress things that he had never done? "So this is to be a mercy killing, then?" David said.

"Of sorts. Better death here than in the Far North where the mad machine dwells. You'd have done well to let dear Mr Tope kill you."

"Tope killed my father, he hunted me all the way to Chapman, and still he couldn't finish what he started."

"I'm not Tope, young man," Sheff said.

"And I'm not a man anymore," David said; there was bluster in those words, and some truth.

Sheff smiled. "You'll bleed like a man, and you'll die like one, too." He set his hat carefully down on the cobblestones. As though he was going to dance around it. Perhaps killing to him was a dance. And, not for the first time, David wondered if death wouldn't be a mercy. Sheff was right, he *was* heading towards something far crueller.

To the north lay Tearwin Meet and the Engine of the World. The Engine was a weapon of last resort against the Roil, and was rumoured to be mad. David's dealings with it had been limited to a single bright burst of consciousness focussed upon him at one of its Lodes, which he had compelled to destroy three iron ships flown by the Roil. He'd shattered them with ice. The Engine hadn't been happy with his use of the Lode. After all, it was the Engine that had punished the Old Men for engaging it the last time. It was the Engine that had turned those who had constructed it, and unleashed its energies, into monsters.

But it was the Engine that Shale needed now. A few weeks, a month, that was all this world had left to it unless the Engine was engaged, and David, through mischance and Cadell's bite, was the only one able and willing to operate it: to set in motion its energies and drive the Roil from the world.

Certainly, there were many willing to stop him – the Old Men included, they hunted him, even now – Sheff was just the next one in line. The funny thing was, as David saw it, he really had no idea how he was meant to engage the Engine. Cadell did, and he wasn't talking.

"I don't think you understand just what I am," David said.

"Troublesome," Sheff said. "Soon to be dead." He nodded his head once. "Gentlemen."

The Vergers to the left and right rushed him at the same time. They were quick, their long knives dancing, but David was quicker.

Still, he didn't quite know what he was doing. The first Verger's knife brushed his arm, and blood blossomed, the second Verger's blade slashed through his jacket, and scraped along a rib. That focussed him.

David kicked out, struck the first assailant just beneath the knee. Bone snapped. The Verger screamed, tumbled to the ground, and David spun, ducking beneath a knife, fists finding the second Verger's belly and his throat. No scream for him, just a gasp and a swift fall.

"See," David yelled. "See!" Though he didn't know why he was yelling it, just that he was angry and hungry, and here, for the first time, he was fighting the knife men that had killed his father, and chased him from his home, and he was winning.

Something heavy struck him between his shoulders, knocked him stumbling forward onto his knees. Strong hard hands wrenched his arms back, until he felt as though they must tear from their joints, and he realized that he would have been better off paying attention to the other men around him.

"Three is always better than one," a dry voice whispered in his ear.

Sheff grinned at him, his blade gleaming in the daylight.

A few streets away people chanted furiously. Something political and progressive, no doubt; the Hardacre folk liked their slogans.

Sheff cleared his throat, spat upon the ground. "A Verger always gets the job done."

The blade pushed close against his throat. Sheff smiled.

Then his face wasn't there any more. Blood and bone spattered over David. And, despite himself, David licked his lips a little. He sprang to his feet, swinging his head backwards, felt the crack of a nose breaking; the man behind him groaned and fell, releasing his hold on David's arms. Blood rushed back into his hands, he closed them to fists.

Sheff swayed before him, a Verger's perfect balance keeping him there as his body negotiated its position with death. The knife clattered to the ground.

"Not this Verger," David whispered in Sheff's ear. David pushed him in the chest, and the man toppled over. "Not Tope, not you."

He crouched down, snatched up Sheff's knife. The Verger behind him scrambled to his feet, knife in hand, eyes blinking. David danced around his guard, and drove Sheff's blade through the Verger's heart – felt the Cuttle-driven flutter of its last beats. "Nor this one, either."

He pulled the knife free, turned his head. "What about you two?"

The other Vergers were running, holding each other up, not even glancing back.

"Don't gloat over the dead," Margaret said behind him. He closed his eyes, waited for the bullet to come. He might have even wished it on a little. Margaret at least had the right to kill him. She didn't fire, of course, and he turned and glared at her. Margaret, pale tall Margaret, greatcoat down to her ankles, rifle still smoking in her hand. As puzzling to him as the first time he had met her in Chapman. In fact, she'd shot something that time, too. Her eyes narrowed, she glared back at him.

"You were following me?" David said.

"Saved your life."

"I was holding my own."

Margaret shrugged, and slid her rifle back into its sheath. "I was bored." She gave a rather wan smile. "Followed you by the rooftops. Almost ran into your friends."

"We'll talk about this later," David said, and Margaret gave him a look that suggested she most definitely wanted to. He gestured at the two fleeing Vergers, still stumbling towards the riots. In the press of all those bodies they'd never find them. "What do we do about them?"

"Nothing," Margaret said. "They won't be hunting you for a while. I think we've killed enough people today, don't you?"

"They wanted me dead," David said.

"Doesn't everyone?"

"I was thinking the same thing," he said, dropping Sheff's knife by his body. Margaret surprised him by picking it up, and wiping it clean on Sheff's shirt. "Useful," she said, almost as though he wasn't there. Her eyes flicked up to him. "Do you mind if I keep it?"

"Not at all."

Margaret slipped the knife into a ring at her belt and smiled a rather Sheffish grin. "Time we left," she said. "Vergers or not, we'd be fools to linger."

David looked at the rooftops. "That way?" he said, somewhat dubiously.

"Of course not," Margaret said, already hurrying down the street, stepping neatly over rubbish. "I wouldn't want you falling and cracking your skull – let's not do the work of your enemies."

David looked at Sheff's hat, and stomped on it. "Try and kill Milde's get, eh?" he said to Sheff's corpse. "Gets you killed instead."

"David," Margaret said over her shoulder without a hint of indulgence. "Hurry."

And he did.

The sound of the riot grew, faded away and grew again; such was the curling nature of Hardacre's streets. They led to trouble as often as they led away from it, but Margaret – efficient Margaret – knew her way even after a few weeks; another corner and the riot may as well have been a hundred miles away. She took them down a side street that ran almost directly to the *Habitual Fool*, the pub they had been staying in these past few weeks. Almost directly meant a meander, and another near-miss with the riot. In fact, one poor fellow ran at them with an iron bar, only to be neatly punched in the neck by Margaret. He teetered there, blinking, so Margaret kicked him in the stomach, looking all the while like she would rather do the same to David.

He stepped over the groaning man.

"I'm sick of being hunted! Talking of which, why were you following me?" David asked, his limbs shuddery; he suddenly and desperately needed some of that Carnival in his pocket, and food, plenty of food. His stomach rumbled.

"I needed to know."

"Know what? That I visit the brothels of Goodlin Street, or that I'm still taking Carnival?"

"I know you haven't been visiting brothels," Margaret said.

David sighed, felt heat in his face. Carnival killed that part of him dead. Besides, his father's friend Medicine Paul had once sent him to a brothel. The experience had been somewhat painful, embarrassing, and terribly awkward; even then Carnival had been his greater craving. "Then what? What did you need to know that asking me wouldn't have answered?"

"I needed to know that you weren't the one doing the killing. Those bodies they've been finding, the ones that started appearing a week after we arrived."

She thought he was capable of that? They turned another corner and he could see the *Habitual Fool* up ahead.

"Well, are you?"

"Of course not," he said. "Of course not. That's Cadell, all of that is Cadell. He's an Old Man; it's what they do. They've hungers when they're alive, persuasive hungers, believe me. But when they die it gets much, much worse."

"And what are you going to do about it?"

"Eat something," he said. "I'm hungry."

He was always hungry, and the sight of Sheff and the Verger dead had only made him hungrier. After all, he was an Old Man, too.

Margaret grabbed his arm. David wrenched free, and turned on her. "Don't get between me and food," he said, with a hiss – all teeth and spittle. "Don't you dare!"

Before Margaret could see his embarrassment, and her

hurt expression could turn to anger, he bolted to the pub, pushing the door right into a poor drinker. The man scowled and clenched his fists, until David smiled at him. "Please don't get between me and food," he repeated.

The man backed away, hands out. "It's nothing. It's nothing," he said.

David wondered just what he saw in his face.

David could feel Margaret's gaze on him. Could feel the question still unanswered.

He knew what he had to do. And it terrified him.

CHAPTER 2

*That time in Hardacre was filled with such desperation and yet
everything moved so slowly. My partner, Whig, and I have waded
through the molasses of civic paperwork before. We've never let it
stop us. I was cocky, but what mayor isn't? We've earned such pride.
I got things done, and in my time, but this wasn't my metropolis.
Every painful step, every stall and stymie was an illustration of that,
as though Hardacre sought to remind me whenever it could that it
wasn't Chapman, that these weren't my people, that my power base
was gone, that my people were gone.*

*I know that Margaret Penn hated me for it, but, at the time, I
didn't quite understand her urgency. David wasn't the only one
being hunted. We all had things to grieve: the profound loss of
loved ones and homes. Nothing was simple anymore.*

There was a will against us, a great and terrible will.

Well, we had terrors of our own. Not least of them Master Milde.

Recollections Recollected, A BUCHAN

THE CITY OF HARDACRE
973 MILES NORTH OF THE ROIL

What little guilt Margaret Penn possessed about following
David evaporated the moment the Vergers had attacked.

David could be angry at her all he liked, but the truth was she had saved his life. With David dead, the Roil could never be stopped. The Roil had destroyed the metropolis of Tate, subsumed her mother into its mind, and taken away everything else that she cared about. She lived for its destruction, and David was so tightly bound in any possibility of defeating the Roil that his welfare had become far more important than her own.

He was the key that engaged the Engine of the World. She needed him alive, and she had to believe that David wanted to live as well. He went on and on about being hunted. But what did he really know about that?

Margaret, on the other hand, was well acquainted with pursuit. It filled her dreams as much as the destruction of her city. Her mother hunted her.

She knew it as surely as the twin moons that shone in the sky. Just as she knew her mother would be relentless in that hunt. Margaret had seen the things that her mother had at her disposal; she'd seen the great works of the Roil, and how quickly it had washed over first her city, and, not long after, the city of Chapman. When such industry was combined with such intellect it was unstoppable.

Almost, and it was that almost that tantalised and horrified her.

If David hadn't destroyed the iron ships that had followed them after their escape from Chapman, she'd most probably be deep in the Roil now, part of the thought within its massed mind, as an ant was part of the thought of its nest.

It sickened her, just how close she had come. And just how dependent she was on David.

She'd followed him, partly to see that he was safe, partly to spy, and mostly because she was bored. They were stuck here in Hardacre. They should have gone weeks ago, left this chaotic little city for the north.

He was taking Carnival again; she had seen him purchase the drug two corners from Hardacre's main square, not hours after he had sworn that he was not. She'd watched the curious dance of the transaction, the doffing of hats, the sleight of hand. The sort of thing you didn't notice, unless you were really looking. Margaret had been disappointed, but at least she knew now. Her hopes were pinned on a man in the thrall of his addiction.

She walked into the pub alone, felt gazes fall upon her. Her skin was too pale and she was too tall. She stood out, no matter how much she hunched over, or how tightly she drew her coat about her.

She couldn't see David, he was probably already in the kitchen. The boy had grown an appetite over the last few weeks. One that was at least the match of their benefactor, Mr Buchan. She lifted her gaze, saw the former mayor of Chapman sitting at his usual table.

Buchan sat, belly creased around the table edge, at the rear of the pub where he could smoke, and eat and watch what was going on. The man saw everything, even when he was eating. And though he didn't own the pub he possessed such a proprietary air you would have thought he owned half the street as well. He gestured at her as she entered, a quick wave in his direction.

Margaret hoped she managed to hide the scowl she knew was building on her face, working its way through muscle that was most often shaped in a scowl anyway. She pushed her way through the pub towards the big man. Once the smell of ale would have annoyed her, now she hardly noticed it, which in turn annoyed her even more.

Buchan's table was crammed with more food than Margaret could have eaten in a week, there was a map folded neatly on one corner of the table, next to a small bottle of map powder. She recognised the map, even folded, the one Buchan claimed to be the only accurate study of the north.

"Margaret, Margaret. What a delight!" Buchan cried, wiping sauce from his lips, map powder clinging to his nostrils. "Food, drink, can I tempt you?" Margaret sat down. Buchan lowered his voice. "David?"

Margaret shook her head. "I don't want to talk about him."

"You two fought?"

"We had a disagreement."

Buchan frowned. "My dear, I know that you feel put-upon. But really, you must nurture some subtlety. Everything about you gives away how you feel, and who you hate."

"I don't hate you," Margaret said.

"And I didn't say you did!" Buchan laughed. "But that is good to know."

"When are we leaving?"

Buchan held her gaze. "Every day you ask me that. And every day I give you the same answer. As soon as we can."

"And you can't see just how unsatisfying that is?"

"Oh, I see it. I see it indeed." He lifted his ale, drained what was left of it with a grimace, looked at the empty glass as though it had somehow betrayed him. "We are all of us frustrated, but just think how much harder it would be if we were in the tents outside the city? Here we are with food and shelter, and some influence."

"You're saying I should be grateful?"

"I'm saying it could be worse. We are doing the best we can, and that that is better than you could hope without us. Keep David on our side, keep him as the dear friend he is, and you will be doing your part, and keeping a roof over your head. It would be a dreadful shame if you weren't to join us on the journey north."

"I'm not fond of threats."

"And I'm not fond of making them… to friends." His gaze flicked to her rifle. "And for goodness' sake, if you're going to walk around those weapons, please be more discreet."

Margaret pushed herself up from the table. "I'll be in my room," she said.

"Margaret, we won't be here forever," he said, voice low. "I promise."

Margaret pushed her chair under the table. "We don't have forever. We may not be moving but the Roil is. You should have never let Kara Jade go."

Now it was Buchan's turn to scowl.

"She was called back to Drift. I could no more stop a pilot from doing as she willed than I could wrestle a Vermatisaur. There was no money that I could offer her to make her stay. The pilots of Drift, they're loyal to the Mothers of Sky, and will be until the damn city comes crashing to the earth."

"You could have tried harder."

"I believe the same could have been said of you," Buchan said.

He was right, but she didn't have to let him see that she knew that.

"Don't look to Drift to save us," Buchan said. "The sky city is having troubles of its own."

"What troubles?"

"There are rumours of a coup. The Mothers have been very quiet of late. Only one has been seen."

Margaret shook her head. "You're talking about the most politically stable government in Shale."

Buchan rubbed his chin. "But everything changes. Hardacre isn't where our journey will end."

She turned without a word, made her way to the stairs and began to climb; not before catching a glimpse of David, his plate stacked with food, the Engineer's ring glowing ever so faintly on his finger. The boy was smiling, damn him. How could he smile? They'd just killed two men.

"Monster," she breathed.

She knew all about monsters. She'd spent her whole adult life killing them. You didn't negotiate with a monster, you couldn't, and she wasn't about to start trying.

And yet, she didn't have any choice. After all, as Buchan had pointed out, David was the closest thing she had to a friend.

CHAPTER 3

After each defeat in the south, Hardacre grew, and the capital of the north truly became that. More blood within the city's veins meant more blood spilled. For when a population grows there are always elements of it ready to take advantage, to murder, and to steal. And as Hardacre's population exploded, those elements thrived. The darkest of those flowered in the weeks after the fall of Mirrlees. The murders were gruesome. Death had never become so lurid.

Added to that were rumours of a Cuttle army massing in the south, driven north by the greater dark of the Roil.

It was a perfect time to be a good fellow such as I. Now let me take you to Miss Gentle's boudoir, where we did not go so gently at all.

Callahan, an Erotic Memoir, CHRISTOPHER CALLAHAN

CITY OF HARDACRE
972 MILES NORTH OF THE ROIL

Something scratched at the window, and for an awful moment, David thought it was *him*. Not Sheff, who was most definitely dead, but Cadell, the Old Man who had cursed him just weeks ago onboard the *Roslyn Dawn*, with a bite,

41

and the Orbis Ingenium: a ring that Cadell had claimed was a universe folded up on itself.

He was everywhere. Cadell was everywhere. Not just in his dreams. Why not a dark shape scraping its nails against the glass, or an Old Man's memories building in David's blood and his bones? And like the Old Man, imprisoned for millennia, David was obsessed with the dimensions of the room that caged him. That was the bit of Cadell in him. Frequently he dreamt of a small room, windowless, with a single reinforced door, bolted shut with something that hurt his head. So often had he had this dream now, that space had come to overlay his own room.

It was three steps from the desk to the window and five from the bed to the window, or three to the door. David knew the dimensions of this little room too well. He'd spent too long in it.

There was another soft scraping against the glass.

David stood up from his desk – where he had been trying to write a letter to his Aunt Veronica – and holding his pen in front of him as though it were a Verger's knife, took those three steps to the window. He wasn't ready for this, didn't know if he would ever be. His hands shook a little despite the Carnival in his veins.

Nothing.

The street below was empty. Perhaps it had been an auditory hallucination. In some people Carnival generated all manner of colourful experiences. David had never taken the drug for that, more its ability to calm. As Cadell himself had implied (well, more than implied), to shield him from the worst sensations of a life subsumed by tragedy. Carnival suppressed doubt, blunted terror's edge. It was what allowed him to stand at the window considering the possibility of the Old Man, and what made it, ultimately, addictive. If David had grown wild with visions and terror every time he'd taken a dose, he wouldn't have taken it.

Cadell was out there, somewhere. David had been expecting it, he couldn't explain how, but he knew this was the consequence of the Old Man's death, and the "gift" he had given him.

Tens of people already dead in the city of Hardacre, and David had yet to bring himself to search him out. He was frightened of what he might find, and what he had to do. There hadn't been much in the way of serious investigation yet; all of these people had been refugees from Chapman, and even a couple from Mirrlees. He'd heard whispers that one of them had even been a Verger.

Carnival kept it at distance and allowed him to study his terror with a dispassion that he could never hope to attain without it.

A source had been easy to find. If you knew what to look for, and the signals were universal, Carnival dealers were never far away, particularly in these darkening days. And the refugees from Chapman's destruction had flooded the market. David had thought that it would be harder to score the good stuff, but apparently a lot of the people who had been carried on the winds had taken it with them. Supplies might drop in the weeks ahead, particularly if the rumours about the exodus from Mirrlees were true. But right now, scoring Carnival was easier than finding fresh fruit.

Getting away from Margaret and Buchan and Whig had proven harder, but he'd managed it, and transactions weren't a lengthy affair. How could he explain to Margaret, hardly a sympathetic ear at the best of times, that Carnival was the only thing that suppressed Cadell's increasing influence within him?

And all it did was slow the process.

Perhaps if he had explained that today, she would have grown more sympathetic; then again, she may have regarded him with even more suspicion.

David's finger brushed the Orbis on his right hand. It was cold, colder even than his fingertips. He'd tried to remove it several times, but it was not just the case of a ring too tight to drag over his knuckle, but that his flesh and the Orbis Ingenium had fused. Indeed it was growing inside him, filaments of that ring were doing things to him, and the more it did, the more he understood its process, and the less he liked it.

Twice he'd tried to cut it off, just beneath the knuckle, only to faint when he reached for a blade. That had occurred early in the transformation, a defence mechanism, he guessed. Now he was curious to see just what was happening, what endpoint lay ahead.

He'd grown a moustache as an act of defiance (in part, it also served to change his appearance somewhat); he couldn't decide whether or not the moustache made him look younger or older.

David didn't know if anyone else had noticed, but he'd also grown an inch taller in the last two weeks, and his shoulders and arms had thickened, which was quite a feat for a Carnival addict. All of it the better to accommodate Cadell, he supposed. He didn't think the Old Man was going to come bursting out of him any time soon, changing the slope of his brow, or the curve of his lips, but he was there, and with every passing day there was more of him.

He stared out the window. Hardacre was so much smaller than Mirrlees; from here he could almost see to the edge of the city. Really, it was barely deserving of the name. Hardacre could scarcely be larger than the largest suburb in Mirrlees, though there everything was out of scale: its levees, its bridges beneath which a whole community could hide and rot. He missed his city, despite the rain, despite the fact that he had been hunted there. Somehow that vastness was easier to encompass than these narrow streets, and houses tacked onto other houses, tall and teetering. Thin curling streets gave out to broad squares, where you'd step from shadow to bright light in an instant, as though waking from a dream, and David's life was becoming too dreamlike as it was.

But Mirrlees was gone now. He couldn't go back, and soon this metropolis would be behind him too, if Buchan and Whig could get them moving again. All of a sudden he experienced a longing for another city, much more ancient and one that he would be going back to, even though he had never been there before. Tearwin Meet, the home of the Engine of the World. Not that he knew what he had to do beyond its high walls. The northern city remained a mystery to him.

A whistle blew in the distance, followed by others. Another body had been found. Guilt gripped him. While he did nothing, people died. He wasn't Cadell; he never wanted that sort of guilt to consume him.

He turned from the window just as someone knocked at the door. Once again he swung the pen in front of him, mightier than the sword and all that.

"David," came a soft voice.

Margaret.

"What do you want?" he asked, trying to inject more urgency into the request than the languid calm of Carnival would allow.

"You know."

David looked at his watch. Midnight had died long ago.

"It's late," he said, trying to sound tired. "Tomorrow."

Margaret sighed. "I've heard you pacing around in there. I know you're as likely to find sleep as I am."

"I don't know what you mean. I'm in bed… you," he yawned, "you just woke me."

"Open this door, or I'll kick it down."

David walked to the door, hesitated, one hand reaching out towards the latch. He considered the veins, raised along his wrist, and the nails that he kept short with a pair of clippers that Mr Whig had provided. It was the arm of a gentleman, the son of a politician, a Carnival addict and a fugitive. His hand shook a little, and he steadied it, though all it did was seem to drive the shakes deeper into him, as though, at his core, all he contained was fear.

"Don't just stand there," Margaret said. "I'm not feeling patient today."

When was she ever patient? She'd spent the last week arguing with Whig and Buchan, demanding why they hadn't already set off into the north.

"You have a second, no more and then I–"

David opened the door because he knew that she would, and if she did it would be a damn sight harder to close again.

Margaret pushed past him, spun on her heel, in a movement as precise and swift as a dancer's, and jabbed a pale finger into his chest. "You can hear them out there, can't you? The whistles blowing?"

David considered her. Much paler than his brown skin, her hair a bone white that still surprised him a little when he saw her. She looked like she had been waiting for just this moment, to come springing from her bed, all accusation and sharp fingers. His jaw moved a little, but he found that he couldn't quite manage to speak.

Margaret grimaced. "What's wrong with you?" she demanded.

David shook his head. "I'm tired. I'm just tired. I was ready to go to bed." And he realised that this time he wasn't lying, he'd been sitting there with his pen in hand trying to think, just how to write what he had to write. Doubting the letter would even reach his Aunt Veronica.

"And sleep, eh. Rest for another day of doing nothing," Margaret spat. She walked to the window and tapped the glass; more whistles blew, louder, closer together, beneath them David thought he could just make out shouts. "Waiting for another night of death."

David felt sorry for her, almost as sorry as he felt for himself.

"Another body will show up tomorrow." said Margaret.

"I would say so," David replied.

Margaret peered at him. "Are you all right? You really don't look it."

David shrugged; honestly, he didn't know. "What are you suggesting we do?"

"We both know it's him," Margaret said, turning from the window. "Don't lie; I can see that you know. We need to find Cadell. Stop him before someone else dies."

David nodded. "You're right, of course. We need to hunt him down, and stop him. Absolutely."

"Are you mocking me?" Margaret demanded. "Because I will not be mocked."

"No," David said, and so what if he was? "But it is too late tonight. I don't think it would be good to find him in the darkness. But tomorrow, when the sun's up, then we have a better chance." He smiled at her. "I'm surprised you haven't gone off hunting him alone."

Margaret shook her head. "I tried, I may as well have been hunting a ghost."

David was shocked. How unlike her to admit a weakness, perhaps he wasn't the only one changing. "And you think having me around with you will give you an advantage? Maybe you're the one doing the mocking."

"Once I'd have laughed at the thought of needing your help. But, David, you're not yourself any more, you even move differently now."

Really, David thought, do I? He came to the foot of the bed, and sat down. Margaret's eyes followed him intently, and not without a little suspicion. He grinned at her. Her lips thinned.

"Whatever Cadell did to you, it's changed you. And not just because you're wearing the Old Man's Orbis." She looked from the Orbis on his finger, to the pen that he still held in his hands, then over at the desk. "What have you been writing?"

"Nothing," David said. Which was close enough to the truth. He'd tried to pen a letter to his Aunt Veronica and failed and failed and failed. All he'd ended up doing was scratching his name in the desk. Ten sheets of paper were scrunched up in the bin by the writing table, on two of them he'd written the word *drown* at least a hundred times. On another sheet he'd scrawled, *Help. They're coming. Hungry.* He didn't even remember writing the words, or whose words they were exactly. His psyche had become complicated of late. He was finding it harder and harder to tell just who he was.

David got to his feet. "You are right, we must do something. We must put an end to this, but we have to be careful. And you're right, I think I can find him." He opened the door, gestured for her to go through it.

Margaret gave him a look that said, amongst other things, *I've seen you tear iron ships out of the sky. You need fear nothing*. But he did, that was exactly what he had to fear.

Instead, as she walked through the doorway, Margaret said, "So what is he, now?"

"He is what he always was," David said. "An Old Man."

"And what are you?"

He shut the door in her face.

The door jolted once, as though Margaret had struck it, or perhaps knocked her head against the wood. David jumped. Maybe he shouldn't have been so rude. No, better she was angry than depressed.

Outside the whistles blew again, loud and shrill, and David could imagine he was home – where the Vergers' whistling would echo like a threat through the dark, and where his father was still alive. And then he was remembering the shrill winds of the storms of Marger Pass, someone shouting at Cadell, and he knew again that his memory had become a chasm, far deeper than it should have ever been.

He slid a hand under the desk and pulled his Carnival from its hiding place.

Nothing better to paper over the abyss, he thought, and laughed.

CHAPTER 4

It was a period of great confusion. The Roil infiltrating cities with ease, and the Old Men bringing fairy tales to life with their murderous hungers. Stade had released them, and he knew what he was doing (how rarely he did not). But that did not make it any less cruel an act. You do not let the old stories out: you do not let them trample the earth beneath their boots.

We may not have understood quite what they were, but the outcomes were all too easy to comprehend. Blood and death, from the moment he sprang their cages.

Remember this, Warwick Milde may have released John Cadell, but it was Stade who did it for the rest.

Accusations, ADSETT & REYNE

THE VILLAGE OF COB
682 MILES NORTH OF THE ROIL

They arrived with the night – silent but for gunshots, and the screams of their victims, though the latter never lasted long.

It was dangerous land, north above the flood plains of Mirrlees, caught between the edges of the Margin and the

Gathering Plains, where the rains fall cold and hard, and death takes a myriad horrible forms. However, there was money to be earned there, salvaging the ruins of a war decades gone. And the people who made it their home were used to horror. After all they picked at its scab, found a living in all those deathly Mechanisms.

Venin had worked as a scavenger and a guard for a dozen years, and he had lived through Cuttlefolk incursions, and a fungal murderous creature known only as the Meer; he'd even survived a night alone in the Margin. (One that had started with five other men. He still heard them calling, some evenings, on the wind – if it blew in from the west.) Rumour was he'd killed a Verger, long ago, had run for his life to Cob, far from anywhere, certainly far from any city justice. Well, there might have been some truth to that, but Venin had never expanded upon it, nor denied it anyway. And talk, as it did, died down.

He'd stayed in the town, and risen in the community's estimation. And if he'd not killed a Verger, there was no denying he had iron in him. Sort of man you could rely on.

Even Venin had considered himself that.

Not any more.

He'd bolted the heavy door at the first screams, all impulse to aid fled. He held his gun in shaking hands, the weapon primed. They will pass me by, Venin thought. They will pass me by.

He'd hardly breathed as first the Starlins next door screamed out their life – and them with a new babe and three younglings – the Wilsons two doors up followed (after the rapid-fire bursts of Caddle Wilson's shotgun).

The screams stopped. And for a few quiet minutes, he

thought he might live out the night – until something sniffed at his door. Venin stepped backwards slowly, crouched down behind a table he had overturned, resting the rifle on its edge, slowly, slowly applying pressure to the trigger.

The door shook against its hinges, once, twice.

Silence.

His breath steamed from his mouth, his fingers chilled. The door creaked, a crack streaked along the floor towards him. What forces could move the earth so?

The bolt slid free, struck the floor and shattered.

The door opened. A figure framed in the doorway, limbs delicate and long, and light that flowed from a hand as though it had turned to silk. Gave Venin enough light to get in a good shot.

He fired twice, the rifle jumping in his grip, banging against the table, like he was new to shooting, like he was just a boy with years ahead of him, and no reputation to uphold.

Boots slapped on the floor, not at all a graceful sound, but quick – like the swift turnings of some mechanism built for speed. Hands wrenched Venin to his feet. His own piss warmed his pants, then chilled in them. The grip that held him was bitterly terribly cold, and it spread to his limbs. He twitched, tried to lift the rifle – instead it fell from his fingers. His teeth chattered. His limbs shook.

Venin looked up into a sophisticated face with pale watery eyes, lit with a fierce hunger. An Old Man's face. The sorrow he saw there shocked him, almost enough that he didn't feel the pain. But not quite.

"It should never have been this way, but the boy, he gave his strength to the boy. Our flesh is cold, our punishment severe, and you must share in that. We need the strength, we need the speed," the Old Man whispered in his ear. "Believe me, I am truly sorry for what I am to do."

But it didn't stop him.

The Old Men stood at the edge of the town, the grass around their feet dying, freezing. Once they had ruled Shale, directed all its energies to science and industry. And they had failed, and they had been punished. The whole world had been punished, and that punishment, in part, meant that no one could dwell on it.

You mastered the cold or it mastered you.

Every town they passed through died. And those lucky few that came upon the remains knew nothing of what had happened there, but death and the quiet relief that it had passed them by. Once, perhaps, these Old Men would have been hunted, but no one possessed the resources or the knowledge to do so any more. And so they were left to race and to devour.

"He's that way," they whispered. "He's that way," they spat, gripped with madness and a wild joy. "Far away, but always nearer."

Fed, but already growing hungry, they rushed from one darkness into another. Heading north, where the boy was. And the thing that Cadell had become.

CHAPTER 5

Things are always complicated.
Hardacre was no paradise. It took a certain grim pride in its lo-
cation, the cold winds that threw themselves down the mountains,
the lazy blue and green curl of the aurora. From such flinty soil a
city had grown. Its people were an odd mix of miners and artisans,
and those many thousands of refugees. They had good reason to
hate the south. In Hardacre they bred them tough and bitter. In
Hardacre they liked to imagine that the south didn't exist at all,
unless they were looking for an enemy, and a reason to unite.

Boothby's Histories & Mysteries, TOLSON BOOTH

THE CITY OF HARDACRE
971 MILES NORTH OF THE ROIL

It was almost 11am before David came down the stairs into
the pub. He'd barely slept at all, and what sleep he'd had
was hardly restful, filled with dreams of a room that bound
him, Old Men running, whistles loud and shrill, and the distant pleading screams of a half-dozen dead. He'd finally
given up on sleeping and watched the morning illuminate
his window, restless but refusing to move from his bed

because that would mean doing things, and unpleasant things at that.

He'd heard Margaret walk past his room twice, but she hadn't knocked at the door again. Something for which David had been extremely grateful, even though he knew he would pay for it.

He'd stayed away from the kitchens, too, to see just how long he could keep his hunger in check. Not all that long, as it turned out, and now, down here, he could feel the saliva building in his mouth. If he opened his lips too wide it would come dribbling down his chin.

He ordered food, quite a lot of it, had it put on Buchan's tab, then sat and waited. It was a struggle not to pick at the half-eaten food left behind by another guest. He managed it, but only just, and that by studying the other patrons.

Not the most salubrious of people, but these were hardly the most salubrious of times.

The pub had swollen with visitors, a lot of them scared and travel-worn. Every day brought new people to the *Habitual Fool*, and new rumours. Cuttlemen had been sighted moving south, an airship of the spying variety had not returned from the east, and a village three hundred miles from here had been massacred, though by what was a matter of some contention. There had been death, so much of it, and not just on the plains. It was easy enough for Cadell's murders to disappear amongst the fatalities, unless you knew what you were looking for, and David did. Indeed, he had no need to look; he could feel it. More disturbingly, he found himself increasingly empathetic with the murderer.

He was on his third plate of steak – raw as he could get it – and beans when Margaret arrived.

"You're late," she said. David thought she looked as tired as he felt.

David shook his head. "I've been here twenty minutes." He gestured at the empty plates, took another swift mouthful of steak.

"Two hours ago I was here looking for you."

"Yes, well, two hours ago I was asleep." Two hours ago he'd been sliding a needle under his tongue, while the presence of Cadell tried to stop him.

"Some people should be so lucky," she spat.

"We both know that sleep comes rare and ill to us. Don't pretend otherwise. You take it when you can get it, and you hope for the best." If you're me, you hope that Cadell won't be sitting with you, he thought, demanding why he was still locked out, why you kept taking Carnival? When the answer was plain and obvious.

Margaret nodded her head. "Well, if you're rested and fed, perhaps we can go hunting."

David looked around the room. "Should we tell anyone?"

Neither Buchan nor his companion Whig had entered the dining hall; David knew they wouldn't be far away.

Margaret smiled. "What, that we're off to stalk a dead man? It's better that they don't know."

"One less worry, I guess."

Margaret shrugged. "I doubt they'll even notice that we're gone."

They left the pub, someone taking their seats as soon as they got up from them, despite the teetering pile of plates.

David took a deep breath of cool air.

It had rained in the evening and the streets were still slick with it. The air smelt of woodsmoke and rain, but not the waterlogged and rotten odours of Mirrlees. Apparently it had been a peculiarly wet year, and while there were plenty of people prepared to swear, loud and angrily, that it had nothing to do with the approaching Roil, their protestations rang far too hollowly. The general consensus seemed to be that people did not talk about the weather.

Every single weather pattern on the planet was driven by the Roil now, though David knew that the rains here would be nothing like those in Mirrlees. Hardacre was too far west of the sea, and shielded by two mountain ranges. To the south, though, the rain would be falling, and falling heavily, the hem of its skirts caught on the mountains. And, further south, where it was dry and hot, Quarg Hounds would be massing beneath shrill clouds of Hideous Garment Flutes, and metropolises would be waking from their slumber.

David shook his head. Ah, how he wished for the days when all he knew about the Roil had come from children's books, pulp adventures, and the drunken ramblings of his father.

"Which way?" Margaret asked. Hands on her hips, suddenly looking her age.

David blinked at her. "I have a sense of something, but not a certainty. The murders occurred in Easton. I suggest we go west, towards New Wall."

Margaret looked at him peculiarly.

"Trust me," David said. "He's not going to kill near his hiding place. Too dangerous."

"And if anyone catches him on the way back from a kill?"

"Then they're dead too. Even now, even diminished, Cadell is more than a match for a couple of constables."

"You and I, though…"

"Think of it as a test," David said. "If we can't manage this, then there never really was any chance that we'd survive to Tearwin Meet."

Margaret had little to say about that, just pulled her long

coat about her. David caught a glimpse of rime blade, and rifle; Sheff's knife was belted at her waist, too. He could understand why she had taken the guns, but the ice blade was good against little but Roilings; sure, she could hack and slash with it, but the thing they hunted would require something more than hacking and slashing with a weapon that turned the air cold.

David took the lead, guiding them down Maddle Street, and onto Devine, where the pubs gave way to shops – bookstores and coffeehouses, haberdasheries and dress shops. The crowds grew around them, jostling, always on the edge of something that wasn't quite despair or rage. The air was filled with the threat of violence, just waiting for something to set it off. The numbers of beggars had jumped in the past few weeks, many refugees, some just people waiting to take advantage. Margaret's presence, though, was all it took to keep them away, and the one or two desperate (or stupid) enough to get in her way were pushed to one side.

Devine broadened onto the market square, and here where produce was on display, fruits and vegetables from the gardens to the west, brought down by barge along the Chortle or Winebrook rivers, David could smell meat cooking, and even more enticing: freshly slaughtered animals. He had to close his eyes to their call – even though all that meat and fat had him salivating – and keep on walking. It wasn't easy, but he managed it. At the far end of the market, where Goodlin Street began, the crowds thinned out, though there were even more beggars, and these seemed darker more desperate – and some of the establishments concerned themselves with other pleasures of the flesh.

If David was alone, he could have found Carnival here. Indeed, he recognised at least three vendors of the drug, though they were keeping a low profile, as several constables were walking their beat. Not that that stopped one of the dealers from tipping his hat to David (who subtly shook his head).

"Look at them," Margaret said, hardly keeping the sneer from her voice. She jabbed a finger at the nearest pair of constables, big men with clubs, dressed in pale blue overcoats. "Like Vergers without teeth, do they make you feel safe?"

David laughed, relieved that she hadn't caught his head-shake, or chosen to ignore it. "Do you think this street would be any louder without them? Not all threats require knives, for some watchfulness is almost enough."

Something prickled in the back of his neck. He turned and looked back at the square, just in time to catch a sudden movement, by the fruit stand. He looked over at Margaret, to whom a painted lady was gesturing furiously, until Margaret gestured something back.

"We need to keep moving," David said. "I can feel something." He pointed away from the markets, no need to alarm Margaret just yet, not when they were in such a crowded part of the city.

They passed through the street quickly, and the buildings closed around them again, grew circumspect. Here the roofs almost touched, leaning in against each other, as though sharing deepest intimacies or salacious gossip. Goodlin Street was so much shorter than Mirrlees' Argent Lane. As they turned into Backel Lane, David began to feel it, and not from whoever or what that pursued them, but a profound, darker awareness.

The part of him that was Cadell responded, as though it felt its mirroring in the distance. David recognised its hungers, because they were his too. But also, for the first time he could feel its wrongness, he had to end it, to take it from the world. What they hunted wasn't Cadell any-more, and in a way that was more brutal, and fundamental, than the way that David wasn't quite David anymore.

"We have to hurry," David said, almost running. They reached the end of Backel Lane, and came upon some in-dustry, men and women working machines, smaller versions of the ones that had constructed Mirrlees' levee.

Along the outskirts of the city a wall was already being built, and before it and behind it, deep channels being dug. Margaret had told him that they were intent upon building a moat, and now he could see it. Already brackish water sat in the bottom of the trench.

David couldn't see the point. The Roil possessed not just snapping jaws and flapping wings, but technologies – iron ships chief among them. More than that, it held cities that dreamed. You might as well dig holes in the ground. The only walls that he knew were effective were those of Tear-win Meet. *So high they almost touched at the top, and the gap itself was shielded with filaments of cold wire; why, when he was a boy he would climb to the top, one way the Great Northern Sea battering at the stony walls, the other land stretching on and on, and you could see the curvature of the–*

David shook away the memory. It wasn't his.

Once again, he felt Cadell's presence, deeper, and more pervasive this time. They turned from the wall, and down another alley.

Then something crashed in the street behind them, not Cadell, nothing like Cadell. There was nothing furtive and sly in the movement.

"Down," Margaret said, and before David could protest, she had pushed him aside.

CHAPTER 6

The Roilings spread swiftly, borne on the winds of war, and by a new species of moth. Why now? Why not after the Grand Defeat? It seemed some dynamic had changed. The Roil was no longer something on the horizon; it wormed its way into the north, borne on iron ships and in the blood of refugees.

Night's Fall, DEIGHTON

THE CITY OF HARDACRE
970 MILES NORTH OF THE ROIL

Margaret moved towards the sound, David behind her. She held the rime blade in one hand. In these close quarters what was literally cold steel seemed the simplest weapon available to her, and the one least likely to lead to manslaughter should the noise prove no threat. Besides, the thought of wasting endothermic shells sickened her. She never knew when her supply would run out, a bullet fired here was one that she could not fire in the Deep North, if they ever made it that far.

David touched her arm, she jerked her head towards him, so savagely that he took a quick step back, and she realised that she had frightened him. Was it wrong that she took so much pleasure in his fear? "I said, get down."

David nodded: an irritating smile grew on his face. "Because, yes, I really need you to protect me. We're being followed," he said. "Have been since we passed the market square." She wanted the scared David back.

"And you didn't tell me until now?" Margaret glanced casually down the street, her flinty eyes narrowed. "Cadell?"

"No, I don't think so. And I could be wrong but–"

Margaret was already stalking back the way they had come.

A woman in her eighties, Margaret guessed, stumbled out from her hiding place; she almost looked as though she were going to crash to the ground. Margaret lowered her blade, but she did not sheathe it. The woman straightened and there was slyness in the movement, her lips turned slightly upwards at Margaret's approach. There was something wrong with her eyes, they were unfocussed. She seemed to look at Margaret and not look at her. Margaret hesitated, then lifted the rime blade higher.

"Why are you following us?" Margaret hissed.

"I'm not sure. The question..." The woman's voice fell away, and she looked at her hands as though the answer might lie there. Then she pulled her shawl tighter about her shoulders. Margaret felt a stab of sympathy, but she ignored it.

"You know what I mean, you've been following us since we passed through the square."

Margaret towered over the woman, fighting the snarl that she could feel forming on her lips. Snarls came more often these days. She tried to smile. "There's nothing to be frightened of," Margaret said. "We do not kill old women."

"Just Old Men," David said from behind her, and Margaret did her best to ignore him, and the ever-increasing smugness in his tone. Where did that come from? Why did it choose to reveal itself now?

The woman didn't look frightened, just confused. She straightened her clothes, took a deep breath, her gaze cleared and she looked at Margaret with eyes wide and suddenly knowing.

And Margaret realised that the woman wasn't confused at all. She'd known exactly what she was doing.

"Not following him. Just you." The woman grabbed her arm with fingers that seemed to burn with their own heat, and smiled. Darkness swarmed over her lips. Her eyes rolled in her head. "We're coming for you, my darling," she said.

Margaret yanked her arm free, eyes wide, that voice – it was her mother's voice. "Hurry up, then," Margaret said, and thrust the rime blade through the Roiling's chest. Her thumb flicked the activation plate, and the Roiling jolted and screamed, or tried to. What came out was dark and fluttering, already dying: Witmoths. Ice streaked her clothes, where the blade touched her; Margaret could feel the old woman's spine grinding against the steel. Margaret grabbed a pistol from her belt and shot the Roiling in the head. The Roiling hit the ground with a wooden thump. She fired again at its chest.

"I think it's dead," David said, touching her elbow.

"She... It shouldn't be here in the first place." Margaret yanked her elbow free. "I said, don't touch me."

"Do you have to kill everything you meet?" David said.

Margaret yanked her blade free. Tapped it against the cobblestones, ice dark with blood and Roil spores dropped to the ground.

"Now we'll never know how it made its way here. Or if it left a trail of infected."

"They always leave a trail," Margaret said.

"Yes, I suppose they do. And it *always* seems to lead to us. Perhaps all we need do is wait." David crouched down, he looked more curious than scared, and picked up a Witmoth. It crumbled beneath his fingers, he grimaced and wiped them clean on his pants. "The moths have become more robust," he said. "They shouldn't be able to hold any form here."

"What, they're resistant to the cold?"

David touched her arm (again!) with his frigid fingers. "Oh, this is hardly cold, but their presence here is disturbing." He peered at Margaret. "Are you all right?" he asked.

Margaret hardly heard him. The Roiling's last few words had been spoken in her mother's voice. Its face had shifted subtly, too.

"Normally you would have knocked my hand away by now."

Margaret did just that. "Yes, I'm fine. What should we do with the body? We can't leave it here."

"You're right," David said. "This street may be deserted now, but people must use it sometimes."

"I'll grab the legs," Margaret said.

David shook his head. "No need. Please, if you would make me some room."

He touched the old woman's face and closed his eyes. The air chilled, ice crackled over the woman's cheeks, it rose crystalline and red from her lips. The corpse stiffened and crackled. David, sweating and breathing hard, took a step back. "Have to do this quick."

He kicked the body with his boot. The corpse shattered as though it were made of glass.

"That was harder than I thought it would be." He panted, and stamped down hard on the shards. "But you were right, we couldn't have left the body here. Someone finds that, gets a moth inside them, and, well, you know what happens."

Margaret still couldn't quite believe what she had seen. There was blood where the corpse had been, not blood exactly, but a sort of black and red slurry.

"How did you do that?" she said. "Cadell couldn't do that."

David shrugged. "Maybe he could, or maybe he wasn't far enough north. We're much closer to Tearwin Meet, and its power is in part mine."

She looked down at the mess. "But that... that is madness."

"Oh, it's nothing really." David took a step forward, tripped, or stumbled, or just dropped. He grabbed at her arm, slipped and almost fell on his face. Margaret pulled him up. He was shivering, and his face had grown almost as white as hers.

"David?"

"I'm f-f-fine."

"Perhaps we should get you home."

"You're too kind," he said. "Far, far too kind. It's the Lodes, well, the absence of them. I was near a Lode the last time I used my powers: it did the hard work."

Something moved in the street ahead, a shadow darting towards them; David pulled himself from Margaret's grip, and took a few steps forward. She moved to get in front of him, and found herself pushed backwards.

"Not this time," he said. "You can't protect me every time."

Margaret opened her mouth, and he shook his head. She had a rifle in hand already.

"If things go badly," David whispered, "run. Actually, I'd start running now. The endothermic shells won't do more than make him angry." He puffed up his chest, stared down the street, and Margaret could see that he'd almost forgotten she was there.

"All right then!" David shouted. "I'm right here!"

He took a step forwards.

Bins tumbled, hard nails scratched against stone walls, heavy boots crashed into the distance. Margaret fired towards the sound.

David grinned. "That scared him." Then he almost dropped again. He turned to Margaret, almost pathetically. "Hurry. Take me back to the pub, before Cadell decides that maybe now is just the time to end this and turns around. Keep your blade ready."

"For Cadell?"

"Ha, no, not a chance, he'd scratch strips from us, then eat them as we died." He patted her arm. "Just in case there's more Roilings about."

There hadn't been any more Roilings about, but plenty of constables and prostitutes, and enough of the latter had whistled at her salaciously on their way into the market square, by which time David was leaning on her heavily. Almost back at the pub, close enough that they could smell the beer, and whatever meat was being served up as meal of the day, David straightened.

"Feeling better," he said. "Have to remember not to do that again. I really should have just done the head. Yes, the head would have been enough."

Margaret still wasn't sure exactly what it was that he had done in the first place. "Still would have left a body."

"Yes, of course. You're right. I won't be so thoughtless next time."

He smacked his lips. "Now, I'm hungry." He looked at Margaret with eyes all too predatory for his face. "We'll catch him tomorrow, Margaret. I promise. Go polish your weapons or whatever it is that you do." She nearly punched that hungry face for being so dismissive, so damn patronising. She was a Penn! Of course, that was precisely what she had in mind.

"And what are you going to do?"

"I'm going to eat, and once I'm done I am going to eat some more," he said. "You're free to join me."

Margaret declined.

CHAPTER 7

The Aerokin are mystery given flight. These great beasts of the sky, bound to their pilots by something deeper than blood or love. Lifespan, sex, intelligence – all is speculation. They are known to change names, size, shape, even pilots over the course of a life that must span decades, if not centuries.

We know nothing of their ancestry. Were they terrestrial in origin, or like the Cuttlemen, from a different world altogether? Certainly they never revolted, though they served only one people, working for others only through the agency of Drifters and their rulers the Mothers of the Sky. History has brought up only two pilots not of Drift blood. Toni Obrey and Max Magrit: the Thieves of the Air. You will find no public record of their existence, but they are still equal parts admired and cursed in Drift today.

Queens & Kings of the Air, COLSON & CREEL

THE CITY OF DRIFT
800 MILES NORTH OF THE ROIL – ALTITUDE 20,000 FEET

There were a dozen Aerokin in the Hall of Winds, but only one of them had her attention – the rest may as well have not existed.

"Finally!"

Kara Jade touched the curved head of the *Roslyn Dawn*, just a few feet from the Aerokin's light sensors, where the flesh was soft and warm. The contact sent a soft prickle through her fingers, and soothed her. The *Dawn* was being washed; Kara could feel the *Dawn*'s purrs running through her body and up her pilot's arms. The Aerokin slid a flagellum over her shoulder, a movement surprisingly gentle for such a huge creature. The *Dawn* could crush her pilot with a single flick, though she never would. Kara and the Aerokin had grown up together, which is why the last week had been interminable.

"I've missed you," Kara said, and the *Dawn* patted her gently.

"Am I being punished?" Kara asked and the Aerokin rumbled warmly, which, of course she would, she loved being cleaned, and not the frigid drenching of the northern storms, but a great warm spray. Soap, hot water and oils were being rubbed into her flesh. The *Dawn*'s wounds had all but healed. She looked better than she had in a long time. Even before they had flown down to Chapman and met the boy, the girl and the Old Man.

She purred again.

Traitor, Kara Jade thought.

Though it wasn't the *Dawn* being called a traitor on the streets. It wasn't the *Dawn* being whispered about in the food halls or on the streets. That was wholly reserved for her pilot. Kara ate in her room now, away from the gaze of accusatory eyes.

Kara's responsibilities towards the *Dawn* had been taken away from her, everything, even cleaning. She was a pilot without her Aerokin, and felt limbless, anchorless. Which, she knew, was how they wanted her to feel. She refused to play their game. The Mothers of the Sky, one and all, could just tumble from the sky as far as she was concerned.

"You'll get soft if you keep this up," she said, sounding as casual as she could despite the lump in her throat. "We're meant to be in the sky, you and me. Not here!"

The *Dawn* batted at her with her flagellum, nearly knocked her off her feet. I suppose I deserved that, she thought.

Kara was surprised that they had even let her walk into the Hall of Winds. But where else could she go? She had a small room in the pilots' barracks, but it was little larger than the bed that it contained, and the single shelf for her book: a Shadow Council novel that David Milde had given her. She thought of him in Hardacre, and hoped he was safe. The last thing she had heard was that he was awake, when she'd left he'd been days in bed, hardly stirring, and she'd expected him to die.

"I did what they told me. Didn't I?" she whispered in the *Dawn*'s ear, a hole no larger than her hand, usually closed over with a thin membrane. The *Dawn* was really all ears. The Aerokin could listen with her bones and limbs just as effectively, but there was something much more intimate in talking to her this way.

"You should have done more than *just* what we told you," a voice said from behind her.

Startled, Kara Jade turned to see Mother Graine. The Mothers of the Sky had kept to themselves of late, hidden away, planning. She'd never expected to see one down here.

"We expect all our agents and pilots, to not merely follow our commands, but to anticipate them as well. Difficult at times, yes. But is piloting ever an easy occupation? The clouds are fickle, the sky an endless challenge. Storms come and must be engaged."

Kara wondered how long the Mother had been standing there, and just how much she had heard. From the look on her face, a lot. At least Kara hadn't given voice to her thoughts concerning the Mothers of the Sky, even as their imagined tumble grew more vivid. She couldn't hide a smile. "I knew that they wouldn't let me in here without a reason."

Mother Graine's expression shifted, Kara couldn't quite tell what it meant. The Mothers of the Sky were unreadable at the best of times, beyond a certain sort of stern abstraction that could be rage or disappointment, or simply not caring at all. That she had managed to detect some sort of emotional response wasn't a good thing.

The Mothers of the Sky were not people to displease; they were more than capable of taking the sky away, and that, for a pilot, was far worse than death. Kara knew that better than most, after all, she had been raised by one who had had her Aerokin torn from her. They hardly spoke now. Hadn't since Kara had been given the *Dawn*. Kara could have found Raven out; Drift was a small city, but Raven could have found her, too. That her older sister hadn't bothered suggested an equal antipathy.

"You should have brought the Orbis Ingenium to us," Mother Graine said.

"So I am being punished?"

Mother Graine shook her head. "Consider yourself in a process of re-education." She rested a hand on Kara's shoulder, a gentle – and what was probably meant to be reassuring – gesture. Kara only found it patronising, but she did not wrench her shoulder away – she wasn't that stupid, not even when she was that angry. "I want you to come with me."

Kara did just that, throwing one last look back at the *Roslyn Dawn*, just in case it *really* was her last look, and she was being taken to the Leaping Ledge to be hurled bodily off it and into the hungry sky.

They walked from the Hall of Winds, past the great tower over the tunnelled rock known as the Caress, and through the main part of the city. Kara was silent all the way, Mother Graine was too, except to call out to the occasional passerby, most of whom who would stop to smile, then look suspiciously, or even worse, judgementally at Kara Jade.

Why? She should be a hero. She and the *Dawn* had flown into the Roil, and survived the fall of Chapman. She'd not only escaped, but she'd escaped with John Cadell, Margaret Penn and David Milde. They'd fought iron ships, and survived; and while that may have had as much to do with Cadell (who hadn't), and the power of the Orbis (she was still confused by what she saw David do in the river by the frozen hill, no one should be able to just slap a ship out of the sky), Kara knew that none of it could have happened without her and the *Dawn*.

She knew her Aerokin, she knew how to pilot her, and if she hadn't, they would all have died. After all, it was her piloting skills that had allowed Cadell to destroy the first iron ship and without her, David would have died, naked and frozen in a river of ice.

Mother Graine led her down stairs of iron and stone, down into the belly of Drift, down through caverns and along narrow tunnels. At last they reached a cavern that opened onto the blue sky; icy winds crashed through the space, loud enough that there could be no argument with the naming of this place. It was called the Howl with good reason.

Here the great filters of the Aerokin were scraped clean, hosed down and washed. Mother Graine led her towards a section of the cavern from which hung thin slivers of fabric. All of them were dark, stained with a black inkiness.

"Here," Mother Graine said, grabbing one of the darkest strips of material; the cloth was black against her cracked brown fingers. "This is why I brought you here. What you see there is the death of our city."

"Filters always darken," Kara said, though she was horrified at the extent of what she saw. "I am so sorry, if these are the *Dawn*'s. I did not–"

"You don't understand. These are inner filters. The inner filters not of the *Roslyn Dawn*, but of the *Meredith Reneged*."

"But the *Meredith* and Cam Shine patrol the north, if she flies within three hundred miles of Mirrlees, let alone Chapman, then she has been blown off course."

"Exactly," Mother Graine said. "The Roil spores are everywhere. Your *Dawn* was much worse than this, but we managed her cleaning. She is hale and whole, and uninfected. That Aerokin is as fine as any I have ever known. The *Meredith*, while of good stock, is not nearly as robust. This is killing our ships. She was choking when she came back here. Dying.

"And it wasn't the only thing we found. I've… we've dealt with that, but you need to understand, Maiden Jade, night comes with a speed none of us could have anticipated. So fast I can barely contain the horror of it. It is winter now, though a winter of such extreme mildness that is in itself alarming, but come the summer, the Roil will spread. More of our Aerokin will weaken and sicken, their lungs clogged with Roil spores, and who knows what changes that might effect, who knows what our Aerokin may become. There may never be another winter, Maiden Jade. And you left the Orbis on the finger of a Carnival addict."

"He saved the *Dawn*," Kara said.

"Without you, he could not have saved his own. Do not mistake self-preservation for charity. He is what he is, a danger to us, and all living things."

"And you want to bring him here?"

"The closer he is, the more control we have, believe me. It is far better that we have him here than in the north. In the north he is a threat to all of us. A Mechanical Winter, my child, you do not want to live through that."

Kara Jade sighed. "All right then, I'm convinced." Mother Graine raised an eyebrow. Kara said, "What do you need me to do?"

"What needs to be done. Be the bait on our trap. Don't worry, I have no wish to harm your friend."

"He's not my friend," Kara Jade said.

"Good, then this should be much easier for you."

CHAPTER 8

Nightmares blew in from the south. Whispers and howls and sav-
agery, that's what the great dark sent before it. And the city grew
afeared, not of Quarg Hounds and Vermatisaurs, nor Vastling and
Endym, but that a deeper dark was brewing; one that even death
could not offer escape from.

The darkest monsters are in our heads; we cage them there but
poorly. They are ceaseless in their rattling of the bars.

Towards a Rudimentary Mythos, MOLCH

The air smelt of rot and the railway sleepers at David's feet
shone magnesium-white beneath the twin moons, but, as
he watched, rain swept up the tracks, bringing dark cloud
with it. No luminous train line any more.

The ground shuddered, a fast rhythmic beat. Train coming. He made to step away, and a hand grabbed his ankle,
held him to the spot. He kicked out, turned, and dropped.
Hit the ground hard, and the hand held on, if anything its
grip surer.

The *Dolorous Grey*'s whistle screamed as the eight-wheeled
train crashed towards him, too late. Too late to stop, and he
too late to move. He threw his hands up, and snapped

awake, scrambling in the dark. His fingers caught in the sheets. The sheets dissolved and he was standing, naked in the cold, though his breath was colder.

Oh, he thought, I'm still asleep.

Space, time, it was all up for grabs.

He could sense them there, in the distance. Roilings, waiting patiently this time, the old woman at the front of them. He could see where all the pieces of her had been put back together. She smiled at him, and a sliver of her cheek fell wetly onto the floor.

"Don't move," Cadell whispered, a cold breath in his ear.

"Why would I want to move?" Though he did just that, turning to face the Old Man.

"Don't lie to me." Cadell gripped David's wrist. "I know when you're lying." He squeezed. David couldn't feel his fingers anymore. "You keep on keeping me out, and that can only end badly. You need me, David."

"Tell me what needs to be done," David said. "Tell me what I need to do in the north."

Cadell grinned. "That's simple. You talk to the Engine, you enter the cage, you save the world."

"Cage?"

"Sh!" Cadell lifted a finger in the air. "There, can you hear that?"

And David could, just; a soft scratching that was almost stealthy.

"Wake up," Cadell said. "Look at all this. Look at all this blood on my hands."

He jabbed a ruddy finger at David. "And yours, too."

David glanced down, Cadell wasn't wrong.

"Wake up."

● ● ● ●

THE CITY OF HARDACRE
968 MILES NORTH OF THE ROIL

David woke, and the scratching followed him. This time
there was no hesitation in the sound, the window rattled
in its casings. He flung the sheets from him, they didn't
melt into nothing, but they *had* frozen to his skin; when
he hurled them away, they took some of his flesh with
them. He dashed the five steps to the window, almost
without thought, and though part of him knew that running away from the window might have been wiser, he
wasn't that David any more.

A bleak face stared in, lit by the twin moons. Cadell's
face, though the eyes had none of Cadell in them, they
were as white as the train tracks in David's dream. There
was something almost comical about it, something too dire
and dark so that it became almost abstract – some rushed
and sinister nocturne. Blood bearded Cadell's jaw like Witmoths had bearded the old woman's. He smacked his lips
almost comically at David. He stood on the ledge outside
the window, fingers sliding along the glass, almost as
though he had forgotten the nature of windows and how
to open them.

David felt a growl building in his throat, he moved closer
to the glass, saw an answering growl in Cadell's face. Was
this where the curse the Old Man had given him was
headed? Surely he had some choice in the matter, though
David could scarcely remember a time when he had had
choice in anything.

"Shall we end this now?" David said to the man in the window. "Do you want to come inside or should I go out there?"

The window was small; the glass thick, and ridged with
leadwork, but David knew Cadell could make short work

of it. He could feel the corpse Cadell's strength. David's body tensed, his jaw ached, and he wilted a little: considered running. Could he even make the door before Cadell was upon him?

And then it was as if the true Cadell was with him, the wit and the wisdom, whispering in his ear. David clenched his hands to fists, chilled the flesh so that it became at once harder and denser; his knuckles thickened with ice, and the blood within his fingers slowed – until his hands felt as though they were something brutal and disconnected from his flesh. Margaret had her guns, and her rime blades, but this was true weaponry.

He tensed, waiting for Cadell to drive his hand through the glass, but the Old Man did not.

Cadell's eyes dropped to the ring on David's finger. David realised that it was glowing, even through the ice. Only the moons were brighter. A cloud passed over them and darkness fell.

Now, he will do it now.

A whistle blew shrilly from the streets below and David was once again reminded of the *Dolorous Grey*. Something smashed on the ground, a roof tile, perhaps, or a stone. More whistles blew and David heard the heavy beat of Cadell's boots clambering over the rooftops. David flung open the window, a pane cracking with a loud pop when it came into contact with his fingers. He looked down at the street; below him ran dozens of constables, heavy clubs in hand. One of them looked up at him, and David nodded, keeping his ice-slicked fingers hidden.

The constable regarded him for a moment, and then kept on after his colleagues. David slumped against the windowpane, his vision swimming. How had he ever thought that he could fight Cadell? Disposing of the Roiling as he had, while effective and showy, had exhausted him utterly. He touched his face with a fingertip, skin and ice fused. He yanked his hand free and took some skin with it.

What am I? What am I now?

David shed the ice from his fists. It was coloured with his own blood and lymph. His fingers ached. He could hardly move them. He brought them to his chest, but there was no warmth there.

He could smell blood that wasn't his own. He peered out the window. There was a puddle of blood on the ledge. Not the sort of thing he wanted daylight to reveal to the world – certainly not to Hardacre's constabulary.

He hurried to the bathroom, filled the bucket there. He scrubbed the blood away as best he could, with fingers that still felt like leaden claws, resisting the temptation to see how it might taste – he knew the answer to that already, the blood scent was in the air. Then he washed his hands in water that was warm, but chilled when it touched his flesh.

Is this my life now? Is this all I am, utterly at odds with my world?

David took a deep breath, walked to the desk, and found his Carnival.

He flexed and released his hands, letting the blood come back to sluggish life. At last, when he could hold his gear with enough delicacy to do what needed to be done, he saw to his addiction.

He half expected Margaret to come bursting through the door. But she did not, and he wasn't sure if he was relieved or disappointed.

He let the Carnival do its work and it didn't matter any more.

CHAPTER 9

She's a city made for rain. She's a city made of rage. She's a city with a rough and seeking tongue. You find it ugly. I find it beautiful.

Hardacre, KEN SLESSEL

THE CITY OF HARDACRE
965 MILES NORTH OF THE ROIL EDGE

The next morning dark clouds rolled in from the north, an unheard-of thing this time of year, coming down from the mountains. The winds had changed seemingly overnight. There was some debate over whether or not they contained rain or snow. The temperature certainly had dropped, but the clouds merely built, obscuring the sky and darkening everything.

The whole city transformed with their arrival, hunkered down, as though it were the beginning of the end. The gardens seemed to shrink, several shops didn't open, a cat gave birth to a three-headed kitten, and weird howls were heard coming from the tent city beyond the town's walls.

Margaret had spent the morning practicing her swordplay.

For all that it was a weapon of last resort, the rime blade rewarded practice. It was heavy, its blade when sheathed in ice heavier still. But she had killed many Quarg Hounds with it. Indeed, she counted herself among the best of her people when it came to the sword. She was certainly the best now, and that made her practice with even more focus than usual. Her arms burning, lungs heaving, she worked through the patterns of the blade, the various rhythms that denoted attack or defence.

But her heart wasn't in it today. Her thoughts couldn't escape the news of the morning. The deaths on Rowdy Street – three killed, half eaten – and the constables that had chased something monstrous to the outskirts of the city before losing both it and five men – pieces of whom had been found with the dawn. The papers were already calling it the Night of Blood.

David was waiting for her in the dining room, having finished off his breakfast. There were several large plates of food, stacked up before him: such a remarkable appetite for such a thin man. Margaret wondered where he fit all that food. It certainly wasn't fattening him up, though he had broadened across the shoulders.

Margaret chewed down a few pieces of toast, and some strips of bacon. "Did you have enough?" she asked him, eyeing his plates.

"Just enough," David said. "Barely enough." He licked his lips, and there was something grotesque about the movement, something unconsidered and un-David like.

Margaret shuddered, and David must have caught some of the meaning behind it because he looked almost hurt.

"Where's Buchan and Whig?" she asked.

"Purchasing more supplies. They say we should be ready to leave in under a week."

Margaret hissed. "They've been saying that for a week already. What good are supplies without an airship?"

"I think this time they might mean it. There's word that a ship called the *Collard Green* is due."

Margaret wasn't prepared to even begin to hope.

David grabbed an orange quarter from the fruit platter in the middle of the table and ate it, skin and all. He stood up.

"I had a visitor last night." He almost sounded guilty.

Margaret leaned in close. "Really, he came to your room?"

"No further than the window, but I suspect he would have entered if the constables hadn't seen him."

"Before or after he–"

He said, "You've heard about the killings then?"

Margaret nodded.

"It was after. The constables didn't start chasing him until after the third death. He'd killed to build his strength, it radiated from him. He'd have taken me easily last night."

"You'd have fought him alone?" she asked.

"And I'd have died, you too. I was still too weak."

"What about now?"

"I'm fine today," David said, stretching his arms above his head; his back clicked loudly. "We'll hunt until we find him. I'm ready."

Margaret's eyes narrowed. "Are you sure? We can wait, until you're strong again."

David swallowed another piece of orange. "Why the sudden change of heart?"

Margaret couldn't quite explain it herself. But her mood had soured today and her desire to put David at risk had cooled. She didn't so much fear Cadell, but the thing David might have to become to kill Cadell.

"I'm fine, believe me, I'm fine. This must be done," David said. "Too many have died because I have done nothing. Besides I really think that Buchan and Whig might really be ready to leave, and we cannot leave him here." As if their guilt wasn't reason enough.

"If he's running from constables he can't be too strong."

"Perhaps, or he's just building. Maybe waiting for me to leave."

"Why?"

"Because when we leave the city, there will be almost nothing that can stop him. Yes, we have to do this today."

CHAPTER 10

Cadell was always the dreamer. But his dreams were nightmares for the rest of us. To call them anything else was an act of kindness and generosity that he did not deserve. He was the worst of them, the terror of terrors.

I dread the steady beat of his footfalls, the dry gasp of his laughter. I met him once; he shook my hand, offered me a drink. I said no. Better sobriety around the man who murdered Sean Milde, and tore the limbs from Vergers as though they were nothing but insects.

I thought about that, and changed my mind. Cadell smiled as he poured me my drink, as though we shared a secret. That smile is the progenitor of more than a few bad dreams.

Cadell, MOLCH

THE CITY OF HARDACRE
965 MILES NORTH OF THE ROIL

Another storm rolled in as they left the *Habitual Fool*, thunder rumbling down from the mountains. David smiled and nodded his head. "Rain reminds me of home, and it'll hide our scent a little," he said, and opened the umbrella,

Cadell's old one with the blade in its handle. He offered it to Margaret, who shook her head and shrugged her coat tight about her. "Suit yourself," he said.

They headed back to the end of Backel Lane and where the Roiling – it didn't do to think of her as human – had followed them. Patrols were out in force, constables armed to the teeth. Men and women with blunt-headed rifles, cudgels, and knives that were the match of any Verger's.

The spot where the Roiling had lain was stained and black, the rain failing to wash these robust vestiges away. David looked at the stain appraisingly, dropping down to his haunches. He could feel that Cadell had been here, had perhaps stood in almost the exact same spot. He could even feel a little of his anger, that such a creature could have come this way. If David hadn't killed it, Cadell would have. David found that a little reassuring. Cadell hadn't changed completely, like these black marks, there was something that even death had failed to erase.

"He will be somewhere dark," David said. "If we were still in Mirrlees, I'd have suggested the Downing Bridge and Mirkton beneath. There he would have had all the food he required, and less fight too."

Then David realised that Margaret had no idea what he was talking about. She'd not seen the bridge, nor the vast levees – outside of tattered books, the pictures dim and hazy, and fronted by men and women in top hats (Engineers all), smoking cigars and patting each other's backs. Even on their flight over the city, all she'd have seen was lights glittering in a flooded landscape: suburbs drowning and those ready to drown.

"Dark," she said. "And I guess deserted, too."

David nodded. "Yes, even now, his capacities so diminished he... it will do its best to hide."

"So, he's an Old Man, but he was before, why does it kill?"

"Everything, well, nearly everything, that Cadell was before, except the hunger, is gone. And believe me, Cadell had killed before, he was just more… selective." David didn't go into any further detail, now was not an appropriate time for such a discussion, and he didn't want to have to earn Margaret's trust again. "What we're hunting is just a shell. The real Cadell died on the *Roslyn Dawn*. He told me to dispose of the remains, but it's rather hard to fulfil a dying man's request when you're unconscious."

"If you just trusted me," Margaret said, startling him; they were both so suspicious of each other. He raised his hands in the air.

"No, no, this has nothing to do with trust," David said. "There wasn't any time. When the Roil sent those iron ships, there was nothing but that threat in my mind. And, to be honest, I didn't expect my actions to be so exhausting. I was naive, but I am not any longer."

And yet, he thought, here they were – the two of them alone, looking for a monster.

They followed the streets, working their way outwards, each street longer, given to a broader curve. David felt they could be missing anything, except the further they walked, the more he could feel… it wasn't so much a presence but a falling away, a rising absence. Cadell hadn't fed again, he could tell that much. The constables' pursuit had weakened him, but he wouldn't stay that way for long. David reached into his bag, pulled out a sandwich, liver and kidney, all that lovely iron. He devoured it, and ate another.

He realised Margaret was watching him. "Need to keep my strength up. Would you like one?"

Margaret declined.

They ended up in the warehouse district. Row after row of deserted buildings crowded around them.

"He's here," David said. "I can feel him, I think." David frowned. "And he's fed again."

But that was the closest they came for hours. They spent the afternoon slowly, slowly walking down wide and empty streets that would have not too long ago rang with industry. The rain fell, and David found himself never quite able to find Cadell, though once they came across a patch of road over which he might have eaten. David frequently made them stop and stand absolutely still.

"He's passed us," he'd say or, "He's very close."

Usually a few minutes later the scent would grow cold.

The day fell into night, lights came on across the city, and still they searched. David guided them back to eat in the city proper – once he had run out of his own supply – devouring huge plates of food like it was his last meal.

"Maybe it's time we went back," Margaret suggested.

David nodded. "Perhaps it's time you did," he said.

"What about you?"

"I'm staying here until this is done," he said. "You're right, too many people have died already."

That seemed to decide it for her. She reached out and squeezed David's hand, a gesture that was almost tender. "As if I can just leave you to die."

David nodded, but he didn't try to talk her out of it.

It wasn't much later that someone screamed.

The scream hung in the air between them. David actually jumped. Margaret could see the pain on his face, even as he smiled at her. "We have him now," he said.

They found him on an empty street near a butchery

closed for the night. The air stank of the slaughterhouse, which was appropriate, Margaret thought.

"He's here," David said.

"Where?" Margaret couldn't see anyone.

There was a crash of glass and the light nearest to them shattered. Margaret heard the next stone as it shot through the air, even saw it just before it hit the next closest street lamp.

Now, only a moon lit the street.

Margaret unsheathed her rime blade, though she didn't activate it, counting on its hard edge.

"Put it away," David whispered. "He's too fast for that."

"You don't know how fast I am," Margaret said.

"I know how swift he is, and, believe me, you're no match – there, there he is." He pointed into the dark. Margaret didn't sheathe her blade.

Cadell crouched in the shadows. He hadn't even bothered to wipe the blood from his lips. He grinned at Margaret, and seeing that face, all that blood, she knew that David was right, there was nothing of Cadell there. Nothing gentle or clever in all that hunger, unless the world itself was just hunger. Margaret had grown up on the terrors of the Roil, but this was an altogether darker thing, and worse, because she had seen some of that look in David. This was no Cadell, but a hollow man, possessed of a mouth, a gut, and cunning. Then clouds passed over the moon, and he was little more than a dark mannish shape.

Rain fell all at once, a great heavy downpour. How could they fight in this? Cadell sprang to his feet and sprinted at them through the dark – and David did something truly annoying. He stepped in front of her.

Margaret had to resist the temptation to cut into his back. David raised a hand, the Orbis on his finger flared with a cold hard brilliance that drew everything around them sharp and clear. It was almost as though the light of another time lit the street, things slowed, and grew a dangerous clarity.

Cadell backed from the light, a blood-covered hand thrown in front of his face, and Margaret could see each drop falling from his fingers to the gravel. None of it lost in the rain. Then things sped up, the light changed subtly. Cadell scurried backwards. But the glow followed him, and his hands couldn't conceal what he had become from it. Another drop of blood splattered on the ground.

"You remember what you are," David said, and Margaret was startled by the pain and disappointment in his voice, as though despite knowing what he was facing, he'd never truly expected it. Cadell halted, lowered his hands, his face long and lupine. None of the sadness was there nor his overbearing mockery and impatience. He truly was cored of everything but the husk. And yet he stopped.

David strode towards him, closer and closer, until they almost touched. "You remember what you are," David repeated. "Though not as much as me. If you honour the man, not the curse–"

Cadell swiped him aside, a movement so swift that Margaret hardly saw it, her limbs already given over to reflex as Cadell darted towards her. So much for David.

Margaret swept her rime blade out, and Cadell grabbed her by her wrist so tightly her bones creaked. She slammed her left fist into his face, it was like punching iron, and yet Cadell reacted. His eyes widened, and dark blood streamed from his nose. But he didn't let go, just yanked her closer. She felt her fingers loosen, the sword starting to fall from her hand. Something moved behind them. Cadell's head snapped forward, Margaret almost buckled beneath his weight.

Over Cadell's shoulder, David's face loomed; blood streamed down a cut beneath his eye. He smiled at her, and, again, there was something ghoulish and un-David like about that grin. He closed his hands around Cadell's head and wrenched him to one side. Now Cadell's fingers released their grip, and David kicked out, driving him away from her – ribs cracked as the Old Man lifted into the air.

David was already sprinting after Cadell, who had landed in a crouch, cat-like. Cadell wasn't running, though. David kicked out at him, Cadell grabbed his leg and, as though it were little more than an afterthought, spun David in a rough circle, before hurling him into the window of the butchery. David went through, headfirst. There was no elegance in the way either of them moved, only strength and speed.

Cadell was fighting on instinct alone and it was giving him the edge.

Margaret let her rime blade drop, pulled free her rifle and shot Cadell in the head. The Old Man spun towards her; perhaps she should have considered running. She shot him again, and then there was no time. He was swinging out at her, and she was using the rifle like a club, looking up at those bloody teeth. She knocked his hands away, heard one of his fingers break as she struck them.

She scrambled back, all instinct herself. His eyes were as dark and empty as an Endym's, and Margaret knew that soon she would follow him down into death. She was out-classed. Endyms, Quarg Hounds, Roilings – she could destroy those, but Cadell was another thing altogether. She flung her rifle at his head, and he swiped it away. She snatched a pistol from her belt and shot him in the chest, point-blank. It didn't even slow him down.

Cadell struck her hard, and she fell to the ground. He pressed one hand against her shoulder, reached down with the other to touch her neck. She raged against that strength, and couldn't move. Her hands closed around the Verger's knife in her belt, she yanked it free, drove it into his chest. His mouth opened and shut. Margaret could hear the breath whistling through his broad nose, she could smell blood and putrefaction on his breath.

The rain stopped. Gutters gurgled, something dripped nearby, and Cadell peered at her, a heartbeat and a heartbeat more. Kill me and be done with it, she thought.

Cadell jerked forward, and then he was rising. Lifted up from behind, David's hands around his neck, the Verger's knife jutting from the Old Man's chest.

"Husk," David said, in a quiet voice that became a growl. "Husk, you are as NOTHING to me!"

David squeezed, and Cadell shook, eyes bulging. He thrashed in David's grip, but David didn't let go. The muscles in his arms flexed with a strength that Margaret could only wonder at. He squeezed and squeezed, and finally Cadell stilled.

David threw the body at the ground, and kicked it. Bones cracked. He kicked it again and again, mumbling something under his breath.

He turned to Margaret. "Are you all right?"

Margaret nodded.

"Good," he said, and he didn't look all right. He looked like he was crying. "We need to end this. Now."

CHAPTER 11

Dead men rise. Dead men fight. Dead men dance throughout the night.

Hardacre folk song

THE CITY OF HARDACRE
964 MILES NORTH OF THE ROIL

David looked down at the corpse of Cadell. It shuddered at his boots, so he kicked it again. I did it, he thought. I managed it. But it's not over yet. And already he could feel the exhaustion pulling at him, felt sick with it.

There was a break in the clouds and the moons shone down, and just to their left glowed the Stars of Mourning: those symbols of sin and forgiveness. That sight steadied him somewhat; reminded him, too, that the corpse was on the street for any passerby to see.

"We will need to cut the... body up," he said, looking to Margaret. "Burn the pieces, and we need to hurry." He tried to sound calm, more in control than he felt.

Margaret was already unsheathing her rime blade, her rifle at her feet.

"No, that's not going to work."

David walked back through the broken window of the butchery. The blades weren't too hard to find.

"This is much better," he said. Thank the Engine for what little Carnival remained in his veins – and there was not nearly enough of it. His hands didn't even shake, and they would, yes, they would. He'd killed what was left of the man who had saved and made him what he was. David wanted to cry out with joy, he wanted to punch the wall with his fist. He wanted to eat, suddenly that was all he wanted, and there was meat here, in the cold room.

Yes, he needed that. Now.

He yanked the iron door open, breaking the lock in the process. Inside he dragged free the least frozen leg of lamb and bit down on it. It was tough work, but he managed it, you just needed to get the angle right, chew with rather than against the grain of the meat. A few bites, then a few bites more. Part of him wondered what it would be like if the blood was still warm.

He heard Margaret calling his name. Of course, how could he be so forgetful?

He took one last bite and walked from the cold room, shutting the door behind him. His stomach rumbled, he chose the biggest cleaver he could find, and a bag of salt, and walked back through the window, almost forgetting to wipe the smear of blood from his lips. His teeth were red with it.

"Sorry, it took me a while."

Before Margaret could say a word, he severed the head from the neck, swinging down in a single swift movement, utterly definitive. "We can't do it here, of course. But this should serve for now."

He lifted the head by the hair. It was surprisingly light.

He grabbed one of the shuddering feet, and began to drag it down the street. "Now, if you could just grab a foot."

Lightning cracked, like a skull hitting stone, and it started to rain. David turned to Margaret. "Just like home," he said.

His side ached. He reached down, fingers finding the source of the pain, and pulled. The piece of glass that came free was almost the length of his forearm. "Not so good," he said. Something squelched and he realised that his boots were full of blood.

He felt light-headed, but still he dragged the corpse behind him. Then he realised that perhaps that wasn't the wisest way to be hefting around a body. There was a wooden box nearby; he dragged it over to them. It was covered in web, which he methodically removed, pinching several spiders to their deaths. He didn't like spiders. He'd once seen a man eaten by them.

David swung the blade with a precision and a brutality that just a few weeks ago, Margaret would not have believed him capable of. She didn't know whether to be impressed or concerned. He carefully dumped the remains in a box.

"We have to take this somewhere and burn it," he said.

"Why not here?"

"People are coming," David said.

"I can't hear anything."

"Trust me."

He hefted the box up. Margaret grabbed the other end.

Twice the box had twitched in their grip; the first time Margaret dropped it, glancing furiously back at David. "Did you feel that?"

David nodded "I was expecting it," he said. "Don't be surprised. It's quite normal."

As though anything were normal, he thought.

She seemed ready for it the next time. Didn't even flinch. They found cover – behind old boxes from Chapman that smelt of rot and the sea – in an alleyway, the closest most deserted place they could find, and put the box down.

Margaret used a few drops of the endothermic chemicals from her shells. As an accelerant it worked well, though Cadell's flesh burned far easier then, giving off a peculiar cool heat. The smoke was thin and oily, and quick to drown in the rain.

David stuck a toe in the ashes, then dumped a bag of salt over them. Surely nothing could have come back from that anyway, but it didn't hurt to make sure.

"One Old Man dealt with," he said without much satisfaction. "Only seven more to go."

"You still think they're hunting you?"

"Yes, I can feel it in my bones. And when I sleep." His voice lowered, though there was no one there to hear it but her, "And they're getting closer."

CHAPTER 12

There is Drift, and then there is Stone, the levitating rock upon
which Drift sits.

It is said that Stone was hurled there by a god, and commanded
never to fall, and so it has remained, outliving even the god that
threw it. Or that Stone was once a god. Or that it is merely a mech-
anism, a great engine, and a conceit. Or that its mechanism is a
god asleep and should it ever wake, our world would be destroyed.

Take your pick.

Undecided Antiquities & the Mirrlees Lion,
SEBASTIAN MERCURE

THE CITY OF DRIFT
1200 MILES NORTH OF THE ROIL

There was a crystal glass of good Drift rum before her, un-
touched. Kara didn't feel like drinking. Actually, she did
(and a serious sort of drunk), but here and now it wouldn't
help. In fact, it might serve to dig her deeper into trouble.
Mother Graine's breath, though, smelt as though she had
no such concerns.

One is not often summoned to an audience with a

Mother of Sky, and this was Kara's third summoning. She did not enjoy it – in all honesty it terrified her – the Mothers of the Sky were meant to command from a distance, this was too personal. Better to be pounced upon by Mother Graine than to come to her chambers anticipating it. And yet here she was again, in the chamber of Mother Graine, with two guards standing outside, both armed with almost as much weaponry as mad Margaret Penn.

There were things that Kara wanted to ask, but knew she couldn't. Where were the other Mothers? They'd not been seen for nearly a month, and normally they would have patrolled the city's outer walls, a stern eye cast to the air. There were rumours of a sickness, something that had passed through the Mothers, and left Mother Graine whole. But Kara could not imagine something that might sicken a creature so powerful as Mother Graine and her kin. Death was something that happened to other people.

"How can you be sure he'll come?" Mother Graine asked, and it wasn't the first time. Kara had to struggle not to roll her eyes, despite her fear.

"He'll come because he's an honourable man," Kara Jade said, tapping a finger against another. "And he'll come because he owes me. He'd be dead but for me and the *Dawn*." And that name caught in her throat, as much as she tried for casual, it just caught. "If we hadn't gotten him, gotten them, out of Chapman, they'd all be rotting there. David isn't one to forget something like that."

And, she thought, he'll come because he's read the double meaning in my letter. Something so obvious that even David couldn't miss it.

"You're saying he's gullible?"

"I'm saying he'll come. What happens afterwards… you didn't see what I saw." Now, she did pick up that glass, and take a quick gulp, it really was good stuff, it warmed rather than burnt.

"Believe me, I am aware of the kind of... power he holds. David is a new Old Man, there's potency in that youth that will keep building for many months yet. He is dangerous, but we can contain him."

Kara put down her glass, half empty. "He tore three of those iron ships out of the sky, and scattered their contents across the ground as if they were nothing but toys."

Mother Graine leaned towards her. The hair on the back of Kara's neck stood up; she couldn't help it, she leant back a little. "Does he frighten you?"

Kara wasn't stupid. What she was really asking was: *Does he frighten you as much as I do?*

"No... yes... I don't know. He's just a boy, well, he was. I don't know what he woke to, after that great bloody rending of the sky. Maybe he's a monster now, but I doubt it, he's still a boy."

Mother Graine sighed. "He is an anomaly, and an aberration, so many wrongs bound in the flesh of one man. And you must remember he was also an addict."

"He never tried to hide that."

Mother Grain's brow furrowed. "Do not confuse candour with truth," she said, almost gently. "It's an addict's strategy. They are not to be trusted."

Kara grimaced. "And what does that make you? Isn't the sky your addiction?"

Mother Graine shook her head. "It is my comfort, it is the presence eternal or near enough. And it would be all for me, if I could believe in one thing. But I do not."

"What is it that you believe?"

"We're all heading towards a doom that only I can stop." She gestured at the glass. "Now, finish your drink."

And Kara Jade did. You can only say no to a Mother of the Sky so many times.

CHAPTER 13

Those of the sky and the land had grown increasingly acrimonious. But that didn't mean that they chose to keep out of each other's affairs. After the fall of so many cities, and with Mayor Stade (who could be said to have given up his city so easily, and against character) in the air to the east, the scope of the drama had narrowed, but the stakes were so much higher.

Wars of Altitude, MOLCH

THE CITY OF HARDACRE
964 MILES NORTH OF THE ROIL

When David finally made it to his bedroom, he sat down, pulled his knees up to his chest and wept. He didn't allow himself too much grief though, before going to his hidden stash and driving Carnival into his veins. A few moments later he was all smiles.

He yawned, and hardly had his boots off his feet before he was asleep.

"Oh, it's you," David said. "Which means I'm dreaming."

He recognised where he was at once. The panoptic map

room, with a map that even the best of map powders could only hope to imitate. He'd been here in a dream, just before he had destroyed the iron ships; in fact, it was in this room that he had first seen them approaching. When did a dream mirror reality so accurately that it became something else?

"Nice of you to join me," Cadell said, rolling a cigarette gently between his fingers. "Some habits you just can't quit, even in dreams."

He gestured to a syringe, red with Carnival, resting on the edge of the map. David swallowed, and shook his head.

"Good," Cadell said. "If you could extend that to the waking world, I need to be let out. You need me. If I'd realised that Carnival would be so effective in keeping me at bay, I would have chosen the girl." Outside a Quarg Hound howled; that had been part of the dream as well. David shivered. "Still there, I'm afraid. I don't know if it's your subconscious or mine that has put it there, just that we might come and go from this place, but it always remains."

"I'm sorry that I killed you," David said, wondering if it was even appropriate to mention something like that to the man whose bones you've just burned.

Cadell slid his cigarette into a pocket. "That wasn't me. I'm dead. What remained was nothing but an abomination. There is nothing to forgive. If the situation had been reversed, I would have killed you without hesitation. Now, no time for this, concentrate, lad. Focus."

He gestured to the map. "Me and my brothers constructed this in our minds. Trapped in our hungers and our cage, we had all the time to make it perfect. And now it is yours, too. So use it!"

David looked down at the panoptic ap, and Shale grew ever more detailed. Here forests swayed in the wind, to the south Mirrlees burned, and on the Gathering Plains, seven gnarled men walked – closer to Hardacre than David feared. His eyes flicked north, to the mountains, and Tearwin Meet, the city with its mighty tower and peculiar intelligence. He felt it stare back, and he looked away. He said, "Why do I keep dreaming this place?"

"Dream? I guess that works. If that works for you, then yes, dream it is. Though I prefer to couch it in more heuristic terms, the map is the least dreamish part of the whole place. For some, a dream, for others an education." Cadell tapped a finger against the northernmost extremity of the map, where the great tower rose, fringed in its mountains. "Tearwin Meet is waiting for you. The Engine is waiting to greet you in its grand hall of mirrors, beyond the steel door."

"I'm stuck here," David said. "Things are complicated. Buchan and Whig, they're doing their best, but–"

"I'm sure they are. But other options approach you." Cadell tapped the map again: a small Aerokin slid into the airspace of the city. Even from above, David could see how easily she evaded the city's defensive airships. She hid comfortably in the clouds, found the darkest routes. "You really need to learn how to get out of your head, or you would have seen it earlier. Another avenue might be opening up for you. Drift has decided to play now."

"And if it does…"

"Be careful, the Mothers of the Sky are not your friends. Nor will they ever be."

"They were your friends once," David said. "I remember that much." And he did, flashes of a past, all gleaming metals and hope.

"Yes, before things became a bit mythical, a bit driven by the curse of a mad machine. You know they once tried to rescue us, in fact, they did. It didn't work. But the past is a meagre ghost, you can't count on it, it's less satisfying than chewing on bones."

"So do I take this other avenue, or not?"

"That is up to you," Cadell said. "I am but another one of those ghosts, haunting the long hallways of your blood."

"So, I've a choice of ghosts?"

"We all do. What's the present but the moans of ghosts past and future? All those possibilities and hope, certainties, and failures, you just have access to a larger store than most. If you let me in." Cadell's face grew cunning. "The sooner the better. You will need me to do what must be done."

David's stomach rumbled, even in his sleep it rumbled, and he looked up, embarrassed at the broad smile of Cadell. "Why am I always hungry?"

"You're hungry because you're growing, and the kind of growth that you are experiencing requires a considerable amount of energy. David, you're going to have to bring that cold to bear on an entire world. You've not even scratched the surface of your abilities, and they are rising in you."

"I'm tired," David said. "I'm always so tired."

"That's because sleep leads you to me. You shouldn't fight it as much. In sleep you can focus on all the things that you need to be, and you can become them."

"I don't know if I want to."

Cadell sighed. "Then wake up. But remember the one possibility that is a certainty." He pointed to the map, south again, where the seven Old Men walked. They stopped, seemed to look up, point at the sky. "They will hunt you until you die, or you kill them. Seven Old Men. Do you think you could manage such slaughter?"

● ● ● ●

David's eyes opened.

Another tapping at the window.

Not Cadell, his point of entry was different now. David hurried to the window, his hands hesitated at the latch. His body ached. He wanted to sleep again, to find that this was nothing more than a dream. That his parents still lived, and that the Roil existed only in the pulp stories of the Shadow Council – leave all this madness to Travis the Grave.

He peered out and saw nothing, heard another quick tapping; David caught a flash of movement, tendrils whipping back into the sky. He swung the window open, and looked up. Something hovered there, above the street.

A juvenile Aerokin, far smaller than the *Roslyn Dawn*. She lowered a single tendril through the opening. Rough flesh, tipped with multi-jointed segments analogous to fingers, gripped an envelope. An envelope with David's name, written with flourishes and curlicues, on it. He recognised the writing of Kara Jade. She'd written him a note apologising for her absence that had managed to be part accusatory – *why in the Roil's name wouldn't he wake* – and rueful – *would have loved to see the north*.

He pulled the envelope from the Aerokin's grasp, the finger-things tapped his arm once and the tendril flicked back outside. The Aerokin lifted a little higher and drifted over the flat roof of the pub. David wondered if she was waiting there in the sky, or simply a messenger.

David looked down at the envelope in his hand. The paper was still warm. He opened it cautiously. His eyes flicked to the end, saw Kara's name there, as he'd expected, then he looked back over it more carefully.

Well, I'm sure you weren't expecting this. It seems I am in trouble. There have been some political reckonings in my city, of the sort that sees a person in prison – if they're lucky, and dead if they're not. And yes, I am lucky.

A man of your particular skills may be exactly what I need. If you could see your way clear to helping me, I would be in your debt – and that's a hard thing for me to say.

The Aerokin that delivered this message is waiting for you, she answers to the name Pinch. *She will not wait long, an hour or two, no more. Should you decide to help out a dear friend, well, a friend at least, please go to the roof. Pinch will accommodate three people, or two if one of them possesses more weapons than is sensible.*

I would not have contacted you if I did not think that my life was indeed in peril.

Pinch contains more information.

I have allies in the city – but I guess you'd get that, because Aerokin (not even little ones) don't just bend to my will – and they will help you get to me.

I am glad you are still alive. You scared us all, even the Warrior Princess (though it's hard to tell).

Yours,

Kara Jade Dawn

David let the paper drop, picked it up, and read it again, looking for some sort of clue, some deeper meaning.

He held it to the light, in case there were some secret script, some warning; he singed the corner, and no revelation came. Here was a way out, a quick escape from Hardacre, which was starting to feel less of a way station, and more a prison.

He took a deep breath, plus a half nail of Carnival, and sought out Margaret.

CHAPTER 14

In many ways both Buchan and Whig were naive. But it is hard to blame them. The world wasn't what it was. Ironically, so close to its ending events were not speeding up, but slowing down, as though everyone refused to acknowledge the cliff they were about hurtle off, or they were desperately trying to apply the brakes.

Buchan and Whig hadn't adjusted yet.

I still feel bad about what we did to them.

Recollections of a Forgotten World, MARGARET PENN

THE CITY OF HARDACRE
964 MILES NORTH OF THE ROIL EDGE

There was a knock on the door at ten past six. Margaret opened it. "You're late."

"Hardly by any real margin," Buchan said, a sheen of sweat marking his brow. Whig followed him into the room, and oddly enough David walked through after them, that smug grin on his face. With all four of them in her room, things were a little squashed. Buchan smelt of beer, Whig smelt like honey. David possessed no odour at all.

"We were delayed," Whig said. "Another meeting with yet another pilot."

"And, once again, no success," Margaret said.

"We will find our path into the north, believe me."

"Horses, why not those?"

"Horses are too slow, the terrain terrible."

"We'd be halfway there by now."

"We'd most probably be dead," Buchan said.

"Yes, I guess there would be few horses that could carry your weight."

Buchan's eyes flared, his cheeks reddened and he clenched one great hand into a fist. Whig stared at her sternly. He said, "There are animals up to the task, believe me."

"I know it's frustrating," Buchan said. "But we are doing our best, our avenues here are extremely limited."

"And that isn't remotely good enough," Margaret snapped.

"I know how it must sound," Whig said. "But we have been stymied at every turn. Sometimes I think that we are truly being stopped from going any further."

"It's true," Buchan said. "Paperwork goes missing, airship pilots that initially seem interested change their minds, or are called off to the east. And the bribes." Buchan wiped his brow. "Ah, I can't even begin to tell you how much they are costing us."

Whig nodded. "Believe us, David, Miss Penn. We are men used to a certain level of unscrupulous dealings."

"We can deal with the best of them. But this is a whole new level of greed, if it is indeed greed rather than something that has been dressed up as such."

"But who would stop us here?" David asked.

"David, there are some people that would rather you

never made it into the north. That perhaps aren't even quite aware of what you are, but know that to let us leave Hardacre may threaten everything that they have built."

"Yes," Whig said. "There are some who believe that, even as a last resort, the Engine of the World should not be used."

"Then why has the Engine been allowed to exist all these centuries?" Margaret said. "Why hasn't it been destroyed?"

Buchan smiled a little wearily. "We lack the means to destroy the Engine, and have for most of that time, if we ever possessed it at all. We are the last and least of our kind, Margaret. Even your great parents, may they rest in peace, were little more than scavengers of old technologies." He raised a finger in the air to silence her before she could respond. "Let me finish, please. We lived in the shadows of our great towers and levees, and though we may have raised ourselves high, it was never nearly high enough."

"Which is why we must use the Engine," David said. "Which is why we must destroy the Roil."

"Yes, we all agree with you. But you must give us more time. When we procure a pilot, we shall be able to make the flight to Tearwin Meet in days. You start walking and the Roil will catch up before you even see its high walls," Whig said.

"We will be ready in a week, no more than that," Buchan said. "For all the delays, for all our excuses, we are finally making progress."

"You must excuse our caution," Whig dragged the pipe from his jacket, tamped down some tobacco. "I know that the wait seems interminable, but even now the distant north is an inhospitable destination.

"The weather is variable in the extreme, and the changes in temperature mean that the ice that coats much of the north has shifted. It can open and swallow you whole, and we've already come so far and lost so much, wouldn't you say, David and Miss Penn?"

"A week, another week," Margaret spat.

Whig said, "Aerokin are hard to fashion out of nothing. We are not the fierce Mothers of the Sky, we are just men – with some exceptions, of course."

"And I would agree if you had nothing. You let Kara Jade go."

"I didn't see you arguing for her to stay at the time."

"I'm not the one organising this journey north."

"Indeed you are not," Buchan said. "Actually, I'm not sure what you are, other than someone that complains and does nothing."

Margaret's jaw moved, she could barely speak, she jabbed a finger into Buchan's chest. "You know what I have done. I could show you what I have done!"

Whig raised his hands. "Please, please, we are all friends here."

Buchan and Margaret swung their heads towards Whig, and said, "We are *not* friends."

The words were spat, with a savagery that surprised Margaret, even as she said them. No, they were not friends, but were they enemies? Buchan's jowls shook, he grabbed a handkerchief from his pocket and wiped at his face. Margaret almost pulled it from his hands.

Whig seemed to wilt. Then he smiled. "Circumstances make friends of us all. Shale grows too small for us to make enemies, a little like this room."

"Then get an airship, or an Aerokin, and get us out of this damn city!" She took a deep breath. "I am going to close my eyes, and count to ten. If either of you are in my room at that point, our friendship shall be tested." She slid the rime blade a few inches out of its sheath, and closed her eyes.

They were gone before she reached three.

She kept her eyes closed a full minute before opening them again. David still stood there.

"What are you grinning at?" she snapped.

"Aerokin are hard to fashion out of nothing, but I think I have a solution to our problem." He passed her Kara's note.

Margaret folded the paper neatly. "Warrior Princess, thank you *very* much." She slipped the paper into David's front pocket. "It's a trap, obviously."

"Certainly," David said; he leant forward in his chair, eyes bright. "It can't be anything but. And yet, if we stay here, you know the Old Men are coming. I can feel them, with Cadell gone, I can sense them even more, and they are not far away."

"How far?"

"That, well, I'm not sure. A sense of foreboding rarely comes with a scale. A day, a week, not much longer."

"So, trap or not, you're saying we don't have much choice in the matter?"

"Yes, and I know for one that Kara must really be in some sort of trouble."

"What? You don't think she would betray us?"

"No, I don't. But right now there is an Aerokin floating above the *Habitual Fool,* and she's waiting to take us away from here, to a person that saved both our lives several times."

"You couldn't take control of the Aerokin?"

"No, my skills don't lie that way. I could kill her mid-flight, I could send her plummeting from the sky, but what is the point of that?"

"All right, we go." She nodded to the bag beside her bed.

"Everything I need is there. Shouldn't we write Buchan and Whig some sort of letter?"

David grinned. "I already have."

He opened the door, ran to his room and came back a moment later with a bag. "I think we were both expecting this, or something like it."

Margaret nodded her head. "Yes, there has been something in the air."

David smiled. "And now there is definitely something in the air, and it is waiting for us."

Margaret grabbed her bag. "So whose window do we take, mine or yours?"

David dragged his bag inside and shut the door. "One window's as good as another, isn't it?"

CHAPTER 15

No one chooses the north. It is almost as though, as a species, we have been bred with some deep antipathy for the ice and the cold. Just as the Mothers of the Sky find it an agony to step upon the land. Of course, it is not nearly as severe as that, and not acknowledged. For all industry, the coal and the oil fields, find themselves in the north. Here too are the Greater Forests (or what once were). We need the north. We work it, but we do not like it. Surely it is forced upon us.

> The North is the North of Course, LANDYMORE

THE UNDERGROUND
875 MILES NORTH OF THE ROIL

Medicine Paul was in a delicate state of internal political upheaval – like a stomach bug, only much worse. Alliances kept shifting. He was nimble, a survivor, but every time he thought he'd found his footing, it had slipped away beneath him.

He'd found himself working for Stade, the man who killed almost all of Medicine's allies. He'd found himself leading Stade's people – though weren't Stade's people his too? – nearly a thousand miles to a secret stronghold in the mountains with the aid of his guard Agatha and her soldiers. Through the predatory gloom of the Margin they'd marched, leaving dozens of dead behind. Then they been captured by – and escaped from – Cuttlemen, fled across the sea of grass known as the Gathering Plains, and finally made it to the Underground.

Within thirty minutes of their arrival Agatha had been executed, and Medicine's authority stripped from him – by people that should have been his allies to begin with. The revolution had come, and he'd somehow been on the wrong side of it.

Since Agatha's execution, Medicine Paul had been left alone. And it was easy enough in the long dark tunnels of the Underground, though that didn't mean he wasn't being watched, or that he wasn't busy. Just that Grappel required nothing of him, demanded nothing but what he demanded of all the citizens of the Underground, that they work and work hard.

Medicine was afforded a single room, a bed and a desk, a toilet in one corner and a door with a lock on it, of the sort that could be picked by even the most indifferent thief or assassin. Medicine had spent his share of time in prison cells, this was no different, even if he could lock and unlock it at will. He knew that wherever he went he was watched, and that for all the size of the Underground there really wasn't anywhere to go.

Twenty thousand people lived and worked here. Medicine was just one of them, and while he worked hard, be it at the infirmary or helping in the construction of inner walls, or the smoothing out of the vent tubes to release heat (while ensuring that something more sinister couldn't find its way back in), he also knew that he was being regarded with a much greater level of scrutiny, and that he would never be trusted.

And why should he? After all, he was from Mirrlees, and it was Mirrlees that had so failed the north and Hardacre in particular. It was Mirrlees that had sent on the refugees from the south.

Work was his only escape, but he didn't have it for very long. Less than five days after their arrival, Medicine became ill.

A mild headache became a sweat, which became the worst fever he had ever known.

He stumbled halfway back to his bed, through the long dark corridors, then fell and kept on falling. When he woke next, he was in his bed, throat burning with thirst, not at all sure how he had made it to the lumpy mattress. He tried to rise, and his limbs shook with the effort, the sheets may as well have been made of lead.

His vision swam, and he found darkness again.

Time passed slowly in the dark. He slept, if such a painful broken thing could be called sleep. Sometimes he was torn from the black and cloying dark with a scream on his lips: Agatha and her soldiers looking on, faces burst asunder by gunshot, a constant horrible accusation.

Medicine had lost many allies in his life, and always he had managed to continue. But now, it seemed, he was paying the cost: dreams as intense as they were terrible, a weariness that seemed to crush him. Then would come the fever, he shivered and boiled. He mumbled at the dark.

"When you die, you can stand here too," Agatha said.

"When you die, you can stand here too," David said, and Cadell, and Warwick, and the boy named Lassiter, who he had sent to his death to save David.

Two whole days he didn't rise from his bed, just lay there

assailed with visions. Horrible blood-curdling things, great waves of darkness washed over him, punctuated by laughter, shrill and deafening in his ears.

Someone came to him, spoke him to in a gentle soothing voice, laid cold cloths against his brow. But when he woke – alone, weak – in the room hardly ventilated, stinking of his fever, his sickness, he wondered if that hadn't been part of the fever, too.

When he finally left his room, it was as a man transformed. What weight had sat upon his bones had bled from him. His flesh was lean and hard, he felt weak, and yet, somehow, a deeper purpose possessed him.

But first he had to eat.

Medicine walked to the common room, guided as much by the smell of food as memory. Everything seemed different – changed as he had changed. He followed long corridors cut into the stone, the ground beneath him shuddering with the vibration of grand works. The mountain was always moving, tiny, almost imperceptible movements that cumulatively were hard to ignore. He'd ridden those vibrations like waves when he had been sick, they'd carried him in and out of madness.

In the common room he stood shocked by the sight of all these living people, he wanted to reach out and touch them, make sure that they weren't a dream. He'd bathed, found some clean clothes in his room, but he knew that he must still stink, as he was left alone. He served himself a little food, meat of some sort, a few limp vegetables, some mashed potatoes. Not much of anything – his stomach must be the size of a pea.

The food was dry and stale, and the most wonderful thing he had ever eaten in his life.

He was just finishing when a boy approached him. The boy could scarcely meet his gaze, kept looking down at his hands. Medicine smiled. Tried not to think of David.

"It's all right," Medicine said. "I don't bite."

"I've a message for you," the boy said. "Grappel would speak with you."

Medicine wiped his plate clean with a slice of bread, chewed it thoughtfully. "Tell him I will be on my way once I've eaten."

The boy hovered there.

"Yes?" Medicine said.

"I'm to take you to him."

Medicine finished the bread. "Grappel the sort to punish you if you don't?"

The boy shrugged, and looked away.

"Very well." Medicine stood up, leaving the plate behind him. "Lead the way."

"You have recovered, then," Grappel said.

"I didn't realise that I was sick. The stress, I've never taken ill that way. It–"

"No, it is to be expected. Almost all of us have suffered from it. It happens to those that come up north. Some weirdness, a contagion. The flesh melts away, and if it doesn't kill you, you find yourself stronger."

"I'm a doctor, I've not heard of it."

"When did you last run a practice?" Grappel said, handing him a glass of Drift rum. "When did you last keep up to date with the journals?"

Medicine took a sip of the strong stuff, winced. "It's been a while since I have actively chased the journals. But, surely–"

"It's something that's little spoken of here. A rite of passage. Why share it? No one would come this way." Grappel cleared his throat, looked at his own rum, but didn't drink. "Did the dead visit you?"

Medicine looked away.

"Of course they did," Grappel said. "They always come. All that is death is in that fever, and you so close to it, you can't even tell the difference. Some people lose themselves to it. Quite frankly, I thought you would be one of them."

"So you called me, to see that I was hale and hearty, and that was all?"

Grappel shook his head.

"I have bad news, I'm afraid," Grappel said.

"Why am I not surprised?" Medicine said.

Grappel sighed.

"Well, out with it! I've people that need me in the infirmary. I doubt that my own fever has seen an end to illness in this place."

"Cadell is dead," Grappel said.

Medicine felt his heart constrict. "Are you sure?"

"Yes, and more than that, the Old Men have been released. They say they hunt the Milde boy."

"David?" Medicine wanted to say that the young man had visited him in his dreams, but he kept quiet.

"Yes, the boy's alive. Cadell, they say, saw him from Chapman to Hardacre. He is with Buchan and Whig. Our spies say that he has changed."

"That's the Carnival, surely."

"No, this isn't the transformation of an addict. There is no sleeping sickness, no madness. He seems more assured, more certain of himself. They still seek to travel north, with the support of Buchan and Whig. To Tearwin Meet."

"Is that a good idea?" Medicine said. "With Cadell gone, what chance do they have?"

"From all reports they seem confident that they could achieve their objectives; the boy is wearing Cadell's Orbis." Medicine found himself instinctively reaching for the place where his ring finger should be, where he had once worn his own copy of the Engineer's ring, before Stade chopped ring and finger free.

"It doesn't matter, none of it does," Grappel said. "We have them in Hardacre, and they will not move."

"Will you be bringing them here?"

Grappel seemed surprised. "A ship, the *Collard Green*, has been sent for that purpose," Grappel said. "Now, the question is, what do we do with you?"

"If you'd wanted me dead, I'm sure you'd have killed me by now. What service can I be?"

"Politically, you're a problem," Grappel said. "Your links to Stade, no matter how transitory, have tarnished you. But there are other things that you can do."

"I'm a doctor," Medicine said. "And I am already doing that. I see to the sick."

"Mr Paul, there are more than human sicknesses to attend to. There's a darkness in the heart of the Project, and I would have you find it."

Medicine looked at the man who had ordered the execution of Agatha and her troops, and was almost certain that he was staring at that very darkness.

"Where do I begin?" Medicine said.

"I've heard rumours of something called the Contest. I want you to find it out."

Medicine nodded. "I've one question," he said.

"Yes, what is it?"

"Who did you see when the fever struck you?"

Grappel lifted the rum, considered it in the candlelight, gold, the ice cubes gleaming. "All of them," he said. "Every single one. Oh, and don't believe it stops. Every night they find me, and every night there is more of them." He finished his drink. "The blood on these hands, Mr Paul. The blood on these hands, you would think me a monster."

Medicine nodded his head, but he didn't say a thing.

CHAPTER 16

"Run," Mollison said.

Travis shook his head. "I run from no one."

Mollison smiled. "Not from, to!" He pointed at the Aerokin leaving the Valley of the Dolls. "We don't get aboard that Aerokin, we're dead men."

Travis was already running. "That, of course, is a different thing altogether."

> Night Council 19: The City in the Valley of the Dolls,
> DICKSON MCUNNE

THE CITY OF HARDACRE
964 MILES NORTH OF THE ROIL EDGE

The window jammed. Margaret sighed, and kicked at the frame, it opened with a crack, wood splitting. The door behind them rattled. David looked at Margaret.

He said, "I may have left the note in a too obvious place."

"Too obvious?"

"David? Margaret?" Buchan shouted; the door shook again.

"You did lock it, didn't you, David?"

He looked back at her. "Of course."

The door boomed. "Don't make me do this!" Buchan said.

"Out," Margaret said. "Hurry."

He slid through the window, not the first time he'd had to. And just as he had that time, he slipped, felt himself go – Oh well, it wasn't going to kill him, just break a few bones, or would it, would he lose the part that was him, and just become the hunger, and maybe that would be easier.

Margaret's hands gripped him by the belt. She yanked him back against the wall, and he found his balance: his bag hanging from one shoulder.

"All moot now, anyway," David said.

Margaret peered down at him. "What?"

"Quite a first step," he said.

Margaret grunted. "Just climb."

Everything was slippery, but there were handholds, and Margaret knew how to find them. David followed her lead, and where he went the water froze. I've become a tipping point, he thought. From water to ice, life to death.

It was still raining. David wondered about Mirrlees, if it was still raining down there, if people still looked up at that low dark sky.

The door in the room beneath gave way just as they clambered onto the roof. David looked down, and into Buchan's face. There was no way the big man was following them, he couldn't have fit through the window.

"David," he said, and there was a pleading tone to his voice that stung. Poor Buchan, always calling on Cadell, and now him. "We can talk this out. You don't need to–"

"We can't talk," Margaret said. "We do this now, or we're prisoners."

David shook his head once. "We really are sorry," he said.

David felt like Travis the Grave. After all, he was always running over rooftops, though Travis was never pursued by his allies. Travis wasn't the sort of man to betray his friends, stalwart and true – nothing had ever muddied his outlook. Fictional characters could choose to be like that, life was never as complicated in books. Goals always clear, or revealed to be in the end. This, all of this, was far murkier, and it had been from the start.

"I'm coming out," Whig called.

Now there was a man who could fit through windows.

Margaret had her rifle free.

"No need for that," David said. "Surely no need for that."

"Where is it?" Margaret said.

"You're heading into the jaws of Death, boy. This is absolute folly, Margaret. Patience, both of you, patience," Whig said, his head peering over the gutter.

"Down, tall man, or you lose your eyes."

"You wouldn't–"

Margaret fired. Whig ducked away.

This was getting too serious, and fast.

"What on earth are you doing?" Buchan's cries stabbed David more fiercely than he expected. He thought, Don't you see, I'm sparing you so much.

"I can't see it," Margaret said. "This could all end in embarrassment."

"*Pinch* is here," David said.

"Where?"

The Aerokin's tendrils dropped from the sky, curling around her and David. They were surprisingly warm to the touch, and while firm, their grip was gentle. Margaret had to trust that they wouldn't just let her go, once they were high enough. Not the sort of thing that came easy to her. She took a deep breath, and pushed such thoughts as far from her mind as possible (not very far at all). In a moment they were lifted up, Margaret's weapons clattering in their bag. The gondola opened wide, like a gummy mouth – and they were slid into it, embraced by the wet-dog-mixed-with-malt odour of Aerokin.

Pinch wobbled in the air, hit by a gust of wind.

Her nacelles shifted and up they went, at speed.

"There really isn't a lot of room in here," David said, as the Aerokin's tendrils slid and shuddered back out the opening with the surety of snakes.

"Larger than the *Melody Amiss*." Margaret's voice was low. "And I spent days in her."

Whig had reached the roof and shook his fists after them. Even from this height, David could see the fear that battled with the anger.

"I feel sorry for them," David said.

"You should," Margaret said. "We owe them a lot."

"And this is coming from the woman who was going to shoot out his eyes."

"David!" Margaret said. "You know me better than that."

"Do you really think it's a trap?" David said.

Margaret snorted. "I think this whole damn world is a trap. Drift or Tearwin Meet, we're rushing towards its jaws, away from those of the Roil. It's what we've always been doing. Things are closing in, they always have been, since before either of us were born."

David whistled. "You really are miserable, aren't you?"

"Death's waiting for us, David. Here or at Drift or in Tearwin Meet. It no longer follows us, but has run ahead."

She pushed past David to the rear of the gondola where it widened, to stow away her bag. The great belly of the Aerokin rumbled and churned above them, generating the various gases for flotation and propulsion. Two bodies and her weaponry made the job considerably harder. But *Pinch* could compensate. Changing her shape, making herself more aerodynamic. Through gas, form and thrust, the Aerokin was capable of quite a lot of lift.

The gondola could accommodate three people at a stretch, just as Kara said. David could see two mattresses at the back. A larder that housed rows of canned goods – beef mainly, a few vegetables, some stewed fruit – beyond it was a small room that contained a toilet, really just a hole that opened onto the sky. And nothing that even resembled a control panel.

Pinch lifted higher over Hardacre, catching the wind of the storm, her nacelles riding with it, driving them west and north. There were rooftops far below. The city was luminous, though it was a softer glow than either Mirrlees or Chapman, all that gas. A northern suburb burned, and David wondered if there hadn't been another riot.

He tapped the membrane, and tried to zoom in, but the rain fell too heavily now or the membrane had yet to fully develop; all he got was magnified blur.

Down below were the hard old fields that fed the city. Rocky ground, and thin hard earth, and yet the city had sprung from them, these fields ploughed and nurtured with an efficiency and skill that softened and sweetened the cruel landscape. Hardacre had become so good at it that they even supplied a large percentage of Mirrlees' food, or had.

David considered that grim grey land; he knew that daylight would shine on fields ready for harrowing, and that four months ago Hardacre had a bumper crop.

Things, perhaps, were never as awful as they seemed. He knew that they were heading into trouble, but he owed Kara Jade this at the very least, whatever the nature of her trouble was. Without her they would never have gotten as far as they had. He liked to think he was a better man than someone who would leave a friend in trouble – even if it meant deserting other allies.

And, finally, they were moving again, crossing a new landscape, putting another city to their backs. David was tired of hunting – it hadn't taken long for that weariness to settle in – and of being in the one place. He wondered if you could ever get so used to running that it became comfortable.

He closed his eyes. Up here, away from the noise of the city, he could feel them much more easily.

Flashes of woodland came to him, trees leaning against each other, gnarled and weary. Screams came near and distant. Mumbled conversation, because the Old Men never stopped talking. Cadell had managed to rein all that in, but David knew how much it had cost him. David could taste death in his mouth, they had killed recently, they were always killing. He felt some sympathy with their hunger, with their rage, even if it was directed at him. After all, whether they liked it or not, whether he liked it or not, they were linked now. And would be until either they died or he did.

Margaret was wrong – Death didn't wait for them, it accompanied them.

The Old Men were some distance to the south-west, but not nearly far enough away. At least now they couldn't catch him for a while. David sensed that even if he made it to the Tearwin Meet, and activated the Engine, they would still come after him, that they wouldn't stop.

His stomach rumbled.

"You better eat something," Margaret said, lobbing a can at him. He snatched it out of the air easily, reflexes so much better attuned to food, even when it was wrapped in metal. The tin opener followed. He caught that too.

Beef, he could sense it even through the can.

"Thank you," he said. "What about you?"

"I'm not hungry."

David envied her.

He ate alone, watching the city fall behind the horizon, his back turned to her because he was ashamed how he looked when he ate. The meat was cold, and salty, there was no blood to it, it was unsatisfying. When he was done, he wiped his face, walked past her and checked the larder, certainly a lot of food.

He opened another can and ate it too.

And by the time he was done, Hardacre was little more than a soft and fading glow, the dark around it possessed of a great and terrible authority.

He hoped that Whig paid good attention to the note David had left him. David worried that he was leaving them buried to the neck in trouble, hadn't he been doing that all along? Since the moment he'd run from his assassinated father – the body still twitching – he'd been leaving behind one darkness after another, and more bodies than he wished to dwell upon.

What did it matter that he was doing it again?

After all, if he failed, then none of them had that much time left anyway. Old Men or Roil, there really wasn't a lot of difference. At least the Old Men wouldn't have them twitching to the commands of Witmoths; the Old Men's one command was die.

Simple.

Even the biggest fool could understand that.

CHAPTER 17

Let us be honest. When all lost their heads, Stade didn't. Madness leads to madness, but his was a particularly rational one. How are we to blame with such distance? With distance, quite easily, blame and analysis are all we have left. Stade rose to power because no one, Engineer or Confluent alike, ever offered a viable alternative.

When others faltered, he remained strong and persuasive. A charm that combined political aptitude with coercion.

Consequences of Defeat, HENBEST & TATE

MIRRLEES-ON-WEEP, TEN YEARS AGO
1500 MILES NORTH OF THE ROIL EDGE

Two days after the great storm when, for the first time in a generation, the mighty gates to the levees had been closed, Stade walked through a city swept clean. But that could never hide the nature of this suburb. Excrement remained excrement, no matter how you scrubbed it.

Tomlinson Pharmaceuticals was built in a neighbourhood less than salubrious, places that Stade tried to avoid because he had grown up in them. He did not like to revisit

the scrambling hell of his childhood, but there were times
that such excursions couldn't be avoided. And he could
trust this work to no one. Two Vergers walked with him, a
new recruit by the name of Tope – who had already proven
himself loyal – and Mr Sheff, an old and canny bastard
Stade had known since he'd first joined the Council. Sheff
knew when to whisper and when to murder, and could
differentiate between the two.

A young boy tried to sell them the latest street drug,
fresh blood obviously, or he would have recognised two
Vergers. Sheff snarled at him, Tope reached for his knife,
but at a headshake from Stade, he slid it back into its
sheath. And the boy, wide-eyed, sprinted for his life down
the nearest alleyway.

Stade smiled, then frowned. He'd been that boy once,
he wished him well.

Tomlinson himself met them at the door. A nervous
bird-like man with owlish glasses that he kept sliding up
and down his nose, an irritating tic that had made it easy
for Stade to hate the man from the beginning.

He led them through a building that was the picture of
industry. Machines whirred, men and women worked at
various conveyor belts, sorting and packaging. Tomlinson's
staff must have numbered at least a hundred people. Obviously the production of salves and map powder was
quite lucrative.

There was no small talk – certainly no talk of the Grand
Defeat. Stade only got that in the halls of Parliament now,
thanks to that damn Medicine Paul. At least Tomlinson was
deferential, he opened the door to his office, a big room on
a mezzanine with a window that afforded a view of the
workers below. Stade wondered if they were as terrified of
Tomlinson as the chemist was of him. At a nod from the

mayor, Sheff pulled the blinds to the window closed. Stade could see sweat beading on his host's brow.

Stade could tell that Tomlinson hated him. No matter how hard the chemist tried to hide it, or his fear, it shone bright in his eyes. Still, he walked to his desk, picked up a clipboard and scanned its contents, as though the mayor was just like any other client.

"All of the subjects have acted similarly under the drug," Tomlinson said. "A low level of euphoria, a gentle calm. Though it can have side effects, a certain haphazardness of character, moments of clarity giving way to confusion. An addict could be quite conflicted, almost mad."

"Everything is weighted with... consequence, Mr Tomlinson."

"To scramble the mind so, it is–"

"Exactly what modern medicine does, and this is a very specific form of medicine. Now, the drug is easy to produce?"

"Yes, and to produce cheaply. We can have it in the... facilities within a month."

Facility was a polite way of saying prison, those groaning, fetid pits where the damned would cling to a drug like this. Stade chewed on his cigar. It would start with the prisons and spread out from there. He said, "Good. The, um, recipe – I want it distributed as widely as possible."

"Isn't that dangerous?" Tomlinson rose to his full height, almost as tall as Stade. "This drug will reduce the will of a city."

"Mr Tomlinson, I am not putting it in the water. " Stade loomed over the chemist, tapped a little ash onto the ground. "Believe me, there are far more dangerous things than this drug you have invented. Far more dangerous things."

Tope cleared his throat. And Tomlinson's eyes grew pleasingly wide.

Stade said, "Of course you have nothing to fear. This is a legal contract."

Tomlinson took a deep breath. He walked to his desk, watched closely by Tope and Sheff. He pulled a file from the teetering pile of notes. "Everything you need is here."

Stade walked from the building; the boy was back on the corner, but the moment he saw Stade and his Vergers, he ran. Tope gave him a look, and Stade shook his head, in a few weeks he would be selling Stade's new drug. Though perhaps not on this corner, there would be too many bad memories here.

The production of drugs was such a dangerous activity, all those chemicals. Fires got out of hand all too quickly. It would be a terrible tragedy of course, and as a mayor who had risen on the back of small business he would speak at the funeral. One did such things for important constituents: it was a sign of respect.

He couldn't risk anyone in Parliament finding this out. Not even Warwick, he wouldn't understand. His friend wouldn't understand a lot of things that Stade had put into action. A week after the Grand Defeat, and still no one seemed to understand that the world was ending.

Rain clouds had gathered. Stade pulled Tomlinson's file under his jacket, and scowled. He hadn't thought to bring an umbrella.

PART TWO
DRIFT

I should have taken David with me, not left him with the monster Cadell. Though in truth where I had ended up was just as danger-ous. The worst thing was all the time I had: to doubt, to regret, to grow fearful. I'd been left alone, my companions murdered, my city squandered for something that was already lost to it, an Under-ground that had been overrun by Mayor Stade's enemies.

We were all haunted by the past, by the ghosts that drift and challenge. In a kingdom of the dead with night drawing close, what else could you expect? I don't think anyone slept easily in those last few weeks. We were waiting, every single one of us, for something to come. Roil or not, we knew it would be bad.

And it was.

Whispers in the Dark, MEDICINE PAUL

CHAPTER 18

There was no city quite like her. When I close my eyes, sometimes all I see are those walls, ice-slicked, and I half fancy that the earth moves to the beat of the Four Cannon. Tate haunts me still.

Fragments of the Old City, MARGARET PENN

THE CITY OF TATE
WITHIN THE ROIL BUT NOT OF THE ROIL

Margaret increased the night sight of her field glasses and swept the horizon, tracking the thin pale line of Mechanism Highway. No matter how she adjusted her field glasses, the convoy did not appear.

In the south-eastern quarter, Sentinels fired at a drift of floaters blown in too close to the walls. The Sentinels' bullets punctured the creatures' gas sacks with a wet slap. Margaret turned towards the sound and watched the last floater, its jaws snapping uselessly, crash to the ground like a burst balloon.

Another threat efficiently dealt with, as all threats were here.

Footsteps crunched on the ground behind her.

"Go home," Lieutenant Sara Varn said, her breath escaping in plumes from cracked lips as she spoke. "You're not meant to be here until tomorrow and I will not have a weary sentry on my wall. Get some rest."

Wrapped in the standard black cloak of Tate's Sentinels, Sara's single concession to Halloween was a tiny silver skull pinned to her collar. She wore heavy spiked boots. Strapped to her back were two ice rifles, while a rime blade and ice pistols were holstered around her waist. Ice weaponry proved effective against the creatures of the Roil, but was inefficient. It took considerable time to charge up and reload each gun, so Sentinels bristled with weapons, swapping and changing from pistol to rifle and (if severely pressed) to blade.

The city itself remained the best weapon.

Ice sheathed the Jut; refrigeration units lipped each merlon, pumping a chill into the air that transformed the cloying warmth of the Roil's winds into frigid gusts.

Sara clapped her gloved hands together and, despite the futility of the gesture, blew on them.

"Of course. While you're here..." Sara pointed east. "A nest of Sappers, staying an inch or so out of range of the main guns."

Flares went up.

Margaret stared at the spot with her glasses. Six of the beasts disturbed the ruined earth. Their huge dark eyes met the light fearlessly. Then Roil spores, drawn by the heat, smothered the flares – and darkness drowned the Sappers again.

"Quite a large nest," Margaret said.

Sara's eyes lit with a grim humour, she clapped her hands together again. "Already under control. We're sending drones out soon. Heavy endothermic bombing, ground breakers. You know, the standard stuff. Odd though, we haven't seen Sappers this close to the city in years, they nearly destroyed the north wall. We got them then and we will this time, too."

Margaret kept her gaze squarely on the Sappers, they did not move. Just stared at the city walls, like they were waiting for something. "When are the drones being launched?"

Sara laughed. "Soon. Just go home and rest. Tate can look after herself without you."

"All right, I'm going," Margaret said finally, and lowered her field glasses, slipping them into a case hung from her hip. Still she hovered there a moment longer.

"I'll send a message the moment they arrive," Sara said.

"The bells are set, so ring me. Three for the moment they drive through the gates."

"Three it is. It's always three, we've done this before many times. Now go."

Margaret climbed to the top of the Wire-tower – the stairs creaking with her every movement – and opened a cabinet in which hung a half-dozen leather harnesses. She pulled out hers and hooked the harness around her chest and waist, making sure the tugs and collars fit snugly; then linked herself to the wire.

She flicked a switch by the side of the tower, smiling despite herself as gears clicked into place. Beam engines hummed, counterweights fell, and the tower rose another couple of yards, making it the highest point of this section of the wireway, lifting her into a zone of hot winds. The whole structure shook slightly, then the wire tightened, lifting her even higher as it did so. Margaret made a final check of her harness; the hooks and wheels were in line, free of tangles and no cracks in evidence. Satisfied, she nodded to herself, then let go. She hovered there for the briefest of moments, a final hesitation perhaps, but it was too late, gravity had its way and she flew, suspended by the humming wire.

"Whatever you do, do not look down," someone had warned her once.

Such advice was absurd! Where else could you look? There were no stars above, just the netting doming the city, and the dark blur of the Roil. Down below, Tate's lights shimmered, distant and comforting, beautiful in their constancy.

From here it was easy to imagine the streetlights as constellations. But these were constellations crowded with people, going to and from work, trudging home in heavy cramponed boots designed for the frozen roadways. Someone, looking up, saw her and waved. Margaret waved back.

Margaret adored the wireway. Of all her parents' inventions, she loved it most. She felt ungainly and too tall, cramped in on all sides, anywhere but here. Here she was free, the wind roaring in her ears, the wheels on her harness sibilant and swift, and the city a sparkling microcosm below.

Pride for her parents' and her city's achievements swelled within her. When she had been younger, she was jealous of all the time they spent away from her. Until she realised her parents were not just protecting the city. They were protecting her.

She reached the next wall, and something slammed against the sky. The Four Cannon burned, and as she watched, the first one tumbled towards her. She tried to release herself from the wire and couldn't.

"You're dead, just like us," a cold-breathed voice whispered in her ear.

She turned and looked at Dale's face. Her first kiss. He had no lips now.

He reached to stroke her face or scratch her eyes, and the cannon fell.

THE *PINCH*
1392 MILES NORTH OF THE ROIL

Margaret woke, the last shadows of the dream clenched around her heart, to a distant detonation.

Where was she? She snatched at the rifle thatlaid beside her. They've found me, she thought, her legs already swinging over the bunk. She nearly cracked her head on the hard roof of the gondola – smaller than the *Dawn*. She blinked, no smell of the pub. And she remembered she wasn't in the *Dawn*, nor her room in the *Habitual Fool*, but that she was in the air nonetheless.

Another rumble in the near distance; and she realised that it was no iron ship, just a storm, and she was still on the Aerokin named *Pinch*, flying to the city of Drift.

She yawned. For the first time in weeks, she had slept more than a couple of hours straight. And while she still felt a bone-deep weariness, it was marginally better. David was snoring in the bed across from her; she looked over at him. His eyes were closed, but his mouth had curved wide with a smile that was almost manic. It chilled her, she would not have been surprised to see Witmoths sliding over those lips, except David's transformation was something utterly different.

He shifted between talkative and quiet. And sometimes he just stared at her, only the gaze possessed an intensity that David had never had. Margaret would glare back and David would shake his head and apologise.

Oh, and his dreams. The boy was always whimpering and crying out. He might possess the power that Cadell had given him, but it hadn't desensitised him to fear. He would snap awake – Margaret's sleep (which was hitched with its own baggage) already broken – the Orbis on his finger gleaming, and sob, till tears and snot slicked his face.

He didn't seem to care that Margaret watched him.

And despite the small space, and the fact that she hadn't caught him, she was sure that he was still taking Carnival. How else could he remain so calm, when every bit of her was itching to be free of this cabin? All he did during the day was read from his small stash of Shadow Council novels. Margaret had tried to read one of them, and found it utterly unpalatable. The books hadn't changed much in style or substance since the ones that her father had read, perhaps a little crueller, a little more violent. All they did was make her yearn for her parents' library, and remind her again what had been lost. But the books kept David occupied, which in itself would be good, but it also made it easy for him to avoid talking strategy.

They had no plan for Drift, for what needed to be done when they arrived. Kara had said that there would be more information in the *Pinch*, but that had been little more than an inventory of supplies. They were going in blind, and as far as Margaret saw it, that was David's fault.

She slid from her bed, landed on her feet lightly and walked towards the control panel – or what would be the control panel at some stage when *Pinch* had matured – as the Aerokin hummed to herself softly. Everything seemed all right – though Margaret really couldn't tell.

Outside it was still dark. She touched the translucent wall and it cleared and she could see in the distance, through the murk, a fire burning down below. Then she realised that it was moving slowly, almost imperceptibly, towards them. She tapped the wall again and watched it shift, drawing the image into tighter focus. She couldn't make out much, other than that it was not one fire, but three. Already they were drawing away from the fire.

Margaret couldn't explain why, but the sight disturbed her. She released the focus of the wall, made the lights a single blur again.

"Worrying, isn't it?" David said from behind her, making her jump. When had he ever been so light on his feet?

"What is it?"

"Who, you mean. The Old Men. They can't get us here, but they can feel me. Just as I feel them, this is as close as we have ever been, them and I." He hunkered down beside her, and smiled, though it was nothing like the smile of his sleeping. "We're quite the pair, aren't we? Hunted by everyone. Far too popular for our own good." He shook his head. "My dreams are always so dreadful these days." He reached across the narrow hall and grabbed an apple, offered it to Margaret; she shook her head. He bit down on the apple, juice ran down his chin. "Horrible, horrible things."

She turned away, looked back out as lightning streaked the sky. She felt the subtle shifting of the Aerokin, the way *Pinch* moved from a parallel path with the storm to a slightly westerly one.

Margaret said, "You didn't look like you were having a bad dream."

David sighed. "That's Cadell. He and I have different opinions on what is good and bad." He took another bite. "Tell me about your city, Margaret."

"Funny, I was just–"

"I think I heard you call out in your sleep," David said. "What was it like?"

And she did. Starting with great towers and the bells,

the wireways webbing the city, and just how much like flying that was, only faster than an Aerokin, the air around you dark as night. The Four Cannon: the rhythm around which everything else was constructed. And then there were the caverns below, ever luminous, smelling of life, nothing like the frozen city above. Just talking about it made her ache.

"Sounds wonderful," David said. "All I ever knew was rain, the smell of rot. The levee walls rising up and up. And everyone afraid that the Roil would come, that the levees would break, or the city just sink into the ground. Do you think there is a person alive in this world that doesn't have a heart drowning in terror?"

"We all drown in something," Margaret said.

"It's all right," David said. "We're moving again. We'll do what we must."

Yes, Margaret thought. Everything's all right. My parents are dead. My city is destroyed. Yes, everything is all right.

And maybe David saw that in her face, because he frowned and turned away.

"It's all right," he said once again, softly, as though to himself.

CHAPTER 19

Drift is everything that Shale aspires to. It's no wonder the bastards are arrogant, they're almost gods. Fly this, race this, lift this, they were always first and best, and quite frankly it was annoying.

They owned the blasted sky. Shame about what happened, none of us wanted that.

A Piece of a Pilot's Mind, Watson Rhig

THE CITY OF DRIFT
1400 MILES NORTH OF THE ROIL

They approached Drift in the early morning, coming at it through a band of clouds. There was nothing secretive about their arrival. Flares went up, there was a fury of flight, Aerokin boiling from hidden hangars, but it was the great edifice of Stone itself that drew the eye. A mountain reversed, flat on the top and jagged below, reaching to a great inverted peak.

Stone's great plateau was thickly forested: houses poked out of the woods, obscured and protected by the forest. And at their heart was a small oval field, by a broad lake that reflected both the clouds and Aerokin above. It was a tinier version of the Field of Flight, though Chapman had modelled their field on this one. And in its exact centre was a single tower, a long finger of stone which David knew was called the Caress. He had always wanted to see it, and now he had. Though part of him, the part in which Cadell resided, remembered seeing it many times.

The hangars were all below, on the hollowed-out cliffs of the plateau, but it wasn't there the Aerokin was taking them. They flew towards the jutting tower of the Caress itself.

Pinch passed over the edge of the city, the shift from open sky to forest, grass, and buildings a dramatic one. The hard light of the sky seemed to soften, as it washed over hard earth. Guns tracked their progress, aimed squarely at the *Pinch*'s flotation sacks. David tried not to think about that too much. Beneath *Pinch* were a few farmhouses made of stone, smoke trailing from narrow chimney. David hadn't expected such a rural setting.

As they headed towards the Caress, David looked down, the sky wasn't the only place that was crowded. A hundred people or more waited on the field below them. Some industrious folk had even started selling fried food on the periphery of the crowd.

"This feels wrong," Margaret said, already walking back to the bag containing her weapons. "I told you it was a mistake to come here."

David couldn't remember her saying any such thing.

"If Kara Jade says she needs our help, then she needs our help."

Margaret snatched up a rifle. "And what hold does she have over you?"

"Nothing," David said, with enough conviction to make it sound believable even to himself. "She saved my life, she saved both our lives. We owe her."

Margaret wasn't listening; she sighted down her rifle. "Nothing handier in a negotiation than a gun," she said. "Except maybe a bigger gun."

"Don't you ever listen?" David put a hand on hers. "We are not to go in there, guns blazing."

Margaret smiled. "You don't know me very well, do you?"

David tilted his head towards her. "You know, you're right. So, are you going to go in there, guns blazing?"

"Of course not," she said, and even she thought she sounded convincing.

The first thing that struck her was the impossibility of it. Rock did not float, and here was a great mountain-sized chunk of it. Her eyes kept seeking out the land to which it was attached, but there was nothing of the sort. It moved in the air, through the air. Then she saw – at the centre of the city – the spire known as the Caress, its shadow reaching out over the buildings. It was said that you could tell time by it, and Margaret could believe that, even if it was the greatest sundial she had ever seen.

Drift's plateau extended at a slight gradient away from the Caress, ending on the steepest gradient of all. Young Aerokin floated and wrestled there, flagella tangling and releasing. And – from the slight excited shudders of the Aerokin that contained them – Margaret could tell it wasn't too long ago that this little craft had played there.

Looking down, Margaret was struck with the familiarity of the sight, and yet how utterly alien it was.

Here was the city of Drift, built on Stone, and yet it floated five thousand feet above the ground. Casting a great shadow over the ground beneath it. Clouds broke on its walls, or were torn apart by the jagged point of its base. Here was a mountain inverted, drifting in the sky.

All at once she understood the arrogance of the people that dwelled upon it.

How could you be anything but, when you had lived in the sky?

The air above it was carnival bright, Aerokin everywhere, in places dozens of them were entwined, an orgy of the sky perhaps, or some more arcane form of communication. Everywhere their bright carapaces gleamed. And beneath them Drifters flew on gliders and wings, chasing the heat. And she was reminded again, and painfully, of her home and the Sweepers that had patrolled the Steaming Vents.

"It's amazing, isn't it?" David said, not even trying to hide the awe from his voice. He almost seemed like the David she had first known. "No matter how many times you see it, it's amazing. And I have never seen it from this angle. If I live to be a hundred, I'll never forget this moment."

And, as if in response, the clouds parted and the sun's light washed down over the city, and it shone like a great jewel from the point of the Caress to the tops of the hangars. A delicate jewel.

Margaret had seen such things deep in the belly of Tate, gypsum jewels that shone in torchlight, but would splinter to the touch. Drift was like that. Frail as the Aerokin.

It's all an illusion, she thought. Scintillating and bright, but so easy to end. She could think of a dozen ways that this city could be taken, even with as few as two iron ships. When the Roil came to this city, it would come fast and violently.

And her mood fell with that realisation, and she turned from the sight of the city, to check over her weapons once again. After all, they had no idea what they would face once they landed in the city.

"So much for a surprise arrival," Margaret said. People down below were pointing. Larger weaponised Aerokin were drawing in.

"I suppose there was never going to be a way to arrive by stealth."

"Yes, but I didn't expect a reception either," Margaret said.

David watched her, and Margaret grimaced at him.

She said, "Better to be prepared for betrayal."

"Long way from the ground if we are betrayed, don't you think? What will you do, if that's the case?"

"Fall," Margaret said. "If we have to fall, then fall we will."

CHAPTER 20

The Mothers of the Sky, who hasn't wondered at their insight or their political control. No government has been more stable, nor, with the exception of two wars, (and that is two wars over six thousand years) more isolationist. What did they do? How did they rule? Truth is, we know little of it. Just that it worked, and worked for a people so contrary and wild. Nothing was arbitrary, nothing ill-considered, they ruled, and they ruled well.

Minions of the Clouds, ADSETT

THE CITY OF DRIFT
1400 MILES NORTH OF THE ROIL

Pinch came down slowly in the field beside the great stony tower of the Caress, her flagella gripping landing pegs set out for her. David couldn't help but gawp at the famous tower of stone, the tallest structure in Shale other than the Breaching Spire itself. Clouds tangled and tore on its edges. Clouds tore and tangled on everything up here.

The Drifters that waited below were delicate, and lean to a man and woman. David was easily three inches taller than the majority of them. They watched *Pinch*'s approach silently, and with a scrutiny that David found unnerving. Just what did they expect to come shambling out of the little Aerokin?

Most of the crowd wore frock coats and capes, with an occasional greatcoat similar to Margaret's. Pilots always dressed in a manner both gaudy and functional, rings gleamed from fingers, brass holsters shone. Their skin was brown like David's. Margaret stood out even more here. In the light her skin was almost luminous. To the rear of the crowd stood men and women armed with rifles, part of some local militia.

Margaret had seen them too, of course; she was already charging her guns.

"Don't be foolish," David said.

"If we're going to die–"

"If they had wanted us dead, *Pinch* could have hurled us into the sky at any time. The moment we got onto the roof, our lives were in the Drifters' hands."

"And we gave them so easily."

Then David saw Kara near the front of the crowd; a woman, taller and older than the rest, stood beside her. David tried to work out her age, but couldn't. A memory spiked within him. He felt his cheeks burn.

"What do you think they want?" Margaret said.

David stared at Kara's companion, tried to access memories that weren't quite his. "We've travelled all this way, I believe that they won't waste too much time in telling us." No luck, he turned to Margaret, motioned to her guns, then the bag of weapons. "Put them away. We're not here to fight. For goodness' sake, those are meant to be our allies down there."

"We're always here to fight. And David, we don't have any allies," Margaret said, though she slid the rifle back into her bag. She did nothing about the other weapons that she had holstered around her waist.

David frowned at her.

"They can pry these off my dead body, if they wish, but that is the only way that I am ever giving them up."

David walked to the fore of the Aerokin. The gondola's doorifice opened for him, admitting the cool air of Drift. He said, "When you decide to die, please don't take me with you."

"If I die, at a time not my choosing," Margaret said, "the whole world will go with me, you included."

"We need to be very careful," David said. "Don't roll your eyes at me." He buttoned down his cape. "And no destroying the world for a while yet."

The crowd stood some distance from *Pinch* – no one coming forward. Indeed, they watched with less than welcoming eyes, until Kara cried out in greeting – the older woman, a Mother of the Sky perhaps, held back.

"David! Margaret! At last, at last, at last!" Kara flung her arms around David, then pulled away, face puzzled. "When did you grow so cold? You're bloody freezing, cold as death."

"I'm all right," David said. "I'm fine."

David could tell that the older woman wasn't used to giving the lead to anyone else, and by the crowd's reaction they weren't used to seeing it given. Only Kara seemed remotely close to natural, her smile the least forced.

"We thought you were in trouble," Margaret said, her bag rattling on her shoulder.

Kara looked at the guns holstered at her belt. "Oh – that, that was a misunderstanding."

"Your letter seemed rather unambiguous," David said.

Kara cleared her throat and looked away. "Politics is very changeable here," she said, her voice low, her eyes flicking in the direction of the older woman. "Like the wind, truths shift."

"Well," David said. "Whatever the truth, it is good to see you."

The older woman smiled at him, and once again David felt that familiarity. It was Cadell's memory. He had shared a past with this woman. Images came to mind, sensations that weren't at all unpleasant. He knew this woman. Cadell had known her, and as intimately as the city. Her dark eyes regarded him steadily, and he felt a jolt run through his body that wasn't entirely unpleasant.

He could see the strength in her, and not just musculature – she was lean, her fingers long, almost delicate, though they moved with a force and a precision that was anything but. She reached out and touched his hand, and there was something electric in the contact. He wanted to pull his hand away only a little more than he wanted to pull himself in closer to her. He did neither, and still her gaze was fixed on him.

"Hello," he said, his voice catching in his throat, but at least he'd managed to speak first.

"Welcome, David," she said, her voice as calm as his thoughts were ragged.

"I don't believe that we have had the pleasure–"

"You know who am. Don't pretend otherwise, eh," she said, and she laughed lightly.

And that familiar laugh thrilled him, in a way that was too unseemly. All at once he felt unsettled, unsure of himself. Who was he? David or Cadell? Could he even tell any more?

"I'm sorry, I didn't introduce you," Kara Jade said, and

David wondered just what she was playing at. "This is Mother Graine, Air Mistress, and Senior Servant."

"Servant?"

Mother Graine flashed him a smile. "We do not rule here, we serve."

"The distinction is subtle, I'm sure," David said.

Again she laughed that glorious and disconcerting laugh. "It always is, isn't it? Just as it's common courtesy to bow to a Mother of the Sky."

"I'm not in the practice of bowing." David nodded towards Margaret. "And don't even bother expecting it of her." It was Margaret's turn to give him a look of warning. He hardly noticed it.

Mother Graine clasped her hands together, stared down at the Orbis Ingenium. "So it is you! The wolf in the clothing of such a dull child."

David blinked. Perhaps he hadn't taken enough Carnival that morning; it had been hard to administer while Margaret watched him. He gritted his teeth, he was going to fix that and soon. "Not quite," he said. "Cadell is buried deep."

Mother Graine nodded, and what may have been disappointment passed across her face. "You are not nearly as annoying as he was," she said at last. "That's something at least. He'd have grabbed my hand and dragged me from this place, and we would have been fighting within a minute."

"You haven't been around him long enough," Margaret said.

Mother Graine stared at her appraisingly. "My child," she said. "I have known him longer than you could believe." She clapped her hands for silence. And it worked. "Here are our guests. David Milde, lately of Mirrlees, and Margaret Penn of the Tate Penns, last of a line of thinkers

– though you would not know it to look at her. We are blessed indeed to have them here. Bid them welcome one and all, let them enjoy our city's hospitality. For they will not be here long, and where they are going will require strength and bravery beyond anything that either has known."

"We've much to talk about," she said quietly, to the pair of them. "But not here. Not now." She gestured to Kara. "Maiden Jade will see to your comfort. We will have a reception tonight, very informal, of course. Afterwards we will talk."

She dipped her head once, and David bowed, stiffly. Mother Graine laughed. "Tonight," she said, her eyes searching his face, and David worried that he was disappointing her. "Please, remember that you are welcome here."

CHAPTER 21

The Mothers of the Sky were perhaps the most influential force in the history of Shale. Forget the Old Men, forget the Council. It was the Mothers that ruled, and they did so with subtlety and force.

Queens of the Air, CASAGRANDE

THE CITY OF DRIFT
1400 MILES NORTH OF THE ROIL

Margaret couldn't understand what was happening. They'd clambered off *Pinch* to see Kara Jade, safe and sound, both of them on edge for signs of betrayal, and now here David seemed to be flirting with a Mother of the Sky.

She glanced over at Kara Jade. Margaret gestured at David and the older woman, and Kara Jade shrugged. It was as though they had ceased to exist.

"We thought you were in trouble," Margaret said.

"A misunderstanding, no more," Mother Graine said, suddenly back in the conversation.

"Yes, yes, misunderstanding," Kara Jade said.

Margaret wasn't very fond of misunderstandings. She

looked over at David, and he stood there, still looking very confused, and not a little flustered.

Mother Graine smiled. "We've ammunition for your weapons, even Chill should you wish it; our artisan chemists are among the best in the world. Though where you're headed I doubt you will require either."

"My guns and my blades kill humans just as well as they kill creatures of the Roil."

Mother Graine patted her arm gently. "Of course they do, my dear. I'm sure you could kill with a glance."

Though if that were true, Mother Graine would be on the ground twitching out her last. "I'll take whatever you can spare," Margaret said. "We've long miles to the north."

"Yes, you do," Mother Graine said. "And though I've not set foot upon the earth in an age, the way to Tearwin Meet is familiar, and perilous. Even to think on it for too long is dangerous. There are forces there that will ruin your mind should you let them." She sighed. "But that is for another time."

"I'd hear it now, if I could."

"Yes, I know, you must be anxious to begin the real journey. We are all anxious to see an end to this, but there are other things we must consider first." Mother Graine looked over at David. "Tonight. We will discuss them tonight."

She left, walking back through the crowd, and they parted for her like water is parted by the bow of a boat: swiftly, elegantly and almost without thought.

"Now, there goes a woman with the weight of the world on her shoulders," David said.

Margaret watched after her. "So, she would have us believe."

With her gone the crowd began to relax.

"Where are the other Mothers?" David asked.

"Mother Graine has always been the foremost voice," Kara said. "But these last months the Mothers have all but disappeared. We are bred to trust them, almost as much as we distrust the earth below, but even that acceptance has been stretched to its limits."

"So you don't think we will see them here?"

"No, not even for you and Miss Penn over there. There is something going on, I guess, plans. Maybe even a new weapon against the Roil," Kara Jade said. "A single Mother is common. Indeed, Mother Graine is all we have seen in the past few weeks. Now, I really must introduce you to a few people before we get you into your rooms. Unless you'd rather go straight there."

Margaret shook her head furiously. "I've been cooped up inside for days. I'm rested enough."

That proved a mistake.

After being stuck with just David, these crowds came as a shock. At first it was exciting, almost energising, but soon, all these people – even with Kara offering some protection – were exhausting. All that noise, questions of the south, of the true fall of Tate: Margaret was forced to consider things that she had been avoiding for weeks.

Finally, Kara Jade led them out of the scrum to rooms within the Caress, and the crowd did not follow. This was the oldest building in Shale, it demanded quiet and respect – and sometimes it got them.

A single doorway connected David and Margaret's rooms. Kara nodded to it, and grinned most salaciously.

"That door won't be opened, I guarantee it," Margaret said primly.

"Of course," Kara said, "from you I would believe it. Though I'd watch this one, seems he can even charm a Mother of the Sky."

CHAPTER 22

There are always factions wherever you go. Get five people in a room, and factions will form. Drift was just a very big room. Yes, we were politically naive, but we were quick to lose that. We had to.

Processes towards New Government, RAVEN SKYE

THE CITY OF DRIFT
1401 MILES NORTH OF THE ROIL

Kara Jade let out a long breath and grinned.

"You," she said, and swung her arms around him, she didn't hold him for long, but David appreciated the effort. "How do you stand her?" she whispered in his ear. Then much louder, "I didn't think I would see you again."

"I never thought it would happen, either," David said.

"And I'm happy to see you, too," Margaret said.

"Of course you are," Kara waved a hand in the air. "Of course you are."

"I'm sorry," Margaret said, "if our parting was a little heated."

Kara laughed. "Heated, I suppose *some* of your threats could be considered heated."

"You left us alone, mired in the politics of Hardacre."

"I left you because I was summoned home. You can be scary, I suppose, but you're nothing compared to the Mothers of the Sky. You saw her, and that was a good day. Imagine seven more, all in a fury because I didn't deliver you to them."

"You were meant to deliver us to them?" Margaret said.

"I think it was implied more than a direct order. Otherwise I would have taken you here immediately."

"So, now we know where your loyalties lie."

"Where did you think they lay? With a pallid, death-hungry bitch and a drug addict?" Kara smiled. "No offence intended."

"None taken," Margaret said archly.

"Count yourself lucky I didn't bring you here at the beginning. David, you were unconscious for days, think about what might have happened then?"

"Well, you've got us here now," David said and smiled at Kara, but she didn't smile back, just a tightening of lips, a deepening of frown.

"Mother Graine says you're a monster. But looking at you, all I see is a young man, with a ridiculous moustache. What are you?" she said, holding his arms. David tried his hardest to keep the cold from them. But what did he know of warmth? All the power that he possessed drew from its opposite.

"I quite like the moustache," he said. "I'm still me, and I'm not. I'm an Old Man in a young body. I'm David Milde and John Cadell, well, Cadell is in there somewhere."

"Hey, Old Man." Kara bumped a knuckle against his skull. "How do you both fit in there?"

David shuddered. "Truth is, I don't know if we even can. But, at the moment at least, we're managing."

"But I thought that Cadell died."

"Yes, and then I had to kill the body."

Kara's eyes widened. "You what?"

"Cadell's body went missing after you left. Without his mind, all it possessed was hunger," David explained.

"You fought Cadell, and you won? That man leapt onto an iron ship, destroyed it with his bare hands."

"We managed. I had all of Cadell's strengths – and Margaret – all he had left were his weaknesses. Hunger is a terrible and frightening thing, but it isn't that smart."

"And are you still hungry?"

David laughed. "I am always hungry. Always, takes a lot of fuel to drive what I am."

"This is so unfair," Kara said.

"Life is always unfair. I've never expected it to be anything else. And since my father died, I've been reminded of this almost a half-dozen times a day. Nothing is fair for anyone now. We're all of us struggling, all of us frightened.

"Hardacre is all but ready to throttle itself, and the situation here, I'm not sure I understand it, but it is a situation, that's for sure. Even the Roil is frightened, or it wouldn't continue its attack with such urgency. I mean, what need does it have for human agents now, and yet it still infects them."

He pulled from her grip. Kara might not have noticed it, but she was shaking. David said, "We're stuck with doing the best we can with what we have. I suppose that has always been the way of it. If I give into my grief now, all I have in my future is madness and killing, and the spectre of Old Men hunting me down."

"*The* Old Men?" Kara asked."Yes, they're after me. Don't

worry, they're still a long way away, but they see me just as abhorrent as I saw the mindless Cadell. They're coming to tear me from the earth if they can."

"Obviously they won't be interested in any of your friends."

That stopped him; he'd forgotten what it was like to have friends. Those had been substituted by suppliers and addicts and little else over the last few years. Even Cadell had been more of a supplier than a friend. After all, what friend would give you this?

"Of course, they're all damned, too," David said. He studied his room: five steps to the door, no window, just a narrow vent. "So when do you think we will be allowed to leave? You're not in trouble, and I'm guessing you will be accompanying us to Tearwin Meet."

"Soon and yes, I'll be facing the headwinds full on with you." She smiled. "Not that I'm much good. Look at these hands, they're almost as soft as yours."

"They'll toughen up," Margaret said. "Now, what do you mean by soon?"

"Tomorrow, I'd guess, after the reception. I suspect that all Mother Graine wanted was to see you were capable of finishing this."

"And I've passed the test so far?" David said.

"So far…" Kara reached into her pocket and pulled out a small device. She pressed it once, and it began to keen, a shrill mechanical sound, like a tiny engine weeping. She looked back at the door, waited a moment, and released a breath.

David raised an eyebrow at her.

"That should work for a minute. Things are bad here," Kara said. "I think there has been something of a coup in the upper echelons. Amongst the Mothers themselves. Not too long ago you would see them all. Now we have Mother Graine alone speaking for them."

"You think she's killed them?" Margaret asked.

Kara looked like she was going to vomit. "No, that's not what I think. That would be unthinkable–"

"And yet…"

"They're trapped somewhere."

Margaret shifted. "You said you were in trouble."

"I'm very much in trouble. Even more so now that we're having this conversation, believe me," Kara Jade said. "But not as much as you." Her eyes dropped to the Orbis. "The Mothers of the Sky wanted that ring, and I think they would have killed you to get it."

"They're going to have to join the queue," David said. "Why did you drag me here?"

"Because I can keep an eye on you," Kara said. "If I'd not gotten you here, they would have sent assassins. And in Hardacre, they could have gotten to you easily. But now, now something's changed."

David thought of Mr Sheff. Had he been working for Drift rather than out of some sense of grievance?

Margaret shook her head. "That logic is utterly flawed. Here we are surrounded by those who would kill him, if by stupidity alone."

Kara smiled, raised her hands in the air, though David thought she looked like she'd rather hit someone. "Here they're relaxed, they don't expect you to do anything. I'm not even sure Mother Graine wants you harmed. And Drift is on a path to the Deep North: every moment brings us closer."

"But we can't stay here, you know what they want to do with me. If they want the Orbis, they'll need to kill me," David said.

Kara patted his arm. "You die, and everything starts over again. We're going to be waiting weeks, I suppose. And how tedious would that be? Besides, the Roil has started to move so much faster than before, it's picked up pace."

"The Roil is like any storm, I guess," David said. "Watch a storm and it hardly seems to move, it glowers and it boils, but it appears stationary. And then, all at once it is upon you. Fury and fire, and you realise the only one that wasn't moving was you. The Roil's moving now, and it's moving fast."

"Been caught out in a few storms, have you?" Kara Jade said. "I know storms, the *Dawn* and I ride them. You won't be caught in that storm, David. Nor would I have Margaret and I suffer the inconvenience of your funeral."

"Thank you for your sympathy," David muttered. "Perhaps you could deliver the eulogy."

Kara cleared her throat. "Here lies a man that was two men, and neither of them up to much. Couldn't hold his liquor for one."

Margaret turned towards Kara. David sighed. "She is right, though."

"Can we leave the joking until we are out of here?" Margaret said.

"Yes, of course. I'm sorry," David said.

Kara looked at Margaret, and nodded.

"Good, then tonight, after the reception we make a break for it."

"Why not now?" David asked.

Kara laughed. "Right now, I couldn't get you out of here. It's one thing for me to sneak through the guarding stations, another for you two. There are traps, patches of bad air, and odd gravities that won't bother me, but will certainly have an effect on you two. I want us to escape, to finish what I know needs to be done, but I don't want to kill either of you doing it. Look, you are safe enough now. Just be patient."

"After the reception, then," Margaret said.

Kara pressed the button again, and the keening stopped. "Now, I've things to attend to. I will see you tonight."

CHAPTER 23

The Underground became the most sophisticated hub of industry in the world, outside of Tearwin Meet and the long-distant Breaching Spire, though to say anything about the sophistication of those regions is to offer little more than wild speculation; Tearwin had last admitted entry eight centuries before, and there are few – if any living – that have stood at the base of the Spire and wondered, just wondered, where it might take them. That is to say the Underground's secrets were technological in nature, as far as politics was concerned, it was as unsophisticated a place as any where women and men chose to settle, united messily by common purpose, but divergent beliefs.

Projections of a Seemly Man, MOLCH

THE UNDERGROUND
865 MILES NORTH OF THE ROIL

The hallways of the Underground leading from one segment to the next were ill lit, in some places almost pitch black. Most of the energy required to keep the lighting running was being funnelled into the defences of the structure, and the construction process itself. Which meant that

Medicine Paul didn't see the fist that hit him in the face, or the next one that had him on his arse.

"What did you do with my nephew?" A light clicked on, and Medicine blinked at the woman holding the torch. He had been waiting for this confrontation for some time, which certainly didn't mean he had been expecting it here. She was always such a surprising person to deal with.

"Hello, Veronica," he said. "Nice to see you, too."

"Where is my nephew?" she said.

"Safe, he is in Hardacre. Cadell took him from the city, there's a ship called the *Collard Green* that has been sent to collect him."

"You did what? That monster, he's–"

"The only option I had," Medicine said, getting up.

Another fist was driven into his chest, but he was ready for it, he stepped backwards, and it only clipped him gently.

"Ah, you infuriating bastard."

He reached out a hand and closed it over her fist. "Trust me, it was all I had left. Your brother–"

"My brother could look after himself, he knew what he was doing."

"Exactly."

"But he isn't here, and neither is my nephew, all I have is you."

Medicine nodded. "I know, I know. I blame myself."

"Are you going to the infirmary?" Veronica said.

"If I wasn't, I think I might need to go now."

"I didn't hit you that hard."

Medicine smiled. Patted dust from his shoulders, and took a deep breath of the hot, dry air – pungent in a way that had become less apparent as the days had passed. "No, you didn't, and yes, I am going. I need to be useful."

"Yes, we all do. It's coming, isn't it?"

"Has been for what's felt like most of my life."

Veronica nodded. "So Warwick is dead? Really dead?""Yes," Medicine said.

They stood in silence.

"I always told him that politics would be the death of him," Veronica said. "Not that I could ever avoid it myself. I'm sorry about what happened to your companions."

"Thank you. Grappel should not have done what he did."

"No, I think he made the right choice. Allow Stade's poison in here, no matter how calm and well reasoned, and we all rot. We might as well open the doors to the Roil."

He said, "I knew them, they were good people."

"Good people that killed my brother, and that locked the gates of the city to the refugees, and drove them to Hardacre. You know, Medicine, the day that happened – that was my last day in Mirrlees; I could not breathe the same air as people that might think that was right. When short-sighted pragmatism overrules compassion, when it is lauded as wisdom. We would have struggled, but we could have built something new, something wonderful. Ah, it still burns."

"That same pragmatism that says it is all right to kill in cold blood those of a different political persuasion."

"That is different. They made their choices. We all do, I'd die for mine, and I know that you would die for yours."

They reached the lift that led to the infirmary, Medicine jabbed the button.

"And do not pretend that you haven't killed for yours," Veronica said. "In these last days all our hands, including those ruined ones of yours, are drenched with blood."

"I do not," Medicine said. "All that I can say is that I am

surprised that you didn't find me until now. My arrival was hardly a secret."

"I found you," Veronica said. "Who was it that nursed you to health when you were sick with the northern fever? I made sure that you breathed. I changed your sheets... now, that was pleasant."

"And you didn't stay to confront me then?"

"No, I couldn't stand to see your face."

"What's changed?"

"Grappel's deciding your future," Veronica said.."

"He's going to kill me, too?"

Veronica shook her head. "He needs a second in command. What you did, taking those people up from Mirrlees, recapturing the steam engine from the Cuttlefolk." Medicine could hardly take credit for that; it had been more seizing an opportunity and fleeing for his life.

She said, "It impressed him. He's going to ask you to join him. I thought I'd let you know first."

"What? I don't want authority. I don't need it. I'm back doing what I should have been doing all along."

Veronica smiled at him. "We both know that's a lie," she said.

The infirmary was always busy. Medicine worked until he was exhausted. This was what he had trained for all those years ago; and now, listening to people, helping them as best he could, he'd found a new joy and a new way of escape from the troubles that beset him. Here he was helping people, even if it was only easing suffering, keeping them alive.

When he was done, still thinking about Veronica's words, he took the lift back down to his room, sat on his bed and unstoppered the bottle of whisky that Grappel had given him.

When the knock at the door came, he was expecting it.

Grappel's messenger entered. "He wants to speak to you now," he said.

Medicine nodded. He knew what he was going to say.

CHAPTER 24

Drift kept itself apart, because it was easy to. But that did not make it an easy city in which to live. It had never unshackled itself from its dependence on Shale for food, nor the sheer cost of moving items to and from the city. It was a state with no resources, but one. And that it ruled ruthlessly.

Drifters: A Brief History, MADELINE MADDEER

THE CITY OF DRIFT
1401 MILES NORTH OF THE ROIL

Margaret sat in her room in the single wooden chair, staring across at the bed and her guns. David had almost immediately gone to sleep – after polishing off several plates of something the Drifters called night-meat, and which David declared was delicious – despite Kara's warnings. He could take care of himself.

She stood up, stretched, and walked for the door.

Margaret had to get out of there, just for a while, and she wanted to know if she could, if they would let her. There were few people getting about and those that were seemed busy, giving her a glance (they all did that), but hurrying on. She found her way to the entrance; Kara had explained the system of lights that signalled the way, and once you knew to follow the amber globes, it wasn't difficult at all. The Caress was built into the ground: the hallways and floors ran through it all in a network, more like a circulatory system than a building. Oddly enough, the way out was different from the way in. She passed empty halls, dimly lit, and bustling kitchens filled with heat. There was even a hallway of statues, stern-faced things that Margaret suspected depicted the Mothers of the Sky, though why there were so many she couldn't fathom.

Finally, down a wide stairwell, she came to a pair of steel doors that swung open at her approach, and she walked out into the late afternoon. Everything sloped gently away from the stone finger of the Caress. Already behind her she could see lights coming on. It would be dark soon, and the Stars of Mourning would rise to the east. She well knew the contours of the dark; it held no fear for her. Not even this curious and wonderful dark she had been thrust into over the past few weeks with its stars and its moons. Tate's sky had only ever been the dark of the Roil and the fumes of the Steaming Vents, and lights reflected off the wireway.

Near the Caress were a handful of bookstores selling the usual array of histories, personal and serious. She saw plenty of Deighton in there, Molck and many others that she did not recognise. There were maps and map powder, too, and a children's book about the creatures of the Roil – the illustrations all a little too cute for her. She even found a couple of Night Council novels and considered getting one for David, though she hadn't seen him read in days. The boy was changing again, growing even more serious.

She left the last bookstore after a few minutes' desultory poking through its stock, the shopkeeper leaving her alone. The city was already cooling down, a mist sliding out from the lake to the east of the city, she could see the mist coasting slowing towards her. The familiar smell of coal smoke greeted her. Fires were being lit on street corners. She stopped at one of them, stretched her hands out over the burning coals, felt her flesh warm a little and turned to stare at the men following her.

They did a double take that was almost funny. Margaret cracked her neck.

Time to deal with this now, she thought.

There were two of them, both big men for Drifters, broad across the chest, guns at their belts. The men were doing their best to appear interested in a shop window filled with flowers.

"You two," she shouted, "what do you think you're doing? Buying me a bouquet, I expect."

They actually seemed to wilt.

"We don't want any trouble," said the tallest one of them.

"You found trouble the moment you started following me, whether you wanted it or not. Perhaps you would like to tell me who you are?"

The two men approached her, hands out, smiling. One said, "It's quite simple, really."

Margaret didn't take any chances. "Yes, it really is," she said. She kicked the first one in the head, and punched the other in the stomach.

They went down far too easily. She yanked free her rime blade, activated the device and pressed it point first against the throat of the man nearest to her. She pulled the blade back when he looked like he might faint

"Who are you working for?" she snarled.

"We're here to protect you," he moaned.

She snorted. "And you thought that would be best achieved by sneaking around behind me?"

"We were told you wouldn't like it."

Margaret let him get up. "You really are terrible at following a person," Margaret said. "I knew you were there almost from the moment I left the Caress."

"It wasn't our intent to scare you. We're Mother Graine's guards, not spies," he said. "We're not employed for stealth."

"Obviously not," she said, and wondered where were the ones that had hidden, which shop had they ducked into, which rooftop did they crouch upon. "And why is Mother Graine so interested in me?"

"The Mothers of the Sky are interested in the welfare of all their guests."

"We would prefer it if you returned to your room," the big man said, rubbing his bloody nose. "For your own safety."

"For my own safety then," Margaret said. "You wouldn't prefer to accompany me around the city. I doubt that I will ever return here."

"No... I... we... your reception begins in an hour."

"Then you had better be quick about showing me this place."

Margaret banged on David's door. He opened it, a towel around his waist. The boy had put on some muscle, not that that meant anything. Muscle could slow you down as much as it could speed you up: she'd proven that half an hour ago.

"Yes," David said.

"There could be trouble."

David frowned. "Just let me get dressed first," he said.

"Before you bring disaster to my bedroom." He shut the door in her face.

"I don't like this," Margaret said.

"When do you ever like anything?" David replied. "We'll have an Aerokin, we can make our way into the north. Everything is turning out for the best, wouldn't you say?"

"I think you're wrong. They had me followed."

"What!" David said with more than a whit of sarcasm. "They had a strange white woman followed?"

"They said it was for my safety," Margaret said, looking down at her bruised knuckles.

"Who did you beat up this time?"

"He had it coming. He was trying to protect me."

David laughed. "Well, who was protecting him?"

"I took it easy on him. I don't like being followed, David."

"Neither do I," David said. "And people have a tendency to want to kill us. Perhaps we should keep as close together as possible tonight."

"Agreed."

"The sooner we're back in the air, the better."

CHAPTER 25

It has been stated that it was the Drifters that halted the development of fixed winged aircraft. That their Aerokin tore them out of the sky, and their spies destroyed such installations capable of the construction of flying machines. Fickle, foolish, vain: Drifters may be all these things, but they were also as ruthless as any Verger, when they perceived it to be required.

Drifters: A Brief History, MADELINE MADDEER

THE CITY OF DRIFT
1402 MILES NORTH OF THE ROIL

Kara Jade knocked on the door to David's room. "You decent?" she called. "You better be."

"I'm ready," David said, scrambling to hide his syringe.

Kara opened the door.

He rose from his bed, affronted. "That was locked!"

"Not to me it wasn't," Kara said, and grinned.

David looked at her. "You've dyed your hair. Are those feathers?"

"Yes, and yes. Don't want to be outdressed tonight. New jacket, too."

"Very smart," Margaret said from behind Kara.

Kara studied her, and shrugged. "Well, at least you've bathed." Margaret was dressed in black pants, a black blouse, and her jacket had a hood. "What are you doing? Going to rob a house afterwards?"

"We go to this damn reception, and then we leave."

Kara nodded. "Agreed. Sooner we get there, sooner this ends."

The reception was held within the Caress itself, a hall extending onto a balcony on the eighteenth level. When they arrived the balcony was already crowded, it was a peculiar thing to see all those heads suddenly turn and regard them as they walked into the room. A peculiar thing, and very similar to an unpleasant experience David had had on the *Dolorous Grey* just a few weeks ago. A dining car filled with Roilings, all ready to turn him into one of them. David cast his eye about for Witmoths. Nothing. Why would there be?

Kara Jade elbowed him, for all the tension of the moment she seemed at ease. David glanced over at Margaret. Even she looked relaxed. What? Had they been at his Carnival?

He'd slept the afternoon away, but it had been a sleep of nightmares, of Cadell demanding he run, that Mother Graine wasn't to be trusted and just where were the other Mothers? What had *she* done to them? Twice he'd woken just as a Quarg Hound was ready to swallow him whole, only to sink back down, dragged there by Cadell's ever-increasing will.

Even here, he could feel the Old Man looking out at the world, studying the people at the reception, tasting their fear, and the sense that all they really wanted to do was forget themselves for one night.

"We'll be out of here soon," Kara Jade said. "Just work through it, and don't mention – oh, no."

"What?" David turned to her; Kara wasn't looking in his direction.

He followed her gaze towards the edge of the party. A woman stood there – almost as tall as Margaret, which made her stand out here. There was something oddly familiar about her, and not from Cadell's memories. David caught her eye, and the woman nodded, before turning her attention back to the bottle she held in her hands. Drift rum of course, dark, glinting like a Cuttleman's blood. She had to be a pilot, they all were here, and pilots drank nothing else.

"Who is that?" David whispered in Kara's ear; she stiffened, turned David bodily in the other direction, before he could even protest.

"You don't want to talk to her," Kara Jade said.

"Why?" David asked.

"She's Raven Skye."

"Raven Skye?"

Kara's eyes boggled. David felt that he had offended her. "I'm sorry. I don't mean to–"

"You must've heard of her."

David shook his head.

"What cave have you been living in?"

A deep dark one, David wanted to say, but he didn't. "Carnival, that's a cave of a sort, I suppose."

Kara's jaw was clenched so tight it looked like she might snap a tooth. "She's the pilot of the *Matilda Ray*."

"What?" Now he *had* heard of her. "S*he's* the pilot of the *Tilly Ray*?"

Yet again, David could see that he had disappointed her. "Typical groundling, knows a pilot's Aerokin, but not the pilot. And *don't* call the *Matilda* the *Tilly* in front of her. She's a bit odd about it. In fact, I think we should–"

"Ah, Kara!" Raven called out, already walking towards them.

Kara winced.

Raven patted her arm. "What, you weren't even going to talk to your sister?"

Sister? Now David looked, he could see the resemblance. Though Raven was a good decade or so older, and about a foot taller; she'd pulled her long hair back, revealing a scar that ran from her left ear, all the way down her chin.

The *Tilly Ray* had been the last ship to leave the Grand Defeat, she'd held the Roil back as the other Aerokin had escaped, and had even managed to pick up more refugees along the way. She'd also been the first Aerokin that Stade had turned away, and the first to land in Hardacre with her wounded. The heroic death of General Bowen and the actions of the *Tilly Ray* were the most famous incidents of the Grand Defeat.

It had been the Aerokin that had drawn the attention, while the pilot had kept a low profile, avoiding mention in all but the most thorough histories, and David rarely read those.

Raven must have been only Kara's age when she'd performed her feats, and just as obstinate. David could understand why Kara might find her sister difficult to be around, two such personalities were never going to get along. And now Raven was coming over; wherever she walked, people got out of her way almost as quickly as if she were a Mother of the Sky. The whole party shifted around her like mice around a salivating cat.

Raven looked down at him. "So this is the addict, the one from the Sump?"

"The Sump?" he asked.

"Long story. But take it from me, it isn't complimentary, addict," Raven said. David smiled, of course it wouldn't be; just looking at her he doubted Raven was capable of compliments.

"Raven!" Kara said.

David reached out a hand. "No, it's true. I had my troubles, but those days are past."

Raven gave him a tense sort of smile, and cracked her knuckles. "So, if I was to shake you, you're telling me Carnival wouldn't come spilling out of your every orifice, pocket, and shoe?"

David realised that everyone in the room was looking at them, at him in particular – the conversation had died down. It was the Carnival that allowed him to lie with such conviction. David lifted his arms. "If you'd like to, but I must warn you, I'm heavier than I look."

Raven laughed. "I'm sure you are." She studied him with eyes as dark as thunderheads. "You're certainly a charmer, so was your father. Don't look so surprised. I knew many Engineers and Confluents when I still visited Mirrlees, before it started to drown. I was sorry to hear he died."

"He didn't die. He was murdered."

"And I am sorry for that." She clapped her hands. "Now, what are you drinking?"

They were all a little drunk by the time Mother Graine arrived, alone. She walked straight over to David, ignoring Margaret as she did. Not that Margaret seemed to mind; she was having an animated conversation with another pilot. And she was smiling.

David thought Mother Graine looked harried, weary, as though she had already had a night of drinking. Raven drained her glass the moment Mother Graine appeared.

Then Raven slid an arm over her sister's shoulder, and pulled Kara away.

"There's something we must talk about," Raven said, leaving him alone with the Mother of the Sky. His head buzzing with drink, and some rather lewd memories of Cadell's; he felt his cheeks flush.

"Raven is so brave," Mother Graine said, watching after the pilots. "It is a hard thing to lose your craft, to have it die. Many don't survive that loss."

"What? The *Matilda Ray* is dead? I'd heard–"

"The *Matilda* was old when Raven took her as pilot. Though she should have had another twenty years in her, she died not long after the Grand Defeat; an infection of the lungs, I believe. Raven hasn't left Drift since."

David thought of that, ten years alone. David thought Margaret would know at least a portion of that loneliness. He guessed he did, too. "People are torn from our lives," he said. "Loves snatched away."

Mother Graine patted his arm. "We've had our share of that, you and I. The dead far outweigh the living in our lives." She sighed, looked around her pointedly. "I can't talk here, and there are things that must be said. Things that only you and I can discuss."

"I agree," David said. "We need to talk, and you need to let us go. We've a long way to go."

"Yes, I understand that. The Engine waits and you fear it as much as you desire it." She touched his arm, and David felt his nerves react in a way that he'd thought was lost to him; or perhaps he had never really known, it seemed so foreign. The Engine wasn't the only thing that he feared and desired.

Mother Graine said, "I understand a lot of things about you. Come with me for a while, I promise people won't mind, I have a bit of influence here." She flashed him a smile, and David's throat tightened, he knew at once, in that moment, he couldn't deny her anything. Plans for an early night fell away; besides, he doubted she could stop him, or even hurt him.

The strength, Cadell's strength, bloomed inside him. And he felt at last that he understood the true possibility of their binding.

"Where do you want to go?" he asked her.

They left the Caress together, the reception still going strong, and already beginning to look like it was going to get messy. Out in the night, David couldn't tell if it was cold, but he guessed it had to be. Mist was rising from the lake (a lake in the sky, that still struck him as so wonderfully odd). People gathered around small fires on the outskirts of the city, guards, he guessed, though they did their best to pretend that neither he nor Graine were there. Graine held his hand, and her grip was warm. She didn't seem to mind the cold.

They walked for about twenty minutes in silence along an increasingly narrow path. The houses thinned out around them, the forest thickened and the stars grew bright. They reached an edge of Stone, and a viewing platform.

"Is this where you push me off?" David asked.

"Don't spoil another night, Cadell," Graine said. "Please."

He gripped the rail to steady himself and an image struck him suddenly, a memory that was not his own: of a third moon rising above a dark and shivering city of stone, and a sea of ice rising and drowning the world, and he could see faces, eyes staring, faces in the ice and they were frozen, but not dead.

"David?" Graine reached out a hand. David stepped away from her.

"A memory, something vivid and cruel. I saw – I don't know what I saw."

Graine nodded. "Sorry, I didn't mean to call him out of you."

David turned his back to her. "He's getting stronger," he said, and looked over the edge, into the dark.

Drift moved in a rough circle over Shale, though its circumference had shrunk with the coming of the Roil, as though where that darkness was the mechanisms of the city feared to go. What the city might do once (if) the Roil enclosed the entire world was uncertain. But then, life in a city in the sky was full of uncertainties. For all that Drift's residents claimed sovereignty of the air, there was much they did not know. For one, was the city capable of eternal flight, or would its engines one day run down and the city fall from the sky?

David felt as though he were falling now.

He turned and looked back at the city, he could just make out the balcony, and the party. Fireworks were being lit. More memories came unbidden, of ancient wars of a vast darkness, crawling, crawling towards towers higher than mountains. He thought, Enough! Enough!

Graine gestured at the sky. "The Roil's iron ships, they'll attack us. We've held ourselves apart from the troubles below for so long, but it was all for nothing. Ah, but the world isn't as it was," Graine said.

"The world never is as it was," David said. "That's the nature of the world."

"We should understand that better than anyone." Graine touched his face. "After all, you are the embodiment of change."

"Seeing you, I'm beginning to understand that better than I could have thought," David said. "Now, please tell me why you brought me here."

"You were never going to be clear of Hardacre before the Old Men came. My spies could tell me that much. Buchan and Whig, they were dithering so, when they should have been more certain, more... commanding. As they were when they ran Chapman. Hardacre's politics are complicated, I guess. And my actions are with precedent. I've once freed you before, long ago. Is it too much for you to remember?

"Though the touch of the earth stabbed at my feet, I went down to your prison and let you out."

And David realised that she was addressing Cadell. Perhaps she had been addressing him all along. He felt Cadell rise a little within him, as though all the Carnival in the world couldn't keep the Old Man suppressed. It was like drowning, and here, with this strange woman, he let himself drown.

David nodded. "It was a mistake."

Graine sighed. "One never knows until one fails. And it wasn't a mistake to free you, just the others."

"If I remember, forty people died as a result of that freedom."

"What did it matter? So many had died already."

David blinked, felt Cadell slide away, as though banished by the memory of that long-ago freedom. "Why didn't you just throw us into prison the moment we arrived?"

Graine gestured at the city around them. "You do not see it? This is Drift. The city in the sky, you cannot run from here unless I say so. Where is your airship? What Aerokin do you pilot? I did not want to frighten you unduly. The frontal approach, that struck me as too dangerous, not for you, nor for your warrior-guardian woman, but for my people. How many of my kind would die before Margaret was overcome? How many could you kill?

"And do not tell me that you didn't expect some sort of assault on your arrival," she said.

"I might have."

"Yes, well, for the first time you were greeted with open arms here. Coercion isn't necessarily the best solution. And it worked. Still, sometimes it's required."

She held his hand. "Let me take you back to the Caress, to my rooms. We have so much to discuss, you've need of strategy now. Old Men hunt you, the Roil hunts you, but I've a way that you can be done with it, and in Tearwin Meet before the week is out."

David let her lead him away from the edge.

In her rooms, they did far less talking than David had been led to expect.

Her lips pressed hard against his. He felt no resistance, just an answering hunger, and this so unlike anything he had known before. It consumed him, made him weak.

She guided his fingers to her thigh, and he felt her racing pulse.

They were naked in an eye blink. And then they were bound in each other, hot and cold combined, and it was hard and rough, and utterly unexpected. By the time they were done, David felt stripped away, worn out, and yet more alive than he could have believed. He traced a finger along the curve of her belly, kissed a nipple gently, and Graine pushed him away.

"That will be enough," she said primly.

"Enough?" His face was slick with her, his senses filled with her. "Good heavens, madam, I thought we had only started."

Graine smiled. "Cadell, my Cadell. I really am sorry."

Her hand flashed out, striking him just above the eyes, and David fell.

"Not fair," he breathed.

"Of course it isn't," Graine said, and kicked him in the face.

CHAPTER 26

Two things does Drift give to the world and they are, without argument, the finest pilots, and the strongest rum.
Is there anything more that you need to know?

A Brief Summary of the Histories of a
Fractured Land, JUSTINE LARHN

THE CITY OF DRIFT
1410 MILES NORTH OF THE ROIL

The reception possessed little formality. Margaret still wondered how people could let themselves get so drunk, and so quickly. Then she had a sip of the Drift rum, and her eyes watered. David wasn't so circumspect. He was soon nearly as drunk as the rest of them.

The pilot reached out a hand. "I'm Cam," she said.

"Why am I talking to you?" Margaret said.

Cam's gaze held hers. "Because you have to talk to someone, and I'm good at talking."

Beads rattled in her hair when she spoke; rings covered every finger: silver, brass, and gold. She pulled back her hair, all those beads rattling again.

"Aerokin are possessed of a singular fury," Cam said. "Sometimes I and *Meredith* fight, sometimes they don't know their own strength. We were both so much younger, scarcely more than children. She never struck me again."

"You don't need to defend your Aerokin," Margaret said lightly.

Cam shook her head. "That is why I live. A pilot would die for her craft."

Margaret reached out and touched her hand. "And I believe you," she said. She wondered what it might be like to be joined with a craft that loved but didn't like you, how that relationship might rage and rush.

"So what are you here for?" Cam asked.

"I really don't know," Margaret said.

"I've been off north, patrolling the edges of the ice plains."

Margaret's eyes flicked towards her. "Near Tearwin Meet?"

"Close enough," Cam said. "Seen the high tower and that damn wall several times through the glass. You come down over those northern mountains, and think you're done for bloody spectacle and then... there, the three mountains and the great wall that links them, rising like a black fist into the sky, and beyond the wall, the sea. It's threatening, don't like things that I can't just glide over."

"And the way was clear?"

"Always is. I could get in trouble for telling you." Cam grabbed her arm, pulled Margaret in close. She lowered her voice. "You a spy or something?"

Margaret yanked her arm free. "No, of course not."

She grinned. "Glad to know, though I'm sure you wouldn't out and admit to it. I like the look of you. Let's get ourselves a drink and then we can chat."

Margaret had to admit that she liked the look of Cam too.

Mother Graine entered the hall, and the whole place quietened. Those nearest dipped their heads in a quick bow.

Margaret watched Mother Graine; a guard came over to her, whispered in her ear. Margaret couldn't hear what was said, but Mother Graine shook her head furiously. The guard stepped back, and she gestured for the door.

Not long after, Mother Graine walked to David, said something to him, and they left the room.

"Mystery piled on mystery," Kara Jade said to Margaret, and not without a touch of jealousy in her voice.

Margaret looked at her oddly.

Kara took another slug of her rum. "Keep your wits about you, Miss Penn," she said.

"I'll try not to follow your lead."

Kara raised a finger in the air. "Do as I say – not as I do." She bent forward and whispered in Margaret's ear. "I'd watch that Cam, she's a wild one."

The rest of the evening passed in a blur of drink and talk. And she stumbled to Cam's room. Talking, laughing, swinging from humour to mad seriousness in what felt like heartbeats. Then she was spilling her guts, and then spewing them. And Cam was patting her back, and then she woke in Cam's bed.

Cam smiled at her, eyes bright with affection and concern. "It's all right. You're safe here, unless you want to be dangerous."

And Margaret did. She really did. Not once did she think about the Roil or Tearwin Meet, or David for that matter.

It was Kara Jade that found her. Kara smirked. "You ignored my warnings, I see."

Margaret felt her cheeks redden. "I... where's David?"

"I was hoping you would know," Kara said. "All I know is that they stopped having me followed. Big men, I believe that you had a run-in with them."

Margaret realised that that the night had never been about her. Something so obvious that she had missed it. They'd taken David.

She swung a punch at Cam. The pilot blocked it.

"What are you doing?"

"Where did you take him?" Margaret asked.

"Whoa, I had nothing to do with that. Nothing! I was merely asked to keep you company. And fine company I found it. That is all."

"We've all been damned and deceived," Kara said, "Distracted. I didn't expect to see my sister at the reception–"

"Is he safe?" Margaret said.

Kara shook her head. "When is David ever safe? That boy attracts danger like lint."

"We'll find him," Cam said. "I don't like being used. The Mothers of the Sky have never acted this way before."

Kara nodded. "Yes, something is very wrong."

Cam threw Margaret's long coat towards her. She caught it easily. "But the world isn't as it was," Cam said. "And I guess we were foolish to think it otherwise. You find David." She looked over at Kara. "I'll get the *Dawn* ready for the journey north, if you'll let me."

"Was going to ask you myself," Kara said.

"Be careful," Margaret said, and Cam laughed.

"There's nothing careful about any of this." She kissed Margaret hard. "I'm a pilot, ain't nothing careful in my life. You fly or fall, that's all there is."

CHAPTER 27

An Old Man once came upon a boy in the street. He patted the boy's head and walked on. When questioned why he didn't hurt him, the Old Man replied:

"He wasn't dead enough."

The man who asked the question apparently was.

Old Men, KINGSLEY APPLETON

THE CITY OF HARDACRE
958 MILES NORTH OF THE ROIL

The trail had led them here, to the city. They stood in the spot where Cadell had died his second death, and mourned the passing of a brother. David was gone, high and fast.

But there were other things to hunt, enemies as ancient as they were. They uncovered nests of Roilings and froze them away. In a single day they found them all, and at the last, facing a host of the dead things, they lost all sense of the boy.

It was as though he had been snatched away from the world.

The Old Men turned to each other, paused in their fighting.

David was no longer there. His presence and the bits and pieces of Cadell were gone.

They neither smiled nor frowned. There was no triumph.

"He is gone," the oldest of them said, then tore off the head of the nearest Roiling. Witmoths spilled from the wound like ants from a nest, but at a gesture, the air temperature fell, cracking nearby stone, and the moths dropped dead to the ground.

Another Roiling stabbed out at him, and the Old Man caught its wrist, ice sheathed the creature's flesh and it screamed once, briefly, and was dead.

"Is that the last of them?" the oldest asked.

"Yes," came the response six times.

Perhaps this was it. Perhaps their task was done, and they could get on with their dying. There'd be a quiet dignity in it. After all, they had cleared the city of Hardacre of Roilings.

"Then we must feed, and–" He felt David again. They all did: the weight of his thoughts and their rage returned.

The captain of the *Langan Twist* waited for Mr Brown of Mr Brown's estates. He clutched the invoice in his hands; he wasn't going until he had all the money that was owed him. Times were desperate, and his business had grown even more cut-throat in the past few weeks. Mirrlees was gone, Hardacre and a few coastal towns the only major outposts – and Drift, of course, but they had no need of his lumpy old dirigible. They had their Aerokin and ways of dealing with the land.

He lived from commission to commission. And even that was getting thinner, this was the first time he had done the Creal and Hardacre run without proper security. His five passengers were stowed away and onboard, but he still needed this payment. He looked down at the invoice, it would see him clear for another month. After that, well, the world might have ended then – and with it his bills. Every cloud, he thought. Every bloody cloud.

If only most of his creditors had been based in Mirrlees rather than Hardacre, he would be free and clear of debt (as some of his competitors had become); but he was a good Northern Airship man, dealt only with northerners, and *they* still expected payment. Month in, month out.

Didn't they see what was happening?

Still, the captain clung to his own ways, which was why he had rejected Buchan and Whig's offer. That and he wasn't given to madness. The way north was dangerous and fickle, and he knew he could never, not even in his most arrogant moments, know the sky well enough to risk those winds.

Now, where was that–

The invoice dropped from his fingers, he reached for it absently, only he didn't stop reaching – and the paper seemed to slide further and further away. How frustrating! By the time his head smacked against the floor, he was already dead.

The Old Man picked him up gently, the body still twitching. He'd only just eaten, and while it never hurt to have a little more, he knew there would be no chance to eat in the sky. They'd come upon the airship fields by accident, but the Old Man was willing to accept serendipity. Before in the city, and for what came after, all that killing and running, they'd not been clear enough of head to consider it, but now, fat on refugees and city folk, clarity was coming back.

The last of the Old Men arrived. He carried a great bag over one shoulder.

"You found the mechanism?" their leader asked.

The other nodded, and wiped at a bloody mouth. "Its owner was more than happy to give it up."

"Then we are ready. We have stripped this town of its Roilings, its Vergers and scum. We have fed and fed deeply. Now we must fly. David is in the air, and we must join him. The time for walking is done," the Old Man said. He nodded to the others, one of them dragging Mr Brown of Mr Brown's estates with him.

The *Langan Twist* rose into the air, and not long after, the screaming began in earnest.

Not everyone could wait.

CHAPTER 28

The Old Men thought they knew everything, the Mothers of the Sky knew more. It's hard not to, when the world is stretched beneath you like a map. Which makes their mistakes all the grander.

Last Days & Last Drinks, MIDDEN JONES

THE CITY OF DRIFT
1411 MILES NORTH OF THE ROIL

"I'm really sorry about this, David," she said with a voice that lacked the slightest whit of contrition.

David struggled to open his eyes, the lids gummed with blood. They came apart slowly. He blinked a scratchy sort of blink. His wrists were bound in iron, his shoulders burned. He tried to touch the ground, and could just manage it, though not enough to support his weight. "What are you doing?"

"You know what I'm doing," Mother Graine said.

David closed his eyes, focussed on the iron shackling his wrists, and the chains that lifted them above his head, and made them cold. Very cold. A bitter sharp sort of chill that built within him and spread out. His breath thickened, the air itself slowed around him. The iron shuddered and rattled. It warped. Slowly, he lifted himself up, and yanked. The iron burst, and he hit the ground hard, breath knocked out of him, almost thinking he might shatter himself, but he didn't. He tore his hands free, took a step forward, and–

He woke in virtually the same position as before, only this time, his toes brushed a puddle of something, melted ice, blood, piss or all three of them. This is not good, he thought.

"You didn't think I was waiting for that, David?" Mother Graine's breath plumed. "Breaking free of that iron wasn't going to leave you in a position of strength, you're too far from the earth and the Lodes."

He pulled on the manacles, just once, or tried to, instead he only managed to swing forward, his shoulders numb, but not quite enough that he didn't know he'd pulled something, maybe broken something else. "Yes, I should have known better."

His stomach rumbled, he was hungry: horribly, horribly hungry.

"That goes for most of the actions of Old Men and boys," Mother Graine said.

"We all make mistakes." He tilted his head to get a better look at the chains. "This is one of them."

"Don't be like that." She stood next to him, touched his face. David suddenly remembered the night before, their lovemaking. His face burned, the first moment of heat in all that cold. Cadell had gotten him into this, where was the Old Man now? He seemed remarkably silent in his veins.

Mother Graine smiled, a grin more chilling than anything his skills could produce. "Now, David, I want you to know that this isn't personal."

"I've always considered death to be extremely personal."

He bit out at her hand, but she had already pulled it away, waggling a finger at him as she did so.

Mother Graine clicked her tongue. "Not for us, never for us."

"What will happen to Margaret?"

Mother Graine blinked. "You really care?"

"Of course I do."

"She will not be harmed. Unless she causes us trouble."

"When doesn't she cause trouble?"

"That personality type is encouraged here, David. Your idea of trouble and ours is different."

Mother Graine fell forward, with a grunt. Margaret lowered her leg. "Not really," Margaret said.

"You took your time," David said.

Margaret nodded at him. Hands held him up.

"Did you just piss yourself?" Kara Jade asked.

He said, "Please get me down."

"I'm doing my best," Kara said, jangling keys. "You didn't see which key they used to lock you up?"

"I was unconscious at the time, I'm afraid."

Something clicked, Kara cried out triumphantly, and David almost fell into the puddle at his feet. "Gotcha," Kara said, pulling him away.

Mother Graine had gotten to her feet. Her face had lost all its humour, but she did not look at all like a person who had been kicked to the ground. You, David thought, are a very dangerous woman, indeed.

Part of him knew just how dangerous, and even now found it thrilling.

"There's no escape for any of you," she said. "Not a breath of it, I'll have you all hanging from iron."

"Escape suggests that we're going somewhere safe," Kara said.

"Believe me, we're not," David said.

"I know what you plan."

"And surely you can't be against it?"

Mother Graine ignored Margaret. She looked at Kara. "It's not too late for you," she said. "You can still turn from this path."

"The same goes for you," Kara said, though her voice shook.

"You have no reason to fear me, daughter. I–"

Margaret struck her hard. Mother Graine stumbled. "I think it's better if you don't talk," Margaret said, and turned to Kara. "Are you ready?"

Kara nodded, looked at David, still so unsteady on his feet. He said, "Just get me out of here."

Mother Graine's eyes burned. "We will hunt you."

"Then you better line up," David said. "The problem, as I see it, is that everyone has different ideas how we should approach the threat of the Roil, or even who should approach it.

"Well, there is only one of me, and I'm not willing to sacrifice myself so that someone else can go and do what needs to be done."

"We need only cut off your finger," Mother Graine said.

David laughed. "Do not take me for naive. That would not be enough. Not nearly enough. This ring will not work on anyone else unless I am dead; dead, and having infected someone. Just who did you have in mind?"

Mother Graine's eyes flicked towards Kara.

"You would have done that to me?" Kara demanded.

She'd have been a good choice, actually, David thought.

"We would have done whatever was necessary. This is the time of doing what must be done, and without hesitation. Do you think you would do this any differently?" Mother Graine said.

"Bloody oath I would."

Mother Graine raised an eyebrow; Kara scowled and turned away.

"What must be done, will be done. You should have trusted me."

"Trust is too rare a commodity these days."

"And yet without it, we will all fail."

"Well, you can trust me to punch you in the face if you don't shut up," Margaret said, stepping between David and Mother Graine.

David sighed. "Kara Jade can accompany me to Tearwin Meet. She and Margaret can see that I get this done."

Mother Graine said, "But you are an addict–"

"Yes, this ring, and Cadell's bite, has made me more than that, but whoever you had forced into taking up this bloody thing would have faced the same problem."

"I still do not trust you."

He looked over at Kara. "Do you trust her?" he asked Mother Graine.

"Yes, but–"

"Then it will have to do. She will be with me all the way, they both will. And at the end we will fail or succeed because of the strength we hold together. We have survived the fall of Chapman, the enmity of all that is powerful in this world. And yet we are still here. Even now, you sought to hold us, and yet we leave here on your fastest ship."

"But before that," Kara said, sliding a pistol from her belt. "Before we do a damn thing, you will show us the Mothers, whole and unharmed, or I will shoot you myself."

Mother Graine led them down long cold hallways, lit by lights that sputtered and smoked, past shut doors behind which echoed the throbs of what David suspected must be engines. Once she demanded that they stop, her head tilted towards the ceiling, and above them boomed out what could only be titanic footfalls; the ground shook, the walls around them seemed to flex and contract. David covered his face with his hands, and whatever it was passed above and beyond them. Two hallways and three flights of stairs later, she hissed for silence and a bright light, buzzing softly, passed by. Mother Graine explained neither, only made sure they continued to descend. Several other times she stopped as though she was lost, but the pauses were brief.

Finally, at the end of a short hallway they reached a heavy iron door. Mother Graine nodded. *In there*. David reached out, touched it and–

He blinked, on his backside. Margaret and Kara were shouting at Mother Graine, all he could hear was the heavy thudding of his heart.

"I'm all right," he said.

Every eye turned to him. He shook his head. "I'm all right."

"I should have warned you," Mother Graine said. "The door's charged."

"Yes, you should." David tried to stand, fell back. "How much of a charge?"

"Enough to kill most people."

"Wouldn't that have been convenient?"

"Honestly, yes." She smiled. "Quite frankly, I still can't believe that you touched it and survived." She gestured at the panel beside it. "It will only open to my touch, I am afraid."

"Do what you have to," Kara said.

The door opened to a room chilled to almost freezing. The room felt at once vast and small, it extended beyond sight in all directions from the wall, and there was something wrong about all that space. David could feel forces at work that warped reality.

Within a dozen yards of them was a cage made of cast iron. Inside, barely moving, seven women stood, their clothes torn and bloody. Despite the cold, David could sense it. Just as he had sensed it in Hardacre, only here it was stronger, almost choking in its potency.

A taste at once familiar and wrong. Here? he thought.

Kara let out a cry. "What have you done, old woman?" She spat, "What have you done?"

She moved towards the cage. David's hand swung out, and he caught her by the wrist. Kara tried to yank her hand free, and he could feel the strength of her: the rough consequence of years of working the ropes, suspended above the air, of climbing and scrubbing, of being everything that a pilot must be; but now, right now – earned or not – he was stronger.

David said, "Stop, look at their mouths."

Darkness gathered and fluttered there, moving slowly, circling the heat of their breaths.

"Witmoths," Mother Graine said. "Kara, I did nothing. The moths arrived with some of the Aerokin from Hardacre. It's a tougher breed, capable of resisting the cold, but not this cold. I had to bring them here, lost two more sisters to it on that screaming mad descent into stone. Men and women died to bring them to these depths. Cadell, we never had the resistance to them that you do. Our blood burns hot like Cuttlefolk, not cold." She touched David's wrist. "I am the only one left."

"And you cage them," David said. "How dare you cage them? Death is the only honour left to them."

Mother Graine straightened, her eyes hardened, and her lips thinned. "You know nothing of cages," Mother Graine said. "Not yet, and when you do, you will rethink the horror of this."

"I know enough to–"

One of the mothers opened its eyes and stared at Margaret. "There you are," it breathed. "There you are." It spun its head towards David, joints cracking in its neck, and hissed. "Saaaa! And there you are, too. We're coming for you."

"Of course you are," David said.

The Roiling blinked. Witmoths crawled from its eyes, fluttered towards David. He lifted a hand, killed them with a touch, though it had him sweating, a briny cold prickle of sweat. The room weakened him, separated him from the great Engine in the north. Every second that passed accentuated that.

"I'm not meant to be here." He turned to Mother Graine and the others. "We have to go, now."

They fled that great hall then. The door shutting behind them, and with it closed, David felt his strength return.

"So now you know," Mother Graine said quietly.

Kara grabbed Mother Graine by her collar and yanked her close. "You kept this hidden. You've left them like that."

"What else was I supposed to do, child?"

"I'm no more your child than any of us. You did not trust your people to this, how can we trust you?"

Mother Graine sighed. "And tell my people what? That they are doomed? That there is no hope? There's honesty and then there is madness."

Kara's face did not soften. She looked like she was going to be sick. She pushed the Mother of the Sky away. "Get us to the *Dawn*. We have to leave this madhouse. I can't take another moment of it."

"Those who have helped you will be punished."

"You threaten me? Even now you threaten me? None of us do this lightly," Kara said. "We know what we stand to lose."

"Kara, my Kara, I don't believe you know what you are giving up. These two, they've lost everything already, but you–"

"Shut your mouth," Kara snapped. "Shut your mouth now. I've lost it all, my city is rotten at its heart. Now take me to my *Dawn*."

"When she dies, you will curse your friends' names for making it happen. You will go mad, worse than anything that the Witmoths could produce, a madness of grief and blood – that's all these two can–" Mother Graine gasped. Margaret removed her elbow from her stomach.

"That's enough now," Kara said, quietly. "Take me to my *Dawn*."

Mother Graine nodded, her eyes hard. "This way," she said, opening another door.

They followed her through.

The door shut behind them. Darkness. There was a soft sound, like wind given bones and whispering papery flesh. Kara's torch clicked on.

The beam of the flashlight cut through the dark, revealing cockroaches in their thousands. David flinched.

"Why do secret passages always seem to be crowded with cockroaches?" David asked. "I don't even know how they managed to get here."

"That's what these things are?" Margaret said, boots crunching down on those creatures not quite quick enough to get out of the way. "I was wondering, but wasn't quite sure. It had always been too cold for cockroaches in Tate. The cockroach and the flea died out when the Roil came."

"They're a lot of fun, until one flies in your face," David said.

"They fly?" Margaret asked.

"Toughen up, you two. We go forward, we get to the *Dawn* and we get out of here."

David could feel them moving all around. Even as he watched, one flew into Kara's hair. She clawed the insect free and flung it to the ground.

Mother Graine sighed. "Not far to go," she said.

David couldn't disagree more.

CHAPTER 29

The last riots were the worst. They swept across the tent city like great waves, driven by tides of discontent, and then washed into Hardacre as though the walls didn't even exist.

Journeys to the Underground, MISTLE & MISTLE

THE CITY OF HARDACRE
955 MILES NORTH OF THE ROIL

Without David and Margaret, the *Habitual Fool* felt empty, for all that it was full of newcomers. Those two had dominated the place, without ever realising it, perhaps wanting to do precisely the opposite. Three days since they had chosen to, escape… no, not escape, it wasn't as if they'd been held prisoner. Whatever it was, they'd already caused ripples. Buchan and Whig had heard from spies of their flight from Drift.

But by then they'd had their own problems: the Old Men had come in the night, tearing through the *Habitual Fool* like death. Buchan and Whig had lost three of their crew to them, but had managed to survive the night, though not without wounds. Each had had to bear long hours receiving stitches and being reassured by a local doctor and historian that the Old Men's bites and scratches did not carry a contagion, and that they were not likely to awaken hungry for blood.

The Old Men had stolen the last of their maps of the far north – those not stolen by David – and a jacket that had belonged to David and been left behind, as it had grown too small.

To Buchan, the loss of the maps had been a devastating blow. They marked the coordinates of death zones; without them, navigating the north was likely to lead to conflagration.

"What do we do here?" Buchan said. "We've spent fortunes preparing for this journey. We've lost everything, and now, even this is taken from us."

Whig sighed. "Maybe it's for the better. I've never liked the cold."

"Standing next to David must have been very unpleasant for you."

"Standing next to what he has become, yes. But you must admit that there's steel in him, and Margaret, too. They may have left us, but it doesn't mean we can't help."

Buchan leaned forward. "What do you suggest?"

"The Old Men still hunt David. We ignored his warning, and managed to survive; perhaps it's time something hunted them, and in the hunting, of course we might just find David, too. After all, it's David they want."

"And just how do you suggest that we do that?"

Whig grinned and patted the blades at his belt. "The old-fashioned way, of course."

Buchan laughed. "Old-fashioned ways for old-fashioned men. I like the way you think, man."

"The Old Men haven't hidden their tracks. After all, they

know no one would be stupid enough to hunt them."

"Until now. Do you think we can kill them?"

"Probably not, but chances are we'll all be dead by spring anyway." Whig unrolled a map of the north. "Buchan, get our crew ready. We've miles to go and blood to spill."

This was taking forever. The Warden of the Air was going through every piece of paperwork more carefully than Buchan thought they really deserved; Buchan would have felt panicked, except he knew that every single bit of that documentation was absolutely legitimate.

Buchan said, "We really are in a hurry."

"You know, you're the first ship we're letting up after the incident,"

answered the Warden

"Yes, I heard of the murders," Whig said, squeezing Buchan's shoulder tightly, whispering at him to calm down.

"Wouldn't have known it was happening, if those bodies hadn't fallen in the main square. By then the *Langan* was on a full head of steam. Those that followed her did not return."

"We're aware of all this," Whig said.

"More than aware, it's coloured our decision to leave the city," Buchan said; a half-truth, which was better than nothing. "We've had enough of the violence of this city. Too much death."

"I do not doubt that, Mr Buchan and Mr Whig," the Warden of the Air said, sounding very much like he did doubt that. Buchan knew he was outclassed; the man was unflappable, years of dealing with Drifters would do that. "Seems there were some folk desperate for the sky. My job's to challenge such desperation." He tapped his clipboard. "Though all this looks all right."

"That's because it is. We've nothing to hide," Buchan snapped. Nothing to hide except their destination.

"Enough of that!" Whig said, squeezing Buchan's arm gently. "Enough of that, or we'll never get to sky."

Buchan relaxed. "My dear Warden. We are just good men, wishing to engage in honest business. Do any of us look like monsters?" He gestured to Whig and then to Watson Rhig, captain of the *Collard Green*. Rhig was nearly as tall as Whig. They knew each other, as it turned out, sharing a distant relative – one who had died in the First Cuttle War, an admiral of the first airship corp. Without that connection Buchan doubted that Rhig would have agreed to have joined in their flight north.

Rhig finally spoke. "I can vouch for these men," he said. "As a captain of some high standing, I can say that I would not be in their employ if their actions were not legitimate."

The Warden nodded. "If you can vouch for these men, then so be it. Your flight is approved. May the skies be safe for you."

The *Collard Green* found its way into the sky, rising over the city.

"To the Underground?" Rhig asked.

Buchan shook his head, smiling as one of his men passed him a plate filled with food. Hearty, warm and very filling. The *Collard Green*'s kitchens were well in order.

"No, my good man. We head north, where the *Langan Twist* was last seen travelling. We've a friend who is in trouble, who may have deserted us, but who we in turn refuse to desert. So, finally," Buchan said. "Finally. Good captain, follow that airship if you please. We'll chase it to the ends of the earth!"

"And what do we do if we catch it?"

"Kill or be killed, I would suggest!" Buchan reached for a leg of cold chicken, and grinned. "Ah, Whig. I know what it is to be alive again!"

CHAPTER 30

Can it be counted as rebellion when there is nothing to rebel against beyond a memory?

Horrors, RAVEN SKYE

THE CITY OF DRIFT
1399 MILES NORTH OF THE ROIL

It was never going to be as easy as they hoped, but even Margaret was surprised when thirty men and women at least, all armed, walked from behind the *Dawn*.

At their lead was the man Margaret had thumped yesterday evening; to their rear stood Cam, her arms tied. There was a bruise across her jaw, her shirt bloody, though Margaret couldn't tell if it was her own blood. Her eyes caught Margaret's, her lips curved just a little. She may have even winked. Margaret reached for her rime blade, and Cam shook her head.

"So you're part of this, too, William?" Kara said.

The man at the lead glowered, though he kept it courteous. It was easy with that many guns behind. "If you could lower your weapons," William said.

"I'm sorry," Mother Graine said, sounding anything but as she shook herself free of Kara's grip. The pilot let her go, as though there was no point in holding her. Margaret couldn't help but feel angry at that. If it were her, she'd be pressing the Verger's knife hard against the Mother's throat. Mother Graine said, "Things were never going to be that easy for you. This is my city."

"You don't think that David won't kill them all," Margaret said.

"If David was so minded, yes, he might. But not before they killed the rest of you."

"And what if I kill you now?" She reached for the knife at her belt.

Mother Graine shrugged. "I'm not important anymore. And everything that must be done can be done without me. One person is ultimately insignificant." Her gaze was firmly on David. Margaret desperately wanted to show her just how significant she was, but Mother Graine was scarcely paying attention to her.

David cleared his throat. "I'd rather not die now. But if it comes to that, well, then I'll die on my own terms."

Mother Graine laughed. "Oh, David. Nothing is ever done on your terms. You will be carried from one disaster to the next. You will see your friends die, and even your success will be failure. Believe me, my little bird, I'm sparing you so much." She turned to Kara. "Kara, my dear, I know you understand. Please get me Margaret's weapons."

Margaret tensed, but Kara folded her arms. "Run for the *Dawn*," she said, and whistled once, short and sharp.

Mother Graine frowned. "You–"

And the *Dawn* was an explosion of limbs. In a single whip-crack, every soldier was knocked from their feet, and Cam with them. The pilot scrambled to get upright, only to be knocked down again, men grabbing her arms, dragging her towards the door, beyond the *Dawn*'s considerable reach.

Kara was already running. She swung her head round, eyes blazing. "I said, run!"

And run they did.

"David!" Mother Graine screamed. "You know that this is wrong."

If David heard her he didn't register it, just kept running. Kara had stopped at the doorifice to the *Dawn*. It opened for David, and he dived neatly through.

William was already scrambling to his feet. Margaret knocked him back down as she passed, snatching his weapon.

Another guard ran at her, and Margaret struck her hard in the head. David peered through the doorifice at her, his face confused.

"What are you doing?" Kara demanded.

"Cam," Margaret said. "We need to get Cam."

But Cam was already being dragged from the hangar, away from the *Dawn*. A limb hurtled overhead, knocked another pilot down.

Kara looked at Margaret, and something resolute and severe passed across her face, an edge of hardness. "No, we don't have time. We can't, we leave now. We'll not have another chance."

Margaret pushed her away.

"Look," Kara said. "David needs you. Cam won't be hurt. Believe me. But if we don't leave now, hell, we're probably going to be thrown into gaol with her anyway. Besides, Cam's never going to leave without her Aerokin. Trust me, between you and her, she'll choose the *Meredith Reneged* every time."

Margaret hesitated a moment more, before running back towards the *Dawn*.

"We need to hurry," Margaret said, and Kara smiled.

The *Dawn*'s limbs struck out and out. Engines fired, even as they passed through the doorifice.

"They got Cam," Margaret said to him.

David nodded. "She'll be all right. What use is it for Mother Graine to hurt her?"

"Mother Graine was ready to kill you," Margaret said.

"She'll be all right. You can't do anything about it now. None of us can. I'm sorry, but that's just the way it is," David said, though he looked about as happy as she felt.

The *Roslyn Dawn* rose gracefully from the hangar, and not a shot was fired, until she was almost free and in the open air. The shot went wide. The *Dawn* fired a burst of shot in response, and every soldier within the hangar dropped to the floor.

Cam was already gone.

"They won't hurt her," Kara Jade said. "Believe me. We don't harm our own much."

The *Dawn* hit the air, bio-engines roaring, the northern wind a sudden beating presence. Margaret could feel the Aerokin working against it.

"There's no one to catch us," Kara Jade said. "You've the fastest Aerokin and the finest pilot on your side. They'd sooner catch the wind than me."

Margaret looked around the familiar space of the Aerokin's gondola. Leaning by the doorifice was her endothermic weaponry. Cam had gotten that much done before they'd caught her. Margaret picked up the bag, scanned its contents, the familiar weapons: swords and rifles that had saved her life so many times.

She found no comfort in them now, just carried them to her bunk at the rear of the Aerokin. She walked back to the doorifice. It opened at her approach, and the slightly cloying, slightly musty smell of the Aerokin faded.

Drift was already a way behind them. No Aerokin had followed, instead they had gathered in the airspace over the Caress.

"They know it's pointless following me," Kara said from behind her.

"This was too easy," Margaret said. "All of it was too easy."

"What are you saying?" Kara rested a hand on her back. This close to the open doorifice, a single push from Kara would be enough to send her falling.

Margaret turned. "Are you part of this, too?"

Kara's face stiffened. "I don't know what you mean."

"Was all this just some elaborate scheme, a test to see how determined David was to succeed?"

"You're seeing wheels within wheels," Kara said. "And none of them make sense."

Margaret flashed her teeth. "So you weren't in on it, then. You're as much a dupe as David. Question is, did you pass or fail the test Mother Graine had set for you?"

Kara frowned. "Look, we made it to the *Dawn*, and she's the fastest Aerokin to ever live. No one, not even my sister, could catch us here. I see what you're suggesting, but as a test, it's far too complicated."

"I don't think so; they needed to see that David – that we were *all* capable of doing this. I've no doubt that if we had failed we'd all be dead by now."

"Think that way, if you must. And I won't argue. In fact, I'd prefer it to be that way."

"Manipulated?" Kara asked.

"We're all of us manipulated, but if what you think is true then it means there's a chance for I and the *Dawn*. We might still be able to return."

"I think you're right," David said from behind them. "I think Mother Graine only showed us that room so I would know that she could have kept me in a place you would never have found me. That room, it did things to me. Weakened me, and the longer I'd have stayed there the worse it would have gotten. There's no way I could have escaped from it. But here we are in the sky again."

"They won't follow us," Margaret said. "We've jumped through her hoops, and ran her maze."

Kara shook her head. "She is the last survivor of her kind. The Mothers of the Sky have always ruled us. Now there is only one. Something beyond terrible has happened, and we are fleeing it."

"We'll make it better," David said.

Kara laughed. "Do you really believe that? I mean, look at you both, Mr and Mrs Grim. Him with his cold hands. And you with those cold eyes. I could drown in the doubt and sadness in this cockpit."

"And you're doing a wonderful job of lightening our hearts," Margaret said.

"I'm not here to lighten your bloody hearts. I'm here to get you north, like I promised I would. And I damn well will."

"And that's all you need to focus on," Margaret said.

David glared at her, then shook his head.

Kara laughed. "It's going to be such a fun trip."

She jabbed a finger at David. "You, cold boy. Get me my rum. We've hours of flying to do, and I'm itching to get drunk."

• • • •

"Is it ready?" the eldest asked, peering at the peculiar contraption.

The second Old Man nodded.

"Will it work?"

"It will work," the Old Man said. "It need only make one journey."

He lifted the machine in his hands, bound it to his body, and let them lead him to the great doors of the airship. Two of his brothers pulled the doors open, and he turned to the eldest one last time. "I will be swift."

"And we will follow," the eldest Old Man said, gesturing for him to go.

The Old Man stepped into the sky. The mechanism bound to him shuddered. It roared. And he did not fall.

CHAPTER 31

The truth about the Deep North was this. There was always
something waiting to stop you. Tearwin Meet might be reached,
but always at a cost. No one had survived beyond its high walls,
and few lived to reach them and return. All we had were a few
rough pictures, including, remarkably, one of the earliest exam-
ples of Immediacism – the artist didn't have long to dwell upon
those high walls. Even the decision to travel north was a danger-
ous one.

> The Trouble with the North, JESSE VANDENBOSCH

THE FREE AEROKIN *ROSLYN DAWN*
1500 MILES NORTH OF THE ROIL

By the end of the first day, even David could tell the *Dawn*
was struggling. Kara stood cursing at the control panel,
mumbling beneath her breath between louder exclama-
tions. She'd gotten drunk and sobered to a terrible
hangover, so bad that she'd downed handfuls of the healing
salve at the heart of the Aerokin – and even some coffee,
which she went to great pains to explain was more valuable
than anything else on the *Dawn*, which was why she

couldn't possibly share any – but apparently her headache was of world-ending proportions.

"What's happening?" David asked.

"Those headwinds," Kara said. "Headaches, headwinds, we're damned and doomed." She swallowed more of the *Dawn*'s gel, washing it down with coffee. She winced. "I'd heard that the winds had picked up, but these are incredible. We're going to have to approach Tearwin Meet, low and slow, and when the winds are at their weakest."

David frowned.

"What does that mean?" Margaret asked.

"Exactly what I said. Higher up the winds are blowing south, we're going to need to follow the earth closer than I would like. The winds down there near the mud aren't much better, but they are better. Up here we'd be faster walking."

"I am being hunted, you know?" David said.

"Yes," Kara said. "Have the Old Men grown wings?"

David smiled. "Of course not."

"The other thing, as much as I hate it, we are going to need to stop for the evening."

"What?"

"The *Dawn*'s filters will need cleaning. A dead Aerokin won't get you to Tearwin Meet, and the winds are blowing fiercer with the evening, but they're dropping out a few hours before dawn. We will reach Tearwin Meet in three days. Surely that's fast enough."

"A day ago I thought I was going to die," David said. "Three days is better than I could hope for."

"Yes, three days to death rather than yesterday," Kara said. "You must be very pleased."

As promised, Kara brought the *Dawn* down just before sunset, the Aerokin fixing herself to the earth with her landing spurs. A ridge rose up before them, offering cover from the wind, but still it roared down from the north. There was a creek nearby, and Kara carried the *Roslyn Dawn*'s filters – black with Roil spores – there.

The wind picked up even more, howling through the trees that lined the ridge. Old growth cracked, dust and wood was sent racing along the plains.

"I don't like this," Margaret said.

"It's a defence mechanism," David said. "The city in the north is cloaking itself in cold."

"And what good will that do against iron ships?"

"There are other defences," David said. "I'm a bit hazy on them, but they exist."

Kara came back an hour later with the filters cleaned, and her fingers cracked. She let the strips dry out in front of the fire. "The damned wind is blasting the spores into my *Dawn*."

"Three days," David said. "And then we can end this."

"And what does that mean?"

"The Roil destroyed. The world turned cold and white," Margaret said.

"Sounds bloody awful," Kara said.

"It won't last. The Mechanical Winter's brief, the spring that follows is long," David said. "At least that's how it's meant to be."

"And if you're wrong?"

"Everything dies," Margaret said.

When the filters had dried, Kara went back into the *Dawn*. "You two," she shouted. "We will be leaving before first light."

"I'll take first watch," Margaret said.

David shook his head. "No, I don't want to sleep tonight. I can rest tomorrow, when we're in the air."

Margaret frowned at him.

"I need you to be ready," he said. "I need you to be awake." He didn't say for what, but she nodded her head, and clambered back into the *Dawn*.

Five minutes after he was sure she was asleep, he slid the Carnival into his veins. At once he felt Cadell sliding away. He smiled to himself and the fire.

He reached out to the flame and could hardly feel a thing. Cadell's Orbis reflected the light, seemed to gather it in. He could see tiny clusters of flame within its heart; perhaps it really did contain a universe. Despite feeling the Old Man's disapproval, he took a little more Carnival, and the ring's light dulled. Keeping the Old Man at bay for another few hours.

The Old Men were drawing closer, he couldn't work out how, but they were. Still they'd be in Tearwin Meet long before the Old Men could reach them. After all, they'd not grown wings! They were still far enough away that he need not worry, for all that he had suggested otherwise to Margaret.

A little deception, there was no harm in it, surely.

The *Dawn* was back in the sky in the near dark of early morning, great lights burning fore and aft, the world grey and old and cold around them. Bit by bit, moment by moment, the darkness succumbed to day, and David felt a deep affinity with that failing and flailing darkness. He felt himself running down, the Carnival he had taken last night was perhaps the last he could allow himself. He needed Cadell as they neared Tearwin Meet. David needed his knowledge, his memories, and he couldn't keep pushing Cadell away. He couldn't give himself the privilege of comfort any more. He did his best to forget the Carnival in his boot, and watched instead the thinning of night, and the land passing by below, a sad and desolate landscape.

The wind from the north built quickly as the sun made its way over the horizon. The flying contraption came up from beneath them. Not an iron ship, but something else, something fast and frail. Something that contained an Old Man.

The *Dawn*'s cannon fired and missed; the winged thing lifted, swinging up, then looping around and shooting straight towards them.

"It's going to hit us," Kara said, even as the *Dawn* dropped. "It's–"

The vehicle struck the *Dawn* hard, the Aerokin screamed and the whole gondola lurched to one side. Kara ran towards the doorifice, poked her head out.

"No, no, no! David, Margaret, I'm going to need your help. Rope up!" She sounded calmer than her body language suggested. "The whole flank's–"

A hand yanked her through the doorifice, flung her away. David caught the look of horror on her face, her hands flailing desperately for a grip, and then she was gone.

PART THREE
OLD MEN

Their words had forked no lightning, but there was always time,
and there was always rage. You could feel it wherever they passed.
Cold as frost, dark as night. Everywhere the Old Men walked the
world bled a little, died a little, too.

Old Men Walking, DAMIEN THOMAS

CHAPTER 32

The Old Men were obviously a construction, a fairy tale. When you are faced with a force as dire as the Roil, it is human nature to construct something just as deadly to face it. The Old Men were madness, because we needed a madness we could claim for our own

Myths of Mirrlees, SARAH TOPE-ESCHELL

THE *ROSLYN DAWN*
1500 MILES NORTH OF THE ROIL

The Old Man pushed his way into the Aerokin; the hard material of the doorifice resisted, muscles flexed along its edge. But the Old Man was stronger, and the doorifice gave way all at once, with a tearing sound. Grimy beads of ice skittered across the floor towards them, kicked there by hobnailed boots.

Margaret could feel the *Dawn*'s shock. The Old Man grinned, a grin far too wide for such a narrow face – as though it could barely contain his hunger – but he wasn't staring at Margaret. His eyes were focussed on David with the heated intensity of a lover.

A cleaver hung from the Old Man's belt: a crude weapon for one so elegant. And there was an elegance about him – from the morning coat he wore to the heavy black boots on his feet; his beard was trimmed neatly; his hands almost delicate, though strong and thick through the middle. Only that smile and that blade – a thing even a Verger wouldn't use – were so raw. And there was a weight to him, a mass that made the floor creak as though it were trying to get out of his way.

"Little brother! At last! At last!" the Old Man said, with such a note of glee in his voice, that in any other situation it would have been comedic, but here and now it pulled the heat from her as effectively as any powers the Old Men possessed. But she did not fumble. She lifted her rifle and shot the Old Man neatly in the chest. The endothermic bullet clattered to the floor. The Old Man turned and motioned towards her, a sort of *you'll be next* gesture, then shrugged, as though she was of such little account.

Her face reddened, though the Old Man didn't see it, he was already facing David again, striding across the deck as though he owned it. "You did not think we would leave you so unharried, even in the sky?"

"Where are the others?" David asked, and she could see he was struggling to keep the fear and despair from his voice.

Kara was gone. We've lost so much, Margaret thought, surely we should be used to it now.

She fired again, a direct shot to the neck. The Old Man gestured towards her with a free hand, not even bothering to look. She felt her breath chill, felt the cold drive her back. She hadn't been ready for that.

"Rupert, where are they?" David asked.

The Old Man stopped, his eyes widened, lost a little of their heat. "So you haven't forgotten?"

"How could I forget?"

"All too easily." Rupert jabbed a long finger at David. "Look at you! Dressed in a boy. Who could guess what you know, what you remember?"

"I remember enough."

"You remember nothing, or you wouldn't seek to do what you do."

"Where are the others?" David repeated, his voice low, calm, but not with the abstracted calmness of a Carnival addict: this was more measured, calculated.

Rupert gestured vaguely in the air. "Near, I will not have to wait long with your corpse. Do not worry, Cadell. We will mourn you. There will be such a funeral pyre, perhaps the last great burning before the world ends. For we are the last great men, are we not?"

David nodded, seemed to seriously consider it, but there was something condescending in the movement.

Rupert frowned.

"We could stop this now," David said. "You don't need to die."

"Death waits for every one of us," Rupert said, and there was such a fever in his voice that he was utterly terrifying. "You most of all, it waits and it grinds its teeth waiting, isn't it glorious?" The Old Man's dark fingers slid towards his belt, grasped the cleaver that hung there and yanked it free. The blade looked familiar – was perhaps even the one which David had used to butcher Cadell's corpse. Rupert swung it square at David's head.

But David had already moved another two or three paces backwards, swift as thought, stumbling further when the cleaver, hissing through the air, struck out at him again. Not used to the speed he possessed.

It wasn't a graceful movement, but it was effective.

Margaret fired again, hitting the Old Man in the face. He scarcely blinked. But this time, he turned, hefting the cleaver, as though it were no heavier than a butter knife. And she fired at his hand. The cleaver dropped away, and with it a couple of fingers.

He wasn't indestructible. Her lips pulled back from her teeth.

"You," the Old Man said. "I have no argument with you. Typical of a Penn."

David swung out at the Old Man with fists that looked to be sheathed in ruddy ice. Rupert let the first fist strike him, blinked again. He punched David in the throat. David scrambled backwards. His eyes widened, he tried to rise, and fell again.

The *Roslyn Dawn* lurched forward. Margaret found herself on the floor, the Old Man standing over her. "It does to be careful of one's footing in such an environment, Miss Penn."

It could have been Cadell talking! She struck out with a boot, made contact with a leg, and felt the Old Man's ankle give way.

She said, "It does indeed."

The Old Man grunted, bent, but he was already regaining his feet, face dark, eyes bright, almost twinkling.

"Take more than that," Rupert said.

"How about this?" Kara Jade struck his back with an iron pipe. Margaret fired another shot. This time a lead shell. Short range. The Old Man's right eye disappeared.

He shook his head, and blood sprayed: thick, cold and dark.

"I'm here, too," David said quietly, and smacked his hand down against the Old Man's neck; bone cracked, but the Old Man danced backwards, almost hitting Kara, though the pilot moved back too. They circled him. Margaret fired a pistol, struck the Old Man in the chest. And this time Rupert moaned.

David had picked up the cleaver. He took a step closer and Margaret unsheathed her rime blade. Didn't bother activating it, she wanted its cutting edge.

"The head, you say?" Margaret said.

"Always the head," David answered; he took a step forward, and the Old Man spat more blood.

"No matter," the Old Man said. "No matter. There are more of mine to come, but there are still hurts that I can offer. I'm a wounding thing, if not the death, your hurting must be my satisfaction."

"Enough of this," David said.

"Enough, indeed." The Old Man snatched out, grabbed Kara around the waist, and slammed his bulk against the window. It bulged, and he struck it again, bearing all his weight and Kara's against it; the material cracked, and gave way, and the Old Man and Kara fell.

Margaret rushed to the edge of the window, looked down. The Old Man and Kara hung suspended by the *Roslyn Dawn*'s flagella. Even as Margaret watched, Kara was wrenched from the Old Man's grip, but not before she gave him a good hard kick to the head.

The *Dawn* groaned, and the Old Man was torn in two; a burst of blood and bone, made almost graceful by the delicate motion of the *Dawn*'s limbs – as though there could be poetry in such brutality.

"The head or that," David said.

The *Dawn*'s limbs twitched and released the broken body, and Kara Jade clambered up them and into the ship.

"No one does that to me," she said, her lip split, one eye closed up and swollen. "Not here, not on the *Dawn*. No Old Man, nothing." Kara looked over at Margaret, her gaze intense. "You excepted, of course. From you it's a compliment. Still kill you just as dead, though."

She might have said something else, but the *Dawn* dropped a dozen feet at once. Margaret hit the roof before dropping to the floor. Kara bent down and helped her up. David had managed to keep on his feet, wrist bound in one of the straps that hung from the ceiling. He looked dazed.

"Get to a seat the both of you, and strap yourselves in," Kara said. "The *Dawn*'s hurt, we're going to have to land."

CHAPTER 33

*Why were they punished so? The Mothers of the Sky were given
their fastness in Drift, but the Old Men were buried, and drowned
in hunger. What creation could be so cruel to punish its creators so?*
  Questions on a Series of Ethical Imperatives, DEIGHTON

THE ROSLYN DAWN
1501 MILES NORTH OF THE ROIL

Wind howled through the broken window.

David let Margaret lead him to a seat. He could smell the
Old Man's blood on his face. He wiped at it absently.

"Strap yourself in, David," Kara said. Margaret had already moved to a nearby seat.

"Your eye," he said to Kara.

The pilot strode past him to the console. "That doesn't
matter now. This is going to be fast and rough. The winds
are building." Kara Jade coughed: a dark bruise was already swelling across her jaw. "The *Dawn*'s been injured.
We were lucky, could have punctured the flight bladders,
could have ignited them; and I think that may have been
what he was trying for, but this Aerokin's different, a new

swifter breed. He struck too low and burst only one of the gas chambers. Still, we need to get to ground."

Already the *Dawn* was listing to to the right.

David managed to get the belts around his waist. They clicked closed; he tightened them around his shoulders. A little wave of panic struck him. The *Dawn* dropped again, the belts tightened around his shoulders.

"We go down now, they're going to get us," David said. "You heard what he said, they're not far behind, and he wasn't lying. I can feel them."

"Would have helped if you had *felt* them a little sooner, don't you think? We don't have any choice," Kara snapped. "We don't land now, we'll fall. And if we fall, we will die for certain. The *Dawn* caught me, not just once, but twice today, and I won't let her suffer for it."

The *Dawn* shuddered and jerked in the sky. Sky and earth were getting closer, the ground looking less an abstract proposition; more a disaster looming.

"Is it too late, already?" David asked.

"She'll be all right," Kara said. "She can just sense the ground, that's all. We're just a bit bruised, she and I."

"How long will we need to stay down here?"

"A day or two at most. The gas chamber will heal quickly enough. We might need to jettison some material. The beds for one, but we'll see."

"They'll hit us in the next twelve hours," David said. "If we can't flee, I'm going to have to fight."

And all of a sudden, he felt a sense of purpose come over him. A focus that he'd never possessed, one that was more strategic, less desperate. He peered at the window, the one nearest him, not the broken one.

Down below, a thin ribbon of river gleamed, in the late afternoon light, rushing over a stony bed that worked its way between a series of low hills. It was a beaten landscape, hunched and ruined, and yet, in that light, it was beautiful. He could see possibilities, ways that the next forty-eight hours might play out.

"There," David said, sounding at once more confident, almost in charge. Kara and Margaret looked at him oddly. "Don't look at me," he said. "Look down. There, near the river, the Malcontent, if I remember correctly. Try and bring us down near the river and the hills."

David coughed, the focus passed, panic filled its absence. There was nothing he wanted more than a nice calming dose of Carnival, but he needed Cadell. He knew he would have done better against Rupert if he'd let in more of Cadell's mind.

"I'll get you there," Kara said.

And she did, in shuddering drops and starts, she and the *Dawn* made it down. The landing was hard, the *Dawn*'s fla-gella uncoiling yards away from the ground, and only marginally softening landfall. But they were down, and whole.

David unstrapped himself quickly, and almost sprinted to the doorifice. Not wanting them to see the fear on his face. The doorifice opened, and David looked out. Here on the ground the beauty of this place was gone, the sun passed behind clouds, the river darkened, the wind howled. It was just cold and wet. David couldn't see how he could leverage a victory here. It was death already.

"I've pistols in the rear cabinet," Kara said. "Enough for the both of us. Margaret won't need 'em."

David shook his head. "You can't stay, Kara. I want you to fly north of here. Find some cover and let the *Dawn* heal. She's too much of a risk here. If we scratch out a victory but lose her or you, we may as well have not fought at all."

"You saying that I'm not good in a scrap?" Standing there, one eye bloody, the other swollen shut; half her face a bruise, she looked as fierce a fighter as anyone could need.

David smiled. "You know I'm not." David shook his head. "The Old Men are hunting me. The *Dawn* is hurt because of me. We need you whole. Stay, and I think we'll all die. Please, trust me on this."

Kara walked to the gun cabinet, retrieved a pistol and handed it to him. "Don't know what good it will do."

David tucked the weapon in his belt. "I can always club someone with it."

He looked at Margaret.

"You can go with her, too," he said.

Margaret laughed.

"Bring your guns," David said. "Anything that fires shells."

She was already hefting her bag onto her shoulder.

Kara handed David a flare. "Use this when they come. If there's anything that I can do, I'll see it done."

David nodded, grabbed a blanket and Cadell's umbrella. "For cover and cutting," he said, yanking the blade free. He also snatched a dozen cans of food, and another couple for Margaret, stuffing them in a hessian bag. He rattled as he leapt from the doorifice.

He could see the scarring of the Aerokin, the place where the *Dawn* was bleeding. Kara followed him, winced, and smeared healing gel over the great black wound. "She'll be all right," Kara said. "She'll survive."

She ran back into the ship, and threw out two mattresses. "At least you will have something to sleep on."

The *Dawn* lowered her two cannon to the earth, leaving only the lighter guns on her carapace.

Margaret touched the coiled conch-shaped cannon

curiously, and David's hopes rose. Kara shook her head. "No good to you. Unless you're an Aerokin, can't be fired, all her weaponry's like that. And right now, even she can't use it."

David glanced cautiously behind him. "You better be on your way."

Kara nodded. "Good luck."

The *Dawn* lifted into the sky. Shorn of the weight of the guns and two passengers, her flight seemed a little easier. She passed to the west and north, and was soon lost to sight beyond the ridge. The sun was edging beneath the ridge as well. The shadows lengthened.

"And now we wait," David said. "They're hours away."

Margaret dropped her bag at his feet. "Night's coming, we need to gather wood, build a fire."

David looked at her, and she shrugged.

"They know we're here. Might as well be warm when I die."

CHAPTER 34

You can never be certain how things will end. There is very little that is logical in the functioning of the universe, and certainly not when it comes to the works of humanity, even when it has been stripped of its humanity. Surprises exist at every turn.

The Conclusion of Conclusion, MILAN ADAMS

THE NORTHERN WILDERNESS
1520 MILES NORTH OF THE ROIL

David shook Margaret awake, dragged her from dreams of Tate. "Five minutes," he said. "I thought it would be longer, but they've picked up pace. They want to get it over and done with, I guess."

It was close to midnight, the air so cold it felt like it could cut her lungs.

David had the fire out. The north wind howled down across the river. The air was bright with the twin moons, and expectant. She could see her breath plume before her. What weapon was best? Rime blade? Rifle? She'd substituted her endothermic shells for simple shot. You could blow a man's face away with a direct hit with one of these, she thought – if you were lucky.

David shook, his teeth chattering.

"I thought you could handle the cold."

"It's not the cold. It's the Carnival, well, the lack of it. It's the Carnival that holds him back," David said.

"So," Margaret said. "You keep him that way."

David shook his head. "No, I can't. We need him now. We need Cadell. This will cost me dearly. To bring him forward is to drive me back."

"I know which I would prefer," Margaret said, and squeezed his hand.

"It doesn't matter what you would, what you want or what I want. We need to do this. We have to, and if that means there is no me after this, then scary as that is, I accept it."

"Is that you or Cadell saying that?"

David smiled at her. "Still time for you to run."

To be so hunted, the both of us, Margaret thought. David stood there, his shoulders straight, one hand clutching the sword that he had taken from the umbrella. He cocked his head to one side and smiled. "Ah, and here they come."

A noise built. A great clattering of engines, a wheezing of machines pushed to their limits. This was an airship dying. Finally, it came into sight, its surface ablaze, passing low over the trees, almost touching the tallest ones.

The dirigible passed overhead, and for a moment they were in shadow. Shots stung the air around them. Margaret dropped to a crouch and fired at the sky. The dirigible was already sliding over the ridge.

"Don't let it distract you," David shouted into her ear. "They're on the ground. They're here!"

David fired the flare.

The land filled with light. He jerked a thumb to the right,

near the tree line. A tall man stood there, dressed in a ragged morning coat, hands flung up against the light.

"To the left, too," David said. "By the rocks." He fired his pistol there, at another man dressed in little more than rags.

"Where are the rest of them?" Margaret said, firing to the right. The Old Man had already moved to cover.

"Some always move faster than others. They'll be here soon enough, Miss Penn."

Margaret blinked.

She asked, "Are you all right?"

"Not at all," David said, and the words were clearly a struggle. "But I am what I need to be."

David straightened, seemed to broaden across the chest, and flashed a smile at her that was both nightmarish and reassuring at once. "They'll come at us in a rush, probably once the flare–"

They didn't wait that long.

In a blur of movement they were upon them. Margaret managed two quick shots, caught a satisfying spray of blood, then her rime blade was unsheathed, a pistol in her free hand.

She fired again, the bullet striking the Old Man in the side of his face. That slowed him, she swung out, and the Old Man closed his fingers around the blade. Margaret lifted her pistol, fired again. Blood sprayed from the Old Man's neck.

She didn't see the fist that struck her.

Only found herself on her back, ears ringing. She snatched out at her pistol, dropped it.

A heavy boot kicked her in the chest.

She felt something break, pain boiled across her chest, but she managed to pull free another pistol from her belt, and her free hand found the rime blade. Time stilled, she rolled backwards. Pain again, waves of it. She could taste blood, her nose streamed. The Old Man stood there, wounded and bleeding too.

He took a step forward, the grass around his boot crackled. Margaret fired.

Another wound, but he didn't stop.

Neither did she. She crouched low, and sprang out, straight towards the Old Man. There was something beautiful in her movements. She knew it, could feel the fluid grace of her limbs, the arc her blade described.

The Old Man moved to block her, but she was already past his guard. She fired her pistol one last time, right into his chest, then cut off the Old Man's head. It fell to the earth. She crouched down, grabbed her second rime blade, and looked at David.

They were talking.

The Old Man had David around the neck, lifting him with just one arm. The other he was using to punch him in the ribs. David's limbs juddered. And yet they talked as if old friends.

"Surely it would be in our interests to work together," David said as blood streamed from his head. His hands were closed around the Old Man's wrist.

"Doing what you do," the Old Man said, swinging, swinging. "You have no idea whose interests you are working for. We cannot countenance the application of the sciences that made us what we are. If I do not succeed in destroying you, the others will try, until you or all of them are dead."

"But the Roil is building. There is so little time left."

"Let the Roil build, let it do what it will do. That is better, let it happen this time."

"I can't and I won't," David said.

The Old Man nodded. "You were always at the heart of the madness, Cadell. Leave the boy alone."

"You're the one trying to kill me."

"Oh, you are so naive. Both of you are so naive. What does it matter?" the Old Man hissed. "What does any of it matter?"

Her first blade she drove through his back and into his heart, the other she hacked into his neck. The Old Man dropped David and turned. She struck his neck again. The Old Man's head fell one way, the body the other.

"It matters a lot to me," Margaret said.

"Get up," Margaret said, reaching down. David gripped her hand with fingers which had grown icy cold, and she almost dropped him.

"The rest are coming," David said.

Margaret nodded to the nearby ridge. "Then we climb that."

She grabbed her bag of guns, wiped her blades free of blood. David was looking at her, one hand rubbing his throat where a dark bruise was forming.

"You'd do well to hurry up," she said and headed for the ridge.

CHAPTER 35

I can't say that I ever really knew David. He was too many things, too many faces. I don't know if anyone could ever really know him. I'm not even that sure he knew himself.

Ice Storm, RAVEN SKYE

THE NORTHERN WILDERNESS
1520 MILES NORTH OF THE ROIL

The stone struck Margaret on the head. David caught the movement a moment too late. She turned, blinked at him once and tumbled. A few more steps and they would have been clear.

Another stone flashed through the dark, but David was ready. He caught it, and hurled it back. Soft laughter sounded from the trees ahead.

"Good throw."

David squinted and could see the Old Man there, half hidden in the branches of a great pine. It was dark, but the Old Man glowed.

David checked that Margaret was still breathing. And she was, though a lump was fast growing on her forehead.

The stone that had struck her had been about the size of a
fist. David picked it up speculatively.

"I could have shot her," the Old Man shouted. "But I am
merciful."

"You're the very picture of mercy," David said.

"And how many men have you killed this day? Men as
ancient as the stony moons. And you snuffed out their
slow lithic lives just so you could breathe a few days
more."

He sat in a lower branch, a coat about his shoulders, as
if he could ever grow cold. The Orbis on David's finger
glowed and the one on the Old Man's responded with a
reflected light. A flickering luminescent dialogue occurred
between the rings that David was only partly aware of.
Like having a conversation smacked into the side of your
head with a flashlight. The sensation passed quickly and
the Old Man looked down at him with an expression that
was almost avuncular.

"Ah, you've led us a merry chase," the Old Man said, and
all at once, David recognised the voice. And it unleashed so
much. He stood unsteadily, buffeted by all that memory.

"Milton," David said.

Andrew Milton nodded his head. "Nice to be remembered."

"I remember you all."

Milton pulled up his coat, blood had darkened and stiffened the sleeves – none of it his own. But he didn't come
down from the tree. David could smell Milton from the
ground, and despite himself, he felt a little hungry.

Ignore it, a voice whispered.

"Where are the others?" David demanded.

"Not far away," the Old Man said. "The fear was that
you might be using explosives, or that a friend of yours

might sacrifice themselves for the greater good. Sacrifice is something you never understood. I don't need them to kill you."

"Rupert couldn't. Nor could Michael or Carver."

"But now, you are alone. Be honest, you have hardly acquitted yourself well. The Old Man's there, but you've stripped away his teeth with that fancy drug of yours." Milton dropped from the tree, landed on his feet easily.

Milton was a good head taller than David, a foot broader across the chest.

David took a couple of steps back. The Old Man matched them, lighter on his feet. He rolled his broad shoulders loosely, bits of dried blood dropped from the coat, onto the ground. David could feel his hunger, feel how it echoed his own. It made his mouth water, his tongue felt thick and heavy, and it stuck to his teeth.

"Weeks we have hunted and devoured, weeks to build our strength to match our hungers. I am ready to tear you apart, it is all that we have wanted for months."

Weeks: had it really been that long since David had left Chapman? There had been slowly passing days, for sure, but hardly that many. He could still remember the great hand rising over the battlements. The Hideous Garment Flutes rushing down out of the dark, and devouring a swirling screaming cloud of birds.

"Do we really need to do this, Andrew?" David said.

Milton blinked. "You never called me that."

"I am different now. Things have changed."

"Which is precisely why you must die."

"What if I agreed not to do it?" the Old Man asked.

"You would not. And, even if you did, your presence alone is enough of a danger. You are an Old Man, old no longer. You are not yourself, but nor are you Cadell."

"Then what am I?"

"Everything that we once were given a new fierce life. Even if you do not realise it, David, you are the destruction of a world."

"But I want to save it."

"So did we. But what is left to save? Perhaps you would like a little of our history," the Old Man said. "After all, you are part of that now. Whether we like it or not."

The Old Man was playing for time. Maybe Milton wasn't as confident as he appeared.

"Can't I just kill you?" David said.

"If you're fast enough, yes. But aren't you curious as to what you are? After all, we have had aeons to come to an understanding. You, on the other hand, have had a few weeks. Don't you want to know why you must die?"

David shrugged. Milton smiled.

He said, "When we did what you have done. When we released the Engine of the World, and sent the Roil back into the darkness, we thought we understood the cost. However, Cad... Mr Milde, we got it wrong. There was death, more death than you or I can comprehend. The Engine itself railed at the terror of its purpose. You may have changed, you may not have been the man you once were, but the Engine can never change enough. And it was as rigorous in what it did to us, as what it had done to the world.

"It captured us. Contained us, and transformed us. Cursed us with hungers, cursed us with life endless (or near enough). And still we thought we could live as normal men. Those days there were twenty of our kind remaining – I am sure you remember them." And David did, he could see their proud faces, hear their voices.

Milton said, "But as the ice receded, as the world revealed

itself to us, what we had undone and what we had made set a madness in our bones.

"Some it affected more than others. Drove them to kill and kill, but we seven, we Old Men, destroyed those who would devour the world that they had saved; and banished ourselves and our hunger to the deep places beneath Mirrlees. We locked ourselves there so that we could not again do what we had done.

"And there was not a day that I didn't regret that decision, even as I knew it to be the wise one. Cadell, though, he was different. He knew that a time would come when the Engine would be required to work again."

"And so it has," David said. "That time has come."

"Yes, but you need to understand. Time or not, it is the wrong path. We have no right."

"We have no right to save our world?"

"No right to destroy this one." The Old Man sighed. "To save it does not save a thing, merely forestalls."

"Isn't that what everything is?" David said. "Merely a stalling action."

Milton smiled. His head dipped a little. "Then we've no more talking to do."

The Old Man crossed the space between them in an eye blink, jaw snapping closed on air. David was already out of reach. Milton's feet dug into the earth, he turned on his heel. David threw a punch, and the Old Man caught his fist and squeezed.

David wrenched his hand free, but not without the Old Man raking his nails across the flesh. David closed the wounds at once. They circled each other.

David's cheeks burned, his limbs felt slow and heavy, despite his speed. The ground was hard beneath his feet. His breath did not plume as Margaret's did. He looked over at her, on the cold earth, forehead bloody and pale. She might as well have been dead. But there, in the cold and the dark, she looked at peace. He felt again the pangs of his addiction, a stabbing ache, at once sharp and hollow, as though it had already torn the flesh from him.

"Caution will not save you," Milton said.

David knew he was right.

What would it be like to let go, to lose himself completely?

It doesn't hurt. Not any more than sadness, Cadell said. Not any more than that. It won't even sting.

Milton moved lightly on his feet; his ruddy lips shone.

"Goodbye, Margaret," David said, and he took a deep breath, left himself to Cadell.

David opened his eyes. Every bit of him was bruised, felt bitterly cold. He sat up.

Margaret was saying something. They were on the top of the ridge now.

"What? What?" he said.

"I–" her teeth chattered.

"I'm sorry," David said. "I went away."

He looked back, and there below them lay the scattered remains of Milton. David coughed, tasted his own blood; when he breathed, it bubbled thick and dark from his nose.

"Two more," he said. "What happened?"

"You killed him. You tore him apart. And then you laughed. David, David, it was the most horrible sound I have ever heard."

"There's still more to come. I should have..."

"You said they didn't matter. You passed me a syringe of Carnival. I don't know where you had gotten it from, and you told me to inject you with that or you would die."

"You shouldn't have."

"What – how could I say no to something capable of that?" She gestured down the hill.

"You have a point," David said. He could feel Cadell at a distance, but not that close inspection he'd felt before – as though Cadell was just leaning over his shoulder. David felt that what he had done was right. Felt, too, the grief. Cadell was wrong. Sadness could cut deeper than any hurt. Sadness could grind the breath from you.

There was no time for grief though. At the bottom of the hill, they appeared: the last Old Men.

Margaret sighted along her rifle. "Are you ready?" she said.

"Of course I am. Margaret, we did all right. No one can say otherwise."

"We might still make it," she said, but David could see that she was having trouble standing. Her breath was as laboured as a horse he had once seen die on a flooded Mirrlees street. She looked like she might at any moment stumble and fall.

Why had Cadell put himself back into the box? Had David really been that close to death, did it really matter?

Now, at least he felt calm, the anxiety had fled from his limbs. He took a deep breath.

Margaret fired, cursed.

"Missed," she said, and slapped another shell into the rifle.

The Old Men sprinted up the hill. Halfway to the top they paused and turned, looking behind them. Margaret fired again, this time striking one in the neck, then even she forgot to fire.

It rose over the hill like a third moon, shining a brilliant light upon the field. An airship from Hardacre: green and grey flags swinging from its belly. Guns swivelled in their emplacements and fired at the Old Men below.

The airship passed overhead Ropes fell to the earth, men and women jumped down lightly, Whig and Buchan with them. Men and women armed with guns and sabres.

"We've some experience fighting these brutes," Buchan said, one great hand clasped around a knife almost as thick as a cleaver. "I believe you could do with some help."

Whig clutched his hat in one hand, firing a pistol at the Old Men below. "Well, answer him, man!"

"Yes," David said. "Yes."

Margaret tried not to smile. "Just don't get in the way."

"So all is forgiven?" Buchan asked. He looked from David to Margaret and back again, and what triumph might have been in his face withered.

Do we look so beaten? David thought. "Only if you will forgive us," David said.

"You don't even need to ask."

Whig reloaded his pistol.

"You're late," Margaret said.

Whig grimaced. "Did you just make a joke?"

The airship circled above, its great searchlights blazing.

"Ready, crew," Buchan roared. "Ready!"

And those last Old Men were running up the hill, throwing cold before them. Guns fired. A wall of death: rifles and pistols all at once. And it took its toll. Still, the Old Men broke through their ranks, bringing their own death with them.

But they were outnumbered, weakened, under constant fire. They could not run fast enough, and always there was David, just out of reach. The first fell to a barrage of rifle fire. The second ran at David, only to be caught mid-air by Buchan himself. With a twist of his arms he broke the Old Man's neck.

And David felt the last of the Old Men go, and a great

wave of sadness – that wasn't exactly his own – gripped him. An age was ended; a whole epoch of existence gone, and they had failed in their singular purpose. But already Cadell was fading, sliding beneath the surface of his mind like some leviathan of thought and memory.

"Well," David said. "We've still breath in us."

Margaret shuddered. "Yes, we do."

"We thought you could use some help," Buchan said.

David grinned a bloody smile and spat a little blood on the ground. "We've not much time," he said. "We need to burn the corpses. All of them."

The Old Men burned fast and almost silently: flesh melted from the bone, bones blackened and crumbled to dust. And these corpses burned much more quickly than Cadell's corpse had. Perhaps their vitality was greater, or just all those ancient bodies pressed up against each other quickened the flames. Oddly, they gave out little heat; instead they seemed to draw the heat from everything around them. A peculiar and disturbing fire, and one that only David and Margaret could bring themselves to stand close to.

David felt something should be said over their bodies, but he wasn't sure what. These Old Men had lived since First Landing. They had defeated the Roil and been punished for it, given over to hunger and madness, and still they had tried to do what they thought was best – and what might have been right.

How was David to know, to judge right from wrong? All he'd known was that he didn't want to die.

Maybe Mother Graine was right, too.

He shook his head, the only way he could see himself through this was to move as though those other opinions didn't matter. They'd all wanted him dead, in one way or another, how could they matter?

"You died for what you believed in," David said. "There's honour in that. Maybe in these times that is all that is possible." He didn't know what else to say, he tried, but his voice faltered. The bodies burned.

Margaret stared at him from across the flames. She looked old, and tired, her skin too pale, even for her, too tight against her bones. "We've yet to see if we can manage the same," she said.

Something rattled in the distance, and she turned her head towards the sound.

"What's that?" she said.

David got to his feet, and felt for a knife. A branch or a twig snapped, someone swore loudly.

Kara came clanking out of the shadows, a pack strapped to her back. A dozen guns flicked in her direction. She threw up her hands up in the air, palms out.

"Friend! Friend! Lower those bloody guns," she cried, sounding breathless as though she had run miles, and perhaps she had.

David shouted at them to hold their fire. Buchan roared out with delight. Even Margaret managed something that approximated a smile.

"You did it," Kara said, the swelling had gone down around her eye, though a bruise covered her jaw line.

"Yes, we did," Margaret replied.

"I brought some rum," Kara said, pulling a bottle from her backpack. "Half the reason I'm buggered. Too damn heavy, five bottles. Now, who wants some?"

"I might just," Margaret said. And she wasn't the only one.

David declined, all he could think of was the Carnival hidden in his heel.

"The *Dawn*?" he asked.

"She will be fine in a day or two. She had no flight in her, I'm sorry. And I'm sure she's mad at me for leaving her, but I had to come and do what I could, even if it meant just burying my friends." Kara smiled, and David thought she was joking, until he saw the shovel jutting from her pack.

She looked over at Buchan and Whig, both hesitating a few yards away. "And I see you had help."

"Yes, we're all back together again," David said. "The happiest of families."

THE MARGIN
FRAGMENT OF THE ROIL

It was a fog of darkness. That first looked like dust, if a dust storm could grow so black. Tornadoes of darkness danced around it, fed by the heat, and its contact with the cold.

And within it great machines walked upon metal legs, each step loud as thunder. Heating mechanisms sat upon their metal heads, round which the Roil spores clung. This was a hardier darkness, but still it required these great things, so far from the Roil. Always this outlier was aware of the darkness from which it sprang: felt its commands flashed along a chain of machines. Such communications were tenuous and fragile, but really all that was necessary. Who was there to disrupt it now?

It split into two great strands of darkness, ready to pinch out the last strongholds of humanity, shift them so that they would become something else, two more dreaming cities.

Those caught in their path were subsumed as a matter of course. Enemies changed to allies with a soft beat of wings, a transformation of neurons, and a new awareness of different imperatives.

To be one with the Roil. To be one with the glorious ending of the world.

CHAPTER 36

The Engines of War moved quickly, racing to finish what had been begun those many years ago. Great battles were fought, many lives lost. And out in the north, a small group travelled upon whom everything hinged – as though they were some door to disaster or salvation.

You would be surprised how often it has happened before.

Simple Stories for Girls and Boys, DEIGHTON

THE NORTHERN WILDERNESS
1519 MILES NORTH OF THE ROIL

The *Collard Green* carried them away from the pyre and to the *Roslyn Dawn*. The Aerokin raised a flagellum sluggishly in greeting. Margaret could tell it was an effort.

"Still healing," Kara said. "She'll be all right in a day or so, it takes a lot of energy to recover from such a wound, even one that isn't fatal."

Since no one was going anywhere fast, they'd made camp.

They'd lit fires, enough for the *Collard Green* and her crew. Someone had gotten out musical instruments, and songs of the Confluents and victory had been sung, some to tunes that Margaret had recognised, if not the lyrics. Political activism had taken on a less combative form in Tate. But the singing and the drinking wasn't just that, they mourned their dead, and mocked the flight ahead of them.

They ate. And ate – Buchan almost matching David in the food he put away. And drank – Whig almost matching Kara.

Margaret worked slowly through her meal, still sore, and now, with some urgency fled, found her mind wandering again to darker things.

To the north, beyond the river, the plain extended, treeless, vast. And it would carry on and on, until Tearwin Meet itself, and the weird tall mountains that she had read about in Deighton's histories. There weren't too many more meals to be had.

When she had finished her plate and passed it to a man to be washed, Buchan came over to her.

"Together again," Buchan said.

"So you finally got out of Hardacre," Margaret said.

Buchan laughed. "It was far harder than we ever expected. I'm sorry that we were so slow."

"And I'm sorry that we left you," Margaret said.

"You did what you thought was right," Buchan said. "I've had plenty of time to consider it."

"So how did you find us?"

"We've been chasing the Old Men since they left Hardacre; they've always kept just ahead of us." He stared into the fire. "Margaret, we saw some terrible things, helped when we could, which wasn't often. We knew – well, hoped really – that if we didn't lose them, we would find you."

"And so you did," Margaret said.

Buchan looked over at David; he was talking to Kara and Whig, the boy's face gleaming with the same healing gel that Margaret had had slathered under her ribcage. Kara's leering application of that had been one of Margaret's more unpleasant moments – but now Margaret was feeling better, more clear-headed. She'd thought she'd not live out the night, and yet here she was.

"Can we trust him?" Buchan said.

"You saw what he did to the Old Man, or what was left of that act. He did that to save me, he could have run, but he didn't. He scares you?"

"He's scared me since the day you brought him to Hardacre, Margaret," Buchan said. "He was little more than a boy when I met him just a couple of months ago, and now he's something altogether different. His flesh barely contains him. I don't know what he is. Man or Old Man, I don't think he knows either. If the flesh is uncertain, what of the mind?"

"What? You're frightened he won't see this through?"

"Frightened that he won't. Frightened that he will." Buchan looked down at his massive hands. "These are terrifying times. The world is drowning. And we're what are left, of those who might be able to stop it. Do you think that what we're doing is right?"

"Of course. The Roil must be stopped at all costs."

Buchan smiled. "To be so young, to possess such perfect clarity."

"The Roil took everything I was, subverted it and threw it back at me," Margaret said. "It didn't just destroy my world, it transformed it, utterly and horribly."

"Stade snatched my city from me," Buchan said. "Turned Whig and I into exiles, and made it so Chapman never stood a chance. I hate the man. I despise him. But I do not want him dead. I honestly believe he thought he was saving us all."

"Stade is just one man. He is nothing in the context of the Roil, all of us are nothing," Margaret said, gesturing at David. "Except him. He can destroy it. He can drive it out, he can engage the Engine of the World, and I will make sure that he does. We survived tonight, I doubt anything is capable of stopping us now."

Buchan smiled grimly. "There, you see; once again, it's the confidence of the young. When all I would be doing is licking my wounds, you're ready to go out and tear the world down."

"When the world deserves such a fate, why shouldn't it be torn down?" Margaret said.

Buchan didn't answer her.

The celebrations, such as they were, had ended hours ago. Kara was out somewhere vomiting into the dark and David sat facing a fire that did nothing to comfort him. In fact, his mere presence seemed to bend the flames away from him. He wondered if anything was capable of comforting him now. Food helped, but barely, he was running a race with his hunger, always chasing some level of satiation that he could never quite reach. Some days, the whole world would have not been enough. He'd seen Cadell, and the Old Men, and found some of that deeper hunger reflected within him. He feared what he was capable of.

Around him people snored. He couldn't sleep. He feared what he would find waiting for him. There was still blood under his nails, despite his furious scrubbing.

He didn't want Cadell there in that dream space, least of all tonight, didn't want to be reminded of what he had done, didn't want it explained to him just how he had managed to tear Milton apart. Just another memory he didn't want.

Oddly enough, he missed Mother Graine. Her absence

at that moment felt more painful than any other loss he had experienced. And she had kicked him in the head.

Sometimes he found it hard to believe that his father was actually dead. His mother, well, he had had years to grow used to that, but not his father. The great grey grumbling presence of him, and the smell of his tobacco. His tendency to launch into long-winded lectures on the correct behaviour of a son of a Councillor, the disappointed tone of his voice; all this coming from a man who had marched away from his friend and joined the opposition, and not only that, but broken into the belly of the Ruele Tower and freed an Old Man.

Maybe he didn't miss him because there really hadn't been all that much to miss. But, no, his father had cared for him. Had loved him in his way. And they'd shared a love of the Night Council novels.

Travis the Grave wouldn't have sat here now, moping, the weight of the world on his shoulders. He'd have been out there, probably at Tearwin Meet itself. The Roil already dealt with, and a nice ale waiting to be drunk. But Travis had a mechanical hand, and the advantage of being fictional.

So he sat despondent and missed the woman who had tried to kill him – for being the thing she loved.

Margaret cleared her throat behind him.

"I was wondering when you might let me know you were there," David said.

"You were brave today," Margaret said, and David couldn't tell whether she was surprised or just stating a fact. David hadn't felt brave. He'd been more frightened than he had in a long time. He stared into the fire, and pulled the blanket tighter around his shoulders, not that it seemed to do a lot of good.

"You have always been so brave," David said.

Margaret snorted. "I fled my family, my city. I deserted them."

"No, that is not how it happened. It might be how it felt, but it wasn't how it happened," David said. "There was purpose in your action. People knew how driven you are, knew that you would make it here. And you have. I fled my father's death, but only because I was terrified.

"I have been an addict for so long. There was no higher purpose to my escape, merely a desire to keep breathing, to get more Carnival in me so that life wasn't so unbearable."

"And you've succeeded," Margaret said. "Here you are, still alive. And you have saved our lives more than once."

David couldn't help laughing. "No, I've only ever run towards death, and not the comfortable death that Carnival could have afforded me: a quiet warm death, away from suffering. No, that would be too easy. Your motives have always been the purer, Margaret. Mine were compromised from the beginning. It's cold here," David touched his chest. "And it's getting colder." He lowered his head to his chest and looked into the fire. "You're the one that's alive. You're the one that's pure of purpose."

Somewhere in the distance, Kara sang to herself, some jaunty thing from Drift that David partially recognised. It should have made him smile, but it just made him feel sadder.

When he looked up, Margaret was gone. She'd left as quietly as she had arrived, and David couldn't help wondering if, perhaps, he hadn't actually imagined her presence by the fire altogether.

He stood up at last, and strode over to Kara. "The *Dawn*, how is she?"

"She's getting better, from now on the sky will heal her far more effectively than the earth. She hungers for flight."

David looked out into the dark, past the gleam of the fire reflected in the river. "So do I. I just want this to end."

"Really?" Kara said. "You want the cold and the death, and the being hunted to end? How remarkable. Who would have thought?"

David sighed. "You don't understand," he said.

"I do, and I will get you to Tearwin Meet as fast as possible." She picked up her pack. "I'm sorry that I had to desert you."

"No," David said. "The *Roslyn Dawn* must come first. Without her, we can't finish the journey."

"You've got Buchan and Whig now, I think you could manage it."

"Their airship might be capable of many things, but the *Collard Green* is a poor second to the *Dawn*."

Kara smiled at that. "Truer words have not been said."

"I'll let Buchan and Whig know that we are leaving now," David said. "It's time we made for Tearwin Meet. It's time we knew what sort of Engine we are facing."

CHAPTER 37

Of all the cities to face the Roil, only one managed to stand un-bowed, cloaked in ice and darkness. It wasn't victory or defeat, but something that many would argue was far worse than either. A violent kind of half-life, a contest where the prize had passed them by

Speculations Approaching a Complete
History, LANDYMORE

THE CITY OF TATE, SOME WEEKS AGO
WITHIN THE ROIL BUT NOT OF THE ROIL

Margaret Penn readied herself for the next wave of the Contest. Her rime blade hummed with its charge, the vibration running up her arm and into her chest, setting up a counterpoint to her pounding heart. She touched the blade with the tip of a gloved finger and could feel its burning chill.

Margaret glanced up at her parents, sitting with the rest of the crowd in the arena above, both in their sixties now, and looking it. Such a thought brought her a momentary pause. She did not like to consider her parents growing older, did not like to consider the certainty of their mortality. We're all going to die, she thought. Just not her parents. Not when she was starting to untangle the mass of contradictory thoughts she had about them, and see them with adult eyes.

Engines whined and the nearest portcullis lifted; the ice sheathing its steel bars gleamed in the light. A Quarg Hound entered the arena through the opening. It was an old beast, big and scarred. Its jaws opened and opened, such a mouth could swallow her whole. It regarded her with intelligent eyes the size of saucers, perfect for the darkness of the Roil, which was why the lights in the arena were suddenly extinguished. Margaret let her mind still, found the calm place between her breaths. There was danger in this. But there had to be, life in the city of Tate was precarious.

The Quarg Hound bounded towards her, its massive limbs a blur. It veered to the right at the last minute before rounding back in towards her. Margaret swung, missed. The Quarg Hound snapped at her, but Margaret had already rolled to the left. She crouched there, blade at the ready. The Quarg Hound charged, and Margaret was dancing away, swinging the rime blade down as it passed her. The blade sank deep into the beast's back. The Quarg Hound yowled, and wrenched its spine so savagely that Margaret nearly lost her sword. She yanked the blade free; there was a rush of claws. Margaret swung her head to the left. Not fast enough.

Margaret's face burned, but she was already swinging, releasing a second rime blade from her belt, and burying it in its chest, the blade on its highest setting. The Quarg Hound stopped, eyes wide, jaw working the air. It fell dead, two swords jutting from its body. Margaret pulled them free.

The crowd cheered, but already another portcullis had lifted, and another Quarg Hound was on its way. Fourteen in one hour. Maybe she was getting a little slow, or the Hounds were getting faster. If the latter was the case, then Engine help them. The Roil had all the advantages as it was.

The Four Cannon fired and the floor of the Penn household shook. Somewhere, beyond Tate's outer walls, in the dark of the Roil, the cannon's endothermic shells shattered, releasing frigid shockwaves that kept the worst of the Roil at bay.

"Sixteen in all, hardly a personal best, dear." Her mother's tone was playful, but it didn't stop her biting.

"They're getting faster."

"We know," Arabella Penn said. "We've noted it on the Gathering Plains, too. Something is stirring; we're having to vary the pattern of our cannonade more frequently. The Roil is reacting."

Margaret winced. Her mother was less than gentle in her stitching.

Arabella pursed her lips. "Oh, did I hurt you? Poor baby."

Margaret ground her teeth.

They'd stopped the Contest at sixteen kills, because the blood from the cuts on Margaret's brow was blinding her, and she'd already passed her nearest opponent by five. She could have gone on, the rime blades had held their charge nicely – her father had improved their fuel cells' efficiency, half the reason behind the Contest was to test new weaponry – but this wasn't the real battle.

The real battle had been lost twenty years before. Almost to the day, and its ramifications echoed through the dark.

The suicide rate was up again, more Walkers than ever – suicides heading out into the Roil. Margaret had only to look outside to know why. She had never seen sunlight, but she didn't need to be told what a loss that was. The city of Tate was wondrous, an ice-bound engine of war and light, strung with its wireways, and guarded by the Four Cannon. But people cannot live in a state of perpetual war;, people cannot stay trapped the way they had remained trapped.

"Do you think it knows about the I-bomb?" Margaret asked.

Arabella shook her head. "Their Roilings have not breached these walls in over a decade. It's bad timing, nothing more."

"So you and Father are going ahead with the tests?"

Arabella smiled. "It has to be done, and soon. If the Roil is… quickening, we need to quicken ourselves in response." She squinted down at her handiwork. "I'm afraid you'll have a scar."

Margaret laughed; her mother could be *very* funny when she wanted to be. Scars were stories here – this one a Quarg Hound, that one the boiling blood of an Endym – not a single resident of Tate lacked for scars from the Roil. Margaret said, "You're still leaving tomorrow?"

Arabella shook her head. "We're leaving tonight."

Margaret frowned, but she didn't say anything. The I-bombs remained their best hope, and hope was a rare commodity in the dark heat of the Roil. Until now.

The battle had been lost twenty years ago. The war might still be won.

PART FOUR
THE ENGINE OF THE WORLD

What deep pulse belies the Engine, what cool and callous thought.
The Mechanism hates itself and hates what it has wrought.

Pronouncements, LANGAN

CHAPTER 38

When the sky is torn asunder, with the mechanisms and their thunder.

You will see what all should know, Shale will fall to just one blow.

One giant world-shuddering blow.

Blow, S. McWayne

THE MIRRLEES AIR FLEET
DISTANCE FROM ROIL INDETERMINATE

Stade couldn't remember the last time that he had slept. There was so much to be done. And he trusted no one else to do it. If he could, he would be out piloting all the airships as well.

He missed Mr Tope. Until the fall of Chapman he had always been so reliable. Stade really couldn't blame the man for his own death. No one had expected the Roil's great rush against the city's walls, and his finest Verger had still managed to get one last message through. And yet, Stade couldn't drive away the hard splinter of resentment that had settled in his heart.

He leant back in his chair, in the airship office where he had spent much of his last few weeks, organising the great logistical nightmare that was his people's journey north. He knew it could be worse – that he could be down on the ground.

Stade considered his maps. Another week at least, and still no radio contact from the Underground, but he had to think of that as nothing more than a problem with their transmission tower, it had never worked reliably. The journey had been a long one. Of course the airships could have made it to the Underground in a couple of days, even against the headwinds, but they had a city's population to protect. A city forced to travel by foot. They had avoided the worst of the Margin, travelling east, then north, but still there were patches of that contaminated forest that had to be crossed.

People disappeared into the night, and some reappeared briefly, drawing others away. The last gondola affected had been clean, but stank of blood. After that, Stade had ordered all airships to keep at least a mile clear of the Margin, and the airship itself was burned.

A small rearguard had stayed behind in Mirrlees; they'd lost contact with them two days ago. The reports up until that point had been one of a city falling frantically into chaos. Their cessation had been abrupt. He had been expecting it, but not so soon.

Stade felt the diminishment of his network with every passing hour. No more could he claim to know every movement of every enemy between Chapman and Hardacre. He was beginning to wonder if he had ever really known anything at all.

A knock at the cabin door startled him.

"What is it?" he growled.

"A problem, sir." It was Moffel, the closest thing he had to a trusted advisor these days.

"I will be right out."

He got up, slid a lozenge of Chill into his mouth.

"And the problem?" Stade said.

Moffel said, "One of the engines isn't operating as it should be. They want your advice on it."

Fair enough, he'd designed the engines after all.

At the outer edge of the airship, Stade, met two men, engines rumbling nearby.

"You called me here because?" he said.

"We thought you should see this."

The Witmoths flew from their mouths towards him. He lifted his arms and sprayed the air with cold, from tubes beneath his jacket sleeves, blistering his wrists as he did so. The moths fell, and Stade yanked free his pistols and fired; both shots went true and the Roilings tumbled over the deck. "Do not take me for such a fool that I do not come prepared," he said to their tumbling corpses.

Though he had been fool enough to come out here. He needed more sleep.

He walked back to the door. It was locked. Stade sighed, pulled the key from his pocket and opened the door.

Moffel was waiting by the door. Stade shot him dead, too.

They found two more Roilings in the crew. Both were thrown overboard. Stade returned to his rooms all rage and fear. He took a lozenge of Chill, just to be safe, and his hands shaking, grabbed the machine.

He let the mechanism fold over his face, felt its spikes slide through the plate of his skull, and into his brain. There was no pain, just a sick-making sensation, as though all this could go so badly, that his sanity, his personality lay on the thinnest, frailest sort of knife-edge.

He'd used this device to control the spiders under Downing Bridge. Ah, that bridge; briefly he was there, back in the city that he had fled, and that hurt him more than Stade had expected – after all, the flight from the city had always been part of his plan to lead his people to sanctuary. However, the gap between his plans and reality had grown wide.

He concentrated, brought his mind under control, shifted it from the city to the belly of his airship, and the airships around them. This fleet was the vestige of the Grand Defeat, and he'd filled the ballast of each with his spiders.

Already thousands of them had released thread to the air, and now he concentrated on them, gaining an image in bursts, and drifts, of the sky from horizon to horizon and beyond.

A drop of blood ran across his chin.

He couldn't do this for too long, or it would tear him apart. But he needed to know what was happening. Stade just had to see where the Cuttlefolk were, if they were a threat, if they were following him, or merely flying towards the Roil – as the first cloud of them had proven to be doing.

And there they were.

There they were.

Not heading towards the Roil or to Mirrlees, but north. Flying north towards his great exodus: a cloud intent on shattering his plans for good.

The sound of Cuttle messengers in flight and en masse was terror scratched out of the air. It was as hard as the wind was hard, the sky had become solid and killing. A thunderous beating of wings and mandibles, and spiked limbs: a storm which had grown brittle and clawed. Such a storm was bearing down on him, and though he had been expecting it, Stade could not avoid the terror of the Cuttlemen's approach.

As a young man, Stade had fought in the Cuttle Wars. So many of his generation had. They'd been men and women fighting a war of cultures – of misunderstandings driven to blood and death. His service and heroism in those wars had led to his election. Heroism, all he'd remembered was the horror. He'd seen troops stripped of their flesh almost before they could fire their guns. Aerokin devoured in the sky, their great cannon useless. He wasn't the only one of his crew to remember such things, but none of them had ever witnessed anything like that which flew towards them.

"How can there be so many?" Captain Jones said.

"Because we didn't do it right the first time," Stade muttered, though he knew that was wrong, that these Cuttlefolk flew with a purpose that wasn't their own.

Witmoths covered their flesh, and fell from them like an inky rain.

"Engage the cannons," he said, and if his voice cracked with the fear of it, no one noticed. "It's time we made the sky bleed."

He reached in his pocket for a cigar, lit it, and unsheathed the knife at his belt, the same blade with which he had severed the fool Medicine Paul's fingers.

"Now, fire the damn things! Fire and fire and fire." The airship bucked and shuddered, and the sky bled.

And still they came. Cannons were never enough. Of course, Cuttlefolk made it onto the ship, and cold-suited Vergers met them with ice guns and frozen blades of the Tate design.

Even Stade himself couldn't avoid the fighting. A Cuttleman broke through the gondola window, and it was Stade that struck off its head, the mayor grinning madly, teeth biting down hard on a lozenge of Chill. He folded his arms around the still twitching corpse and hurled it out in the sky.

Cannons fired. Ships fell in flame and smoke and detonations, but the Cuttle messengers took casualties too, and theirs were in far greater numbers. The battle was over within half an hour. Two ships gone down, plus another slowly sinking, and one without radio contact.

The slowly sinking airship veered to the west. The silent one followed. Stade had another airship pull alongside it, and it too grew silent. There had been five Vergers on that ship and none of them called back in. The three airships pulled away.

Stade took no chances on another ship, he had all three shot down. He sent out a directive for all crew to have Chill at the ready. He could not afford to lose more ships.

Nor was he prepared to abandon the masses that the airships themselves were protecting.

Two days at most and they would reach the Undergound. Stade only hoped that it was still there. Despite the lack of radio contact, he had no other destination. There was no other hope. They reached the Underground or they all died.

And word had finally come to him of an approaching Roil mass, a finger of the Roil itself, two miles wide by three. It was covering the ground behind them at an incredible rate.

If they didn't reach the Underground in three days, this small finger of Roil would be upon them. And small though it might be, it was still enough to crush them.

CHAPTER 39

*"Of course, Shale possesses a hollow core," Travis the Grave said.
He flexed his hand, the movement generating a short puff of steam.
"Where else do you think all the monsters come from?"*

"And where might we find entrance, Mr Grave?"

*"Where all the curses and madness of this world originate. In
the distant north, in Tearwin Meet."*

> Night Council 18: The Hollowing, JB BRICKENHALL

THE DEEP NORTH
2000 MILES NORTH OF THE ROIL

Two days from the river and David became aware of the
slow rise and fall of the world, and the landscape beneath
them began its curious simplification. They reached the
place where the last forests thinned and became nothing
more than low wind-burned trees and grass, and these in
turn gave way to clumps of some grey matter that seemed
to sit halfway between grass and lichen.

After that landscape became raw stone, grey too – except
when it rained, short icy showers that turned the stone
blue or black. Three times they passed over Lodes – like

the one David had used those weeks past – and each time, looking down, he could feel the Engine of the World staring back. David couldn't read the expression, but it was at best ambivalent, at worst disapproving.

Each Lode (as though they possessed transformative powers) brought a little more of Cadell to the surface, too. Memories waltzed through him that weren't his own. Conversations, jokes and slights that made little sense to him, though he knew Cadell understood them. Certain unfamiliar mannerisms became less so; the way he walked sometimes felt wrong; even the way he looked out at the world, as though Cadell was trying to use his eyes differently from how David used them. Objects in the distance grew clearer, peculiar lights haloed the stony earth below. When he pointed it out, no one seemed to see it.

What he noticed most of all was an ever-increasing smugness. Cadell was getting what he wanted, or trying to hide behind it. He pushed away the disapproval, hoped that Kara hadn't seen it.

The world stopped its rising and falling, and just seemed to fall, as though the entire north was focussed on – and leaning towards – a single point. For two days, as they followed their slow flight, nothing changed below them, but for the stone, or the occasional animal, never larger than a fox, scurrying from sight, eking out an existence in what must be the harshest of environments.

David felt the great curvature of the world too, though here, yet again, it felt as though it was only curving in to one point.

Change came at last, a hint, revealed in increments, of a great upthrust of stone.

Tearwin Meet.

It grew on the horizon, and beneath them, that sensation

of falling at first accelerated before shifting, as though the earth itself had stopped to crane its neck and look up. And still it seemed that they would never reach the city; that no matter how far they travelled against that terrible and monotonous gale, they could draw no closer.

And when David slept, Cadell was there, and that increasing sensation of falling: him falling into Cadell or Cadell falling into him. David had nothing to hold onto, it was happening whether he wanted it or not, and it was accelerating.

"I'm coming back," Cadell said during one particularly deep slumber. They stood in the map room, Cadell circling the world like a moon.

"I know," David said, wondering if he wasn't just substituting one form of powerlessness for another.

"The clouds are peculiar today, don't you think?" Cadell tapped the panoptic map with his thumb.

David's gaze was drawn towards a single dark finger of cloud.

"Peculiar, that's no cloud."

Cadell nodded his head smugly. "The Roil's got its legs. Now it's decided to go walking. And where would such a thing go walking?"

They both looked at the range, and the one mountain that contained the Underground.

"The cloud is moving swiftly, three days, no more, and it will reach the Underground."

"Why not Hardacre?"

"It doesn't see that city as a threat, it has already lost, as far as it is concerned. No matter how this turns out, Hardacre will cease to be."

"And we can't stop that?"

"You are doing your best to now. But it is better to think

of what lies ahead. Tearwin Meet. The Roil itself is important, but we cannot influence it anywhere but here. And by we, I mean me."

Cadell reached across the map, grabbed David's head and began to twist.

David's eyes snapped open. He was in the *Dawn*, Margaret watching him from the other bed. "What curious dreams you have," Margaret said.

David grimaced. "If only they were merely curious." He stretched his arms above his head, yawned. "Are you rested?"

She shrugged. "All my weapons hold a charge," she said. "All I want is to look down on the Engine of the World."

David smiled. "You don't look at all rested."

"Neither do you."

Yes, he thought. Maybe it hadn't been such a good idea. Maybe you couldn't rest before such a thing. Not when the drug you depended on for calm was leaching out of your body. But he had tried.

He yawned. "Where's Kara?"

The toilet flushed in the cabinet nearest them, followed by the sounds of furious scrubbing. A half minute later, the door swung open. "Can't a person use the amenities without half the world talking about them?" she said.

David felt his face slip into a disapproving expression that wasn't his own. "I'm touched that you think I'm half the world," David said.

Kara grimaced.

"We're almost there," David said. "I need you to be ready."

"A pilot is always ready," Kara said. "Ready or dead. Now, ready for what?"

Margaret peered north. "Just what is that fire?" she said quietly. David turned to her.

"What fire?"

"The one streaking towards us."

David made a gagging noise. "Ready for that," he said. "Kara, could you veer to the right, please?"

"Starboard, veer to the starboard. Why should I – oh." She began her curious conversation with the *Dawn*, fast and furious, but not without its eccentricities. She touched the control panel twice, and the *Dawn* almost seemed to shiver, rather than fly, starboard.

The flaming ball swung past them, almost perfectly between the *Dawn* and the *Collard Green*, close enough that they could hear its screaming descent; the air smelt burnt.

"That makes no sense," Kara said. "We're flying in the safe zone."

David sighed. "I'd forgotten this," he said.

Margaret sighted along her nearest rifle, pointing out into the void. "Forgotten what exactly?"

"Well, forgotten is probably the wrong word, Cadell had forgotten it, or I'd suppressed the bit that knew. This is the problem. This is the problem when you fight it. We're almost there, and I still only know half of what I need to," David said. "But it doesn't matter now, this far north, and with the Roil expanded, the safe paths have changed."

"What do you mean changed? Or have you suppressed that, too?" Margaret asked.

"There is only one set of coordinates that will have us reach the city by air without being shot down. Well, a range of coordinates."

Another ball of flame cruised towards them. "I take it that we're not exactly following those coordinates now," Kara said.

David closed his eyes. Margaret wondered just what it was that he was considering.

"No," he said. "No, we are not. But we're close. It's going to slow us down a little."

"Fabulous," Margaret said, "when we have so much time to spare."

"Won't have any time if one of those bastards hits," Kara said.

"Bear to the north-east," David said. "Just a little more, and we will be safe." He turned to Margaret. "And signal to the *Collard Green*, they have to follow us."

"Watson's no fool," Kara said. "He'll know to keep on our tail."

"But just in case."

"Ah, you risk offending him, but just in case."

Margaret went for the flags. "Which ones?" she asked.

"The red, the green and the black," Kara Jade said. "Means follow right on our arse." She smiled. "Look, he's doing it already. Clever little fellow. Flash those flags, Margaret, give the bastard something to complain about. Now, David, are you sure that this is the right way? I'm not too keen to die engulfed in flames as a result of your incompetence."

David couldn't help but laugh at that. "Believe me, I'm sure. It will add a half a day to our journey, but we'll make it. The defence mechanism has tolerances," David said. "As long as we travel within those, we will be all right."

David's memory proved better than he had thought. They were shot at several times more – each time Kara glared at him – but none came as close as that first shot.

Soon the great mountains, and the city between them, dominated everything. The path they followed kept them zigzagging towards it, drawing closer with painful slowness. Twice, they almost touched the mountains and the wall, though Tearwin Meet remained hidden; only the central tower of the Engine of the World was revealed, rising above the wall.

And here the winds grew fierce and twisted, curling around the mountains and the city's walls. The wind battered at them, the *Roslyn Dawn* struggled in its grip, but did not succumb.

"We can't stay up here long," Kara said.

"We don't need to. Not today."

"How do we get to that?" Margaret said, gesturing at the tower.

"Today, we can fly over it. Kara, don't drop below this altitude. Everything beneath the height of the walls is well guarded," David said. "And even I am unsure of the path required to bring you to safety."

"Why am I not surprised?" Kara said.

"And please, signal to the *Collard Green*. They're not to follow us."

Kara whispered at the *Dawn*, and the Aerokin lifted, rising up over the wall. At its top was a narrow walkway. David was struck again with an ancient memory, of guards set at regular intervals along the wall, and a great dark storm building on the horizon.

The winds stilled, as they flew over the city, the tower to their right. David pointed at the tower, and the fine mist of wires that surrounded it. "We need to make for the door at the tower's base. We'll have to go from the walls and walk in, the tower is too dangerous to descend itself." He smiled. "It's coming back to me. Bit by bit."

Flying over Tearwin Meet, and looking down, David had the impression again of a vast consciousness, and one that was directed at him. Only this time, he wasn't looking at it via the panoptic map. There was anger and curiosity in that gaze, and strangely enough, amusement.

"Perhaps we should land now," David said.

"I *could* try to land in there," Kara said.

David shook his head. "Try and the *Dawn* would be torn apart, trust me, Kara. I *know* this. You might not see it, but the top of the walls are webbed with wires sharp enough to shear through her."

"We could climb it now," Margaret said. "Just drop us on the ridge. The narrow walkway circles the wall, and down we go." Her face was pressed against the window, she'd tapped her section to complete magnification. David peered down with her, not that it revealed much, the city beneath the walls was hidden in shadow. Nothing but gloom, though it was a gloom that seemed to stare back.

"I'm used to the dark," Margaret said.

David shook his head. "Not now. Not yet." He looked over at the walls. "Kara, just how much rope do you have on the *Dawn*?"

"For climbing?"

"Abseiling," he corrected. "It's how we... they used to get to the ground."

"I've got miles of the stuff. As fine and strong a thread as you could imagine." She followed David's gaze. "I hope you're not scared of heights."

"We'll find out tomorrow, I guess."

The *Dawn* passed over the city and came to its edge. And David was reminded of one more thing, here they truly were at the end of the land. Beyond the northern wall of the city was a great dark sea, one that could be followed all the way north – until one headed south, seeing nothing but a small island chain known as the Unremarkables, before reaching another frozen sea and the southern tip of Shale.

"Do you think they would find us if we just set off over the sea?" David said softly.

Out there a dark shape breached the water, followed by another. David frowned, then realised that it was a pod of whales. The sight was somehow heartening and heart-breaking at once. The wind struck the *Dawn* again, and they were out of the city.

"They'll find us anywhere," Margaret said. "Which is why we should turn the *Dawn* around and jump down onto the lip of the wall, and climb, and do it now."

David shook his head. "We climb. But not today," David repeated. "Today we land, Miss Penn. Today we rest, just outside the walls. I'm not quite ready yet." He looked over at Margaret, and hardly noticed that she was looking at him not with anger, but curiosity. "You'll have to use the flags again," he said, and pointed to a space on the ground, just outside the walls. "We're going to need to land there."

The *Collard Green* already looked like she was making for the landing space, though Margaret did as she was asked.

"And fly carefully, Miss Jade," David said.

Kara mumbled something, but David didn't hear her. The wall took up too much of his attention for that. Though as they descended, he felt a little less of the scrutiny of the Engine beyond it.

They sank slowly. Perhaps too close to the spiked walls of the city, as though Kara was making a point; David could see just how sharp those spikes were and he knew those edges could cut flesh with a touch.

Here at the boundary of Tearwin Meet, his sense of scale had to adjust constantly, it was like nothing he had ever seen before (and yet the part of him that was Cadell knew it too well); and he a citizen of a metropolis given over to excess. The grand levees of Mirrlees, the broad hulk of the Downing Bridge, these were nothing more than toys against the reach and span of Tearwin's walls.

They rose spindly and tall, looking like stone, though constructed of something far stronger and lighter. You could swing an axe at those walls, David thought – if you could get past the dense mass of cutting edges, thrusting out at all angles like monstrous thistle heads – and not leave a mark. Though there were signs of decay and age, in places furred colonies of fungus marked the wall, or forests of some sort of hardy vine. David even fancied he caught flashes of graffiti, ridiculous drawings of men and women, and curious beasts. He rather hoped someone had climbed up here, just to mark the walls. Their size alone required some kind of magnificent defiance; the climb itself was something to be admired.

As they sank, the city's walls only grew grander, thicker, more densely spiked. And looking up, at the top of the walls, it looked less like a walled city than a colossal smokestack. Indeed, wisps of cloud added to the impression as they trailed from its peak.

We cut and we cut and we cut and we cut.
  We keep the peace on the edge of the knife.
We cut and we cut to save your life.
We keep the peace along the blade.
We cut to be merry, we cut as we're bade

Verger Folk song

CHAPTER 40

And what was happening in the south? We only have speculation, rumours of dreaming cities, but no real indication of what such things might be like. The Engine hid behind its walls, and the Obsidian Curtain was just as opaque.

South of the Border, DEIGHTON & CRUX

THE DREAMING CITY
DEEP WITHIN (AND OF) THE ROIL

Tope opened his eyes.

He'd failed.

He should have been dead. His last memory had been the leap into the liquid nitrogen in Chapman.

And yet, he could feel his own pulse, and deep beneath the surface on which he lay supine (breaths all a shudder) was an echoing beat, as though the earth itself was alive. Perhaps even more so. After all, he had spent his life containing his passions, honing them to such an edge that they might strike out at the enemy, wherever and whoever that was.

He had failed in that task, just as he had failed to die.

He felt a moment's frustration at that failure, and a

moment's anger at the relief that followed, and the realisation that he had never wanted to die. But his life had
never been about what he wanted. Whose life was?

"You are awake, then." The voice that spoke those words
was soft, but authoritative. Nearby curtains twitched. His
gaze flicked towards the movement.

"Yes." Tope knew there was no point in pretending otherwise. That voice denied deception. "Where am I?"

"You know where you are."

And he did, he lay in the terrible dark of the Roil. His
skin burned, the flesh itched. But all of it meant one thing,
that he wasn't dead. That he was very much alive.

"Yes, I do," he said.

"Don't you wonder how you survived?"

Tope shrugged. "I've seen many wondrous things. Killed
my share of them, too. I stopped requiring the whats and
whyfors a long time ago."

There was a sense of pleasure in the response. "You're a
Verger, for you the knife is all."

"The knife is all."

"And it's knife work that we require."

An image grew within his mind, possessed of that same
beat: it flashed and flared and faded. He said, "The boy..."

"Is a boy no longer."

Tope wondered just how long it had been since he had
last opened his eyes.

"Weeks have passed, only weeks," the voice whispered,
gently mocking. "But for him, and this world, it has been
an age – your home would be unrecognisable to you. And
the boy, though he might not look it, has become a monster.
The world is greatly changed. You say you have seen wondrous things. But you have not seen anything like this." The
curtains parted, and he realised that they hadn't been

curtains at all, but winged creatures that went howling through the window – and the Dreaming City was revealed to him. He saw its engines, felt the rushing thought that informed it all, that was his thought and its thought. Here he was a single organism made up of many organisms, that were also part of this city, that were part of many cities. He felt in himself a deep yearning for that, to be part of it, part of the whole, because he wasn't, not yet.

"This was once known as Carver. It was the first metropolis to fall to dreams, now it is just one place of many. Here all is possible, here matter shapes to our dreaming. Though in truth we dream no more. We have woken. And when the dreamer wakes, dreams are realised."

Tope realised just how foolish Stade had been, to think that he could resist this. One thing to hide and fight against a senseless force of nature, but this was vast thought, of a scale that no one man was any match for, schemes within schemes as tightly bound as any clockwork mechanism, and infinitely more cunning. This was the future, and it was beautiful.

"The boy would destroy this new world. He would wipe it from the face of the world, and with it the seed of all hope."

Always the boy! Always the ruination of things. If only he had killed him that first night. The father should have been the one spared, the boy was always the danger. It amused him that the Roil – and Stade's desires – had boiled down to this one thing. He smiled.

"I will kill him," Tope said.

"Yes, we believe you will." The voice sounded very pleased indeed. "There is a vehicle waiting for you, a ship of fire that will burn as bright as any star. It will take you to the north."

He looked about the room and saw it at last. The figure, obscured by Witmoths, they scurried about its flesh, slid in and out of its mouth and nose. Tope couldn't tell whether it was male or female. All sense of that had gone. It was merely Roil.

"There will be a woman with him. Pale-skinned, tall."

"I know her," he said. "I have seen her. She tried to kill me."

"But she did not. You are to give her this gift." A single moth flew straight for him. He batted out at it, then re-alised that was exactly what it had wanted. He felt it slide into his skin, just beneath the wrist, a hot sliver of moth. Something that was quite different from the other crea-tures that filled his blood.

"You are to be kept of single mind, until this is done. Then we will decide whether or not you have earned our gift."

The Roil lifted its hand, a fist now, clenched around a belt of knives. "You will need these," it said, and tossed them to the ground.

"The knife is all." Tope walked to the belt, scooping it up and strapping it around his waist – all his knives were there, the cutting and the driving, the thin slivers of steel that he was adept enough with to unpick locks. The knives that had been tools of his bloody art, the ones he had used to kill the boy's father. "Yes, the knife is all."

At least for a little while longer.

A door opened, another figure appeared, or perhaps it was the same one, because when he turned there was no one behind him. "This way, this way." It gestured through the door.

Tope was led through the city. Saw those wonders up close, the mechanisms that bound it, and it was the most beautiful thing he had ever seen, and he was a part of it. Wherever he went he would take it with him.

An iron ship waited at the city's heart – the first less than beautiful thing he had seen, though it possessed an undeniable elegance – a door in its belly opened, and Tope stepped through it. The ship was ringed in seats: all taken, but the one closest to the door. Tope sat down in it. The ship shuddered, and began to rise. Windows – that Tope guessed were a vestige of when this ship might have been designed for humans – opened like eyes. The Dreaming City fell away. He felt the acceleration push at him, a weight against his chest.

"How long?" he said.

Eight hours until the city is reached.

Tope closed his eyes, and dreamed of killing the boy, and finishing his job.

CHAPTER 41

We never developed an adequate defence against the iron ships. Fortunately their production must have required certain rare elements, for no more than fourteen seem to have been produced. But even that was an adequate number to conquer a world; there wasn't much of it left.

Machineries, GASKELL & SLIGHT

THE OUTER WALL OF TEARWIN MEET
2100 MILES NORTH OF THE ROIL

Buchan and Whig waited at the base of the tower. Their airship, the *Collard Green*, bobbed hard against her lines, though she was in no danger of striking herself against the jagged wall. Watson was too good a pilot for that.

Whig was dressed in so many layers that he almost looked as big as Buchan. He slapped David on the back, hands thick with several pairs of gloves.

"You did it," Whig said. "You got us here."

"With a little help from the pilots, thank you," Kara said. Watson – who stood by the *Collard*, checking the lines to see that they were secure – grunted. David couldn't help but smile.

"What?" Kara said. "It's bloody true."

She was shivering.

David realised they were all shivering, except him.

"You lot," Buchan said, "time to get under cover. We'll die out here."

Near the base of the wall was a sort of overhang. Their men had set up a perimeter facing the landscape of ice and stone. The stones were frangible and layered. They crumbled underfoot. David knew that this was why the single continent was called Shale. It had been the first thing those first people had seen, fields of rough stone in every direction, shale as unwelcoming as the dark between the stars.

There was little wind though, this low down. The sea could be heard clearly here. David could all too easily imagine all that bristled stone toppling over. He tried not to think about it too much, there was nowhere else for them to go, except over those walls. David considered the final minutes of his father's life, the time when David had to choose to run or to die. He'd chosen flight then, but had never expected it to lead to here.

"What's done is done," he said.

Margaret smiled darkly at him. "I know what you mean," she said.

Of course you don't, David thought, but he smiled back. They were here, he could reach out and touch the wall of Tearwin Meet – if he wanted it to tear open the flesh of his palm.

"I'm sorry," David said. "We'll leave before morning. But I'm still not quite ready."

"When will you ever be ready?" Margaret said.

"When I do this," David said. "I don't know if there will be much of me left. When we cross that wall, and descend into the city, I don't know if it will be me that does it, or if it will be me that will come back."

"The Engine transforms everything, but so does the Roil," Margaret said. "We've made our choice, we've settled on a side."

David wasn't sure he had, but he nodded his head.

The air was salt-sharp and stinging, and it felt like just breathing could cut.

He felt Cadell's memories, too – of a childhood here, staring out at all that grey stone.

Shale's beginning had been difficult, and cold. And so had Cadell's, but he had grown strong, and ageless, and the city had spawned twelve metropolises.

It seemed appropriate that whatever rebirth the world would have would begin here.

David glanced over at Margaret, as they walked beneath the overhang. "We will do this soon. Before the dawn," he said. "I promise you."

She nodded, but David could see the anger there. After all, she had been the one that had yearned for this moment. David had only been driven to it.

"So, what must be done?" Buchan asked. The big man wiped map powder from his nose; they'd been considering the one map of Tearwin Meet they possessed. David had refused the powder, the map itself was so folded and old that the creases had become shadow roads and buildings: it was too easy to get lost in them.

Besides, the map powder only made him crave Carnival more.

"You've never told us what we can do once we were here."

David shook his head. "I never told you because I wasn't sure. I still don't know. It may be as simple as turning a switch, but I doubt it. The one thing that I am certain of is that the rest I need to do alone – well, with Margaret's company. I don't think she would ever let me enter Tearwin Meet without her," David said.

"You can't expect us to," Buchan blustered. "We have come all this way."

"What I expect you to do is let me finish this. Margaret will be coming with me, she is all I'll need."

"I could send my crew with you. Whig and I, we could–"

"And they would die, and you would die. I couldn't protect them, and in there they would need protecting."

Buchan wiped at his nose, David thought the big man might be about to cry. "After all that chasing, all that rushing to your aid, and we are no use."

David tried not to smile. "You saved us from the Old Men, you escorted us here. You've done all you need. All that can be expected of you. And I did not come here just so that you should die, or worse, get in the way, and kill us too."

"So we sit here and wait?"

"No," David said. "Not exactly." He pointed to the overhang. "You wait beneath that."

"It's dark in there," Buchan said.

"Yes, but it's warm. When the Engine is engaged, there will be no safer place, you should survive here."

"Should?" Buchan asked.

"Might, should, won't – I don't know," David snapped. "There are no guarantees any more. We are here. We have made it, and that is all. And that is all we have to understand." David realised that he was shouting.

Buchan took a step back. "Then you can tell the damn pilot."

"Of course," David said, and he got to his feet.

Watson Rhig sat beneath the shade of his gondola. He smoked a pipe, offered some to David, who declined.

"Not my poison," he said.

Rhig laughed. "No, I would imagine that it isn't."

"You flew well," David said.

"I'm a good pilot," Rhig answered. "Not such a good compatriot. You know I was meant to take you back to the Underground."

"Why didn't you?"

"I guess the question is: how could I? Let me tell you, David, that your aunt is safe, and Medicine Paul; well, they were when I left them. That should be some comfort to you." Rhig gave his pipe a good hard knock, stuffed it with some new tobacco, tamped it down, and took his time as pilots do. "I saw what you and the girl did to those Old Men. Knew that I had no choice but to throw in with you lot. If anyone is capable of surviving Tearwin Meet, I'd imagine it's you."

"You think we can do this?"

The pilot lit his pipe with a match, and puffed a moment. "I know you can, Mr Milde. And if you can't, then it wasn't possible in the first place." He smiled. "And yes, I'll move the *Collard Green* under that damn overhang."

CHAPTER 42

Without good leadership, pride, a sense of destiny, and a little fear, a city will fail. A city will fall. As long as we keep strong, keep to our purpose, keep to my purpose, we will not succumb as the other cities have.

Should we falter, then we will all die.

Brute & Noble Governance, MAYOR STADE

MIRRLEES-ON-WEEP
ROIL EDGE

Another bad day.

Business had been non-existent this last week. The city was emptying out, deflating like a burst tire. After the Chapman disaster everyone was heading north, most had already gone weeks ago with Mayor Stade's fleet.

It was the Grand Defeat all over again, only this time much worse. There was little hope that the people of Hardacre would greet them with open arms. Stagwell Matheson had considered leaving but there was nowhere else to go, even if his staff had decided otherwise.

The door remained open only out of habit. No one had

walked through it the last two days, and he doubted any customers would again.

At least the rain had stopped, as ominous as that was; the sun, even hazed with what people told him were Roil spores, was cheering. Though what the sun revealed was less so. The months of constant rain had scarred the city and there was no one left to heal it. The air stank of sewage and dead things and while the rain had hidden such smells – or at the very least dulled them – the sun lifted them up, seemed to take a delight in their acrid pungency.

And at night, and during the day, there could be heard always a distant screaming. And sometimes the sky grew slick and black with the Cuttle messengers. When that happened he kept inside his shop.

Once a Quarg Hound had passed by, its wide eyes taking everything in. It had yapped out something that might have been a kind of warning, and then it had bounded away. Stagwell had watched it all from behind his counter.

There were whispers of a sickness, a spreading madness; that people were not to be trusted. And while there had always been sicknesses, fevers and chills, such was the nature of modern city life, this was an altogether different thing.

The city had been left to the insane. So while he had not had any customers that day, Stagwell found some comfort in the solitude. The few people he had had in the bookstore over the past week had become increasingly desperate or desperately odd. Many times now he had locked the front door, and hid behind the shelves, rather than let some oddly shambling man or woman enter the shop.

Stagwell dusted the biography section, the presence of these collections of lives – simplified and analysed – calming him. At least here was something solid and unchangeable.

The shop jolted, a sudden terrible spasm. Mayor Stade's *Brute and Noble Governance* fell to the floor, his stern face staring up, and Stagwell almost tumbled down with it. The beams in the ceiling groaned and the building had another petit mal.

He ran to the front of the shop and stuck his head out the door. There were few people on the street and of those that were, fewer remained upright.

The earth quaked again, and Stagwell watched it ripple towards him along the street. He clutched desperately at the door frame and managed to keep his footing. Inside the store, shelves juddered and books crashed to the floor.

His line of sight extended down Main Street and where it ended on Harris Heights, across the River Weep. The earth rippled again and the ground flexed, then bubbled, and the air twisted and grew black with wreckage and broken buildings. A great fiery hand burst through the earth and with it fire and stone struck the sky, shooting up and arcing down. The nearby River Weep hissed, and steam crowded the air – and something else with it that was smokey and flitting. And that something was racing down the street, fanning out, hunting. People screamed, or laughed, or screamed and laughed – and fell down, before they rose on limbs shaky at first, but gripped with a new purpose.

From the top of Ruele Tower, something flared with a great cold light. The air chilled, the smoke fell from the sky, and the hand shuddered and dropped, smashing back through the earth. A bomb, some sort of miniature Engine of the World, Stagwell guessed.

Snow fell, the air chilled.

He rushed inside, but he wasn't the only thing that had fled the cold. Darkness rushed towards him on tiny dusty wings.

All he felt was relief, stronger even than the pain. Relief that it was all over, that he did not need to worry about what to do, that he did not need to care.

A hot old voice whispered in his skull, and suddenly Stagwell Matheson was laughing and getting matches and setting all those tumbled books alight.

By midmorning the retail sector was blazing, by that afternoon the whole city burned, and the sky was dark with ash and smoke.

And thus, before the Roil was even a smudge on the horizon, was the old city of Mirrlees-on-Weep finally taken.

But it wasn't without cost to the Roil.

The Witmoths, the nerves along which the Roil strung its thought, knew for perhaps the first time in twenty years a setback. And though there was no one there to see it, the Roil felt it nonetheless.

The currents beneath the earth were strong and deadly even to Vastkind, but deadlier still was the land above. Each time it burst through the earth, that cruel void, so absent of pressure, threatened to tear it apart. It sank down, stunned and wounded by the upper world, by the cold thing that had flared in the sky.

Down. Down. Into the rushing heart and heat of the world.

Above the surface was a universe of which it desired no part. The forces were too soft, hardly forces at all, and its mind – so attuned to the ebb and flow of electromagnetic fields – could feel the emptiness, the thinning out. And it reacted to it in horror and agony one final time.

Let the chattering children play out their game.

Such pain drowned out their commands – her commands

– and slowly, it sank back into the mantle: all glorious heat, all glorious pressure.

It sank and it dreamed its stony terrible dreams again.

The iron ships streaked across the sky. Six of them, though three turned to the east before the dawn, travelling somewhere that Tope did not know. Drift or Stade's precious Underground, perhaps.

The other three followed precise coordinates, the fastest flight path to Tearwin Meet – and toDavid and the girl Margaret, to whom Tope felt a perverse paternal instinct, that, even as he knew it was not his own, had become almost as strong as that hatred he had possessed for decades. He struggled with the battling desires, the beating warmth, the chill disregard. He knew that if he did not possess that first command – to kill the boy, to crush out what it was that hid within the addict's blood – then this new love would destroy him, would tear him open and make something so different that he would not recognise it at all.

He sat, face still, not moving a muscle. A belt was stretched tight across his chest, and the ship's acceleration pushed him into the chair, a hand as certain and as strong as the Roil within him.

The fiery ball missed the first ship, streaked right over it and crashed into the second. It disappeared in a series of bursts, bundles of fire and flame knitted together with strands of smoke.

Tope didn't even blink, as one last great explosion tore through the sky.

Twice more they were fired upon. Neither ship was struck, and their companion's wreckage became a ruddy blur on the horizon. A second barrage occurred an hour later and another iron ship fell, smoking and broken to the earth, landing with a boom that never quite caught up with Tope's iron ship.

He watched the ruin of that craft fade into the distance and wondered if he would live to strangle David after all.

They were fired upon at hourly intervals, but this time the ship seemed prepared, or the weapons weren't, because they managed to evade the flames. And when an hour and a half had passed since the last burst of flames, the iron ship slowed, mountains grew curled and cruel out of the earth, and a wall almost as high, and Tope knew that they had arrived.

CHAPTER 43

The Engine. Even now I cannot say that I understand it. What a marvel it was, and what marvels were we to have made something so far beyond us.

Engines, DEIGHTON

THE OUTER WALL OF TEARWIN MEET
2120 MILES NORTH OF THE ROIL

Margaret took the last guard duty. She'd had an evening teeming with dreams of the Roil, Tate and its fall, or worse, a Tate unchanged, but empty of everyone but her, a city driven by clockwork – like her father's great Orrery that had mapped out the expansion of the Roil. And that clockwork had hunted her.

She was relieved to escape to the chill monotony of peering beyond the overhang – no one seemed to be sleeping – as though only bad dreams walked these stony fields. Buchan nodded at her over a steaming cup of tea, gestured at her to come and talk, but she shook her head. She wanted to be alone.

Margaret looked at the curving wall, spikes jutting from

its surface. For all that it was constructed on a scale beyond anything she had ever seen before, it reminded her of the Steaming Vents of Tate. She wondered if it would prove to be a similar draw to the agents of the Roil.

Death lay ahead; she felt it in her bones. It had trailed her from the moment she'd heard the ringing of the bells that had signalled her parents' return, and then, somehow, it had overtaken her. But now, at last, she headed towards it directly.

Death, whether the city welcomed them or not, how else could it be anything but death? Perhaps she had never really been hunted by it, perhaps she had been hunting it instead, a great and glorious death that would take the whole world, too.

The wind had stopped some time ago, but it somehow felt colder. She looked into a sky as clear as glass, and bright, despite the twin moons having set an hour before. The stars were cold and distant. Instructive, she thought, in that a greater darkness bound them and that they burned, for all their multitudes alone.

She thought about Cam, felt a sliver of guilt, and hoped that the pilot was safe. Margaret thought of her kisses again, was stung by the memory, and her yearning. She let herself circle the memory, as the *Dawn* had circled Tearwin Meet. It was a good simple hurt, and she had too few of those.

At that moment she wanted everyone to die, and everyone to live; she wanted doom and joy in equal measure, and the cold dark, filled with the distant rumble of the icy sea, seemed to offer that.

She laughed, the sound startling her, and stared again across the dark and rocky plain.

"What a lonely world we save," she whispered into the night. "But what else is there?"

There was no answer, of course, but she found something in the cold places of her heart. And if the answer was
unsatisfying, still it was an answer. She pulled her coat
around her shoulders and watched the night.

David found her a few hours later, while Buchan and
his crew were still sleeping.

"Time to go up," he said.

"Should we wake Buchan and Whig?"

David shook his head. "Let them sleep, who knows, it
could all be over before breakfast."

Kara Jade was already with her Aerokin. The *Dawn*
stirred, shifting her body heat, breaking ice from along her
spine. Coffee brewed in a great pot and Kara passed them
both hot mugs of the stuff, black as the sky. Margaret
curled her hands around the mug, and smiled.

"Enjoy it," Kara said. "There's not much left."

Margaret took a mouthful – it was good and strong and
warm, and she suddenly realised just how cold she had been.

"So, this is it?" Kara said.

There was an excitement in the air, even Margaret could
feel it.

David smiled at Kara. "Yes, it is."

The *Dawn* shivered, more ice sloughed from her flesh,
and suddenly they were in the air. Ten feet, twenty.

"Going to be a slow rise. Are you sure you wouldn't
rather just get drunk?" Kara said. "I've plenty of rum for
that coffee."

"We'll leave that for when we're done," Margaret said,
and Kara laughed.

"I will hold you to that," she said.

Margaret looked down. Whig and Buchan stood below,
holding torches, waving them at the sky; they looked so

alone down there, they could have been the last two men in the world. And she was reminded of the last time that they had left them by fleeing in the *Pinch*. Margaret found herself waving back, feeling a little stupid as she did so. When she stopped, she realised that Kara was looking at her, the smile on her face unreadable.

"You're all sorts of surprises," Kara said.

Margaret put on her cold suit as they rose, stripping and redressing quickly, as though she were a gun to be broken and remade again. There was still a small charge left to the suit, though she didn't activate it. She slid her clothes over it; her greatcoat she slipped into her bag, too dangerous to descend wearing that.

David could see the dark material of the suit jutting out at the wrists. He looked at her. "What are you doing wearing that? Where we're going it will be cold, colder than cold."

"It keeps me warm enough when it's not activated. I left Tate in this suit, and I will finish what I set out to do while dressed so."

"Fair enough," David said. "Though if you expect me to take some Carnival, I will have to disappoint you."

"You take Carnival, and I'll cut your throat."

"I'd expect nothing less from you," David said.

The *Dawn* stopped at the top of the rocky wall. The wind was building, just the first few gusts, but there was the promise of more. Far to the east, the sea glowed with the coming sun. The *Dawn* stayed steady, absolutely still, as though asserting her mastery over the sky. Margaret slipped her empty mug into the small sink at the back of the gondola, stared at it a moment.

Her gaze fell upon the east, and she wondered if they need

perhaps wait for the sun to rise – that starting without seeing it one last time was wrong. After all, she had known so few sunrises, didn't she deserve this last one? There was something so right in the idea that she opened her mouth to suggest it.

But David spoke first. "Are you ready?"

She nodded and he passed her a great coil of rope, the thin strong stuff of the *Roslyn Dawn*, grown by the ship herself. He had another looped around his shoulder.

"Yes," she said, and walked to the doorifice, it opened and the cold rushed in, such bitter terrible cold. Her fingers ached at once, her lungs seemed to constrict and burn.

"It will be warmer below," David said, touching her back gently. The coldness of him seeped through, she pulled away from his touch. "Not much, but a little."

Not for you, she thought. "All the more reason to do this quickly."

"Good luck," Kara said.

"You too." David kissed her gently on the cheek.

Kara hugged him tight, then did the same to Margaret, and Margaret surprised herself by letting her. "How will I know if you succeed?"

"You'll know," David said. "The world itself will draw a mighty breath. You hear that, you take cover."

Kara looked at Margaret. "Keep each other safe."

Margaret wanted to say that there was nothing safe in what they did. Instead she nodded, and leapt out through the doorifice and onto the edge of the wall.

David followed, landing lithely. He crouched on the narrow walkway, a hammer in hand, and drove an anchor into the wall. Three hard blows and it was done, to his apparent satisfaction.

Already the *Dawn* was sliding away and down, and

already the dawn was breaking the horizon, a light washing over an icy sea. And so Margaret saw the sunrise as she'd wished. Somewhere distant a sea creature let out a cry at once mournful and triumphant, and Margaret knew how it felt. Another night survived, another day to endure, the world had yet to grind it down.

The wind grew then. It pulled at her hair, and her great-coat, and snatched the sound away.

David grinned at her, and she grinned back at him.

He locked a karabiner into place, then played out the weighted line, down, down, down.

He sighed, and in a voice more Cadell than David declared, "The last time we used rope, it didn't go so well at all. And yet, here we are."

Margaret nodded, hardly listening, looking down at the city below, and the webwork of razor-sharp cold wire that protected it. For a moment, all she could think of was Tate, and its network webs and wireways.

"It's like going home," Margaret said.

"For both of us, eh," David said, though Margaret could tell there was little of David here.

"Shall you go first?" David said. "You'll be safe, just don't venture too far from the wall."

Margaret clipped her harness and her line onto the rope, and let gravity do what it always did. Within moments, as the muscles in her arms and legs worked at the wall, she felt herself grow warmer. She looked up; already David was a dot on the wall.

She dropped in leaps and bounds, and it was like she was back on the wireway. Ice shards fell with her, and she knew that she would have to get well away from the wall when she reached the bottom, or David was likely to kill her with the ice he'd bring down.

When she reached the bottom, she yanked on the rope three times; then ran from the wall, finding cover a few yards distant. She took her weapons carefully from her bag, checked their charges, and waited for David to descend.

And ice fell, such a rain that anything within the city surely knew that they were coming and would be waiting. She looked at her guns and her blades. She was ready, too.

When he made it down, he grinned a great grin: part delight, part terror. "Made it." He looked past her shoulder, at the city beyond. "Finally," he said. "Finally."

Tearwin Meet drowned in the shadow of its walls. The sounds of ice sheets cracking echoed all around them. Tearwin Meet itself was no more than a mile in diameter, as wide as it was high. The tower that was their destination sat squarely in the heart of the city. And down here on the ground, Margaret couldn't see the tower, but for the occasional glimpse, between this tower and the next.

She had to rely on David, that he knew what he was doing. But with every step into the city, it was as though a wall was rising between them, and like the Engine's tower, she was only catching glimpses of David.

The buildings that lined the streets were tall, some ran to thirty stories, many were linked by narrow walkways, further reducing the light. Awnings stretched out from each building – they seemed at odds with the great structures from which they sprang, but Margaret could imagine tables laid out beneath them, people eating and laughing. People had lived here once, before the Engine had driven them away.

It looked to be a simple thing to walk to the heart of the city, but within that half-mile was a network of ring roads and dead ends, of roads sinking beneath the earth and rising again back at the wall, having curled without them even noticing. It was a maze as complicated as the Engine of the World itself.

But it was a maze that David said he understood.

"We follow the path laid out for us. We always do," David said. "When we reach the tower, there will be a door at its base. We need to find that door."

"And what do we do then?" Margaret said.

David's eyes widened, and then he gave her a condescending smile, and patted her arm. "We step through it, of course, Miss Penn. Because that is what doors are for."

Something snuffled in the distance. Margaret pulled her rifle from beneath her coat, but whatever it was, it did not reveal itself.

David looked towards the sound. "Let it be," he said. "It will not attack unless it perceives us as a threat. That gun looks rather threatening, wouldn't you say?"

"It's meant to look threatening," Margaret said.

Again that blasted smile.

"We need to hurry," David said.

And the road dipped, and led them into darkness, though David's Orbis glowed in the dark with a feverish light. The shadows around them grew long and danced, and it was suddenly very easy to believe in ghosts. Twice Margaret fired at what she took to be movement, but was only the flickering reflection of the ring.

"Calm down," David said, after she had wasted another round. "We are not threatened. Not yet. I will let you know when we are."

They came back out into the light again, and found themselves at the base of a low hill, though the road did not directly lead to the tower, they could see it up ahead.

● ● ● ●

They heard the iron ship's approach as a thunderous drone, a ceaseless noise that they recognised almost at once. Ice showered from the walls behind them.

David's eyes widened. "No, they couldn't."

But they had. She had. Margaret knew who had sent this ship.

It crashed down at them, through the protective web-work, metal snapped and screamed, iron tore with the sounds of a million metal teeth grinding and scraping. And the ship itself did not stay together, but detonated overhead.

David stood there, watching it all.

"Cover now," Margaret said, throwing David towards the nearest of the awnings. Shrapnel fell.

A second craft shot through the opening, though it made it further before detonating. Then a final iron ship crashed down. This one passed overhead, and was gone from sight. The earth shook with what Margaret assumed was its landing.

"The bloody things cleared a path for it," David said. "They'll be on us in a few minutes."

Margaret looked at the tower: at all she had fought for. "Then we'd best run," she said. She pushed David in front of her. "Go, find us the way. I'll be right behind you."

And David ran. Margaret primed her weapons. Whatever was coming, whatever her mother had sent, she would be ready for it.

CHAPTER 44

So Stade lived to see his life's work realised. That was a gift, you could say, and a punishment. I would feel sorry for him, but really, the man cut off my fingers. He deserved everything that he got.

Maybe we all did.

Confluent, MEDICINE PAUL

THE MIRRLEES AIR FLEET
DISTANCE FROM ROIL VARIABLE

Stade stood in the radio room, hunched next to the nervous radio operator. The poor man had had only bad news to report until now. They had received at last a signal from the Underground. In Stade's darkest hours, he had grown to believe that they had travelled all this way and at such dire cost for nothing. And now, as they travelled within a few miles of the mountain that contained the Project, he'd been vindicated.

"We can see you," a voice murmured over the radio.

Stade frowned. "As can we. Sam, is that you?" he said. "The bulk of the refugees will be at your gates within the hour. I'm afraid that we have the enemy behind us."

"You are not to approach," the voice said. "This is Grappel of the Underground, subsidiary of the free state of Hardacre. Our weapons are trained on you. You are not to approach."

"But I made this," Stade said. "All of it. I made this."

"Yes, you did," Grappel said.

The ships floated above the horizon. Thousands stood beneath them. And they had not moved for hours. Medicine and Grappel stood in the observation tower above the Underground.

"You have to let them enter," Medicine said.

"These people killed my family," Grappel said bitterly. "I owe them nothing but death."

"Those are my people, not soldiers, not your enemy. You can't leave them to die," Medicine pleaded. "They don't even understand what's happening. Please don't repeat the crime of my city. Not everyone supported Stade's stance, for many it was a dark time in history, a terrible time."

"And your people did nothing. The gates stayed closed to us, they trained their guns on us, and we marched. We marched into the north and so many of us died."

"But the Roil is approaching. You can't leave them there."

Grappel shook his head. "I can and I will."

"Think of them as what they are," Medicine said. "Workers. Enough people to make the Underground what it must be, the last stronghold of the world. You leave them out there, and all you are doing is giving the enemy more troops. They are not your enemy now, but they will be."

Grappel frowned, lifted a pair of field glasses and looked south. Behind them the horizon was darkening. He walked from the observation platform, and Medicine thought he had lost this argument, that his people were doomed.

A couple of hours later Grappel returned.

"Look," Medicine said. "If you won't let my people in, then let me out there. Let me die with them."

Grappel smiled. "You'd like that, wouldn't you? You are right. It doesn't sit well with me, but you are right. These people do not deserve to die, and we certainly do not deserve more enemies. There's a reason why I've elevated you, Medicine. Sometimes you talk sense.

"Let them in, though if one of those airships so much as dips towards the ground, shoot it down."

Grappel stood at the iron gates, flanked by his guard, as the Mirrlees folk began to enter.

There was a flash of steel and the first guard fell, but not before he grabbed the Verger and tumbled with him.

"Shut the doors," someone cried.

Medicine began to run to Grappel.

Then the second Verger rose above the crowd and hurled his knife at Grappel. The leader of the Underground crumpled.

Medicine reached Grappel and the Verger turned, another knife in his hands.

"Well, here I'm granted no small mercies," the Verger said. "First a rebel leader and now a Confluent traitor."

He pulled back his knife to throw it, then groaned, blood spilling from his throat, and fell to the ground. Grappel stood above the Verger, a bloody knife in his hand.

He looked at his guards. "Medicine is in charge. I transfer my powers to the cripple. It's the end of days, anyway, what does it matter!"

Then Grappel toppled and Medicine was calling medics, leading Grappel to his rooms, then sprinting back to make sure the refugees had entered and that there would be no recriminations. There was no time and too much to do. But later, he swore, they would hunt the Vergers down.

Outside, the refugees milled. They had nowhere to go.

"Get them inside now!" Medicine roared, thrusting his head through the portal, glaring out at the shadow approaching. He felt all the fear within him uncurl. And for a moment he stopped, and was certain that he would turn and run as deep into the mountain as he could go.

Instead, he ran down to the gates and began mobilisation of their heavy weaponry. The machinery already primed began its swift build to lethalness. Whatever happens, he thought, we will make them feel the cost of this conquest.

The Roil mass was already on the horizon and it raced towards them, but this Roil was different, it did not extend as far as the eye could see, east and west. It was a narrow band of dark, no wider than a mile, though that was wide enough. Above it floated huge airships, or creatures like Aerokin, from which were hung vast mirrors, and before it the ground blazed.

This was no scorched earth retreat, but a scorched earth assault. There was no secrecy now, neither his nor the enemy's. The word he'd been receiving – from the few spies they had left – suggested this was only a small finger of the Roil fuelled by these airship engines. In fact, it had broken off from the main body of the Roil, which remained on the outskirts of Mirrlees.

Medicine wondered if it had been Stade, bitter at the loss of his Underground, who had given the game away. Medicine would not have been surprised; he had left the Underground in disgust.

It was someone else who first saw the aircraft to the west of the Roil mass. A small fleet of airships: Mirrlees craft launching endothermic munitions into the guts of the darkness.

Even now, Stade was fighting to protect his refuge.

And then Medicine ordered the guns to be fired as the darkness came into range. And the ground shook as endothermic matter was launched into the Roil, punching holes in the darkness the size of houses, but the Roil did not halt in its progress, just kept up its march towards them.

The Underground doors opened and then, up out of the crowd, the Wit smoke lifted. Men calmly turned the hoses filled with icy water onto the crowd. All through the Roil mass, people fell screaming to the ground.

"In," Medicine shouted at those still standing. "The rest of you in."

"Damn it. Fire the cannon. Hurl ice out into the darkness," Stade roared. "I did not risk all to see the Underground fail, and should we live out this battle, then you never know, the bastards might yet let us in."

The first barrage struck a Vermatisaur, sluggish this far north of the Roil. It crumpled and fell from the sky.

The whole crew cheered.

And then the iron ships came and launched their fire into the *Daunted Spur*'s great target of a balloon and gas cells ignited, raging in all that horrible heat.

And Stade fell with his ship, burning.

"Fire at the mirrors," Medicine yelled. "They drive it on. Strike them from the sky!"

The cannons fired. One after another, blasting the huge mirrors. And as they tumbled dreadfully from the sky, the Roil itself began to diminish.

"Now, into the Roil. Into the Roil with everything we have."

And all at once a hundred cannons fired ice and snow, and all manner of state-of-the-art endothermic matter – and the Roil stopped its forward progress.

Medicine allowed himself a smile.

"We might yet hold onto this place. We might yet have a chance," he said.

CHAPTER 45

Big Engines and little, that's what it comes down to. That is what we have lost, the little and the big. And why did we lose them? I would gather that the answer is simply this: The little and the big are difficult things to hold onto. Think of sand, think of something finer than sand, it would slip through fingers no matter how tightly it was grasped. And how does one hold a world? It would take more than gloves and a large stick to do it properly. How could one do it and remain human? We are human and thusly we did not.

The Engine of the World, DEIGHTON

TEARWIN MEET
2120 MILES NORTH OF THE ROIL

Something howled from behind them, David jumped (was this what it was like, to feel engaged, to feel threatened by the world? He missed his Carnival!). The street behind was empty, well, the part they could see. Though David could see another street, crowded with memories; he blinked and they were gone.

"Stop doing that," he whispered, and for once Cadell seemed to listen. "Can't see it," he said more loudly.

The Quarg Hounds had been hunting them, drawing closer, as they'd made their slow way up the streets of the frozen city. The central tower felt no nearer.

"It's not quite close enough yet," Margaret said.

Margaret slipped a rifle from her back and handed one of her pistols to David, who handed it right back.

"I don't need it. Why let me waste bullets?"

Another howl, closer.

"Get ready," she said, so calmly that David almost resented her. Even now, even with all that he had become, the sound held terror for him. Dragged him back to the *Dolorous Grey* and his woozy flight from the Hounds, made his bones grow spiky with fear, and lit the spark of all too recent memory.

And now he no longer had Carnival to keep it at bay. He closed his shaking hands into fists.

Something broke free of the nearby shadows, claws clattering on the ice, heavy enough that they pierced it with each footfall.

The creature was made of ice, around machinery of some sort. David recognised it at once, a Mechanism of the Engine. It snarled at them and Margaret swung her endothermic rifle towards it. David grabbed her wrist, half expecting her to drive her elbow into his throat. She nearly did.

"That's not going to do much good now, is it?" he said. "The damn thing's made of ice. Besides it's on our side, sort of."

Margaret hissed at him, but lowered her weapon.

The Mechanism ran towards them, and crouched as though to leap. David lifted his hand, the Orbis flared and the Mechanism stopped, though its icy jaws clamped open and shut, and its limbs juddered.

"It's all right," David said, and walked towards it.

Its great head shuddered a moment, then lowered. David reached out and touched its brow, and the Mechanism let him. It was cold to the touch, like him. He remembered these creatures now, remembered the great packs of them that had circled the city, fighting Quarg Hounds.

"Cadell," a voice whispered in his skull. "The Old Man returns."

"I know you," David said, and the guardian made a deep rumbling that might have been a laugh.

Margaret stared at him, her rifle pointed at the creature's skull. David shook his head.

"It remembers me. Trust me, it will ensure our safe progress through the city," David said.

Something howled from behind them, as loud as a pistol shot, and Margaret and David turned towards the sound, almost colliding with each other in the process.

The Mechanism turned its head slowly, regarding the street behind them with heavy eyes.

This time Margaret fired her rifle.

The Quarg Hound was unlike anything David had ever seen: part animal, part machine. He knew at once that it had not been born, but made from a motley of living things and components. A Roil-beast engineered for the cold. Sheathed in iron, the Quarg Hound shook off the ice pellets, its huge eyes narrowed.

"Wasting my bullets there, too," Margaret said petulantly, though she kept her gun raised.

The Mechanism leapt past them and crashed into the metal Hound, David stood and watched as the two monsters struggled, rolling and thrashing, jaws clamped around each other's throats.

The Mechanism slammed the Quarg Hound hard against the nearest wall. The concrete cracked, and the Hound whimpered. Steam crashed from it, black blood spilled, and the Mechanism let the corpse drop from its jaw.

Then the Mechanism turned towards David, and he could see where it had been injured: a long wound ran along the side of its face.

Another Hound howled in the distance, and another. They appeared.

"Run," the Mechanism said. "Run. I will do what I can."

It shook itself once, and ice spilled from its great back. And then the Quarg Hounds were upon it, snapping and snarling and dancing.

"Time to go," David said.

Margaret didn't argue.

Into the heart of the city they sprinted, along wide streets, far too wide – so that they felt exposed, their backs an all too easy target for whatever might be following them, be it Quarg Hound or Roiling, or a Mechanism whose programming had gone wrong. The general direction they followed, the one that David's fragmented memory suggested, led them further uphill. And twenty minutes later, they found themselves much higher up, and closer to the central tower, its top gleaming with its mother-of-pearl brightness.

Margaret didn't like leaving herself so totally in another's hands; not that she didn't trust him, just that she felt useless, even that she might be slowing him down.

Several times he had stopped, turned left or right, rather than straight ahead, whispering, "Too dangerous for the both of us" or "They'll never let two through here."

It seemed that there were many ways to reach the heart of the city. Margaret wondered if they weren't taking the fastest, but the safest. David had stopped again. To catch his breath, he said, and here they had a clear view of the area that they had already travelled.

From this elevated position Margaret, with the aid of her field glasses, could see back the way they had come. The ice beast lay there, a flopping mass of metal, greasy with fluid, and behind it she could see a single Roiling.

A man, broad in the shoulders, strode across the ice, too distant to make out. Though there was something familiar about the Roiling. A little part of Margaret chilled at the sight of the figure, her lip curled. This wasn't like the lumbering mad things she had encountered at Chapman. Its steps were purposeful, and she knew its purpose was her and David.

"Roiling," she said.

David smiled at her. "Then it's a good thing that we're almost there."

They sprinted now. Around another corner and another, and David started almost to run. "We're nearly there," he said. "Nearly there. Around this bend, we'll come to a doorway."

And they did, they came upon the tower at last.

David laughed. "See! See!"

"I see," Margaret said.

And the door stood there, at the base of the tower. Such a tiny door, with no handle or keyhole, but a door nonetheless.

"So how do we–"

The Quarg Hound barrelled out at them from the shadows, knocking David to the ground, and leaping onto her, so that she fell upon the flat of the rime blade – the movement activating it and burning her back with cold.

The beast snapped at her neck. Margaret reached into a pocket, her fingers closing over the lozenges of Chill. She grabbed as many as she could, swift as her hands would let her. The Quarg Hound stretched its jaws wide and Margaret threw the Chill into that dark maw. Its eyes blinked, pupils expanding until they looked like they might burst, and then it shook its head, and gagged. It rolled from her, making that dreadful gagging noise, loud enough to deafen her, and its mechanisms whined. Then it dropped to the ground, stood up and dropped to the ground again.

Margaret got to her feet, unsteady, the ice-sheathed sword now in her hand, watching.

When the Quarg Hound was finally still, Margaret ran to it and struck off its head with her rime blade. Three hard blows it took through armour and bone and muscle, and she howled as she did it. And then, when the head had fallen to the ground, she threw the dark mass away, ichor raining from the mouth and neck, down the street.

"Let them know they've failed," she said, turning to David.

"Maybe they'll stop coming," he suggested.

"No, they'll never stop. Which is why we came here. They'll never stop until we're dead and they're dancing around in our corpses."

And then the door opened, light spilled out.

David stood there as if mesmerised. Margaret fancied that she saw a figure beyond the door. She took a step towards the light, and David stopped her.

"You can't go through here," David said. "I'm sorry, I don't think Cadell wanted me to remember that, until now."

Margaret looked at him, almost brought the blade to his throat. They had come this far, and she couldn't go through.

"I've just felt it," David said. "A memory, a warning. You can't come through this doorway. It will kill you. It's a final trap, a test you see. It will only recognise an Old Man."

A Quarg Hound bounded around the corner, its great

eyes narrowed. Margaret could hear another approaching. David walked beside her.

"We can take them," he said.

Margaret smiled. "I don't doubt it, but it's too risky."

She looked down at her weapons. Checked their charges, more than enough to do what was needed. They backed closer and closer to the entranceway.

"Go through the door now," she hissed. David opened his mouth to speak, but Margaret wouldn't let him. "We're not here for ourselves. Go, boy. Leave me to this, because I cannot do what you must. Believe me, if I could I would, and there would be no hesitation."

Then his face hardened and he nodded. "Margaret, I–"

"Move!"

"I can't," David said. "I won't leave you here."

Margaret flashed her teeth at him, fired her rifle at the first Hound's head. It dropped on its arse, and clawed at its face. "I know what I'm doing."

And she had never felt wilder, or more confident.

He stood there looking at her. Margaret could tell David was struggling with Cadell inside him, the fool, to struggle so now: just because he had grown a spine. He moved to stand beside her. "I won't leave you," he said. "We fought the Old Men together, we survived the fall of Chapman."

"You damn well will," she said, and then she turned swift and smooth and kicked him hard in the stomach.

Not what David was expecting at all, obviously. He fell back through the door, and the door closed.

CHAPTER 46

Drift fell and faster than we could have feared. In the sky we had never felt threatened, had believed ourselves to be the threat. But we were so wrong.

The Sky is Falling, RAVEN SKYE

THE CITY OF DRIFTA
ROIL EDGE

The Caress shattered, broke into great shards of stone that rained death upon the city. Cannon fired all along Drift's walls, but the iron ships were too fast. Mother Graine counted eight of them, and even as she watched another three scarred the sky with their incendiary flight.

A hundred Aerokin guarded the skies, flagella clutching guns and incendiaries, but they were nothing compared to this. All they could do was fight and die. An iron ship was struck and it fell, diving into the woods, setting alight everything it touched. Trees that were hundreds of years old burned.

Mother Graine hurried along Mina Street. Raven waited for her in the training hall. Her students were there, a hundred or so nervous pilots. Their clan parents were in the sky.

"They want to fight," Raven said. "We all want to fight."

Mother Graine didn't know whether to laugh or cry at these children and their teacher, so desperate to meet their death. "No, the hangars are destroyed. The Aerokin within are dead."

"We must arm ourselves."

Mother Graine shook her head. "No. It's too late for that. Raven, you're going to have to take them deep into the Stone. You know what it's like to lose an Aerokin, and survive, and this is far worse. You have to show them how."

Raven nodded, then her eyes widened. "And where will you be?"

"I'll try and follow, believe me. But there are things that I must attend to," the lie came out of her mouth easily enough. "I must see to my sisters."

She left Raven to gather together the pilots, and as many others that still lived. She walked back up through the winding ways of the city, passing death and destruction. Helping where she could, though there was little that she could offer now.

She reached the broken stub of the Caress. Hoping that the lower levels remained intact, she opened a reinforced door. She came at last to a familiar set of stairs and then down, until she reached the room near the heart of Stone where her sisters were imprisoned. Graine could hear them within, crying out with a dark joy. Perhaps sensing her outside.

She still didn't understand how she had managed to escape while the others had been taken. Luck, perhaps; she was neither the most cunning, nor the most skilled at governance. She knew that she had made mistakes. But what else could she have done? There was no time for general elections, no chance to build confidences and allegiances, other than those she had had already in place. It didn't matter now. All of it was undone.

Graine stared at the panel set into the wall a long time.

"I'm sorry," she said, and then she pressed it, just so, fingers drawing out the right patterns. She felt the stirrings of a mechanism deeper within Stone, then a sudden rising chill. There was a sensation of vast energies at work, peculiar forces grinding soft and vast against each other. The stone shuddered, Stone shuddered. And she knew that all across the city of Drift, people would be pausing, listening, disturbed by the motion of energies old and ill understood, even by her. The reasoning behind most of their technology, the old grammars of science, had been lost to the Roil.

That's what happens when children rule. All of them, Mothers and Old Men alike, had been scarcely in their twenties when the Roil had come. Sure, Cadell had been a little older – proud and oh-so-strong – but what is a handful of years? Nothing when faced with what followed.

Her sisters screamed once, then were quiet.

She waited ten heartbeats, then opened the door; the room within was empty, wasn't even quite the same room.

All at once, she felt more alone than she had believed possible. She leaned briefly against the wall, and took a single deep breath.

Graine had seen the world shift and change beneath her. She had watched it expand, seen centuries of development as humanity and Cuttlefolk recovered from the Roil. But always she had watched at a distance. It was as though she had had two lives: one brief, a normal span, and then this endless passage of time. Well, it had never been endless; it was coming to an end now.

She turned and climbed the stairs again. At one point

she heard Raven and her charges descending. Graine took the next doorway, and hid until they passed. Her history and theirs was a different one now, and she didn't want to muddy its beginning with her presence, or find herself tempted to follow. She couldn't be a part of it. She had just killed her sisters. She didn't deserve to be a part of it.

She came out of the Caress through a different door, and walked the same path she had taken David along just a few days before. The grove of trees was almost completely alight, a great finger of flame, and smoke rising into the sky. Smoke hid Witmoths, and all around her were newly made Roilings.

Graine looked at the sky, then the corpses of her kin. Dead now. Motionless, until the Wit smoke found them, and she could not bear to think of that, it hurt her even more deeply than the loss of her sisters.

Punctured Aerokin tumbled screaming to the ground. Guns fired and were silenced. Men and women laughed the shrill mad laughter of the Roil.

She hurried through chaos to the edge of Drift, here, above the Peek, where the drop was steep, no rough spurs of Stone jutting out just the sky. Cold air rushed past her, tugged at her clothes.

And she stepped over the edge.

A Cuttle messenger snatched at her, caught her as she was falling. Witmoths boiled from its mouth; she reached up, hands burning with the heat of them, and snapped the creature's neck. Its wings stopped, though its limbs tightened around her.

Down, they tumbled, spinning over and over. And the moths flew around her, but the air was cold and they fell so fast.

The fall was a long one, just as her life had been long, but nothing is forever; the earth found her in the end.

CHAPTER 47

That something so small should forge something so big is the paradox of Minnow technology. Minnows are tiny machines. Smaller than the eye can see, I swear it. There is no doubt that once they did exist and in such abundance that they built a world. Consider these, the Hour Glass of Carver, Mirrlees' Ruele Tower, the Bridges of McMahon, all our greatest municipal structures and they are as nothing to the power of minnows. Mechanical Winter was a minnow-constructed thing, just as is the Engine of the world. I have seen it all. Drunk on visions, I have seen it all.

The Engines of the World, DEIGHTON

THE ENGINE OF THE WORLD
DISTANCE FROM ROIL VARIABLE

The door closed in front of him. If David hadn't snatched his fingers from the door edge, they would have been cut off. As it was, it struck his head hard. He felt his nose break.

He stared into his own face, and the reflection of the cloud of dust his falling had unsettled.

Blood streamed from his nose, and dust coated the blood. I'm still here, he thought, Cadell's yet to–

Then his reflection smiled.

Not the sort of smile he even thought his face was capable of.

You got what you wanted, David thought. You've won.

"Didn't we both want this?"

He whipped his head around. A hundred Davids stared back at him with a hundred smug smiles. He fished in his pocket, yanked out a handkerchief and wiped the blood from his face. Blood disappeared a hundred times.

All he could hear was his own breathing loud in his head, his heart beating hard in his chest. Neither was amplified.

The air stank of ozone; it tasted of metal tangy as blood, or was that just his own blood, running down the back of his throat?

He stood there, dazed, uncertain of what he needed to do.

Shouldn't he know what to do?

He took a step forward, and the dust puffed up. All the Davids repeated the movement. He stopped, only this time one of the Davids reached out and took his hand.

"I'm sorry," the mirror being said, "but this is going to hurt."

He wasn't wrong.

David blinked; he didn't know how long he'd been on the floor. His tongue was swollen. He thought he might have bitten it, he couldn't remember. If someone had told him just then that he wasn't David, that he was someone else, he wouldn't have argued.

A hand touched his shoulder. This time there was no pain. David scurried forward, slid along the floor and rolled, hands bunched into fists; no one was going to stab him in the back.

Cadell smiled at him, that same smug smile David had seen reflected back at him.

"You're not dead, you know," Cadell said. "Death is quite unlike this, trust me."

"Then what am I?"

"You're all manner of possibility." Cadell gestured to a wooden bench beneath a tree of bone and cogs, on the edge of a great brass road that stretched into infinity.

"What is this place?" David asked.

"Convenient," Cadell said. "It is the world contained within the Orbis. The Great Brass Highway. It's the infinite folded in on itself. It's convenient."

Cadell looked up beyond David, frowned, bit at his lip. "Oh, I really thought I would have more time. Infinity, even compressed into a ring, is a rather a lot."

David turned. Saw the figure running towards them across some impossibly vast space.

"The Engine," David said.

"Yes, the Engine. Well, part of it." Cadell sighed. He almost looked embarrassed. "David, things aren't quite as you believed."

"What, we're not here to destroy the Roil?"

"No, not that. Only it isn't we. It's you."

"What?"

"I needed to get you here. Just you. I needed to make sure that you would survive the journey here and go through that door. But the rest is up to you. You and the Engine, of course."

"And you did this, why?"

"Because I had no choice. I never expected to die on the *Dawn*. Don't look at me like that, David. None of you people do, and me, I had even less reason to; after all, I had managed not to die for thousands of years. I'd been so good at not dying that I believed it couldn't happen. Well, I was wrong. I'd always meant to take someone here, just not you. After all, I'd promised Medicine that I would see you to safety, and I meant it."

"Why didn't you choose Margaret?"

"I meant what I said about her. I don't trust her. Perhaps I was wrong not to. But I couldn't be sure. Just be happy that I didn't kill her."

"So what do I do?"

Cadell opened his mouth to answer, and then he wasn't there any more.

"That's not his role," the Engine said. "That cannot be his role. He is gone. And you, the flesh and blood, remain. You have to choose."

The Engine moved sinuous and direct, not like ice, but something more fluid, light grown cool and slow.

"You've made it to me, David," it said. "You must be very pleased."

"My friend beyond the door. You have to let her in."

"I'm sorry, that's not how this works." The Engine shook a finger in his face. "We don't *have* to do that. We don't have to do anything. You've choices to make, and that isn't one of them."

"And if she dies…"

"She dies. She dies, and you can spend your life grieving for her. If you are capable of grieving for anyone."

"Let her in."

"No," the Engine said.

David opened his mouth, and the Engine slapped him hard. Knocked David down with the blow, lifted him back up.

"I could pull out your lungs before you opened your mouth to scream. There isn't time," it said.

David's head pounded with what he would have considered, before today, to be the most horrible headache possible. He wiped his face and his fingers came away sticky with blood, much more than last time: it spilled from his nose, his lips, and his ears. His clothes were covered in blood, and vomit. His whole body had become a bruise or a wound.

"I'm sorry," the Engine of the World said, helping him to his feet. "There isn't time to clean you up. There isn't much time for anything. You've done well to get here. Cadell did well to get you here, but that is not enough. This last great choice must be your own." It pointed to a cage that sat in the middle of the room, dark metal, hooked and barbed as the walls to Tearwin Meet had been.

David looked at that cage.

"I guess I have to go in there," he said.

The Engine nodded. "Most cages are a prison, this is a liberation. If you make the choice to enter it."

David took a deep breath. "I'm ready," he said.

"Are you? I think not. There is much you do not know, let me illustrate. The Witmoths are not of the Roil, at least, they weren't at first." The Engine paused. "David, this world was made with the raw matter of another. Minnow technology, microscopic machinery did the making. The Witmoths were just our most perfect creation. We designed them as a weapon to be used against the Roil itself, to link our troops more effectively, to bind them in strategy, and instead, it was absorbed, and after that the Roil began to think.

"There's all manner of secrets and secret histories and histories of secrets."

David pulled himself together, got unsteadily to his feet and stared dubiously at the cage.

"And what does that do?"

The Engine laughed lightly. "It engages me," the Engine said. "It releases all that I am. The memories in you and the memories in the ring."

"It releases Cadell again?"

"In a way, yes," the Engine said. "History is a very different thing in this world of ours, David. Not at all what you might expect of it. It bears a rather peculiar weight. Over and over the cities have been remade. The people rebuilt, the Roil beaten back. It is in this city that all your memories are stored, cleaned of all but a vague knowledge of the Roil, then returned to their cities – in bodies rebuilt by minnow machinery.

"It is history as a set of ever diminishing circles. Repeating and repeating, and I'm afraid to say, I don't think it can contract any more."

CHAPTER 48

Death was coming. Just no one knew how. Nor that it would be so pervasive. I remember those last days clearly, even before the earth began to shake and those last Roil machines came over the horizon, on their titanic legs, all rage and fire. There'd been a quality to the air, a light positively elegiac.

Doom Patrol: Nights and Mornings on the
Last Mountain, Ursula Madrigal

THE OUTER WALL
2098 MILES NORTH OF THE ROIL

Buchan and Whig sat around the fire, heads almost together, and Buchan's hands nearly touching the flame. They looked up at the dark walls that Margaret and David had crossed almost half a day ago. "All this effort, and here we wait outside," Buchan groaned. "Everything that we have done and once again, we're left waiting."

Whig patted his arm. "We made it this far, don't discount that. We saw the pair of them to the edge of the wall." He pointed at Kara, who sat hunched over, polishing her boots. She'd been polishing them since she'd brought the

Dawn back down. Polishing and polishing, not saying a word. Whig said, "It's much harder for her."

"But still, all this waiting."

"Quiet," Kara hissed.

"I did not mean–" Buchan said.

"I said, quiet. Another one's coming, an iron ship," Kara said; she ran from cover. "Fourth one today, and it's coming back."

Buchan and Whig followed her. They watched the ship curve around the valley, then shoot straight up into the sky. It dipped, then plummeted beyond the wall.

"That's it," Kara Jade said. "I'm going up there."

"And what are you going to do? David said to–"

"I don't remember David paying me to go on this expedition," Kara said, sliding her fingers into her gloves. "I'm a free agent. And they're my friends."

"But–"

She looked at Buchan significantly. "You want to come?"

Buchan shuddered. "No, we will guard the base of the wall. Just in case."

Kara cleared her throat, and spat on the ground. "Yes, just in case. I understand."

She strode across the gravel, boots gleaming in the red light of sunset. At the edge of the overhang, she turned, and this time there was no mockery in her expression. "Good luck, gentlemen."

"Be careful," Buchan said.

Kara laughed, loud and clear in the cool air. "If I was ever careful, ever cautious, I would never have come here, neither would you."

Buchan couldn't argue with that.

She was hardly free of the overhang when the ground shook, and ice tumbled from the great wall. A piece that was almost the size of her crashed to the stones nearby and shattered. Kara ducked back under cover as more pieces fell.

"Something's happening," Buchan said.

"You don't say," Kara said. "The Engine," she said, and her smile was wide, and grim. "It has to be."

"And you?"

"I'm still going up. Four iron ships, I reckon there's a path into the city."

The *Collard Green* had already been dragged into the darkness, but the *Roslyn Dawn* had refused to go into the dark, and Kara couldn't blame her. There was something ominous about that space beneath the wall despite its warmth. For all David's declarations that it was safe, it threatened her. Kara was of the sky, as much as her Aerokin. Wide open spaces welcomed her, but that dark, it was old; it seemed to know something and seemed ready to swallow her without hesitation – perhaps the stories that David had told about the Downing Bridge and its malevolent spiders had affected her more than she'd thought.

She folded her arms and walked back to the *Dawn*.

Buchan shouted after her. "Do you have a death wish, girl?"

Kara Jade smiled. "I think you have me confused with Margaret. The *Dawn* will keep me safe."

The *Dawn*'s doorifice was already opening. Kara could see Buchan's large form in the dark beneath the overhang, and could just make out Whig's slender figure behind him; touching his shoulder, talking to him quietly, no doubt, but with a strength that all Whig's conversations possessed.

She stroked the belly of her Aerokin. "Just you and me," she said.

The *Dawn* sighed, released her grip upon the earth and began to fly, rising high and fast. Outside it was cold and dead, but here, wrapped in such perfect life, Kara felt warm, she felt like she was home.

All alone in her *Dawn*. Finally alone – and never alone.

She couldn't help smiling. Death wish, no! This was all about life!

CHAPTER 49

There was desperation in those last moments. When things tipped over, and everything became mad, both sides did things that were... regrettable. Such is it at the ending of every war. How can forgiveness even be considered? Because it must be. Genocide is the only other option.

Compassionate Hatreds, STAFFORD ENWIN

TEARWIN MEET
2100 MILES NORTH OF THE ROIL

They were upon Margaret almost at once.

Her vision narrowed, grew focussed only on the moment: a weakness in the enemy, a break in defence, the turning of teeth or claw. Margaret was back in Tate – in that amphitheatre where she had been wounded, but never beaten.

She struck the first Quarg Hound in the neck, once, twice, and it fell dead. its blood mingled with the snow: a bloody ash.

The second Hound lashed out – and she was ready for it, ducking beneath its great claws, driving the chilled blade into its belly, pulling away as it fell on the sword; already swinging the other blade up and down, and onto its neck. The blade caught on armour, but she found her balance at once, struck down again, and watched the Quarg Hound's head drop to the ground.

She kicked it away, and heard footsteps behind her. She had spun around in her fighting, no longer had her back to the wall. She remedied that problem, turning on her heel and throwing a blade from her belt towards the sound.

A man there ducked. And the blade clattered off a wall.

"You," Tope said. "Where's the boy?"

"I know you," Margaret said. "You're too late. He's inside, the door is shut."

Margaret jabbed her rime blade at the two dead Quarg Hounds. "I killed these. Do not think of me as incapable of killing you."

"Oh, I know your capabilities. You and I, we are much the same, steeped in blood. Wouldn't you agree?" Tope slid his knife from its belt, his other hand gripping a pistol. "The boy now, he is something altogether different... undeserving."

"I don't care. He has made it to the Engine of the World. He has walked through the door. I've delivered the bomb, that is all I ever needed to do."

Margaret loosened her sword arm, swung the blade once, twice. Tope shot her in the stomach and she toppled to her knees, dropping the rime blade. She reached out towards it, her fingers touched the hilt. Tope gave her an almost sympathetic smile, and dragged the sword away from her.

"Miss Penn, people walk back through doors, too," Tope said. "And when he does, I will be here. I am a patient man."

Margaret went for a gun at her belt, and he shot her again. She fell on her side.

"That's the problem when you try and fight someone else's fight. This isn't between you and I, it never was. You think me cruel," Tope said. "And I am cruel, that's a Verger's remit, to be cruel when the rest of the world cannot. But this is given with love."

Margaret's world had shrunk to Tope. "Would you just shut up," she said.

Tope's lips pursed. He shook a finger at her, then lifted his arm higher. A dark spot on his wrist bubbled and spat. Skin tore free and from the wound a single moth detached itself, shaking out bloody wings. "See, I am also a bringer of gifts."

Margaret found some vestige of strength. She yanked her last gun from her belt, the wound in her belly tearing (though she did not scream), and fired, not at him – because he was right, this had never been between him and her – but the moth.

The shot went wide. The Witmoth, however, didn't. Margaret flung up her arms too late. It struck her face and slid with all the certainty of a death towards her eyelid. It was fluid and razor-sharp. It burned. She dropped her pistol, clawed at her face. Tope might as well not be there, the wound in her stomach did not exist, only this blazing pain.

"Hello, my darling. I'm bringing you home," her mother said, and Margaret felt such joy, the absolute happiness; she had a mother again. She struggled against the thought: it was a lie. A trap for her mind.

There was no pain. Tope was smiling almost beatifically at her.

Margaret stood up, almost toppled again. Gritted her teeth. "And what if I don't want to go?"

"You have no choice, my darling. None at all."

● ● ● ●

She blinked; she was sitting inside the iron ship. Tope wasn't, she knew that he would be back there waiting for David, and if he walked back through the door, David would face Tope's knives.

She felt calm. Was this how David had experienced Carnival? She could think, she could rage, but it was all at a distance. As though she was watching someone else. David, she had to warn him!

Margaret rose from the seat.

She blinked. She was back at her chair.

She looked down: her fingers brushed her belly, dark forms held the wound closed, Witmoths more substantial than any she had seen before. They hissed at her touch. How long had she been... whatever it was that she had been?

"They will heal you." At her feet was a bloody bullet. "The wound was cruel, but it's nothing that I can't repair. Margaret, my Margaret."

She stood again, took a step, and blinked.

She was back in the seat.

This time she'd pulled buckled straps around her shoulders.

"You'll hurt yourself," a familiar voice said. Her mother's voice, but it came from a different face altogether. Anderson, the head of the Interface, smiled at her with her mother's smile. He reached out and grabbed her arm before she could undo the straps.

"He should not have hurt you that way, but a rough instrument was what was needed. He will not be coming back with us." Anderson looked down at her belly. "You will be healed, made whole, and of the whole. I will heal you, my daughter."

Margaret yanked her arm free. "Let me go."

"Hush, I have given you some autonomy, but you are

mine now, and we are part of the whole. As you should have always been. I've missed you, my love. But now I can care for you."

The ship shuddered, she felt it lift, and narrow windows grew out of slits in the wall, letting in light. She watched Tearwin Meet's wall slide past, as the ship traced its path back out of the webwork that protected the city.

The space within it was primitive, nothing like her *Melody Amiss* or the *Roslyn Dawn*. In this sort of ship nothing but basic comforts were required. This ship fought and flew, as little more than a disposable barb of the Roil; not even as valuable as a limb, something to be spat out in anger, or with the cruellest of cunning. Steam swirled around her, such a contrast to the frozen world beyond the iron ship.

"Be still now," her mother said. "Or you will hurt yourself."

Margaret clenched her jaw. "No, I—"

Anderson tightened her belts, she could barely move. The open windows completely revealed the ship in greater detail. All around the edge of the craft sat Roilings, facing inward, and every one of them looked at her with the eyes of her mother.

"Where is Father?" Margaret asked.

She felt the answer first as a wave of bitterness and grief that crashed against her – so hard that she raised her hands to her face. "Your father is gone. When he destroyed Tate, when he used the I-bombs, he tore away his chance at life, at union, he tore himself from the both of us."

"If only he'd managed to kill you, too," Margaret said.

"He did," Arabella said. "My body was destroyed, but I didn't need my body any more. The Roil doesn't require bodies, only thought, such warm and wonderful thought.

It took a while to master it, but I have, my darling. And you will too."

They reached the top of the wall, and there the *Roslyn Dawn* waited. Two bursts of flame. The iron ship shuddered a moment later, the ship creaking and groaning. The metal bulged inwards, but did not give, no matter how much Margaret wished it to.

The iron ship was quick to return fire.

Accurate and powerful fire, for the *Dawn*'s engine nacelles blew, as did a large section of the fore skull. Her flagella thrashed at the air, and the Aerokin tipped and fell into Tearwin Meet.

The iron ship's engines fired, and they were already putting distance between them and the walls of the city. Margaret turned and watched the last flash of the *Dawn*'s limbs as she tumbled into the metropolis with its razor-sharp wires, and was lost to sight. The iron ship raced south towards the Roil, towards the purest thought of her mother.

CHAPTER 50

History is a mess of argument. As though it's never quite what it should be. The pieces of a jigsaw cut crude and without thought of the future.

It's the historian's job to make them fit with eloquence and arrogance, and if that doesn't work, a sledgehammer will suffice.

Palimpsests & Powders, DEIGHTON

TEARWIN MEET
DISTANCE FROM ROIL VARIABLE

The Engine of the World held David's hand.

It said, "Time and time again the Roil has been beaten back. But this time something different happened. This time the Roil grew so quickly – it was just forty years ago that the Roil conquered this world and was frozen from it. Normally centuries pass before I do what I must.

"And every time, I am activated by someone like you, driven by one of the Old Men, cast from their prison in desperation, just as unknowing as the rest of you. Last time it was Milton and a man called Stagwell Matheson." The

Engine smiled. "A humble shop clerk, would you believe. This time you came to me with Cadell."

"And if I say no now?" asked David.

"You will walk back through that door, and die. But you will die knowing that the Roil can have its world, that humanity will be scoured from it, or fused wholly with it."

"And if I walk into the cage?"

"You will be given this choice again. And you will know this world as you have never known it before."

"And will I die?"

The Engine shrugged. "Perhaps."

"I don't want to die," David said. "I don't want anyone to die."

"Death is a given," the Engine said. "But realise this. The Roil has already washed over Drift – the last Mother fallen from the sky." David felt himself fall with that news too. Mother Graine was gone. It said, "Hardacre burns in the south, and a great army crashes against the Underground – that secret place that was never a secret place: a wave of claw, tooth, flame and shadow. And that stronghold will not long remain so.

"To do nothing is to kill all that remains of your world. Are you prepared to let that happen?"

David stood there, looked at the door, then the cage. Thought of the Underground and the people that still fought, and he realised that he wasn't. That he had come all this way for Margaret, for Cadell, for Buchan and Whig. He had killed Old Men. All of it feeling he had no choice, and now, now... he realised that he did have a choice, and that it was the same as theirs.

Without another word, David stepped into the cage.

The cage was dark: it smelt of the dark. Icy and smothering

at once. David half imagined he could see stars, points of light that danced and circled.

"I don't want to do this," he said, but he knew that for a lie. From the moment he had fallen from his window ledge, choosing to run instead of lie still and die, he had wanted this. No, that wasn't true, he'd wanted this even before that. When his mother had died, when his father had frozen him out, without ever meaning to. Carnival had offered solace, but this, this was true relief.

Here he could stop a world. Reset it, and make it what it should be. What a monstrous wonderful thing that was. He had a choice, and he had made it. He had no choice at all.

"I'm ready," he said. The cage closed around him like a fist. A thousand tiny spear points drove into his flesh. Pain, a terrible jabbing pain, and then they began to move.

He shrieked and pushed his hands against the bars and hissed at their stinging energies. The world dropped on him from a great height and at a great speed.

His heart stopped, but the cage tightened further, energies fired and set it beating again.

Blood ran from his eyes and the cage fed the bloody teardrops back into his body. And he screamed – once his heart started beating again – and he could not hear his scream, though his throat threatened to tear itself apart.

The machine gripped him and he stretched, became something that was not him – that the borders of his being could not even begin to contain. Distant engines engaged, machineries more powerful than anything of which he could imagine. But he knew at once that his kind had imagined them, had engineered them.

All this catastrophic force.

And, suddenly, he wanted it to stop.

The machine stung him, ground him down, and ripped his being to shreds until all he could feel was the vast cold of the universe.

I am dead, he thought, ruined by this Engine.

The Stars of Mourning blazed distantly, disinterestedly – – David realised that there was no mourning there — and dimmed. Weird masses were exchanged, great bodies vaster than this world circled each other faster, collided and did not collide, brushed past each other or flung away into space, gravity shifting their cores, and energies were stolen from their movement. He flew above it all, watching, though not really understanding, because the information crashing into him was too pure, and he realised what he had become.

Not dead. But Death.

And it was too late.

The machine unleashed its fury.

Margaret stared through the window; something was coming out of the darkness and at horrible rate. Instinctively she brought a hand up to the glass, covering her face. Around her the Roilings began to moan, and the ship increased its speed, pushing her back in her chair. But it was not fast enough.

Suddenly she could move again, totally of her free will. She slipped a lozenge of Chill into her mouth, felt it sting against a cracked tooth. The thing on her arm yowled and slid free, it shuddered on the floor a moment. Then the creatures holding her wound together, and released their grip.

The iron ship jolted as the ice front struck it, glass creaked and cracked. The craft itself began to flex, the pilots moaned, though they still kept up their flight. But there was a juddering uncertainty building within the ship's movements.

As she watched, one of the pilots dropped to the floor and the iron ship tilted with it. Witmoths rushed from its mouth and ears. They hovered senselessly before falling dead. Andersonhad fallen too; his hands clutching at his ears, his mouth open and screaming silently, dark blood streaming from his cracked lips.

"Hold on," Anderson groaned through gritted teeth.

"What's happening?" she asked, though she suspected she already knew the answer.

"We cannot take you to your mother," Anderson said. "We failed. The Engine has been engaged.

"We are losing so much, so swiftly. All this wisdom and all of it dying," Anderson said, and his voice grew thick with concern. "We must land, while we still have a mind to do it. I did not come here to kill you, Margaret. Nor would I see you dead even now."

Margaret slipped another lozenge of Chill in her mouth and the iron ship came down hard, jarring her bones, tearing open her wound even more.

And this time she screamed.

CHAPTER 51

And around, not thunder bound, but riotous and loud
In rushed quick death, and icy breath, a vast and killing
cloud.

Engine Cantos, ANTHONY WARDELL

THE UNDERGROUND
A ROIL EDGE

The ice front hit, shearing through the Roil. The mirrors
on the airships cracked, then fell in shards upon the earth,
and the walking machines fell too.

The Engine's been engaged, Medicine thought. We've
done it. David's done it.

The men at the front cheered and then stopped, falling
dead, the blood freezing in their veins. At the rear, those
soldiers close to the outer doors turned and ran, but all
died before making a few steps. Their bodies sheathed and
then smothered with ice.

It's killing them, Medicine thought. Our salvation, it's
going to kill us all.

"Shut the doors! Shut the doors," he cried, thinking it

already too late. The air had suddenly stilled, his breath came in clouds, his eyes started to sting.

"Shut the doors. Shut the doors," the cry went up, breaking that silence and suddenly the iron doors closed. And no one knew how close a thing it was.

But that was for later; now Medicine watched, eyes wide, as the Roil collapsed; within a few moments it was gone, and ice covered the window. He felt himself witness to something that he didn't quite understand, something that was bigger and crueller than he had ever expected.

David, Medicine thought. Oh, David, what have you done? What did we make you do?

All along the continent, Lodes came to life, lit by the Engine of the World; like neurons fired by David's raging thought. Releasing their cargo of cold, stilling the fury of atoms for just a moment, though that was all it took, creating instant permafrost.

Round and round the fire the stationmaster danced, his circles describing some sort of victory. And then the cold struck, freezing the air, killing the Witmoths within him instantly. He fell and with him tumbled his family, their fevered eyes closing over with cold.

And in the ice, curled up together, though dead for weeks, they died at last.

Lode B1914, already woken but weeks before, roared this time to full strength, and flattened the wet land around with cold. Plants died. The little creek – down which David and Cadell had run from the Quarg Hounds – grew brittle and still.

Tate's Lode flared uselessly, the cold cracking the city's

walls again, hurling out Quarg Hounds, plucking Endyms and Floataotons from the dark sky.

The Margin's Lode flared with chill effulgence; the River Weep snap-froze. And factories died, their cells bursting with the cold, swift and painless death, but death nonetheless. Cuttle messengers fell from the sky. The Cuttlefolk army froze in its bivouacs.

Where the Roil fastnesses – those dreaming cities – rose into the heavy sky, they felt the cold's coming as a swift and terrible diminishment of thought. The Roilings moaned in anticipation of their doom, and knew at once the terror that they had not known since the Wit smoke had caught their souls. The fear of death.

The engine that sat at the heart of McMahon rumbled a few more futile heartbeats. The ceaseless inventions tumbled uncontrollably: bombs, shields, pieces of weaponry, mewling creatures with bleeding eyes and fevered breath. And then it stopped. The Penn woke from the dreams that caged her and her first thoughts were of her daughter. And in her next, she knew her daughter was safe, if only for a few moments more. And she knew a brief happiness.

A moment of stillness.

The ice struck, as the nearest Lodes boiled and bubbled with pure cold. All thought was stripped away and there was not even time for sadness.

Just an end.

Deep in the south, Vermatisaurs crashed into the sky – crammed with terrified and battering Hideous Garment Flutes and Endyms, snatching and scratching and biting at each other's flesh. And then the giant beasts turned tail and flew, raced to the volcanic mountains at the equator, where it was still hot for a few moments more at least, the ice crashing in from north and south. Most did not make it, but there were still enough that they were crammed into caves, the last ones sealed the holes in mountains with their own frozen flesh – their many heads describing a hundred different agonies – and so a few survived.

They had seen this before and would see it again. And their brains bubbled with bitterness and a hunger for revenge and fire, and just hunger; and, as they fell into the deepest of sleeps, their dreams were filled with both.

But few creatures made it. Most were caught in the fury of that racing front – a cloud of dirty ice – an obsidian curtain flung back on itself, dotted with the broken remains of Quarg Hounds, Floataotons, Hideous Garment Flutes and Endyms. And all manner of more exotic creatures: dreamlings, faunitaurs and cadinows, the latter hurling down bone instruments in dismay and losing their music to the ice.

The cold stilled, and the sun shone down on a cloudless world made sluggish and white, when all before had been dark and swift.

Carnelon had been taken. It had seen it, dark canisters that spread a purposeful madness. It had known not to go near. And with Carnelon's fall, some deeper evolutionary mechanism was activated, weeks spent hidden in the hills, in a cave dark and deep.

It looked at its young, they mewled and scraped and fed upon the corpse of one of their winged brethren, grown too old for flight and fattened for food. The Cuttle messenger had become meal.

It sealed the cave mouth with materials extruded from its mandibles, and struck the wall in the points weakened for just that purpose: stone fell. And the cave mouth was as if it had never been a cave at all.

Then it clutched the dead messenger in a claw and dragged the corpse deeper and deeper into the mountain. Let the world tear itself apart, it had its young and that was all it would need in the belly of the world.

From the belly of the world they had sprung and the belly of the world would contain them again. Let the world turn and burn or freeze. It would keep its brethren safe.

In his place at the heart of the storm, David sensed it all and found himself lost, so fragmented that he feared he would never put himself back together. Even that fear was almost impossible to hold, it slipped through the widening halls of his mind, and he watched it go, without realising that he was watching it, scarcely conscious of anything at all.

But a voice, Cadell's voice, whispered sternly in his ear. "It is done. You can stop now." A dry hand clasped his. "It is done, you have done it. Wake up."

David looked up and saw his mother – as she had looked just before the disease took her – and he could not tell if she was smiling or frowning. But there was love there all the same. And that was his memory, not Cadell's, his alone.

"Wake up," she said. "Wake up."

David gulped at the air like a drowning man. One of his eyes was swollen shut, and he was back in the cage, the taste of blood in his mouth. His whole body was stained with the effort, scoured and made squalid by it all. He just wanted to be clean, to be stripped of all that filth, and now, now that he was himself again: he wanted to escape his thoughts. He wanted to cry, but it seemed beyond him. He opened his mouth, and his crusted lips moved, cracking with the motion.

"Let me out," he said thickly, and leant heavily against

the door. It swung open and he fell through the doorway
to the floor.

David lay there, his head boiling with thoughts, the after-
shock of all the raw energy of the Engine. He wrapped his
head in his arms, cradled it, hunched over. At last he let his
hands drop.

"What have I done?" he whispered, teeth chattering. He
stared down at his bloodied nails, the ruined palms of his
hands.

"Frozen the world to death," the Engine said. "But it is
not the end. The storm will pass."

"And then what do I do?"

The Engine looked at him as though he were a dullard.
"Wait."

David recoiled at that answer. Wait: so that all this could
happen again. He did not understand how that was worth
it. "But surely there is something more than that? I do not
want to construct another broken thing. The Roil will return, our technology, our heat will call it."

The Engine laughed. "The world is always broken. My
power does not extend beyond the crust. I cannot still the
heart of this world. To do so would destroy it utterly."

David looked out at the frozen land beyond the city.
"What did we do just then?"

"Stopped the Roil."

"But at what cost?"

The figure raised its hands in defeat. "I am a machine,
David. I do not understand these questions."

"Then it is up to me to find the answers."

"I doubt you will like the world you have made," the
Engine said. "No, it will not be at all to your taste."

"I didn't think I had any choice." David said. "Everybody
kept telling me I didn't have a choice. And what is choice

anyway?" David realised that he was babbling, he stopped and looked down at his hands. His fingers were coated with blood. His cheek had been torn open at some stage in the process, he pushed his tongue against the wound, felt it poke through the side of his face.

"Perhaps you didn't," the Engine said. "I hope that gives you some comfort."

David wanted to hit this awful thing, but he saw the single tear that tracked its cheek, saw the shudder passing through its body. And he was too tired, too exhausted, and he just wanted to stop, to fall into some kind of sleep.

"I was made for this," the Engine said; it bent down and picked him up. "I am only ever whole when I ignite all my Lodes, but it is a dreadful thing. Already I am fading, the defences of the city crumbling, not to be rebuilt until I sleep."

"How long do you sleep?" David asked, thinking how that sounded like the most wonderful thing in the world right now.

"As long as it takes, and never as long as the last time, but I would rather sleep forever. I would rather never wake again. Because when I wake, the world must end anew."

"This will not happen again," David said, resolutely. "We will not pick up the pieces and rebuild our world, merely to break it down again."

He remembered something he had seen. Margaret was gone, and the *Roslyn Dawn* had crashed into the city.

"Kara, I have to get to her," he said. "I have to find her, and Margaret."

"Margaret is beyond the city now," the Engine said. "I do not think you would like to find her."

"It doesn't matter what I would like, I have to."

The Engine smiled. "See, you are beginning to understand."

The Engine led him to the doorway.

David walked to the door, took a deep breath, tried not to look at the ruin of his cheek. "Let me out," he said. "It's time to see this new world I've made, and make something of it."

"David," the Engine said as the door opened. "You might find that this new world has teeth."

David stepped through the doorway, and the door shut behind him.

"Hello, David," Tope said, and he was already throwing knives.

David dropped and flung out his arms. The first blade passed overhead, the second struck him in the arm.

"Looks like you're having a bad day," Tope said. "Where's your face gone?"

David grasped at the cold, snatched at it, tried to freeze his flesh around the wound, but the pain was too much. Instead, he pulled the knife free and dropped it to the ground. Blood followed the steel: splattering and clattering.

"Ah, I've been waiting for this day a very long time. I died and was reborn just so I could experience it. The Roil had me, and lost me. And now, here we are, the world ending. All ambitions undone, except this simplest of ones. The Roil is dying, and this world with it, but here I am. My little wish fulfilled."

"Not yet," David said.

"No, not yet, but soon." He ran, charging at David, lips curled back with a cruel and dreadful savagery.

David yanked the knife from his belt, the one Margaret had given him, Sheff's long killing knife, and Tope stopped. Just within reach. And for the first time in those implacable eyes, David saw doubt.

"I know that blade," Tope said.

"Then you know he's dead." David snapped his hand forward and buried it to the hilt in Tope's chest. The Verger shuddered. Ice, released at last in desperation and fear, sheathed David's hand, sheathed the knife, and crackled up and along Tope's flesh.

"He's dead, and so are you." David pulled his hand free, and struck the Verger hard. He shattered in a burst of crystalline blood.

David let the broken knife fall and ran. Kara was still out there.

In the end, it was easy and terrible, for the *Dawn* had scattered in her fall. Bits of Aerokin were everywhere. He walked where the bulk of her ruin appeared to be.

He could smell the rank terror of her death, even above the ozone crackling of the engine: a raw and horrible ending for the *Dawn*. But where was Kara?

She couldn't be dead. The Engine had told him that she wasn't dead. But what did it know of life?

And then he saw her. Curled up, wrapped in the foremost flagellum of the *Dawn*. Kara was breathing. And that horrible ending became something somehow beautiful, and he did not want to disturb it. But nothing beautiful lasts forever, and only pain could follow this. He touched her face gently and called her name. Her eyes flicked open and the pain within them was a greater hurt than anything that David had ever known.

His voice died in his throat.

"What happened to your face?" Kara said.

David shrugged, the pain was getting worse, but there was nothing he could do. Not here at the end of the world.

"She's gone," Kara said. "I'm sorry, she's gone. I saw her, she was in the ship, the one that..."

It took David a moment to realise she meant Margaret.

CHAPTER 52

She was a hero. And through her was the union of land and sky. She was my sister, but she became so much more. The greatest pilot, and that was only the beginning. If you have time, read. If you do not, make time.

She would be the greatest of pilots. And not for her loss, but for where it took her. Where it took us all. What finer vistas than Drift? We were so high and dismissive of the slights of the earth that we forgot to look up.

Memoirs, RAVEN SKYE

TEARWIN MEET
DISTANCE FROM THE ROIL INDETERMINATE

"There," David said, pointing at the wall, and leaning into Kara's shoulder. She knew his face must be burning; his jaw had swollen dramatically in the last couple of hours. "Just here." He sounded so tired.

The passage back through the city had taken forever, or it felt like it – even without the threat of Quarg Hounds. David was barely able to walk, Kara hardly wanted to. The *Dawn* was behind them, dead. She would never see her

Aerokin alive again. The only thing that kept any movement in Kara was that the *Dawn* had struggled to save her life: that she hadn't let her pilot die, and that David needed her so much.

She'd even entered her darling Aerokin one last time to find what was left of her healing gel, slapping a palmful of the stuff over his jaw, and storing the rest in a container at her belt. It must have been doing something, because it burnt, and though David had already suffered so much this was almost the worst of it. If Kara hadn't needed him so, he would have just sat down in the snow and died. If he hadn't needed her, he was sure she would have done the same.

Kara virtually carried him to the stony wall, a section just like any other, and quite close to the part that he and Margaret had clambered down. She ran a hand along the wall, and hit it hard with the meat of her palm. The stone rang out like a bell, and she stepped back, holding David upright as the sound died.

"Hollow," she said. "So, we stand here, and..."

The stone parted, as though it were nothing more than a curtain, opening onto a tunnel and admitting a howling terrible wind that cut through their clothes, gnawed at their flesh, and nearly bowled them over. David shivered beside her like an old man.

"Another bloody tunnel," Kara shouted into his ear.

"Yes, another one."

They stood there a few moments, bent over against the gale as it did its best to knock them to the ground. But, unsteady as they were, they did not let it.

"We better keep moving," David said at last.

The journey through was dire. The wind only got louder and colder and stronger. It blasted against them until Kara thought she was going to die, frozen to death, hollowed out.

Her bones felt frozen. Her eyes kept sticking closed. Only David was warm, she pulled him forward, kept him moving.

At the mouth of the cave, they looked out into the snow – it was already growing dark, and growing even colder.

"So this is what victory looks like," David said, teeth already starting to chatter. Just hours ago he would have laughed off the cold, he would have created it. But he wasn't that David any more.

"We aren't going to last long out there," Kara said, sounding like she didn't care.

"We won't have to," David said, and pointed.

The *Collard Green* cruised over the ice, low and fast. And Kara had never been happier to see a dirigible. Her great lights traced the wall of the metropolis. And then those lights shone upon them, blinding in their brightness.

Kara yelled at the top of her lungs. David did too. And the lights stopped, stayed fixed on them.

"Now," Kara said, "we're going to need to get away from the wall, or she'll smash against it."

She lowered him to the ground, the lights following them, and he sank in the snow to his knees. Kara dropped beside him, hands reaching under his arms. The snow actually felt warmer than the air.

"Keep moving," she said, and she couldn't tell whether she was talking to him, or herself. So he did, one painful step after another. A hundred yards from the wall, Kara stopped. "This is good enough."

The ship made her way towards them, dragging what looked like several anchors, her engines working loud and hard against the storm, the gondola passed over their heads, her lights washed over them.

Buchan looked down and he chortled.

"We found you. With nothing but two moons in a snow-storm to guide us, we found you," he said, or, at least that's what David thought he said. David couldn't hear much of it. "Can you climb?"

David nodded his head.

"We can climb," Kara shouted. "Or I can climb for the both of us."

Rope ladders dropped to the ground, and slowly they made their way up them. At the top, Buchan hugged them both, pulling them inside, slamming the door behind them.

"Your face," Buchan said. "What happened to your face?" He was already reaching for bandages, pushing them into place over the wound.

"It's all right," David said. "It hardly hurts at all. How did you find us?"

"A voice – the Engine, I guess – told us that it was safe to leave the overhang, and that we would find you here." The gondola creaked, the airship jolted, headed alarm-ingly close to the great spikes of the wall. Buchan gave a frightened-looking grin. "Well, it was right about one thing."

Already the *Collard Green* was turning, her engines roar-ing. We're not out of this yet, David thought.

Buchan looked at Kara. "The *Dawn*?"

Kara walked away, and Buchan left it at that.

David left Kara to herself.

"And what of Margaret?" David asked.

"I think you had better worry about your own health," Buchan patted his back. "An iron ship passed back over the wall a few minutes after Kara left. It... passed the *Dawn* and raced south. I'm guessing that she was on it.

"But that doesn't mean that we can't get her back. After all, we've won, haven't we?" Buchan looked out into the maelstrom. "Cadell was right. I did not even begin to comprehend how awful this would be, the sort of destruction it would cause."

David nodded his head, knowing too much, his own body numb with horror at the dreadful thing he had done.

"Not everything is destroyed," David said. "There will be pockets, around the Lodes, or in valleys perhaps, that the Engine did not drown in cold."

Buchan grimaced. "Really, would you want to be alive in this?"

"We are," David said. A sudden Carnival pang slithered spiky and cold through him, he bent over with the pain.

Buchan grimaced. "Are you all right?"

"Just the Carnival."

Kara came back to David, holding a shoe. "You might need this," she said, gently. "I took it from her, from the *Dawn*."

He looked at it hungrily. Not everything was different about him. He lifted it from her hands, and gently slid back the heel. All of the Carnival was there. Saliva built in his mouth, here was an end to pain. He pulled the paper containing the drug free from its hidey-hole, then walked to the gondola's door, opened it a moment, and threw the drug out. It fell away into the dark.

Kara was watching him.

"If I live through this. If *we* live through this, then I am going to need a clear head." He winced again, another burst of pain.

Kara reached out to him, and David gently pushed her away.

"Things are going to get much worse, and quickly," he said, quietly.

No one tried to tell him otherwise.

CHAPTER 53

And the Engine turned and the snow and the ice came, and we all fell down. Those were dark days. But there was some that got back up again. There always are. Praise the mad bastards, or none of you would be here looking out at the unfamiliar constellations.

Pieces of a Fragmented War, LANDYMORE

THE FAR NORTH

The iron ship had landed on its roof. Margaret's ears rang, the wound in her stomach burned. She crawled around the ship, looking for a way out.

She wasn't the only survivor. Anderson lay by the door, hands clenching and releasing. His breath rattled in his chest. He looked at her, tried to speak, but couldn't: all that came was a wet-sounding cough.

Margaret slid over to him, across buckled metal, and held his hand.

He squeezed hers back; she could feel his life leaving him. But she knew that she didn't have long for this world, either. She felt a sharp sliver of bitterness. Who'd hold her hand?

The ship shuddered, there was a muffled bang, either

rocks falling on the craft, or an engine exploding. The iron ship lifted a few feet, and fell, windows shattering, and was still. Explosion, she guessed. Snow melted and trickled through the broken glass. She could smell gasoline: the ship might go up any minute. A quick death, what was wrong with a quick death? They'd won, hadn't they?

Anderson sighed, eyes still trained on her. A look that Margaret recognised, a brief stare, wavering but so strong.

"Mother–"

Anderson squeezed her hand again; hard enough that it almost hurt.

And that was it.

His eyes did not close, but dulled. His fingers no longer gripped hers back. Gently, ever so gently, she laid his arm across his chest. "You can rest now," she said.

Margaret stared through one of the cracked windows at the falling snow. There were mountains out there and caves. She circled the ship again, and found a cabinet filled with blankets. She wondered if they had been brought for her. There were also several sheets in there. These she pulled out, ripped into long strips, and tied around her wound – not that it would do much. She knew she was dying. She grabbed a pair of blankets, wrapped them around her shoulders and walked to the doorway. She turned the handle, and put her weight against it.

The door swung open and she fell out onto the ice and snow. The contact was hard enough and painful enough that she blacked out briefly. But, cruelly, that wasn't the end. Her eyes flicked open, she gasped with the pain. The cold began to numb her, a small mercy, that. What was she thinking? Where could she possibly escape to?

She considered crawling back into the ship. But it contained enough death already. She couldn't bear to add to it, and already the ship was cooling, she would freeze just as easily within it as without.

And she would bleed to death before that.

Her teeth began to chatter. She was going to die in a few minutes at best. There were worst things than death, she had seen them, but that didn't mean she wanted an ending now.

Then she saw the gasoline dripping down the side of the craft. It took her several attempts to free a lighter from her belt, another couple of fumbles to actually light it. She threw it at the ship and the gasoline caught in a sudden rush of flame.

She'd half expected it to explode, but she was spared that for now: just fire and warmth.

She hunkered down, blankets around her shoulders, and watched the iron ship burn.

The winds had died down a little, though dark clouds building on the horizon suggesting they would be back soon. David looked down from the gondola and pointed towards the smoke.

"See," he said. "I told you. She's down there."

The ship jutted out of the snow, steam and smoke gusting into the air. The *Collard Green* approached slowly, dropping anchors when they were within a few hundred yards.

"Perhaps you should let us look," Buchan said.

"And spare me what?" David asked, and there was the ghost of Cadell's irritability there. "I've seen too much already to be spared anything."

He clambered down the ropes, falling the last few steps to the snow. But he was back up on his feet at once and wading through snow towards the iron ship.

And yet, when the time came, David hung back, and it was Buchan, face masked, that looked through the open doorway.

"There's dead here," he said. "But she's not among them. Though I did find this." He lifted up one of Margaret's rime blades.

"Maybe she's back in the city," Kara said.

"No," David said, "if she was I would have known. She's here, and nearby."

It was Buchan that found her, half buried in the snow. "Too late," he said. "We were too late." Kara and David ran to her side.

Margaret opened her eyes, just once. She might have even smiled.

"Get her into the *Collard Green*," Kara said. "Get her inside now."

They lifted her into the airship, careful as they could in the rising winds, and warmed her. She woke as Buchan looked her over, declaring that he knew a little of doctoring; he stopped the moment he came to the bullet wound, frowned and slid the sheets and blanket back up to her neck.

"You were lucky you didn't lose your fingers to the cold." Buchan smiled, though he couldn't conceal the worry in his eyes. "So are we friends now?"

Margaret smiled thinly. "I think you can say that, you bastard."

Buchan laughed.

Margaret reached up and brushed his hand.

David looked down at her. Her lips were bloodless, eyes strained as though she were sick.

"You're alive!" Margaret said. "But what have they done to you?"

"Nothing," David said. "Nothing. I did that to myself."

"What do we do now?" Margaret asked.

David sat down on the bunk next to her and told her and Kara what he thought had to be done. Buchan listened at a distance, but the man was subdued; he'd hardly spoken since he'd looked over Margaret.

"So," Margaret said. "If that is what you think is right, and I agree with you. Then we must go to the Underground. But if you could please hurry, Buchan's skills at doctoring don't extend this far, I think." And then she showed them the extent of her wounds, and David realised that he could smell her death. There was still enough of Cadell within him to recognise it for what it was.

She laid her head down on the pillow and smiled. "Don't worry, I think I am ready to die."

"No," David said. "No, you are not."

"There's enough of the gel to keep her together," Kara said. She looked over at David. "But not enough for the both of you."

"I'm all right," David said. "I'm all right. Buchan, we need to go, and now. She's dying."

He said, "David, I give you my word, I will get her there in time. I may have not been able to get you out of Hardacre, but I can get you out of this. I know the way to the Underground."

And so does Watson, David thought.

Buchan said, "And it's where we are heading, as far as I know it is the only place where there might be food and supplies, and doctors. We've maps and charts, and the in-struments on this ship are more than up to the task – and though the landmarks are for the most part gone, the mountains are hard to miss."

"So is that storm," Kara Jade said, nodding towards the dark snow-filled clouds rushing towards them. "If we stay here, we're dead. If we fly into that..."

"Optimism is a virtue in such instances, Miss Jade. I would suggest we hold to our course and think only of what lies beyond the storm."

PART FIVE
THE UNDERGROUND

CHAPTER 54

Monteroy Bleaktongue breathed raggedly. Though his wounds were not fatal, he had been worn down by them. His bones seemed anxious to break the surface of his flesh. He'd become a creature of angles and pained breaths – a caricature of geometry. "Mr Grave, don't you see? You have failed. We have failed. Everything is undone."

Travis the Grave shook his head; blood stained his teeth, and bubbled in time with his breaths, and he knew he had too few of those left now.

"Monteroy, you're wrong as usual. Endings, they are just be-ginnings. And until the great engines of the universe run down, it will always be so. And who's to say what will happen after that greatest ending of all? No, Monteroy, there are no endings. Not even the cage of our flesh can make it so."

Shadow Council 24: Endings, DICKSON MCUNNE

THE UNDERGROUND

It had been Grappel's idea to set up the floodlights in the snow: sweating beacons aimed into the sky.

"We've no reason to hide now," he'd said to Medicine

from his cot in the infirmary. "Let those who remain find us. The more bodies we have the better."

It was sometimes hard to believe that the world had suddenly changed so much. Here in the Underground it was still all business, all struggle, but it had been that way for years. Though the urgency was gone from it, and the fear. The Engine had turned, the worst had come, and they were still alive.

Beyond the great iron gates the old world was gone. Sometimes, in the day-to-day business of the Underground it was a struggle to remember that. Thousands upon thousands had died, but it was still all so abstract. And when Medicine tried to bring it in, frame it with faces and friendships he had had, it became too painful. David was gone, and Agatha. There'd been no word from Hardacre, so they had to assume the worse there.

Better to focus on what lay ahead, on the many tasks that had to find resolution, so that many thousands more wouldn't die as well. But sometimes he took himself out to the lights. To remember and honour what had happened. Most nights there was a crowd at the outer wall, standing, craning their heads to watch the coruscating tubes, and wait to see just what might come out of the darkness.

Because, nearly every day, since the lights had been activated, things came.

Medicine lifted his head towards the dim sputtering and the sharp fingers of light caressing the horizon. An airship. The third that day. And this ship he recognised.

"It's them," he said. "It's the *Collard Green*." And he knew that they would be on it.

The *Collard Green* landed, in an ice field aswarm with airships at mooring masts. Medicine did not know how long the ships could last without hangars, and there was no way that they could broaden the cavern mouth to the Underground – facilitating flight had never been part of the idea behind it. They were doing their best to construct covers, but the weather was horrible, even now, some days after the Engine's activation. Though the mooring masts were made of reinforced steel, one of the ships had already been taken away by the wind.

He knew he would have to negotiate with Drift – word had just reached them that there were survivors in that city, too – or they might as well let the ships rot. One thing he did know with absolute certainty was these airships would be the last of their generation. There simply wasn't enough cow gut to make the gold-beater's skin. There'd soon enough be pilots and airfolk with no ships to work.

Medicine thought of all that pent-up energy, all those pilots's egos. Yet another administrative nightmare to add to the menagerie.

But before then, once the worst of the storms had passed, the ships would be sent out. To Mirrlees and Hardacre to Eltham, and all the other townships, searching for survivors or at the very least, bearing witness to what had happened.

David clambered out of the airship, shivering as the cold air struck him; his face stung. Twice the wound had grown so horribly infected that Whig had had to drain the pus from it with a syringe. Kara had held his hand through that ordeal.

The flight had been awful; several times he'd thought they were going to die, despite Watson's assurances that he could survive anything. Indeed, the look of horror on Watson's face (and echoed in Kara's) was enough to make such assurances null and void. What's more, the ship had constantly required clearing of ice, around the clock, done in shifts that even David had been unable to avoid.

And all the while he had suffered the pangs of Carnival withdrawal. The screaming aches, the nightmares, more savage and cruel than he could imagine. Once on the ropes he'd actually let go, only to be grabbed by Kara and bundled back inside.

"You're not dying on me," she said. "No one dies on me. Not now."

And still, when his time came around again, he staggered out and worked on the ice. The hard work ground away his thoughts. The wind cut through them all with a dreadful indifference. And Kara – finding him as some sort of project – found relief from her thoughts, too.

Margaret alone had stayed in bed. Sometimes she would speak, but no one was ever entirely sure that she was speaking to them. Once she demanded her guns, another time her mother. Kara looked after her, too. With a kindness and a sensitivity that David found surprising and utterly wonderful.

No one dies on me.

And no one had.

And now, after that, here were so many people, unfamiliar faces one and all, until he came to Medicine. David nodded towards him and tried to smile. The former leader of the Confluent party looked at him and David thought he was going to cry. There was a hesitation there, perhaps a guilt, but not fear.

"You're safe," Medicine said.

David nodded. "I'm safe." He moved slowly, every part of his body ached, his face burned. "But Margaret..."

"Your friend?"

Two of Buchan and Whig's men were carrying Margaret out on a stretcher. Solemn and slow.

Medicine looked at the woman. "Infirmary, now," he said, and sent a man to lead them there. David made to follow, except Aunt Veronica was hugging him, squeezing him so tight he thought he might break a rib. She stepped back and grimaced.

"David, David! You look terrible," Veronica said.

"Would people stop telling me that?" he said.

"I mean it. You look terrible, and if I can't tell you that, who can?"

David put an arm around her, let her bear his weight. "You don't look so good yourself."

Veronica huffed. "Look a damn sight better than you do! Though a scar is good on a man, and that will be a *good* scar."

David touched his jaw, the wound still burned.

"I'm so sorry," Medicine said. "This didn't turn out how I expected. Cadell was never meant to..."

"You did what you thought was right," David said. "I'm here. I'm here now."

"But if I hadn't..."

"If you hadn't, I'd be dead."

"Time to get inside," Kara said from behind him. "And not another moment on that bloody ship."

His aunt looked from David to the pilot and back again, and gave him an enquiring look. He shook his head. Still, she raised an eyebrow.

"I've heard a lot about you," Veronica said. "Raven Skye's sister, and just as wild."

Kara stared at her blankly. "We're here," she said. "We've made it."

"Home for now," Veronica said, and she didn't ask about Kara's Aerokin. David loved her for that.

"So are you letting us in?" Buchan boomed. "I'm tired and hungry and have spent far too many hours in the air. Let us in and be done with it."

"Of course," Medicine said.

They moved onto the gantry and David stopped, and his breath stopped in his throat.

"Here it is," Medicine said. "I bet you never expected to see it."

"No," David said. "But I think we all expected things to end badly. And who could say that it hasn't? The Roil was coming, whether we did anything or not. All the denial in the world could not stop it."

"A lot of people made it here, David. Because Stade had constructed this place, more people survived then we had a right to expect. Whatever I think of the cruel bastard, I have to give him that." Medicine regarded David a little more closely, though David wasn't sure how the man felt about what he saw. "You look different, and not just that scar."

"I feel different." He looked down at the ring on his finger. It was just a ring now, its mechanisms worn out, soldered together by the final engagement of the Engine of the World. "It's the Carnival, I guess. I stopped taking the Carnival."

David took it all in, the extent of the Underground. Surely this city was as big as Mirrlees, maybe bigger. Tunnels ran wider than football fields deep into the mountain, stretching further than he could see, scaffolding covering their walls, surrounding other tunnels, leading deeper into the belly of the world. Machines worked non-stop and everywhere there were people. Some paused to watch them curiously, then got back to their work. Life hadn't stopped just because the Engine of the World had turned.

David, for all his exhaustion, watched them intently. Here was the seed of something. Not his own redemption, but a world's.

Margaret's stomach still pulled where the stitches had been, she was still weak. But finally they had let her see this Underground with David and Medicine Paul.

He'd prepared her a little for the world beyond the infirmary's walls.

But, it still proved a surprise.

Margaret sighed, her eyes widening at what she saw, the curvature of streets, the whine of machinery, the distant glimmer of ice shields, the chaos of pipes – all with arcane uses, though ones she knew she could guess at. All of it familiar.

"I know this place. I know this place," she said.

Medicine chuckled. "Of course you do, Miss Penn. Where do you think they got the blueprints? This last great project of Stade and the Council of Engineers would be nothing without the city of Tate, and the Penns. We have survived because of your family.

"It can be a dismal stink hole of a metropolis, too hot in some of the caverns, too chilly in others; and the lice, let me not start on them. But until the cold passes, when and if it passes, we can survive here," Medicine said.

"No," David said. "We must do more than survive. This must be the start of something new. I've seen what our people have done, what we're capable of. And I know what we must do. Just how to do it? That's the question."

"And what is that?" Medicine asked, raising an eyebrow.

"Build ships that cross the dark above," David said. "And leave this place. All our industry, all our work, must be directed towards that one task. It is more than a lifetime's work, and we must complete it in less. We do not belong here, and every day that we remain is a continuation of an ancient evil. It must end."

"Then where do we belong?" Medicine asked.

"Maybe we don't belong anywhere but up there. Cadell's people designed us for this world, or the world that they constructed at any rate. But that world itself was a lie, something they built on and from the bones of another." He smiled. "And those bones will never rest, nor should they. This is the Roil's world. If there is anywhere for us, it is out in the greater darkness. It is time to dismantle the Engine of the World, and build instead Engines to the Stars."

"It's a dream worthy of Travis the Grave," Medicine said.

David smiled at Margaret, and it was a grin as patronising as any of Cadell's, but she could forgive him it. "Not at all. This is no tale in which just a few face the perilous journey, this will be a story of an entire people. All of us have suffered, this whole world is a world of suffering, but we will see an end to that. We have to."

When she was strong enough, Margaret spoke to the head horticulturalist – after all, she was well acquainted with the difficulties of subterranean agriculture – who was at first sceptical, then excited by her suggestions. They talked until she was exhausted. Margaret left him scrawled notes, only allowed to leave once she promised she would return the next day.

She'd already remembered and modified her parents' lighting system and she knew that they would be proud.

That afternoon Medicine had shown Margaret her room, it wasn't much, but it was hers. And she knew that she wouldn't be going anywhere for some time. She imagined the stark walls covered with her designs.

In a few months she knew she would travel with David to Drift. He was anxious to explore that ancient city's catacombs, perhaps study the workings of its grand engines.

David had changed and it wasn't only Cadell's influence there.

She sat in her room, holding her father's notebook. He had loved her, as had her mother. Even at the end she was certain of that, the Roilings had never attacked her as hard as they could. Perhaps even then her mother had had an inkling of what was about to happen. Perhaps they had seen the end and desired her survival. She found some comfort in the thought.

She looked at her guns, and that book: all that she had left of Tate. She closed her eyes and tried to visualise the city. It did not come to her as clearly as she would have liked. She could feel the memories fading, the horror of it all, but also the good things of that life. Sometimes she'd pause and wait for the rumble of the Four Cannon, but it did not come. But even that did not happen so often now.

Tate remained alive in her, and while she lived, she could not lose it completely. And if David was right, if the metropolis would grow again, then she would see it once more, though it would be different, it wouldn't be her city.

She should be resting; there was so much to do.

But being a Penn, she put her father's book down, got up off the bed and sat at her tiny desk, so unlike her parents' grand table in the library. She took a deep breath and began to modify another one of her parents' designs – she was finding them so easy to remember now – and as she worked, thinking of her mother and her father and their old vast library, she began to cry.

CHAPTER 55

From heat to cold, Shale was fury. And we are the first to know that. What a curious thing that is. And what a storm that change brought about, three years and only now is it ending. I write this in the anticipation of a spring. Forgive me my excitement. I never expected to live to see it, and yet I, and yet we, have.

Recollections of a Storm, DEIGHTON

THE UNDERGROUND

David's new room was small, far smaller than the one he had had in his father's house, or even the room at the *Habitual Fool*. But it was his, and somehow, unlike the others, it did not feel like a cage. He'd already managed to find a few books he hadn't read and these were piled up, all wonderful potential, next to his bed.

One day, David knew he would sit down and write his own story. It would be a rough-and-ready work, that writing, for he did not possess the finer points of art and history, but it might help the pain. That was the worst thing of all, the pain of what he had done and the guilt that came from wanting it gone. He'd destroyed a world: he didn't deserve to lose the way it had marked him.

He'd worked all day, helping Medicine in the infirmary. It was little more than getting things when Medicine demanded them, but it was good work, and the sort that meant you met a lot of people. David was never going to be a doctor, but it was a start at building something. And, as they worked, he could talk to Medicine Paul. And they had. Catching up on each other's lives, both adjusting to just how much the other had changed in just a few months. With Medicine, Veronica, Margaret and Kara, it was like having a family again. Though that was only the beginning. He had a whole people to care for, and to protect.

He crawled into bed, and slept. And one last time he dreamed a dream that wasn't.

David knew this place.

Cadell was there, or the shadow of Cadell.

The panoptic map was dark, though David could see clouds swirling across the map's surface, wiping it clean. There was nothing to see here any more. No rain clouds over Mirrlees, no Mirrlees at all, just that scouring whiteness.

"You did good, Mr Milde," Cadell said, distracting him from the map. "Better than I could have expected."

"You lied to me," David said.

"Surely you're used to that." Cadell patted him on the back. "Would you have done it if I hadn't?" His face split with something that might have passed as a smile. David could see that he didn't care, not really.

"I might have questioned it more deeply," David said, hearing the lie before it came from his mouth, then watching the words tumble down into the sky, the vowels in white, the consonants red and green – it was a dream, after all. "I might have found another way."

Cadell shook his head. "The Roil doesn't negotiate." He looked at his pocket watch. "And it will come back. And, worse than that, the cities will be reborn, reseeded, the people there risen whole from the earth with new-sprung memories.

"In a few years when the snows recede, you will find a new Mayor Stade. A new Council, all with memories and histories leading up to the Roil. The Engine will have edited those bits out. There will be many puzzles for you to solve, and histories for you to unpick, and I am sorry that I cannot be there with you. Except, of course, I will be, only I won't know you, and I will be in a cage with the other Old Men.

"Remember, once, how I told you how you would never understand the things that I had seen and done, that I would rather that you didn't. I meant that. Not just because it put me in a bad light, but because of what it would do to you. And I was right. Now, I think it is time that we said our farewells, don't you?" He started folding up papers, turning down switches with his long pallid fingers, so that the light in the panoptic map room dimmed even further.

David shoved his hands in his pockets. "If you want forgiveness, I can't give it to you."

Cadell laughed, as though that might just be the biggest joke in the world; he wiped at his eyes, then looked at David with a genuine fondness.

"You and me share that, David. Regardless of how we have come to that sharing." Cadell stretched and his bones cracked. The Old Man winced. "Neither of us expects to be forgiven. The universe continues regardless, it's a big old thing, the universe, and it doesn't give a damn." He yawned, and started for the door.

"When you slept," David said, his voice stopping Cadell as he reached for the door handle, "there was always a tear, running down your cheek. Why were you crying?"

"Why was I crying?" Cadell laughed again, softly, his eyes gentle, though they still possessed a terrible hardness. He dropped his hand from the door. "That song, the one I had you hum when I was dying, the one I hummed back at you: 'The Synergist's Treason' it was called."

"Yes," David said. "I remember that."

Cadell patted David on the arm. "I lied when I told you I heard it in my childhood." He smiled that smug smile. "I wrote that song, it was vanity – nothing more – that had me demand that you sing it to me. It is the memory of my life bound in music. Dear boy, after the things I've done, and not just once, wouldn't you cry?"

David woke, his face wet. It was dark; the lights outside had been dimmed in turn with the diurnal sequence. He lifted his watch to his face and the radium hands blurred into view. Three o'clock. He pulled his arm away, and it was as if the watch had never existed, he could be staring into the heart of the Engine's cage again. If he closed his eyes and concentrated, he could feel the ground trembling, another storm assailing the mountain perhaps, or heavy machinery – despite the dimmed lights, the Underground never really stopped, it was a mechanism almost as complex as the Engine itself.

"It's over," he said softly, his face aching with the movement. There were drugs he could take, to deal with the pain, but David refused them. He was done with hiding from the pain.

"All done," he said into the dark.

But, of course, it wasn't.

Something cold pressed against his side, he reached down, and found the Orbis, its edges rough and already flaking. He rubbed the finger that had borne it, and there was nothing to show the ring had ever been there. His thoughts, too, were less crowded, no longer wedded to the Engine of the World and its Mechanical Winter. The sadness that welled up in him was a surprise. Part of him had grown used to bearing all those memories, and now they were gone, it didn't quite know what to do. He'd become smaller, no need to contain Cadell anymore. But that didn't mean his ambitions had shrunk.

He put the ring on his bedside table. Perhaps Medicine or Buchan would like to study it, this last vestige of the Old Man. One thing he knew for certain, he would never wear the Orbis again.

He stared into the dark a while and, in the dark, he fell again to sleep.

It turned out he had little choice regarding the Orbis. He woke to find that all that was left of it was a circlet of dust.

A universe reduced to nothing.

David stood with Kara and Margaret.

He touched his jaw with a gloved hand, and pressed at the ache. Kara squeezed his other hand.

"I can feel her out there," she said, and David squeezed her hand back.

"Are you sure?"

Kara gave him such a dirty look that it was hard not to smile, even with his aching jaw. "I'm a pilot, I know when an Aerokin is coming."

Medicine was already walking out into the snow, his footsteps tracking towards to the landing fields. A cold wind whipped his coat around his shoulders like an Endym's wings. David's coat was buttoned to his neck. The last of his meagre tolerance for the cold had gone with the ring.

The first Aerokin was coming.

Almost everyone that was not on duty was there to see its arrival. Margaret had even dragged herself from her work in the gardens, her hair tied back on her head, skin almost as pale as the snow. Her coat managed to stay tight around her, barely moving with the wind, as though she had fostered an iron discipline even in her clothes.

A week before, they had received radio transmissions from Drift, fragmentary, and vague: something about an emissary. And now an Aerokin had been spotted.

Mr Buchan and Mr Whig stood with them on the landing platform, watching the wonderful flying creature arrive. This brought back such fine and horrible memories. The last Aerokin David had seen was dead, her pilot cradled in her flagella.

This one was larger, bulkier. Carrying what Kara described as winter ballast, extra layers of fat and what even looked like fur. The wind gusted towards them and David could smell the Aerokin, her familiar odours, evoking something that was once happy and sad within him.

"It's the *Meredith Reneged*," Kara said, voice catching in her throat. David squeezed her hand again. "Shine Cam's Aerokin."

"And a fine ship she is, too," Buchan said. Kara glared at him.

"I thought you were busy writing your memoirs and your secret history," David said.

Buchan grimaced and waved his hands dismissively. "Not now, there's too much work to be done, what with overseeing the retail sector of this fine city. History is written and history is made, and I'm of a mood to make it, young man. After all, we hunted Old Men, all of us, and we survived. We journeyed to the ends of the world. I need time to let that sink in."

Kara flashed him a smile. "Or you're just a lazy old bastard."

Buchan snorted, patted her on the back. "There is that, too," he said.

David considered Cadell's words again, of what must come after the ice and the snow, and wondered what was happening down south, what perhaps stirred and grew beneath the snow. The thought of Mirrlees and all the cities remade by minnows filled him with no little terror – would he find himself back there an addict? Would he see his mother and father again?

But that lay in the future. A whole people with a whole fabricated history, one that started and stopped and stumbled and slipped, always coming against the Roil, always being beaten back by it.

But now they'd forced a change. There were so many possibilities, for the twelve metropolises lost, and for the Roil itself. It would return, after all, it had never really left, just been driven down again, and David had no doubt that it would come back faster next time, it had learnt a lot in this iteration. David knew that's what he would do.

But they had learnt a lot, too. The great wound of this world had to be healed and not with fire, ice or war.

They were being given another chance.

Margaret Penn stood across from David and he was startled by what he saw. She was smiling, and in her eyes there was something he had never seen before.

He saw hope.

About the Author

Trent Jamieson is an Australian Fantasy writer, and winner of two Aurealis Awards, whose *Death Most Definite* series has attracted rave notices.

Trent has been writing fiction since he can remember, and selling it since the mid-Nineties... quite a long while after he started.

He works as a teacher, a bookseller and a writer and has taught at Clarion South where he was described as "the nicest guy in Australian Spec Fic", shattering the reputation he was trying to build as the "Hard Man of the Australian Writing Community".

trentjamieson.com

ANGRY ROBOT

We are Angry Robot.

Web angryrobotbooks.com

ANGRY ROBOT

WHO NEEDS FOOD?

Own the complete Angry Robot catalog